Saving Hope

"*Saving Hope* is a story straight from the headlines. Missing teens, a Texas Ranger Dad, and a woman who just wants to make a difference in the lives of the girls she loves all come together in an explosive story that will make you turn the pages as fast as possible to get to the end—which has a nice twist that you won't see coming. Just make sure you have plenty of time to read because you *won't* want to put this one down. A fabulous romantic suspense."
—LYNETTE EASON, bestselling, award-winning author of the Women of Justice series.

"Through crisp writing, Daley paints lifelike characters engaged in a believable struggle that kept me turning pages to the satisfying ending."
—RICHARD L. MABRY, MD, author of *Lethal Remedy* and the Prescription for Trouble series

"Margaret Daley's *Saving Hope* is a beautifully told story of second chances with very real characters who stayed with me long after I finished the book. I'll be looking for more Texas Rangers stories from her!"
—ROBIN CAROLL, author of the Evil series and the Justice Seekers series

More Books by Margaret Daley

A Love Rekindled (Love Inspired, April 2012)
His Holiday Family (Love Inspired, December 2011)
From This Day Forward (Summerside Press, September 2011)
Hidden in the Everglades (Love Inspired Suspense, September 2011)
Protecting Her Own (Love Inspired Suspense, June 2011)

Saving Hope

Men of the Texas Rangers Series

Margaret Daley

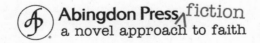

Abingdon Press fiction
a novel approach to faith

Nashville, Tennessee

Saving Hope

Copyright © 2012 by Margaret Daley

ISBN: 978-1-4267-1428-3

Published by Abingdon Press, P.O. Box 801, Nashville, TN 37202

www.abingdonpress.com

The persons and events portrayed in this work of fiction
are the creations of the author, and any resemblance
to persons living or dead is purely coincidental.

Published in association with the Steve Laube Agency.

Library of Congress Cataloging-in-Publication Data

Daley, Margaret.
    Saving hope / Margaret Daley.
        p. cm. — (Men of the Texas Rangers series ; 1)
    ISBN 978-1-4267-1428-3 (trade pbk. : alk. paper)   1. Texas Rangers—Fiction.   2.
Texas—Fiction.   I. Title.
    PS3604.A36S28   2012
    813'.6—dc23

                                                                        2011031795

Printed in the United States of America

1 2 3 4 5 6 7 8 9 10 / 17 16 15 14 13 12

To all the Texas Rangers who protect the people of Texas

*A special thank-you to Ron Pettigrew, a Texas Ranger,
who answered my questions*

Acknowledgments

From the very beginning I have felt the Lord wanted me to tell this story. If I can help one child avoid being a victim of a predator, I will have accomplished what I set out to do. Thank you, God, for giving me that chance.

I want to thank my agent, Steve Laube, who believed in me. I also want to thank Barbara Scott, who bought the Men of the Texas Rangers series, and Ramona Richards, for being a wonderful editor to work with.

I can't forget my husband, Mike, who has been a great support throughout my thirty-year career as a writer. Also, to my critique group (Vickie McDonough, Jan Warren, Caron Smith, Therese Stenzel, and Gloria Harchar), who has been with me from the beginning of this series when it was only an idea.

1

*R*ose gripped her cell phone so tightly her muscles ached. "Where are you, Lily?"

"At—Nowhere Motel." A sob caught on the end of the last word. "Help—me." Lily's breath rattled, followed by a clunking sound as though she'd dropped the phone.

Rose paced the small bathroom at Beacon of Hope. "Lily?" Sweat coated her palms, and she rubbed her free hand against her jeans.

Silence taunted her.

What have you done? But the second that Rose asked that question, an image came to mind of her friend lying on the dingy gray sheets in the cheap motel, wasted, trying anyway she could to forget the horror of her life.

"Lily, talk to me. Stay on the line." Pulling the door open, Rose entered her room. When she saw her roommate, she came to a stop.

Cynthia's wide-eyed gaze fixed on Rose for a few seconds before the fourteen-year-old dropped her head and stared at the hardwood floor. Rose crossed to her dresser, dug into the back of the top drawer, and grabbed a small, worn leather case.

She pushed past her roommate and headed into the upstairs hallway.

Striding toward the staircase, Rose dismissed her roommate's startled expression and focused on the crisis at hand. "Lily, are you still there?"

A sound as though someone fumbled the phone and caught it filtered through the connection. "Rose, I need—you."

"I told you I would come if you wanted to get out. I'll be—"

A click cut off the rest of Rose's words. *No, Lily. Please hang on.*

Rushing down the steps to the first floor, she quickly redialed the number and let it ring and ring. When she approached the program director's office, she finally pocketed her cell, took out her homemade tools, and picked the lock, a skill she learned to give her some sense of control over her life. In the past she'd done what she had to in order to survive.

Guided by the light through the slits in the blinds, Rose entered Kate's darkened office and switched on the desk light. A twinge of guilt pricked her. If Kate found her in here after-hours, how could she explain herself? Especially with what she was going to do next to the woman who had saved her and taken her in.

Kate's gonna be so disappointed in me for stealing—no, borrowing—the van. She's put so much faith in me. But I've got to save Lily. I promised her. When I bring Lily back here, Kate will understand.

Rose used her tools to open the locked drawer on the right. Pulling it out, she rummaged through the papers to find the set of keys at the bottom, then bumped the drawer closed with her hip.

I have no choice, Kate. Please forgive me.

The memory of the words, *I need you,* spurred Rose to move faster. She had to get to her friend. Get her out . . . finally. Bring her to Kate.

Clutching the keys in one hand, she turned off the lamp and carefully made her way to the office door. She eased it open a few inches and peered out into the short hallway. The empty corridor mirrored the feeling inside her.

When would it go away? When will I feel whole?

After she checked to make sure the office door was locked, she hurried toward the side exit of the building that housed the residential program for teens like her. Outside the summer heat blasted her in the face even though it was past midnight. Her heart pounded as hard as her feet hitting against the concrete. Sweat beaded on her forehead as she rushed toward the parking lot to find Beacon of Hope's van. The security light cast a yellow glow on the vehicle at the back of the building. Visions of her friend slipping into drug-induced unconsciousness, no one there to care whether she died or not, prodded her to quicken her steps.

I won't let you down, Lily. She was the reason her friend was where she was right now, stuck in a life that was quickly killing her.

As Rose tried to unlock the white van, her hands shook so badly the keys dropped to the pavement. Snatching them up, she sucked in a breath, then another, but her lungs cried for more oxygen. With her second attempt, she managed to open the door and slip behind the steering wheel. Her trembling hands gripped the hot plastic. After backing out of the parking space, she pressed down on the accelerator and eased onto the street in front of Beacon of Hope. With little driving experience, she would have to go slower than she wanted. She couldn't get caught by the cops. This was her one chance to save her friend. If all went well, she could be back here with Lily before morning.

She tried to clear her mind and concentrate totally on the road before her. She couldn't. Memories of her two years as a prostitute tumbled through her mind, leaving a trail of regrets. One was having to leave Lily behind.

Nowhere Motel—her and Lily's name for one of the hell-holes where they'd had to earn their living. A place—one of several used when they were brought to Dallas—near the highway on Cherry Street. A place where inhuman acts happened to humans—young girls who should be dressing up for their prom, not their next trick.

She'd escaped only because she'd been left for dead on the side of the road when a john discarded her like trash. But the Lord had other plans for her besides death. A judge had seen to it that she came to the Beacon of Hope program, and Kate had given her a glimpse of a better life.

And I'm gonna start with rescuing Lily. I'm not gonna let her die. She's gonna have a chance like me.

Rose slowed as she neared the motel, two rows of units. Bright lights illuminated the front rooms, which maintained an appearance of respectability, while the rooms in the back were shrouded in dimness.

After she parked across the street from Nowhere, she sat in the van staring at the place, its neon sign to welcome travelers taunting her. Sweat rolled down her face, and she swiped at it. But nothing she did stopped the fear from overwhelming her to the point of paralysis. Memories of what went on in the back rooms of the motel threatened to thwart her attempt to rescue Lily before it began.

I owe her. I have to make up for what I did to her.

She pried her hands from the steering wheel and climbed from the van. After jogging across the two lanes, she circled around to the second building that abutted the access road to the highway.

The sounds of cars whizzing by filled the night. People going about their ordinary life while some were barely hanging on. A loud, robust laugh drifted to her as she snuck past the first unit, heading for room three, the one Lily always used at Nowhere. Someone opened a door nearby and stepped out of a room ahead of her. Rose darted back into a shadowed alcove at the end, pressing her body flat against the rough cinder block wall. Perspiration drenched her shirt and face. The stench of something dead reeked from a dumpster a few yards away. Nausea roiled in her stomach.

Two, sometimes three, of *his* guards would patrol, making sure the girls stayed in line. She wasn't sure this was a guard, but she couldn't risk even a quick look. She waited until the man disappeared up the stairs, then hurried toward the third unit. With damp palms, she inched the unlocked door open and peeked through the slit.

Dressed in a little-girl outfit that only underscored Lily's age of fifteen, she lay sprawled on the bed, her long red hair fanning the pillow, the sheets bunched at the end. Her friend shifted, her eyes blinking open. Groaning, she shoved herself up on one elbow, only to collapse back onto the mattress.

Footsteps on the stairs sent a shaft of fear through Rose. Her heartbeat accelerated. She pushed into the room and closed the door, clicking the lock in place. She almost laughed at her ridiculous action as though that would keep anyone out. But she left it locked.

The scent of sex, alcohol, and sweat assailed her nostrils and brought back a rush of memories she'd wanted to bury forever. For a few seconds she remained paralyzed by the door as memories bombarded her from all sides. Hands groping for her. A sweaty body weighed down on top of hers. The fog she'd lived in to escape.

She shook them from her thoughts. *Can't go there. Lily is depending on me.*

Turning toward her friend, she started across the room. Lily's glazed eyes fixed on her. For several heartbeats, nothing dawned in their depths. Then a flicker of recognition.

She tried to rise, saying, "Rose, so sorry . . ." Lily slurred her words as she sank back. "Sor—reee."

"I'm here to get you out." Rose sat on the edge of the bed. "You've got—"

A noise behind her and to the left cut off her next words. She glanced over her shoulder as the bathroom door crashed open, and *he* charged into the room.

"Did you really think I'd let you go?"

His gravelly voice froze Rose for a few seconds. King never came to Nowhere Motel. Too beneath him. He should be—

Finally, terror propelled her into action. She scrambled off the bed and ran for the door. She grappled for the lock, her sweat-drenched fingers slipping on the cold metal.

King slammed her against the wall beside the door—her only escape route. He pressed her back to hold her pinned, the scent of peppermint sickening her. He loved to suck on peppermint candies, and she'd come to hate that smell. The aroma enhanced her desperation.

Words from her street days spewed from her mouth. She twisted and tried to buck him off. He thrust her harder against the wall until she couldn't catch her breath. Lightheaded from the lack of air, she went still.

"You'll always be mine. That john paid for losing you." Her pimp threw the lock on the door and opened it. "Tony."

Oxygen rushed back into her lungs and with it returned the frantic need to get away.

But before she could make a move, King's fingers clamped around her upper arm so tightly she thought he would break it. A six-foot-tall guard appeared in the doorway as King dragged her across the room and flung her on the bed. One of her arms flopped then bounced on the mattress near Lily. Her friend's head lolled to the side. Her eyes closed.

"Hold her." King withdrew a syringe, filled with a clear liquid, from his pocket.

"No," Rose screamed and scrambled over Lily's body. She *had* to get away. She wouldn't go there again.

Tony lunged across the bed and grabbed her leg. His fingers dug into her ankle. Inch by inch he hauled her to him. Lily moaned as Rose slid across her, but Lily's eyes stayed closed.

Can't give up. Rose kicked free and launched herself at the guard, raking her fingernails down his cheek.

He struck her face with his fist. Pain radiated outward from her jaw. Her vision blurred. A metallic taste coated her tongue. The room tumbled through her mind, as if she'd been stuffed into a dryer in the middle of its cycle. The ringing in her ears drowned out what Tony said. Throwing his body over hers, he trapped her on the bed.

Can't—

Her pimp loomed over her. Through the haze, she saw the malicious grin as King gripped her arm and yanked it toward him.

When he held up the syringe, her heart beat so fast she thought she would pass out from the hammering force against her ribcage. She gasped for a mouth full of air, but it wasn't enough.

"No, please not that," she whimpered as he jabbed the needle into her arm.

2

As Kate Winslow jotted down a note at the bottom of a letter she'd received, the door to her office at Beacon of Hope opened. She glanced up.

"Where's the white van?" Harriet, one of the teachers on staff, asked from the entrance.

"In the south parking lot."

"It's not there. I'm supposed to take the girls to the ranch today. We went out there to leave and couldn't find it."

Kate pushed her chair back and caught sight of the barely open right-hand drawer. Pulling it toward her, she searched beneath the papers for the vehicle's second set of keys. Nothing. Finally, she pulled the drawer completely out and dumped the contents on her desk. Still nothing.

"Someone took my keys."

"And stole the van." Harriet covered the distance to Kate's desk. "One of the girls?"

"Anyone missing?"

"Not from my group."

Kate inhaled a deep breath, holding it for a few seconds before releasing it slowly. "We need to do a check. Was everyone at breakfast?"

"No. Rose and Beth were missing. Rose often doesn't eat breakfast, and someone said Beth wasn't feeling well."

"I'll take Rose's room. You check Beth's."

Dread gnawed at Kate as she climbed the stairs to the second floor where the girls often gathered when they weren't busy. Rose had been in the program six months and was really doing well. Kate didn't want to see anything go wrong with the sixteen-year-old's path to a better life.

So often when she received a teenage girl in the program, her physical wounds were healed because she'd come from somewhere besides the Dallas area, and it took a while for the system to send them here. But not Rose. She'd been found by a couple nearly dead on the side of the road just south of the city. Her face, still bruised and cut from the beating she'd received, took weeks to heal. Weeks during which Kate had grown attached to the child. Even more than the other twenty-three girls she housed at Beacon of Hope.

At the door to Rose's room, Kate knocked. When half a minute with no reply passed, she pushed the door open and entered. After she made a visual sweep of the area—noting Rose's made bed—Kate checked the small bathroom the teen and her roommate shared with the girls next door.

Why would Rose take the van? Has she run away? That doesn't make sense, not after our heart-to-heart conversation yesterday.

Kate inspected the closet, full of the teenager's clothes, then pulled open the dresser drawers to see if anything was missing. Everything seemed to be there. Rose wouldn't leave without taking her possessions. She had so little, but she'd always taken special care of what she had.

So what are you doing, Rose? Going back to your old life?

That just didn't seem possible. Rose had begun to have dreams of what her future could be. Yesterday she'd talked about what she was going to do after she got her GED.

Maybe Rose was in the infirmary. Hope flared in Kate. She swung around toward the door and left at a quickened pace.

A minute later, she entered the small infirmary. Harriet, one of the school staff, stood talking with the nurse on duty who was wrapping an Ace bandage around the ankle of a student. Beth lay on a bed next to them. There was no one else present.

Visions of what Rose had looked like when she'd first come to the program flashed into Kate's mind. How the young girl had survived such a beating still amazed her. Fear for her charge clawed at her composure.

If she's back on the street, what will happen to Rose if her ex-pimp finds her? The question chilled her. She shuddered, hugging her arms to her. *I have to find her before it happens.*

Kate signaled for Harriet to step into the hallway. "Rose is missing from her room. I'm going to talk with her roommate while you do a thorough search of the building. Get Jillian and some other staffers to help you. Before we do anything else, I need to know that she's gone for sure."

"I'll tell my girls to wait in the rec hall. Her roommate, Cynthia, is part of my group. I'll send her to your office."

"Let's keep this quiet for now, just among the staff." There were no bars on the windows or locks to keep the teens inside at Beacon of Hope, because she never wanted the girls to feel like criminals. The teens had to agree to come to the voluntary program. They weren't forced, but that didn't mean some didn't feel they had a choice really. She knew she still had to contact the police if someone left on her own. They were still minors, and, legally, they were runaways. But she didn't have to report the van stolen by Rose. At least not until she had exhausted all possibilities concerning the girl. The teen didn't need any more problems.

"We've done well. Remember the success stories. They outnumber the ones who go back to the streets."

And Rose was going to be one of those success stories. Why did you leave, Rose? If I knew that, I might know where you went. "You're right, but sometimes it's hard to remember that when you lose someone special. Rose has so much promise."

"Don't forget there are few places like Beacon of Hope in the United States. The police and courts are beginning to see the need for this type of program. Where are the teens most people have forgotten going to go for help if we aren't here?"

"I'm afraid back on the streets or in the morgue." *That's why I'll do what I need to get results. Someone has to care.*

As Kate strode to her office, she passed a group of teenage girls in the large foyer of the building. With only a nod and a general greeting, she didn't stop to talk as she usually did.

Rose's dream for her future played in Kate's mind. *I want to help girls like me have a better life. I want to make a difference like you.* Tears had shone in Rose's eyes as she'd confided that to Kate yesterday. For the first time Rose had hugged Kate and cried as though she were reliving every horrible act done to her.

But the teen still hadn't told her who her pimp had been. Every time she had tried to get Rose to talk about him and discover something to help the police find him, Rose would clam up, say she couldn't remember anything before she woke up in the hospital. The fear in the child's eyes tore at Kate's heart. Rose knew more than she was saying.

In her office, which overlooked the street that ran in front of Beacon of Hope, she surveyed the room, wondering if anything else was missing. She often met with the staff or some of the teens around an oak table set in the corner with its four comfortable beige padded chairs. She tried to keep meetings as informal as possible. The chocolate-brown leather couch on the opposite wall became her place to crash after a long day. The rest of the area was completed with two wooden file cabinets, a desk, and a set of bookcases between two windows that lit the area with streams of sunlight. Bright posters of locations around the world adorned the mint green walls. This was her home more than her small apartment on the third floor of the shelter. Nothing was out of place or missing.

Her gaze fell upon the books that lined her shelves. What about the hidden cash she kept for emergencies? She crossed the room and retrieved a thick volume. Inside, concealed among the pages were four twenties and two tens. Nothing missing. Her hand shook as she slipped the psychology book back in place.

She had a bachelor's degree in social work with a master's in counseling, but nothing she'd studied at the University of Texas had really prepared her for what she'd faced each day with the teenage girls here, all former prostitutes, some as young as thirteen. She'd remembered when she was eight, her parents gave her an expensive, antique porcelain doll. Her dog had knocked it off the table, and it had smashed when it fell on the marble floor in the large foyer of her childhood home. She'd spent days trying to glue all the pieces together. Her result had gaps in the porcelain face, pieces too shattered to be glued back in place—same as the girls she worked with, some of whose hopes were so shattered she hadn't been able to fix them. Remembering this incident only renewed her determination to do more in the future to help put them back together.

The door flew open. Harriet and a petite brunette hurried into the office. Cynthia kept her head down, her shoulders slumped, until Harriet left them alone.

"Have a seat please." Kate waved the fourteen-year-old to the chair in front of her desk. She took the other one beside it and turned it so she faced the young girl. "Do you know where Rose is?"

No answer. Cynthia hunched her back even more as though drawing in on herself. The child had been at Beacon of Hope for three months because her parents had given up on their daughter, and the only person she'd warmed up to had been Rose.

"Cynthia," Kate waited until the girl peered up. "I think Rose is in trouble, and I want to help her. Is there anything you can tell me about where Rose might be?"

She shrugged, averting her gaze. "She got a call right before she left last night. She never came back to the room."

"Do you know who she was talking to?"

"Not sure but it sounded like the person was in trouble." Tears crowded the teen's eyes. "I know I shouldn't have eavesdropped on Rose, but I don't want anything to happen to her."

"Neither do I."

One tear slipped down Cynthia's cheek. She scrubbed it away, dropped her head, and stared at her lap. "She was nice to me." She peered at Kate. "When she didn't come back—she's in trouble, isn't she?"

"I don't know." Kate pushed to her feet, not sure what to do next. Leaning back against the front of her desk, she clutched its edge.

Unless Rose turned up soon, as much as she wished she didn't have to, her next step would be to go to the police and file a missing person report. No good would come of it. The teen would be considered a runaway, especially because of her background. In her gut, Kate was sure Rose hadn't returned because something bad had happened to her—not because she chose to run away or go back on the street.

If she could just get some kind of lead, maybe she could find Rose. "Cynthia, did she ever tell you anything about her old life? Who her pimp was?"

Shaking her head, the fourteen-year-old twisted her hands together in her lap and kept her gaze down. "She said she didn't remember."

"I think she was remembering. If you recall anything about where Rose might be or who her pimp was, please let me know right away. If Rose is in trouble, I need all the information I can get to find her. Anything, no matter how insignificant, might help me."

"You're gonna look for her?"

"Yes, if I have something to go on. Think back to any talks you two might have had. It could be something casual Rose said."

"I'll try." The teenage girl yanked on the long sleeves of her shirt—over and over.

Was she cutting herself again? Kate approached her, all her actions in slow motion. That didn't stop Cynthia from flinching away, her eyes wide. She pressed her arms to her chest.

"Let me see your arm. Please." Kate forced calmness into her voice while the injustice of what these children had gone through raged inside her. From the beginning, Cynthia had been one she was afraid she would lose. Until she had paired the girl with Rose. She had made a difference in Cynthia.

Rose's roommate stared through her, as though she were somewhere else.

"Please."

The teenager uncurled one arm and presented it to Kate. Slowly she pushed her white cotton shirt up to her elbow. Angry red slashes, many old wounds but a couple of fresh ones, marked Cynthia's skin. Kate unrolled the sleeve and covered the cuts.

"Why don't I walk you to the infirmary to have the nurse look at your arm? I don't want you to get an infection."

"I'm all right." The girl hung her head, her words mumbled so low it was hard for Kate to hear her.

"Humor me."

"I guess so." Cynthia shoved to her feet.

Kate moved toward the door and opened it. "You know you can talk to me any time, 24/7." Since she lived at Beacon of Hope, she was available even in the middle of the night for any crisis that arose. She wished that Rose had come to see her last night. Then maybe she wouldn't be missing, possibly in peril.

"Yes, Ms. Winslow."

"Remember it's Kate. I'm here to help you."

Cynthia shuffled past her into the corridor and followed Kate in silence toward the infirmary. She wanted to put her arm around Cynthia and tell her she wasn't alone anymore. She had someone to turn to now, even if Rose never came back. She'd been surprised the child had let her see her cuts. Maybe one day she'd get through to her. Every failure to reach a girl left a mark on her that she couldn't erase.

Lord, one crisis at a time. I know I want to solve all the problems at once, but Rose is my immediate concern. Help me find her before something bad happens to her.

తౖ

The screen door banged closed behind Wyatt Sheridan as he came out onto his porch and strode to the wooden railing. Setting his mug on it, he surveyed the ranch that had been in his family for over a hundred years. When he had the time, he loved riding his horse over his land. He dreamed of raising quarter horses when he retired from the Texas Rangers.

Rows of black fences and green pastures with a few animals grazing in them stretched out from the left and right of his house. A gravel road led to the highway three hundred yards away. His Lone Star Ranch was his refuge in a world gone crazy. Not far from Bluebonnet Creek, a small town twenty miles northeast of Dallas, he stayed connected to the world out there, but when it got to be too much, he always returned here and rode over his property until he could put to rest the demons that hounded him.

Taking a swig of his black coffee, he hoped it did the trick after being up most of the previous night in a stakeout that led nowhere. He winced at the bitter taste as it slid down his throat. His mother had made the coffee, trying her hand at being domestic, again. It was never gonna happen.

He took another sip and finally pitched the mug's contents over the porch rail. A butterfly fluttered around a bush his mother had planted to attract them. That had been when she was in her gardening phase, which had lasted all of two weeks last year. Much like that butterfly, his mom flitted from one project to the next, never staying long with any of them.

The sound of the screen door squeaking open, then closed, drew him around. "You're up early." He glanced at his watch. "You don't get up before seven even when school is in session."

"It's too hot to ride later." His fourteen-year-old daughter set her tan cowboy hat on her head. "It's in the high nineties before noon."

"That's August in Texas. Who are you going to ride with?"

"Kelly. I'm meeting her in the south pasture. Are ya gonna make the rodeo this evening?"

"Sure, I have to see my gal compete. How about your grandma? Is she coming?"

Maddie shrugged. "I never know what Nana is gonna do next."

"I suspect she doesn't either. Have you seen her this morning?"

His daughter descended the steps. "She told me last night she'd be gone by five-thirty. I think her latest hobby is bird watching."

He chuckled. "Who's into bird watching?"

"Chuck."

"Ah. That explains her interest."

Maddie crossed the front yard and headed for the nearby barn. One of his current assignments with the Child Rescue Task Force, dealing with child prostitution, made him thankful every time he was with his daughter that she was sensible, normal, caring. When Maddie disappeared from view, he made his way inside to make real coffee, not this tasteless tar his mom thought was drinkable.

After brewing some and filling his mug, he started toward his bedroom. His daughter had reminded him he had some chores to do around the ranch before his meeting with the Dallas police. He stopped in mid-stride halfway across the large kitchen. His mother stood in the entrance, her face twisted into a frown.

"I thought you were bird watching. Not many out at seven?" Wyatt blew on his coffee then took a sip. It was perfect.

"Chuck and I had a difference of opinion this morning."

He gritted his teeth then asked, "What about?"

"My talking. I don't understand why I can't talk while bird watching. I can't just sit there and wait. My arms were getting tired holding the binoculars up."

With his mother dressed in a bright orange shirt, tan shorts, and orange sandals with heels, he couldn't imagine her blending in with any type of terrain. "You weren't gone but an hour. How long were you sitting and waiting?"

"Five minutes."

"A record." He pressed his lips together to keep the rest of his comment to himself.

"What's wrong with talking?"

"Nothing, Mom."

"My name is Carrie. I've been telling you and Maddie to call me that. Mom and Nana make me sound old. I'm only fifty-five. I was so young when I had you, practically a child myself."

He fortified himself with a gulp of caffeine-laden drink. "Your name is Caroline. Where is Carrie coming from?"

"Carrie and Caroline are close. I like Carrie better. Makes me sound young. Like that country-western singer that won *American Idol*."

"I have to check a fence before I leave. I'll talk to you later." He passed her in the doorway.

"That's the trouble with being out here in the boonies. No one to talk with."

"Why don't you join another ladies' club or something?" He hurried his step, realizing when she started on that tirade he'd never get anything done.

"Why don't you move into town? Bluebonnet Creek is small, but it has some people. Better yet, Dallas. Don't the Texas Rangers have people in Dallas? We certainly know it has its share of crime. If not, I would settle for Garland, where Company B's headquarters are."

He paused, came back to his mother, and kissed her on the cheek. "I promise we'll talk tonight. You can have my undivided attention then."

"Where's Maddie?"

"She's riding Star Champion. Meeting Kelly in the south pasture."

She swung around. "Then I'll go and talk to her."

"But, Mo—Carrie . . ." It was useless. His mother crossed the dining room and was in the hallway. It wouldn't make any difference what he said. She would do what she wanted, even joining her granddaughter and her friend on a ride.

His cell rang. He unclipped it from his belt. "Sheridan here."

"I'm heading to a crime scene. A rancher found a white van abandoned on his property," The familiar voice was Daniel James, his FBI counterpart on the Child Rescue Task Force.

"Since when do you investigate abandoned cars?" Wyatt strode toward his bedroom, hearing his mother singing a song by the country-western singer she'd named herself after. Singing it off-key.

"Since there's a young girl found near it. The sheriff sent me a picture of the victim. She was reported missing last year in Oklahoma."

He pushed the sound of his mom's fading voice from his mind. "Where?"

"Not too far from you off Highway 78." Daniel gave him the directions.

"Be there in half an hour." Wyatt stuffed his cell back into its belt case and grabbed his gun, wallet, and car keys.

In the kitchen, he jotted a note on the dry-erase board by the wall phone, letting his daughter and mother know where he'd be. For a few seconds, Maddie's smiling face as she started for the barn popped into his thoughts. Another parent would be notified a daughter wasn't ever coming home. He'd wanted to make a difference in children's lives and had asked to be assigned to the Child Rescue Task Force, but sometimes he questioned his sanity when he'd approached his captain about it. His daughter was his life. How would he be able to deal with it if something happened to her?

3

$\mathcal{A}$ half hour later, Wyatt pulled his silver Ford F-150 off the country road and parked behind Daniel's black SUV. The crime scene techs were crawling all over the area like ants on their hill. Not far from the pockmarked highway sat an older white 8-passenger van. Along the side, a deep groove ran its length as if someone had keyed it. As he approached the FBI agent, Wyatt noted the vehicle's Texas tag number. Then his gaze fell upon the flat back tire, the other one stuck in a muddy patch of ground.

"Is that where they found the body?" Wyatt gestured to the left toward a cluster of men and one woman standing in a grove of trees.

"Yeah. I had them wait until you came to transport the body." Daniel started forward.

"How'd you identify the victim so quickly?"

"I've been monitoring the missing girls in this region. That one stood out to me. She disappeared about a year ago. She was fourteen at the time. Her parents had insisted she'd been kidnapped, that she wasn't a runaway. They hounded the FBI office in Oklahoma, demanding they find their daughter. She vanished. One classmate said she had been hanging out with a new group of friends and had a secret boyfriend. Older. None of her classmates knew the friends or boyfriend. The case sent up a red flag to me."

"So you suspected she'd been wooed by a recruiter?"

"Yeah." Daniel stopped in the middle of the meadow, took out his cell, and passed it to Wyatt. "This is the photo the parents used for the Amber Alert. She fits the profile of someone the recruiter would go after. Not overly beautiful but not unattractive."

Wyatt stared at the picture of a young girl with red hair pulled back in a ponytail, a big smile and large gray eyes. But what caught his full attention was that look of innocence in her expression. His own daughter with gray eyes and long dark red hair came to mind. The two similarities knotted his gut. He tore his gaze from the photo. "How old was she when this pic was taken?"

"The month before. You see it, too."

"The innocence. Yeah. That seems to attract a certain predator." His grip on the phone strengthened, his jaw clenched so tightly pain streaked down his neck. Finally, he released his hold and gave the phone back to Daniel. "They're getting younger and younger."

"You know the statistics. The average age has become thirteen."

Maddie isn't much older than thirteen. The fact drove a sharp blade straight through his heart.

Daniel continued his trek across the pasture. "I don't think they expected the body to be found so fast. It was buried in a shallow grave."

"You think the death was recent?"

"The medical examiner says within the past twelve hours. He'll know more after an autopsy is done."

"How was the girl found?"

"The rancher saw the van when walking across the field with his dog at dawn. While he was checking out the van, his dog began sniffing the ground. Then it raced toward the trees and started barking. When the rancher got there, the animal had dug up part of the body. That's when he called the sheriff."

Wyatt paused and turned back toward the van. "So the suspect drove into this field at night got stuck and a tire went flat?"

"Maybe he left the road because the tire went flat and ended up stuck. The end result was the suspect decided to ditch the van here and bury the body."

"A change in plans? Maybe. If that's so, then I wonder where the suspect was heading with the girl."

Daniel resumed his trek toward the cluster of people in the grove. "We'll ask him when we find him."

"Has the tag number been run?"

"Yep, and that's the interesting part. It belongs to Beacon of Hope, a program for teenage prostitutes. I've heard good things about it."

Wyatt knew a little about the privately funded, nonprofit organization. It was gaining a top-notch reputation for working with former teenage prostitutes from all over the Southwest. He'd considered talking with the program director to get her insight on what was happening to these girls on the streets. Possibly even interview some of the teens now that he was on the Child Rescue Task Force. It had been on his long list of things to do. "When was the van reported missing?"

"It hasn't been."

"Maybe it was stolen last night. It's early yet. Maybe they haven't noticed it's missing yet."

"Maybe everyone is sleeping in."

Wyatt chuckled. "Sleeping in? What's that?"

"Beats me." Daniel stopped next to a crime scene tech who stood over the dead girl, lying in the unzipped body bag.

Wyatt fixed his attention on the teen. Ordinary features arranged in a pasty death mask surrounded by her stringy red hair. Her gray eyes vacant and staring straight up at him as though to beg him to find the person responsible. He blinked and averted his gaze from the body.

This isn't Maddie. He had to remember that. He had to remain detached if he was going to do his job. His hands curled at his sides. There was nothing innocent about the victim's face now, and he intended to discover who robbed her of that. The sound of the tech zipping the body bag echoed through the stand of trees.

Slowly, Wyatt flexed his fists. "Any physical evidence gathered?"

"Footprints were destroyed by the rancher and his dog." Daniel gestured at the ground nearby. "There are some at the van that might belong to the suspect and a set walking off toward the road. I have some deputies canvassing the places up and down the road to see if anyone saw someone last night."

"What if the suspect had a partner who picked him up? If this is part of a prostitution ring, there was probably a partner following to give the driver a ride after dumping the van."

"Probably. What's down this road?"

"Woods. A lake."

"Drive the van into the lake? That could work."

"Yeah."

Daniel moved back while two deputies hefted the body bag and carted it off toward the road. "We'll scour the area, talk to everyone we can find. Let's hope someone saw something."

"And I think I'll pay Beacon of Hope a visit and tell them their van has been found."

After staring at the sheet of paper for ten minutes and not remembering anything she'd read, Kate closed the file and pushed it away. It wasn't any use. She couldn't do the normal day-to-day work running Beacon of Hope when Rose was missing. Now for thirty-eight hours, not that she was counting or anything.

Yesterday she'd spent her time talking to the girls and discovering no one knew anything beyond what Cynthia had told her. She'd gone to the police station and filed a missing-person report, and she knew beyond checking the city hospitals, morgue, and juvenile detention center for Rose, nothing would be done. And she'd already done that herself. She still hadn't reported the van missing, however. She would have to soon. But she kept praying that the teen would appear at Beacon of Hope with the vehicle.

The sound of her office door opening caught Kate's attention. An older woman with short black hair, wearing a designer sundress with a short-sleeveed jacket entered. Based on her stern look, Kate resigned herself to the fact the next few minutes wouldn't be pleasant.

"Mother, what are you doing here?" Kate rose from behind her desk.

"Harriet just told me a girl is missing and so is one of the vans. What is going on, Katherine?"

"Are you asking as my mother or the head of the Winslow Foundation?"

"Both."

"Rose left here two nights ago around midnight and hasn't been back."

"And she took the van?" Her mother marched to the couch along the far wall and eased onto it, crossing her legs.

With a sigh, Kate skirted her desk and took the other end of the sofa, trying to relax back against the cushion. But nothing she did mitigated the tension woven through her. "I don't know for sure."

"But you think she did?"

She nodded.

"What do the police say about the van?"

"I haven't reported it missing yet."

"Why not? You can't protect *them* when they do something wrong. This is what thanks you get for trying to help *them*."

Her mother's icy emphasis on the word *them* produced a constriction in Kate's chest. She delayed replying—forcing oxygen into her lungs. "The teens I'm trying to help are young girls who need someone to care about them. To protect them."

"They—they are prostitutes."

"Former ones. Often these girls have been lured into a situation they can't get out of easily, especially if there isn't somewhere they can go to get assistance. So many of them are throwaway kids, children who their parents don't—"

Her mother fluttered her hand in the air. "I heard all this before when you came to the foundation for money."

"And I appreciate your financial support, but I need more than that." *I want you to believe I can make this work.*

"The only reason I agreed is because your father thought it would be a good tax deduction, and he didn't want our friends to think we didn't support our own—even in foolish endeavors." Her mother's sharp gaze zeroed in on Kate. "So what are you going to do about your van?"

"If it isn't found, I'll use my own money to replace it."

"You mean from your grandmother's trust fund."

"Yes."

Her mother clutched her Prada purse. "She didn't give you that money to throw at a cause like—like—"

"Don't go there." Kate pushed to her feet, her head throbbing. "Thank you for coming, but as you know, I've got a lot to do."

Her mother remained seated. "Like what?".

Kate glanced away, resisting the urge to squirm under her mother's intense scrutiny. Finally, she knew there was no way around the truth. "I'm going to go look for Rose."

She shot to her feet. "Katherine Winslow, you will do no such thing."

Kate winced at the all-too-familiar reprimand. "Thank you for dropping by." She started for the office door.

At the entrance, she turned back toward her mother who still stood by the couch. Her stare drilled right through Kate. An uncomfortable silence seemed to plunge the room's temperature. She refused to allow her mother's usual techniques to get to her.

A minute later, her mother gripped her purse in one hand and crossed the room, her gaze never leaving Kate's. She'd lived through many attempts at intimidation by Laura Winslow, the matriarch of her wealthy Texas family. *This is no different, and I'm not giving in.*

At the door, she straightened her shoulders and looked down her nose at Kate. "I can pull my funding."

"Then if I have to, I'll use my whole trust fund to keep the program going until I can find someone else who believes everyone needs a second chance."

Her mother blinked, doubt flickering into her eyes. "Let the police do their job."

"That's not enough."

The haughty façade melted. "I'm not going to let you put yourself in danger."

"You can't protect me forever. I'm in the Lord's hands. I have His blessing in this endeavor."

"We'll see about that." Her mother jerked the door open and nearly collided with a six-foot man poised in her way.

Surprise crossed her mother's face for a few seconds before she recovered, drew herself back, and angled to the side. "Good. Someone to talk some sense into you." Without another word, she marched down the corridor, the sound of her white high heels clicking on the tile floor.

Kate watched her disappear from view before turning her attention to the stranger dressed in brown cowboy boots, tan slacks, white short-sleeve shirt, a black tie, a white Stetson, and a gun in a holster on his belt. She finally fixed upon the silver star pinned over his heart. A Texas Ranger. His presence filled the doorway and locked her attention on his neutral expression, not one indication of why he was at Beacon of Hope.

Rose? Did he know something about her? "May I help you?" Dread settled in the pit of her stomach. Had Rose been found dead?

"I'm Wyatt Sheridan with the Texas Rangers." He pulled his wallet out of his back pocket and flipped it open to show her his ID. "I need to have a word with you."

She stayed rooted to the spot for several seconds. Hope that he knew anything concerning Rose evaporated. Surely, the local police hadn't called a Texas Ranger in on a missing teen's case—one they hadn't thought was a kidnapping.

"Ma'am?"

His deep Southwestern drawl yanked her back to the matter at hand. "Yes, come in." She stepped to the side, gripping the edge of the door. After closing it, she faced the Texas Ranger with eyes like quicksilver. "Can I help you with anything?"

"I hope so. Are you aware that your white van is missing?"

"Yes. Have a seat." She waved her hand toward the chair in front of her desk while she took her seat behind it. "I wasn't aware the Texas Rangers would be interested in a missing vehicle."

"So it hasn't been stolen?" He leaned back as though this was a casual conversation about the weather. "Who took the van?"

"Why do you want to know?" She pulled her chair close to the desk and folded her hands on its wooden top—to keep them from trembling. *If Rose had been found, he would have mentioned that first. Which means she wasn't with the van.*

"It was found this morning in a field."

"Good," she managed to say while inside questions assailed her, ones she didn't want to ask out loud. *Where is Rose? Where was it found? What did that mean for Rose?*

"Why haven't you reported it missing? Who took the van?" His calm voice belied the intensity behind his queries.

"I'm not sure who took my van."

His gray eyes narrowed. His mouth pinched into a frown. "Who do you *think* took it?"

She glanced down at her keyboard off to the side on her desk. "A teen staying at Beacon of Hope." She lifted her gaze to his. "But I have no proof it was her."

"Who?"

"She goes by the name Rose Garland."

"Goes by?"

"She was found near Garland, Texas, beaten badly. Her injuries caused quite a bit of trauma to her brain. She had holes in her memory. She insisted her name was Rose but couldn't remember her last one. She couldn't or wouldn't tell the authorities anything that happened to her other than she'd been kept against her will and forced to have sex with different men. No names. Nothing. Rose decided to go by Garland. So far no one has come forward to ID her."

After removing a pad and pen from his pocket, the Texas Ranger leaned forward. The chiseled planes of his tanned features settled into an unreadable expression. "But you think she knows more?"

"Yes. I think she has been regaining her memory lately."

"The police couldn't find her parents?"

"No. There wasn't a missing person report about anyone who fits her description. No match with her fingerprints was found either. So she ended up here. This is a last-ditch place for some girls, and I work with the authorities and parents or guardians to save as many as I can."

He wrote a note on his paper pad. "And she hasn't said anything to you about her past?"

"Nothing that tells me who did that to her. The rest of what has transpired between us is confidential." She squeezed her hands together. "Tell me why you want to know about Rose."

"Because we found a young girl's body near your abandoned van."

Why didn't he say that at the beginning? Her heartbeat accelerated, pounding a rapid staccato. *Please Lord, not Rose. I could have helped her. I had such hope for her.*

She collapsed back in her chair. Words swirled around in her mind, refusing to form a coherent comment after his declaration. "Rose is dead," she finally murmured.

"I don't think it's Rose."

The thundering of the pulse in her ears muffled his voice, and she strained forward to hear his quiet words. "You don't think it's Rose?"

He nodded.

"Why?"

"She has been identified as Lillian Harris from Oklahoma. She was reported missing a year ago."

"But Rose might not be her real name. Although she remembered that, it doesn't mean it's her given name. I felt Rose was hiding something. I sensed she knew more than she was letting on. A lot of these girls have been terrorized and are frightened of being found and forced to go back to that life. Some never speak about it. Others finally do."

"Lillian's family was actively looking for her. It doesn't sound like Rose's was."

"Still. I'd like to be sure it isn't Rose in the morgue."

Surging to his feet, Wyatt unhooked his cell phone from his belt. "I can show you a photo of the girl who is dead. Just a sec." He strode out into the hall, his voice too low for Kate to hear who he called or what he said.

The pulsating pain behind her eyes increased. She kneaded her fingertips into her temples. *If it isn't Rose, what do I do next? That means she abandoned the van and did what? Where would she be? Why was a young girl found near the van? How is Rose involved?*

The click of the door being closed as the Texas Ranger reentered her office brought her head up, and her shoulder-length hair fell away from her face. The somber expression on his craggy face underscored the seriousness of the whole situation. The teens she'd worked with came from a horrible, terrifying life, but this was the first possible death of one of her girls while under her care. The thought of what he was about to show her iced her blood.

He covered the distance to her desk and slid his cell across its surface. A beautiful young girl maybe thirteen or fourteen with long red hair in a ponytail, alabaster skin, and large gray eyes peered back at her. The beaming smile caught Kate's attention and broke her heart.

Her lungs ached from holding her breath. She finally blew a long breath out and said, "That isn't Rose. I've never seen her. You think she was mixed up with prostitution?"

"We'll know more after the autopsy is done. But it's a definite possibility, especially since she was found near your van that was probably taken by Rose. So if this isn't Rose, do you have any idea where she is? What connection Rose would have with Lillian Harris? How did Lillian end up dead not far from your van that you think Rose took?"

"No idea where she is, but this fits what Rose's roommate told me about that night Rose left."

"What happened?" He took his phone and slipped it back onto his belt.

"Rose got a call late. Her roommate, Cynthia, got the impression the person Rose was talking to was in trouble."

"Do the girls have phones in their room?"

"No. There's one they can use in the rec room and some have cells—usually prepaid ones, which are more affordable for them. They like the freedom of having one. Some of the girls have part-time jobs. Rose was one of them. She'd started working at a fast-food restaurant across from the park last month. We start bank accounts for the girls with jobs, but allow them to hold out a part of their paycheck for their own use. The first thing Rose bought with her money was a GoPhone. She was so proud she had saved up for it."

"Besides going to work, where else did Rose go while she was here?"

"She went to church with me on Sundays. The students go on outings on the weekends and sometimes during the week if it has to do with their schoolwork. We have several accredited teachers here associated with the school my church runs. These girls are working for their GED or a high school diploma. Their program is tailored for each girl's individual needs. The same with any medical or counseling needs. Some attend counseling sessions here, and we have a nurse on staff. Others go to see people in private practice we have agreements with. Rose refused to go to talk with anyone outside here."

"So, she's usually with someone associated with Beacon of Hope except at work?"

"Yeah. I have three staff members besides myself who are available to supervise the outings. There are a few businesses where the girls can work, all places where I know the manager. They are all within a couple of blocks of here. This isn't a prison. I don't want the girls to feel like it is. As they progress through the program, they are given more freedom and opportunities." The intensity pouring off Wyatt Sheridan made her feel she had to justify everything they did at Beacon of Hope. "We're here to help the girls, not make them feel like criminals. They're the victims."

"Which restaurant?"

"The Ultimate Burger."

He wrote something down on his pad. "I'd like to talk to Cynthia."

"She isn't here right now. She's on one of those outings I mentioned. They aren't due back for another hour."

"Then I'll go to Rose's job and talk with the people there. I'll come back to interview Rose's roommate. If there's anyone who Rose is close to, I'd like to talk to them too."

"Cynthia should be back by three."

"I'll be here then." He stood. "Do you have a photo of Rose?"

"I can run one off."

"Send it to my email address. I'd like to have it on my cell." He took out a business card and wrote on the back of it, then handed it to Kate.

She glanced at the address then at him. "Then you're going to look into Rose's disappearance?"

"Yes. If Rose was the one who took your van, there definitely is some kind of connection."

Hope took root inside her. Maybe Rose had a chance. *Please, Lord, help us get to Rose before something happens to her like Lillian Harris.*

Kate followed the Texas Ranger toward the door. "I think Rose is in trouble. I'm so afraid her pimp found her, and she's right back where she was six months ago." *Or dead.* That thought sent a shudder down her length. "I'll help you anyway I can."

After opening the door, Wyatt turned back and tipped his hat, some of the severity easing from his expression. One corner of his mouth tilted up. "I appreciate that, ma'am."

"Kate, please."

"I'll be back—Kate."

⊰◈⊱

Rose struggled to clear her mind, but her thoughts wandered around in a circle, a fog wanting to drag her down again into the void. Slowly, sensations came back to her, followed by clarity. The suffocating scent of mold and dust. The roughness touching her skin. The dryness of her mouth. Her last memory before she succumbed to whatever King had given her.

Her eyes inched open. Blackness surrounded Rose like a tomb. So dark she couldn't see her hand a few inches from her face. The damp coolness of the stone pressed into her back. Her jaw ached. She grazed her finger across it and winced. Rolling to the side, she pulled her legs up and hugged them to her chest. Tears welled up in her and flooded her eyes.

The Deprivation Room.

How long have I been here?

Wet tracks streamed down her face. *He'll keep me here until he breaks me or*—she wouldn't think of the alternative.

I'm not letting you win, King.

Then she scanned the inky wall enveloping her, and fear stole her next breath and the one after that. An invisible band about her chest contracted. Her fear morphed into terror, threatening to send her over the edge.

Can't let it.

What would Kate do?

Thinking about Beacon of Hope and Kate calmed some of the panic. She wouldn't die friendless. Kate cared.

Why didn't I ask her for help? Why did I think I could rescue Lily alone?

Because I've always been alone.

Fresh tears jammed her throat when she remembered her friend on the bed, forced to lure Rose to Nowhere Motel. *Lily is blaming herself. King will use that to control her even more.*

Shoving herself to a sitting position, Rose reached out until her fingertips encountered the rough texture of the wall. Then she began inching along the perimeter, stopping only when she felt the smooth surface of the door. After trying to open it, she examined the handle and lock.

A thought flashed into her mind. She slid her hand into her back pocket and discovered the small, flat pouch with her tools she'd used on Kate's desk. Hope shot a dose of adrenaline through her.

She knelt on the hard stone floor and felt around until she managed to insert her homemade pick into the lock. Her arms shook as she held her tools up working on her escape. Hunger gnawed her stomach and weakened her, but she would do this if it was the last thing she did.

I won't go back to my old life.

Frustration caused her to hurry her movements. One of her tools slipped from her grasp and fell to the ground. She patted the stone nearby. Nothing.

No! She began sweeping both her arms over the floor. *It's got to be here.* Her fingers touched something long and thin.

She dropped her head against the cold stone, waiting for her heart to slow its rapid beating. *Thank you, Lord.*

When she went back to the door, this time she drew in several calming breaths and then proceeded methodically. The sound of the lock tumblers clicking filled her with renewed hope. She shoved her tools into her back pocket then inched the door open. A bright glow blinded her. She closed her eyes, then eased her lids up little by little until she'd adjusted to the light.

Across from her, shelving made of wood planks lined the wall. Off to the side a staircase offered her the way out. Rose pushed out into the basement room, but a sensory overload bombarded her and she stumbled.

4

August in Texas. There was one word to describe it. Hot. Wyatt opened the door into Ultimate Burger, and a blast of cool air surrounded him, beckoning him inside. The aroma of grilled hamburger meat reminded him he hadn't eaten lunch yet, even though it was nearly three.

After a quick scan to assess where the exits were and how many people were in the restaurant, he approached the counter and looked over the menu plastered above him on the wall. "I'll take a number two with a sweet tea."

The teenage girl, probably sixteen or seventeen, behind the cash register punched the appropriate buttons and said, "That'll be five dollars and seventy-two cents." She peered up at him, a certain dullness to her eyes and a slowness of movement proclaiming her boredom. "Anything else?"

"No." He paid for his order. "Is the manager here?"

She twisted around and called out, "Gloria. Someone's here to see ya." With a glance over her shoulder at his chest, she added, "Police."

Behind him the only two customers in the place scraped their chairs back, dumped their trash in the big container by the door, and left. As they did, four young people—three girls and one boy—came into the restaurant and sauntered toward the counter.

"Can I help you?"

Wyatt sidled to the left to let the group order and shifted so he faced them, but could still glimpse the older lady who must be the manager. "Gloria?"

She nodded while her gaze strayed to the three girls and one boy. A frown pinched her thin lips together.

"Is there a problem?" he asked in a low voice, tossing his head slightly in the direction of the group.

The manager leaned toward him, still staring at the young people. "They're troublemakers. Come in here to get cool and hardly buy anything, but stay for a long time. Can you do anything about that?"

"What kind of trouble have they caused?"

"Loud. Laughing. I think they're making fun of me."

"If they do anything illegal, I'll do something about it. I need to ask you about one of your employees."

"Rose Garland. I can't believe the police are doing anything about her being gone."

"Why?"

"You know—because of what she was."

The accusing tone in the manager's voice nettled Wyatt. He straightened and retrieved a card from his wallet. "Rose is missing. She may be in trouble. I need to know if anything recently happened here concerning Rose. Did someone she might not have wanted to talk to come in here?"

"You're worried about her? She can obviously take care of herself while you can't do anything about these hooligans who like to loiter here."

"Have you said anything to them about leaving after they finish their sodas?" He slid his glance to the group sauntering toward a table by the front plateglass window.

"Well, no. Look at them. Tattoos all over them, their hair spiked. One of the girls wears a dog collar and the boy is so large. I'm not dumb."

Wyatt counted to ten slowly in his mind then said, "So nothing out of the ordinary has happened with Rose lately?"

"No. She used to talk to them."

"How did Rose interact with them?"

"Like she was their new best friend. The grubbier a person was, the more Rose responded to them."

Wyatt slipped his card toward the manager. "Why did you hire her?"

"Because I was told to. My boss likes to feel like he's doing something good for the community and help the girls from Beacon of Hope. That and he likes the lady that runs the place."

"Is he around?"

"Him? Come here? Maybe once a month to check up. Otherwise, I don't see him."

"So he doesn't know Rose?"

"No, he pretty much gives Kate Winslow free rein to suggest who she thinks is good for a job here. I tell you, I'm not one bit surprised that Rose went back to her old life. She only makes minimum wage here. Not much to live on."

"Thank you. If you think of anything else, please call me." He touched the brim of his cowboy hat then headed toward the group of teens.

Their laughter vied with the sounds of his footsteps. The boy stopped talking and gave him the once over, catalogued, appraised, and dismissed. Wyatt continued his trek as the rest of them fell silent and stared at him.

"I understand y'all like to come in here a lot." Wyatt hovered near the young man, who sat with shoulders hunched, head now dropped forward, eyes downcast.

Silence greeted his opening remark. Hostile looks pierced him. One girl, the tallest and very thin, narrowed her gaze on his silver star.

"I could use your help," he said with a smile. "Y'all look like you're aware of things going on around here."

The tall girl blinked, her attention swinging to the teen across from her. Finally, she peered back at him. "You aren't here to throw us out?"

"No, why should I?"

The boy raised his head. "Because she doesn't like us." He fluttered his hand toward the manager, who glared at the group.

"Nope. Y'all aren't doing anything wrong."

"What kind of help do ya need?" the tall girl asked and sipped her soda.

"Do you know Rose Garland?"

A couple of them shook their heads.

But the boy's brows slashed together. "The girl who works here? Long blond hair, pretty?"

"Yes."

"She isn't here. I haven't seen her in a couple of days. Usually she's here by now." The teenage boy cupped his hands around his drink.

"Yeah, Cal. You're right," the girl across from the tall one said, "She told me she was working as much as she could so she could get a car one day."

"Have you noticed anything unusual concerning her? Talking to someone who wasn't a customer? Upset about something?"

Cal frowned, his body tensing. "Why? Is she in trouble?"

"She's missing."

"A runaway?" The tall girl slurped the last of her soda.

"No, I think someone's taken her. That's why I'm asking around so anything you can tell me even if it doesn't seem important might help me find her."

Quiet blanketed the group as they peered at each other.

"Something happened?" Wyatt pulled up a chair and sat, wanting to make it clear he was staying until they told him.

Cal hung his head while he ran his forefinger and thumb up and down his straw. "Nothing here. From what we saw, she worked hard then left. A white van came and picked her up when she got off work. At least the times I've seen her leave."

The word *but* dangled in the air between Cal and Wyatt. "But something happened somewhere else?"

"One day her ride was late, and a young girl I've seen in the park sometimes caught Rose's attention. Rose ran across the street into the park and hugged the girl. They talked a few minutes. When Rose saw the van coming down the street, she grabbed hold of the girl's hand. But the girl yanked herself away. She started to hurry away, but Rose stopped her and pleaded with her. When the girl shook her head, Rose gave her something."

Wyatt held Cal's gaze. "What?"

"Don't know. A piece of paper I think. It was hard to tell. I was on the other side of the road in the park by that time."

"What did the girl look like?"

"Red hair. Pale. She didn't look too good."

Lillian? "Have you seen the girl before that or since?"

"A couple of times in the park. I think she's . . ." Cal averted his gaze and stared at the tall teen catty-corner from him.

"You think what?"

"We think she and a couple of others are turning tricks in the park," the tall girl said.

"Why do you think that?" Although the thought didn't surprise Wyatt, he wanted to know what made the group come to that conclusion.

She looked at him as though he were crazy. "The way they acted, and the fact the men and the girls would disappear for a while."

"Have you seen any of them lately?"

The teens shook their heads, except for Cal who said, "This has happened before. A group of girls come for a week or two, then leave."

"Is it ever the same ones?"

Cal cocked his head to the side. "No, not that I've seen. You might ask around."

Wyatt rose and took out four business cards. "If any of you remember anything else or see anything happening in the park that I might be interested in, please give me a call. I think Rose is in a lot of trouble and needs help." He studied each teen for a few seconds before he started for the door.

Cal caught up with him halfway across the restaurant. "You really think Rose is in trouble?"

"Yep."

"The others don't know this, but I talked with Rose the next day about the redhead in the park. Rose got upset at me and told me to mind my own business. Later I saw her crying in back of this place."

"Did you say anything to her then?"

"No. She made it clear she didn't want my help. Shut me down real fast."

"How was she after that toward you?"

"I didn't see her after that. She hasn't been to work since that day."

"Personally, I'm glad you didn't mind your own business. Thanks."

After going back to the counter for his food, Wyatt exited the Ultimate Burger and stared across the street at the park. The sun streamed down on him, baking him in the heat of the day. When the glare of its rays off the windshield and chrome of the nearby cars blinded him, he reached into his pocket and slipped on his sunglasses then crossed to his truck.

His cell rang as he climbed into the cab. He noticed the number and smiled. "Hi, honey."

"Dad, you should be home by now. I need to leave soon for the rodeo."

He'd forgotten. He shouldn't have, but whenever a child was involved in a case, he lost track of time. "I'll be a little late. I got caught in Dallas. Can you get Nana to take you to the rodeo?"

Her heavy sigh came through the line loud and clear. "Again?"

"I promise I'll be there to see your competition. Can you go ask her? I know she was going too."

"Fine. She's in her bedroom getting rid of all her bird-watching things."

"The binoculars?"

"Well, that and the books she bought, as well as that outfit Chuck had her buy. You know the one that was camouflaged so she would blend in. I wouldn't be surprised if she cuts it up into little rags to use while cleaning. She hated that."

"So Chuck and her are over for good?" he asked as he heard a knock on wood.

"Looks that way," a long pause then, "Nana, can you take me to the rodeo grounds?"

"Sure, sweet pea, if you remember to call me Carrie. Is that your dad?"

"Yes."

"Why is he going to be late again?"

"Don't know. Thanks . . . Carrie. We need to leave in half an hour. I want to be there early."

The sound of something ripping filled the air. "I'll be ready just as soon as I carry this box out to the trashcan."

"I told Dad you'd throw that away." His daughter giggled. "Dad, she can take me. Why are you gonna be late?"

"A new case I'm working on. Nothing you need to be concerned about." He unwrapped his burger, probably cold now.

"Don't say that! Whenever you do I get worried."

The second he said that last sentence, he'd wanted to take it back, especially when Maddie's voice held a frantic edge to it. "Hon, you don't need to worry. All I'm doing is interviewing a girl. No big deal."

"Are you sure?"

"Yes. See you at the rodeo grounds."

When he hung up and laid his cell on the seat next to him, he took a bite of his hamburger and washed it down with a gulp of tea, then cranked the engine and pulled out of the parking space. Out of his rearview mirror, he noticed the four teens leaving the restaurant with the manager coming to the door to watch them. The group moseyed toward the street and intentionally ran across just in front of a car that had to brake to keep from hitting them. Gloria's piercing gaze zeroed in on him. He wondered if those teens came into the restaurant just to see the manager's reaction. Wyatt laughed at the thought. It would have been something he'd have done as a teenager.

Five minutes later, Wyatt parked in the same place at Beacon of Hope and finished the last bite of his food. The interview with the teens at the Ultimate Burger kept spinning around in his brain. Was the redhead Lillian? What had Rose given her? Why was she crying the next day? Did Rose know the girl because they had the same pimp? Did her ex-pimp know where Rose was?

Wyatt went in search of Kate Winslow. Without finding Rose, he doubted he would get too many answers to those questions. He might never. If Rose had talked with Lillian, was their encounter the reason the young redhead was found dead this morning? Would Rose's body be discovered too? He needed to talk with Daniel to make sure they search the surrounding land for another body.

When he approached the director's office, he saw the door open. He found the woman standing at her window looking out. He cleared his throat.

She swiveled around. Her dark brown eyes flared for a few seconds. "Oh, you're early. I thought you might be Cynthia. I'm having Harriet bring her here."

He entered. "Does she know I want to talk with her?"

"No, I wanted to wait until you came. If she's given time to think about you talking with her, she'll get nervous and upset."

He cocked a grin. "I have that effect on some."

She gestured toward the table. "Have a seat. I hope it's okay that I sit in on the interview."

"I want your input. You've worked with these girls for a while and know them. Your presence might make them open up more to me."

"Then would you mind if I conduct the interview? I think Cynthia will respond better to me asking the questions than you. She doesn't do well with strangers."

"Sure. If there's something I need to know, I can ask at the end. I mainly want to know what happened the night Rose left with the van." Wyatt took a chair. "I was hoping to stay after talking with Cynthia and interview a few more girls, but I have a family obligation."

Kate chuckled, her whole face bright with merriment. "I know about family obligations. I get pulled into one at least once a week."

"Pulled in? That's an interesting way to put it."

"With my mom—that's the only way to put it. Laura Winslow can run over a person faster than a herd of stampeding cattle."

"I've read about her in the newspaper. She is a force to be reckoned with in Dallas."

"If it's a large charity event, she has her fingerprints all over it. She runs the Winslow Foundation and takes her job very seriously."

"Much like you?"

Kate's gaze fastened onto his. "Yeah, much like me. I guess my mother and I are more alike than I care to admit."

"I can't say that about me and my mom. She's like that runaway train bounding down the mountain. *Full steam ahead* is her motto, without checking to make sure the brakes work first."

"Your mom sounds the exact opposite of mine, who plans everything down to the tiniest detail. I've seen a show about swapping wives for a week. How about swapping mothers for a week?"

"Shh. Don't let them hear us say that. We'd never hear the end of it."

Her soft laughter stirred something in Wyatt—something that he'd buried a long time ago when his wife, Rebecca, had been murdered. He never wanted to care again about someone that way.

A sound out in the corridor drew his attention toward the entrance. A petite girl about Maddie's age appeared in the doorway with an older lady behind her.

"Thanks, Harriet. Come in, Cynthia, and have a seat." Kate patted the table in front of a vacant seat.

The girl's eyes grew round as she stared at the silver star he wore. "I haven't done nothing. I don't know nothing," she mumbled and stayed put, even placing one foot back as if she was going to whirl around and flee.

"Cynthia, you aren't in trouble. Ranger Sheridan is here to help us find Rose. You want us to find her, don't you?"

The scared teen nodded once then rested her chin against the top of her chest.

"He wanted me to ask you a few questions. You don't have to answer any of them if you don't want to, but you may know more than you think. Will you join us please? It's your choice."

Kate's soothing, coaxing tone relaxed him. He hoped it did the same for the child. Out of all the girls he'd seen in the house, this one looked the most vulnerable.

A minute ticked away before Cynthia shuffled toward the table. When she reached to pull the chair out, her long sleeve shirt rode up her arm, and he glimpsed several lashes, one red, done recently, and two healed on her skin. What had this child gone through in her short life? All he wanted to do was go home and hug his daughter and never let her go.

Cynthia jammed her sleeve back in place and plopped onto the seat. She kept her head down, her hands in her lap.

"If you get uncomfortable, remember you don't have to say anything. We're here to help Rose, and you can, too. Nothing else. Okay?"

The child gave a quick nod.

"I've told Ranger Sheridan what happened the night that Rose disappeared. Have you been able to think of anything else that might help us?"

"No," she mumbled in such a low tone that Wyatt had trouble hearing her.

"Do you know who Rose was talking to that night she disappeared?"

"Someone in trouble. Not sure who."

"Did Rose ever receive any other calls on that phone?"

The only indication Cynthia heard the question was that she ducked her head down even further. Wyatt shot Kate a look, urging her to probe her reaction.

Kate leaned closer to Cynthia, next to her but not crowding her. "Who called Rose? Lillian?"

"I think so. The night before," a long pause, then, "No, it wasn't Lillian but Lily."

"Did you hear what was said?"

The teen shook her head, finally peering up at Kate. "I only heard the excitement when Rose answered. Then she left our room."

Lily was probably Lillian. Wyatt shifted in his chair. He had a connection between the dead girl and the missing one.

"And you didn't overhear anything in the hallway?" Kate asked.

Tears glistened in the girl's eyes. "No. When she came back into the room after talking with Lily, she wouldn't say anything. She was upset. I should have asked her what was wrong. I didn't want her to get mad at me."

Slowly Kate reached toward the child and placed her hand on her shoulder. "You were a good friend to Rose."

"No, I wasn't. She's gone."

Kate lifted Cynthia's chin so the girl would look at her. "What you told us could help us find her. Thank you for that."

Cynthia closed her eyes, one tear running down her face.

"Any time you need to talk, you know my door is always open. Rose might not be here right now, but I am."

The teen swiped her hand across her face. "Okay. Can I go now?" Her gaze darted to Wyatt then back to Kate.

"Sure, I'll see you at dinner." Kate smiled warmly at the girl.

Beneath her grin, Wyatt sensed the exhaustion the past couple of days had produced in Kate. The gesture didn't reach her brown eyes, a lackluster hue. A furrow of concern above her nose telegraphed the effort it took Kate to maintain the smile as Cynthia hurried toward the exit.

The second the girl disappeared through the doorway, Kate's expression fell. A long breath hissed from between pursed lips. "Did I miss anything?"

"You did fine. We now know Rose had been in contact with Lily on more than one occasion. What if Rose wanted to go back to her old way of life?"

With a violent shake of her head, Kate shot to her feet. "No. She didn't. I've worked with these girls long enough to know when one is teetering on the brink of going back. I've lost my share to their old way of life, but that wasn't Rose. She wouldn't choose it willingly."

"So you think her pimp gave her no choice? Used Lily as a way to get to Rose?"

She walked toward her desk and spun about on her heel. "Yes. This is the man responsible for her being left for dead by the side of the road. This is a man Rose could identify, if she wanted to."

"Why hasn't she?"

"I think she would have when she really thought of herself as safe." She collapsed back against the desk. "But she wasn't safe, was she? I try to keep them safe. Now they'll know it's not possible."

The defeat in her voice hovered in the air between them. Wyatt surged to his feet and closed the distance between them. "No one is one hundred percent safe, ever. Not even the President of the United States."

"They need to feel that way here."

"She wasn't taken from here. She left. There is a difference, and you'll help the girls see that. We can't control everything as much as we wish we could."

Her chest heaved as she gulped in a deep breath. "I know that. I fought that a good part of my life. You're right, there will always be some things out of our hands. But I'm not going to let these guys who prey on children win. Not as long as I have a breath."

The fervent appeal in her voice struck him, zapping him with a connection that took him by surprise. That was how he felt. His approach came from a different direction, but they fought the same battle. Knowing a little about her privileged background brought his respect to the foreground. She could have stayed in her nice little safe environment and never gotten her hands dirty. But she hadn't. What made her open Beacon of Hope?

"You aren't the only one wanting to stop the predators. That's why I jumped at the chance to be on the Child Rescue Task Force. I have a daughter who just turned fourteen. I want a better world for her."

"You know that's close to the average age for one of these girls to go into prostitution. That's not right. They should be worried about things like getting a boyfriend, what clothes to wear to school, the pimple that broke out right before the big dance."

"Our children are growing up too fast. They're in a hurry to be adults."

She quirked a smile. "If they only knew all our headaches."

"I'd like to come back tomorrow and talk with some of the other girls. What's a good time?"

"After three. I want to keep their schedule as normal as possible. Some will be going to work, but a lot of them will be here."

"I'll start with people Rose has hung out with."

"That's easy. Everyone. She was popular in here. With all she's gone through, she cared about the others, and they knew it. That's also why Cynthia responded to her."

"Good. I should have the autopsy back on Lillian Harris by then. We're checking out the area where we found the van. Also, I'm going to drive around some of the parks and see who is there."

"Why?"

"A teen I interviewed at the Ultimate Burger said a small group of girls come to the park for a short time and then move on. Where do they go? I think Lily was one of them and Rose connected with her. That's probably what prompted Lily's call the night before Rose left."

"That makes sense. I'll see you tomorrow. I want to check on Cynthia and reassure her she has done what she can to help Rose."

"Yeah, she's given us something to start with. Now I get to go watch my daughter ride in a rodeo."

"What does she do?"

"Barrel racing is her favorite event. She's really good at it." He made his way toward the hallway.

Kate followed him and paused in the doorway to her office. "That's something I wanted to do as a girl, but I never did."

"What kept you from doing it?"

"My mother. A Winslow would never participate in a rodeo. Too dirty. Too undignified. Of course, look at me now. I—"

A scream sliced the air, curdling Wyatt's blood.

5

*H*earing the sound from above froze Kate for a few seconds. Her heart skipped a beat, then charged forward as she headed toward the stairs behind Wyatt. The sight of him drawing his gun caused her to stumble on a step. She caught herself before going down on both knees. Pushing herself up, she kept up with the Texas Ranger.

Three girls stood in the entrance to Rose's room. One of them pointed inside, her hand quaking, her face ashen. She saw Kate. "It's Cynthia. I think she's dead."

More people poured into the corridor from every direction, including Harriet. While Wyatt forged his way through the girls crowded around the doorway, Kate waved to Harriet. "Take them downstairs. We'll handle this. Get the nurse." She forced as much calmness into her voice as she could manage, but she shook with the implications of what the child in the doorway had said.

Please don't let that be true.

As the students filed past the door, they all tried to look inside. Kate hurried toward the entrance, glimpsing Wyatt reaching down to feel for a pulse at the side of Cynthia's neck. Blood covered the blue spread on the bed where Cynthia lay.

Stomach churning, Kate pivoted and blocked the last few girls' view of the scene while Wyatt called 9-1-1. Now that the hallway was empty, the thought that Cynthia was still alive gave Kate courage to turn toward him.

As Susan, the nurse on duty, rushed inside with a green bag of emergency supplies, Wyatt stepped back from the bed. "I've called for help. They should be here in a few minutes."

After assessing the situation, Susan opened her bag and dug around in it until she found gauze and passed it to Wyatt. "Apply pressure on the wound to stop the bleeding."

While Susan took care of the right wrist, Wyatt followed the nurse's direction and pressed down on the wound on the left one. Kate came to Wyatt's side.

As he held the gauze over Cynthia's injury, Wyatt scanned the room. His gaze latched onto the desk. Nodding his head toward it, he asked, "Are those marks new?"

Kate looked toward where he indicated and found grooves cut into the edge of the desk. "Yes. They weren't there yesterday morning when I came up here to check on Rose. This is new. Cynthia has cut her arms before but never furniture. She's hasn't cut herself much in the past six weeks. And she's never tried suicide. I should have realized she might do this. Rose's disappearance hit her harder than anyone else in the house."

"How about you? This hasn't been easy on you either."

She clenched her teeth. "I can't help it. I'm supposed to protect them. Who else is going to look out for these girls?"

"I am," Wyatt whispered.

Surprised by the strength and will behind those two words, she stepped nearer. "Why? Most of the cops I've talked with haven't cared much for my girls. What makes you so different?" Rage built up in her as though all those times she'd tried to get the police to see these teenagers as children, not adults, deluged her with frustration.

"I have my reasons." He closed his mouth and stared at the door.

Two EMTs rushed into the room and attended to Cynthia, stabilizing her before moving her to the stretcher.

Kate trailed behind them. "Which hospital?"

"Mercy Cross," one of the paramedics answered.

"I'll follow the ambulance." Glancing back over her shoulder, she said to Susan, "Can you take care of this?"

"Yes. Don't worry. I'll stay and answer any questions the girls have. I've had experience with suicides."

"Thanks." Kate started down the back staircase that would take her to her office.

Wyatt followed a few steps behind her while he talked on his phone. When he finished, he caught up to her. "I called this in. They're sending an officer to fill out a report. He'll come to the hospital after checking here."

"Now they care." In her office, she fumbled for her bag in the desk drawer. She couldn't get rid of the image of Cynthia lying on her bed in a pool of blood. It shuddered through her. As Kate retrieved her handbag and hunted for her keys, she dropped her purse onto the floor, her items inside spilling out.

Wyatt took her bag and keys and cupped her hands in his. "I'm driving. I'm not needed here, but I think you need someone with you."

"I can do this by myself."

His fingers squeezed gently around hers as if to say she wasn't alone. "I know. Humor me. I want to be there." He scooped up her items from the floor and gave them to her. "Let's go."

She heard his words as though spoken from a long distance. The sight of the blood took hold in her mind and multiplied until all she saw was a bright red. *I should have foreseen Cynthia trying to commit suicide. If I hadn't been so focused on Rose—*

"Kate?"

He grabbed her upper arm, jolting her attention back to the present, to the fact she might lose Cynthia. She shook the visualization of the attempted suicide from her thoughts and hastened toward the corridor. "Come on. I need to be there."

❧

Kate paced from one end of the waiting room to the other. She grasped a cup of coffee, taking a sip every once and a while. Finally, she winced and tossed the drink into the trash, then resumed her trek. "What am I doing? I hate cold coffee. I actually hate coffee."

"I think it's called wearing a path in the floor." Wyatt wanted to take her hand and guide her to the chair next to him. The ordeal of the past few days had etched tired lines into her face and prompted his urge to ease her worry. But there was little he could say that would—because the fact she had two students in danger wouldn't change with mere words.

She stopped in front of him. "Why is it taking so long? I've never been good with waiting."

"Most people aren't, but it might help you to sit and rest. When you are allowed to see Cynthia, she's going to need you at your best."

"I'm not even sure what that is anymore." She remained standing, her hands opening and closing at her sides.

Wyatt rose, near enough to her to smell her scent of vanilla. A memory of that aroma jarred him, throwing him back into the past for a few seconds, to his first house as a married man. To a room lit with vanilla-scented candles. To his wife before him with love in her eyes. Her image materialized in his mind, only to shimmer for a heartbeat then disappear.

"Wyatt?"

Kate's soft voice dragged him back to the present. He took her hand. The brief shock as they touched dissolved his earlier memory. He tried to capture the vision of his deceased wife again, but all he saw was Kate and her needs.

"Sit," he finally said to the query in her expression.

"I'm not a dog you can command." A weary tilt to the corners of her mouth took the sting out of her words.

"I'm very aware of that." He tugged her toward the chair next to his. She let him guide her down onto the seat. "Cynthia lost a lot of blood, but she was alive when she was brought in here. They are very good at their job."

"I should have realized she might do something like this. But I was so preoccupied with Rose, I didn't consider it. I've let Cynthia down."

Like I did Rebecca. What could he say to Kate to make her feel better, when he knew exactly what she was going through? "All we can do is our best. Sometimes it isn't enough." He'd told himself that many times since his wife's death and hadn't believed a word of what he'd said.

"I can't accept that. Not when I have twenty-four girls in my care. I should have called in Jan Barton right away."

"The renowned child psychologist?"

"Yes. She's a friend of my mother's. They went to school together. She's seen some of the girls in the past. I was so caught up in finding Rose that I didn't see the needs of the other girls. I can't afford to do something like that again." She retrieved her cell from her purse, then she stood and walked a few steps away to make her call. Her back held rigid, she lowered her voice to talk.

Wyatt blew a long breath out and leaned his head against the wall behind his chair. When he'd gotten up this morning, there'd been nothing unusual about the day before him. He had some leads in a case that he'd been working on for a month and had planned to track a couple of them down. But this had an urgency to it. For six months, the task force had been gathering evidence against lowlifes who lured young girls into prostitution and kept them in line through drugs, threats, and confinement. What they needed was the people behind the pimps—the ones protecting them and funding this major operation.

The song "The Good, the Bad and the Ugly" sounded and jerked Wyatt forward. Glancing at the number calling, he quickly answered his cell. "I forgot. I'm so sorry, Maddie. I got caught up in an emergency."

"Then you're okay?" Fear laced each of her words.

"Yes, hon. I'm at the hospital, but I'm not the patient."

"Nana and I were worried. I told her I would call and make sure everything was okay."

That was so like his mother to let Maddie make the call. Mom didn't like to deal with anything that might be emotionally messy. "Have you competed yet?"

"No, but I should soon. I've got to go."

Maddie hung up before Wyatt could say anything else. He stared at the cell in his hand. More and more his job interfered with his family life. He'd let Maddie down again. She was the most important person in his life, and there were times he wished he had a job with more normal hours.

"Is something wrong?" Kate asked, coming back to sit in the chair beside him.

"That was my daughter. I should have called her to tell her I wouldn't make the rodeo. Whenever I don't show up when

I'm supposed to, she worries about me. That's the part I hate the most."

"I'm sorry. You should go. I'm fine here by myself. Maybe you can make it before it's over."

Wyatt glimpsed the clock on the wall in the waiting room. "No. I'd be too late. Besides, how would you get home?"

"A cab. I'm a big girl and can do it by myself."

Twisting toward Kate, he looked into her eyes. "No. I want to make sure Cynthia will be all right. You're not the only one who blames herself for what Cynthia did. I was sitting in on that interview. Was my presence what pushed her over the edge? Most girls who've been on the street avoid the police any way they can." He flicked his silver star. "It's kinda hard not to figure out who I am."

"I think it has more to do with losing any security she has felt at Beacon of Hope with Rose disappearing. Plus she knows the odds of Rose being found."

"Alive?"

Kate nodded. "She was left for dead six months ago. I doubt the person who lured her into prostitution wants Rose walking around free from his domination. Rose was a loose end he was probably trying to tie up."

"I wish she had talked to you about what happened to her."

"Whoever controlled Rose put the fear into her. The police quietly looked for a family, but it wasn't publicized she was found on the side of the road. I was hoping her pimp might think Rose was dead. But if she met someone she knew in the park, that might have changed everything."

"Do you think she died with Lillian?"

"Maybe. Was the girl beat up?"

"No. I think it was an overdose. There were track marks on her arms. The autopsy will have to confirm the cause of death. Tomorrow my FBI counterpart on the task force is bringing in a cadaver dog to search the area where Lillian was discovered. If there are any other dead bodies in the field, the dog will find them."

"There are dogs that can sniff out dead bodies in the ground?"

"Yes. There are even some that can detect a dead body in water, which will be our next move. The small lake at the end of that road needs to be searched."

"Do you think they used the lake to dispose of bodies?"

"Maybe. It has to be checked out."

Wyatt caught sight of a doctor approaching them. "Miss Winslow?"

"Is Cynthia all right?" Kate gripped the arms of her chair.

"She's alive and will make it, but I'm admitting her to the psych floor for further evaluation. I see other cuts on her."

"She hasn't attempted suicide before, but she does cut herself. She's been going to counseling to help her with that. When can I see her?"

"She was quite agitated, and I sedated her, so not before tomorrow."

"Can I at least look in on her? Is she up on the psych floor?"

"We'll be moving her in a few minutes. She's still down here." The doctor looked toward Wyatt. "Are you here for professional reasons?"

"Yes."

The emergency room physician frowned before swinging his attention back to Kate. "Miss Winslow, you can see her for a few minutes before we take her up."

"Thank you. Is she in the same room they brought her to?"

"Yes. I'll let the nurse know it's okay." The doctor made his way into the hallway.

"I'll wait for you in here then take you home."

"You're not coming?"

"No, I think you need some time alone with Cynthia."

"She's sedated." Kate started for the doorway. "But you're right. Even if she can't hear me, I need to talk to her. You should go on home. See your daughter. I can take a cab."

The bleak look in Kate's eyes reminded him of the times he glimpsed himself in the mirror especially right after Rebecca was murdered. The man who had stared back at him had been inundated with guilt. And no one had been able to help him. Not even the Lord. It had eaten at him for years until his daughter had demanded his participation in her life. But the guilt was still there, buried deep inside him.

❧

When Kate entered the hospital room in the ER, Cynthia's pale face captured her attention first. Then the bandages on both of her lower arms. And finally, the blood infusion she was receiving.

She moved slowly toward the bed. Cynthia didn't deserve to be in this room. She shouldn't be here, but was because Kate had neglected her and focused on Rose.

Bowing her head, she closed her eyes and pictured the young girl healthy, laughing, and involved with others. "Father, please heal Cynthia and bring her back to us. Give me a second chance to do what is right by her. Keep Rose safe and help us to find her. Amen."

When she opened her eyes, the unhealthy gray pallor of Cynthia's face mocked Kate. *And please, Lord, give me the strength to do whatever needs to be done.*

An idea began to form in her mind and take hold. She could use her contacts to ask around about where Rose might be.

As Kate emerged from the room, she found Wyatt lounging back against the wall across from the door. He pushed upright, a smile on his face.

"Okay?"

She nodded; her throat choked up with emotions from seeing Cynthia, but also from the fact Wyatt had cared enough to be waiting outside the room.

"Ready to leave?"

Kate swallowed several times and said, "You're stubborn, aren't you?"

"Yep. I'm not going to leave you here to call a cab." His grin grew. "Besides, I wanted to hear how Cynthia was."

"If only I had gone upstairs sooner, I could have stopped her."

"Cynthia hadn't been gone long from your office."

"When she left us, she must have gone directly up to her room and cut herself. At least she's got the help she needs."

Wyatt strode toward the exit. "She's had that for a while. You've provided her with the therapy and counseling she's needed and been there for her when others haven't. You've been reaching troubled girls when the system we have couldn't. Not everyone is out there on the frontline trying to do something about a growing problem. The girls are getting younger and younger. This is a problem not only in the United States but around the world."

After he opened his truck door, Kate climbed into the front seat and watched him round the hood of his vehicle. The glow from the security light in the parking lot emphasized the strong lines of his face, his well-built physique, his confidence in how he carried himself. Economical movement—nothing wasted.

He had a daughter. Did he have a wife? When he talked, she didn't think his daughter's mother was in the picture. Was he divorced? Suddenly she put a halt to the direction her thoughts were going. What she had worked for the past years was start-ing to unravel. She couldn't afford for that to happen. The program was her way to give back. She needed the girls as much as they needed a place to stay, an opportunity to better their life.

Once he slipped into the cab, he turned the ignition on and drove away. "While you were with Cynthia, I called the police and talked to the officer who responded to the call about the suicide attempt. I took care of everything. If there are any follow-up questions, he'll contact me. You won't have to deal with them right now."

In the shadows, she studied his profile. "Where have you been when I needed to cut through red tape?"

At a stoplight, he threw her a smile that kindled a spark in her. "Having a good working relationship with the local police is important to a Texas Ranger. We're partners. Besides, the situation was pretty straightforward. Nothing magical to it."

"However it happened, thanks. One less thing to worry about."

"I figured your family was tight with the chief of police. I'm sure you would have been fine."

"My parents are friends with him. Not me. I prefer not to ask them for help." Only if she absolutely had to for Beacon of Hope to stay in business.

"Mmm. That sounds like there's a story behind that comment."

Preferring not to discuss her lack of a real relationship with her parents—at least her mother—Kate focused on the pass-ing terrain and said what had been on her mind previously, "I hope your wife won't be too upset that you missed the rodeo because of work." The second she uttered the inane comment she wanted to disappear. Not a very original way to find out if he was married. And what business did she have even to ask in the first place? It wasn't like she was looking for a date or anything.

"No. My wife died nine years ago."

"Oh, I'm sorry. Who helps with your daughter when you get involved in your work?"

"My mother. When I had trouble being a single dad, she came to live with us. Maddie was seven, and over the years there are times I'm hard pressed to distinguish the child from the adult."

"It sounds like you have mother problems like I do."

"Not problems so much. Just opportunities to learn patience."

Kate chuckled. "I like how you put that."

Before she asked too many personal questions she had no business asking, she clamped her jaws together and watched the street as Wyatt neared Beacon of Hope.

When he pulled into a parking space in the back of the building, Kate had her hand on the handle and the door open before he'd switched off the engine. "Thanks for the ride."

But as she marched toward the back entrance, Wyatt joined her. "I want to make sure everything is all right. No more problems. Okay?"

"Sure. I just hate keeping you from your family."

He reached around her and pulled the door open. "The damage has been done. It was my choice, and I'll stand by it."

She had a feeling he was that kind of guy. He didn't make excuses about his mistakes but owned up to them and dealt with the consequences. Very different from the one serious relationship she'd had. Paul had been a nice enough person. Although his family was one of the oldest in the Dallas area, he wasn't caught up in the wealthy world her parents frequented. That was the problem in the long run. Money had been more important to him than her. He'd accepted a great job with one of her dad's businesses, but the catch was he had to leave immediately for Africa for several years and her father had made it clear he didn't want his daughter accompanying him. Once her dad got his hooks into him, she'd heard less and less from Paul. Then the next thing she'd discovered when reading the newspaper was that Paul was engaged to a woman from South Africa.

Inside the foyer, the silence was ominous. "Where's everyone?"

Tension whipped down Wyatt's body. He didn't draw his weapon, but he positioned his hand near it. "Where are they usually at this time?"

Kate checked her watch. Surprise flitted through her. "It's almost eleven. I didn't realize it was that late. Most are in their rooms for the night. Some are probably even asleep."

The click of heels echoed down the long hallway to the right. Twenty seconds later, Susan appeared in the foyer. "Good. I promised the girls I'd tell them as soon as you returned."

"Where are they?"

"In the chapel." It was a room she insisted on having at Beacon of Hope. She'd wanted the girls to have a place where they could go and pray if they chose to any time of the day.

"All of them?"

"Yes and I have to say it's crammed. That room isn't meant to hold so many people. I'd just come out to write you a note and pin it on your office door. Your mother called several times in the past hour and wanted you to return her call whenever you got back from the hospital."

"You told Mom I was at the hospital?"

Susan shook her head. "She already knew. How's Cynthia?"

"She's going to be all right, hopefully. They're keeping her in the hospital for a while."

"I expected that. I'll tell the girls. They need to go to bed. These past few days have been hard on everyone." Susan's gaze bored into her. "Especially you. After you call your mom, this nurse is telling you to go to bed and get a good night's sleep."

Yeah, as if that's possible. "I'll try." Then she turned toward Wyatt. "Thanks for the ride. Come by tomorrow after three if you still want to talk to the students."

"I do." He tipped his hat toward Susan and Kate then left.

Kate stared at the closed front door. The last person she wanted to talk to was her mother.

"I can continue to field your mom's inquiries if you want."

"I can't do that to you." Kate sighed. "Putting it off won't make it go away. Thanks for the message. If you could tell everyone how Cynthia is doing and have them go to their rooms, I'll make the rounds tonight and answer any questions they have after I talk with Mother."

As Kate trudged down the corridor toward her office, she heard Susan say, "Which means you won't get any rest."

What she'd said was true. But then after what had happened earlier, she didn't think she could sleep anyway, especially not after a confrontation with her mother. In her office, she plopped down in the chair behind her desk and reached for the phone. Her hand trembled, and she squeezed it into a tight fist to still the quaking.

A minute later, her mother came on the line. "It's about time you called."

"Mercy Cross Hospital was busy tonight in the emergency room. I didn't know you wanted to talk with me. You have my cell number. Why didn't you contact me that way?"

"This isn't a conversation we need to have where people might overhear it."

Kate shot forward in her chair. "Why?"

"I'm pulling your funding starting immediately."

6

The glare of light from a lone bulb dangling from the basement ceiling assaulted Rose's eyes. She closed them for a few seconds, then with her hand partially shielding them, she slowly eased her eyelids up. The staircase loomed before her. She moved toward freedom.

Dank, musky air enclosed Rose from all sides. Sweat rolled down her face in rivulets. The urge to run up the steps went through her. But the disorientation she'd suffered in the room plagued her. She had to be smart if she was going to escape. She couldn't make a sound. Creeping up the stairs, she latched onto the railing, her legs wobbly from exhaustion and lack of food.

How long had she been in the Deprivation Room? It could have been hours. Days. Even weeks. Time had come to a halt in the darkness with no contact with the outside world.

At the top of the stairs before the door that led out, Rose reached for the knob. Her hand shook so badly that she paused and curled it then flexed it to steady herself.

She tried again to grasp the handle. Again, the trembling started in her fingertips and quickly spread up her arm and throughout her body. She hugged herself and dropped her head, closing her eyes.

I can do this. I have to. I've got to save Lily and get back to Beacon of Hope.

The words echoed through her mind with a hollow ring as though to taunt her with her foolish dreams. How in the world had she thought she could get Lily away from King? She was one girl against a man who had an army of people to help him keep his merchandise, as he loved to refer to the teens working for him, in his possession.

You can do anything with the Lord on your side, Rose.

The sound of Kate's calm voice floated through her mind, nudging the doubts to the side. Kate had been right. In the six months Rose had been at Beacon of Hope, she'd completed her freshman year of high school course work and had gotten a job. She'd started a saving account for a car. She'd helped others, especially Cynthia.

I can do this.

Lifting her hand, she tried again. Her fingers gripped about the metal knob, cool to the touch, and slowly she turned it to the right. She held her breath until her chest burned. She exhaled in a rush.

Inch by inch she eased the door open enough to squeeze through the gap. Cool air-conditioned air bathed her damp face and drew her forward out into the empty hallway. Muted, gray light pooled at one end of the hall while the other beckoned her with darkness.

So far so good. As carefully as she had opened the door, Rose closed it, not a sound made. Scouting out the area in front and behind her, she determined the fastest way to escape the house—she hoped. Then she slinked down the corridor, passed King's office, toward the dim illumination, her ears attuned for any noise.

The chimes of a clock struck and a small gasp issued from her. She halted, not a muscle moving. Then the timepiece echoed a second and third clang and stopped. Three at night or in the afternoon. She couldn't tell, and that gave her a sense of disorientation as if she was back in her cell.

After several heartbeats and quiet ruled again, Rose tiptoed a couple of yards and turned the corner. Before her was a wide foyer with a large round table, a bowl of cut flowers sitting in the middle of it. Behind it, massive double doors sporting brass handles, called to her. The darkness in the narrow windows on either side of the doors told her it was three in the morning. Her first break. It would be easier for her to flee under cover of darkness.

Again, the impulse to race across the entry hall and out the front door rose up inside her. No, patience was what she needed. Kate would be proud of her for not hurrying through a task that needed to be done right. Over the months, she'd taught her to assess all her options then decide what to do.

She crept painstakingly slow across the foyer and placed her hand on the knob. She began to turn it when a thought struck her and she froze. What about the alarm system? Could it go off if she opened the door? In her eagerness, she had almost forgotten.

She searched the dark shadows for the security system. A tiny green light glowed in the dimness a few feet from the entrance. She made her way toward the beacon. There was just enough illumination, coming from a room off to the side so she could decipher the numbers on the keypad and the fact that the security system wasn't on. This meant that King was home. He often didn't arm it unless he was gone. She sagged against the wall in relief because she still had a chance. Most likely King was in bed, but more importantly, the alarm wouldn't go off and alert his minions to a break-in. In her case, a breakout.

Quickening her pace slightly, she crossed to the front door and reached for the handle. The closer she came to escaping, the faster her heart thudded against her ribcage. Its rhythmic beat pulsated through her head, a loud tempo that drowned out her harsh breathing.

She inched the door open. The hot night air rushed in. The scent of the outdoors gave her the courage to hurry a little more. Almost free. Her mouth watered at the thought of getting away.

This time she would do things right. She would get to a phone and call Kate. Tell her about King and where she was. Maybe Kate could bring the police, and Lily could be freed too. That heady thought pushed her even faster out onto an all too familiar large porch. Moonlight streamed across part of its wooden planks, casting its softness onto white wicker furniture at one end, while the other captured the blackness and held on to it.

She started forward, no longer as cautious about making noise. A sound to her left snagged her attention. A red glow in the dark that hadn't been there seconds before sent her pulse speeding through her.

She whirled around and collided into a wall of muscle. Arms encircled her and pinned her. As the sound of footsteps neared, she was swung around, facing outward. Facing the red glimmer that moved closer toward her. Out of the shadows materialized King, lifting a cigarette to his mouth. He drew in the smoke then blew it out, making rings.

The scent of tobacco accosted Rose's nostrils. It reminded her of the times she'd had to be with a man and her stomach flip-flopped. Bile rose into her throat.

King dropped the cigarette and ground it beneath his boot, then raised his gaze to hers. "Did you really think I was gonna let you escape?" He laughed, its insidious sound hammering at her composure. "I thought it would be fun to see how long it would take you to pick the lock and try to leave. Over a day. That's why I left you your tools. You must have gone soft while at that place. Did you really think I didn't know you had them?"

She tried to jerk away, but the hands that held her dug into the flesh of her upper arms until she cried out.

"That's okay. I can toughen you up. Give you a reason to think twice before trying to leave me again."

She gnashed her teeth together. "Where's Lily?"

"Ah, don't you worry about her. She's served her purpose."

The icy thread in King's voice knifed through Rose, and she shuddered. "What do you mean?"

He nodded toward the man behind her. "Now for our first lesson in following my directions."

❧

"Why are you pulling the funding, Mother?" Kate asked, her grip on the phone so tight her hand ached.

"I heard what happened today."

The disapproval she always heard from her mother came over the line loud and clear. Kate collapsed back in her chair behind her desk. "What did you hear?"

"The suicide attempt by one of your students. The police were called in. The Winslows don't get involved with the police. This school/shelter thing, whatever you call it, is getting too messy and . . ." Her mom's tersely controlled anger sputtered to a stop.

"How did you hear?" Was it someone at Beacon of Hope, the police, or the hospital? The thought that a person reported to her mother about what happened bothered her. If it was the police or hospital, that was one thing she could accept even though she didn't like it, but if it was someone here, she needed to figure out who. She couldn't have a spy in her midst.

"That's not important, and you won't be able to use your trust. Your grandmother put a clause in the trust that said I had final say on how you used the money until you're thirty. That's not for a while yet."

Shocked by the news of the clause, Kate nearly dropped the phone. "When did she do that? She never said anything about that when she told me about the trust fund."

"Did you really think I would give you unlimited access to her money without some safeguards? I convinced her to add it not long before she died. It wasn't hard after that little incident in Costa Sierra."

"Little! I'd hardly call it something little when a young girl from the village was sold into prostitution because the parents didn't have enough money to live on. All I wanted to do was buy Maria back and give them money so they wouldn't sell her again." That incident changed her life over twelve years ago— gave her a purpose other than being a rich, spoiled debutante who did what her parents deemed appropriate for her station in life.

"You went to find the man the father dealt with. You could have been kidnapped for a ransom. I didn't want you to go on a mission trip in the first place, but the sponsors assured me it was safe. I shouldn't have given in to you. I regret that every day."

The face of Maria would haunt her as Rose's did. Kate fortified herself with the knowledge she wasn't going to give up now. She would find a way around her mother. "It's been a long day. May we talk about this tomorrow?"

"It won't change anything, but come to the luncheon I'm having on Saturday. We can talk afterwards. Good night, Katherine."

Kate punched the off button and let the receiver drop into her lap. Drained emotionally and physically, she closed her eyes, her arms falling to her sides. She'd always depended on her trust as a fallback in case her mother pulled the funding for the program. Her mother made sure she was kept in the dark about the added clause. Kate had known she didn't have any access to the money until she'd turned twenty-five, but not this. Her mother probably did it so she wouldn't go out and seek other donors for Beacon of Hope. This way her mother remained in control, which was paramount to her.

She'd go on Saturday and use that time to approach others to fund her program. The luncheon was for one of her mother's pet projects—Mercy Cross Hospital. She was raising money for a new children's wing, and yet her mother didn't care about the girls at Beacon of Hope. It was all in the image. The Winslows weren't allowed to sully their hands by actually working with the downtrodden, especially after what happened in Costa Sierra. Throwing money at the cause was acceptable, but that was all.

She couldn't turn these girls away, not now when she was making some progress. They deserved a second chance. She personally had enough money to keep the program open until the end of the month. That gave her three weeks to come up with a miracle.

An image of Maria, when she'd last talked with her, crowded Kate's thoughts with all the feelings from joy to sorrow she'd experienced on that mission trip. They'd just finished painting the new church/school building for the village. They sat outside under a cluster of palm trees, relishing the slight breeze, drinking water from the new system, and giggling about a boy Maria liked. She'd teased her new friend about having a crush on Pedro. Maria's cheeks had reddened, and she'd averted her gaze. Maria had been fourteen and innocent. That all changed that evening when the large man with a scar on his left cheek came to the village, recruiting girls for his business.

The frightened look in Maria's eyes as she was dragged away by the man would stay with Kate always. She'd come to see if Maria could come out and talk. Kate had loved to practice her Spanish with her friend. She never even got to ask. Instead, she hid in the bushes watching the scene in disbelief, at first not sure what was happening. Quickly that changed, but Kate was too late to stop the man.

Susan appeared in the open doorway of Kate's office. "I gather by your expression that your conversation with your mother wasn't a good one."

"No." Kate pushed herself forward in her chair. "Come in and shut the door."

"This doesn't bode well." Susan took a seat in front of the desk. "What's going on?"

Susan had been with her from the beginning and had the same passion for Kate's cause. She lived in another apartment on the third floor. Surely, she wasn't a spy for her mother. In fact, she couldn't see it being anyone at Beacon of Hope, which meant her mother had found out about Cynthia from someone at the hospital or the police. "I need to tell someone, but I don't want this to go any further than this office. I don't want others to worry, especially the girls."

Her friend frowned. "This doesn't sound good. Is it about Rose?"

Kate shook her head. "Mom's shutting down the program. I have enough to keep it open for a few weeks, but that's all."

"I've got some money saved. Maybe it will help."

Kate tried to smile but the effort took too much energy. "Thanks, but besides looking for Rose, I'll now have to find some funding to keep this place open until I turn thirty. That's when I get my trust fund, no strings attached."

"That's over two years away. How are you going to come up with that kind of money to keep the program open?"

"I'm my mother's daughter. She's a master at fundraising. With the Lord's help and what I've learned from her, I'll get the money." *I have to.*

"If anyone can, it'll be you. I came to tell you the girls have gone to their rooms. They're much quieter than usual, but that's to be expected."

"I'll go up and talk to them. Pay each one a visit."

"That's good. They need to see you." Susan rose at the same time Kate did. When she came around from behind her desk, her friend gave her a hug. "You aren't alone. I'll help any way I can."

"Thanks. I needed to hear that." Then Kate remembered Wyatt sitting in the waiting room today when he should have been with his daughter. Suddenly she didn't feel as alone as she had been.

◈

Wyatt parked his truck in front of his house, glad to be home after a very long day. He glanced at Maddie's bedroom window. It was dark. He thought she might still be up so he could hear about her competition. At least tomorrow, they could share their usual early Friday morning ride before he had to go out. Then he could find out how she did and try to make up missing the rodeo to her.

When Wyatt let himself into his house, he noticed the light on in the kitchen and went in search of who was up at midnight. He entered the room. Sitting at the table in the breakfast nook, his mother peered up at him.

She lifted a mug and took a sip. "It's about time you got home. Do you want some tea? I can fix you some."

Wyatt winced. "Some of your herbal—uh, tea?"

"Yes. Green tea is good for you. You should try some."

She so rarely imparted "motherly" advice that he had to clamp his jaws together to keep from chuckling at the time she picked. "I'll pass." He stepped back a pace. "Well, I'd better go to bed. I have a full day tomorrow."

"Don't you want to know how the rodeo went?"

The determination on his mother's face put him on high alert. "I thought I'd ask Maddie tomorrow morning."

"She isn't here."

After dealing with this case concerning child prostitution, the news that his daughter was somewhere he didn't know pricked his wariness. He drew himself up straight. "Where is she?"

"At Kelly's spending the night."

"We usually ride Friday morning."

His mom set her mug on the table. "I know how much you look forward to those rides, but she was so disappointed you weren't there tonight that when Kelly asked I said yes. Sit, son. Maybe we should talk."

"About what?" He hung back by the doorway, too tired to have this conversation, especially if she was going to tell him what a bad parent he had been tonight. He already felt that way.

"Maddie wants to get a tattoo."

His mouth dropped open. "There's nothing to talk about. It isn't going to happen. It's against the law to get one in Texas. I know there are places she could go that ignore the law, but I won't let her. Period."

"It wouldn't be too big. I have one."

"You're not my fourteen-year-old daughter. What she does when she turns eighteen is her business, but not as long as she's under my roof."

"I told her I would talk to you and try to get you to see her side. It isn't a regular tattoo but a henna one."

Wyatt strode to the table but remained standing across from his mother. "In this case, her side doesn't matter. I don't care what kind."

"All her friends are getting one. She doesn't want to be left out."

"Are they?"

"That's what she said."

He gripped the back of the chair in front of him and leaned into it. "So if all her friends were going swimming in shark-infested waters, it would be okay for her to jump in too."

"Shark-infested waters? Where did that come from?"

He wasn't even sure himself, but suddenly he felt as though he were swimming around in shark-infested waters and desperate to keep his family on the shore. He shrugged. "I'll talk to her. I'll make her understand."

"As you said, she's fourteen, Wyatt. It won't be as easy to dictate to her as it was when she was little."

"Mom, what are you saying?"

"Don't go charging in, telling her what she can and can't do. At least pretend to be listening to her first."

Like his mother had listened to him when she'd gone off on one of her escapades. "Sure. I'll listen." He pivoted to leave.

"I know I wasn't the most ideal mother to you, but you've given me a second chance with Maddie."

His movement halted mid-stride. Throwing a look over his shoulder, he studied his mom, a shadow of regret in her eyes. He loved his mom, but they were very different people. "What's this about second chances?"

"When I married Howard, I left you with Grams that summer and went on a two-month honeymoon. I was too caught up in the moment to see I should have spent time with you, preparing you for the change. You were only eleven. I should have given you a chance to tell me how you felt about me marrying another man after your father died. I know you didn't think your dad could do anything wrong, but I . . ." Her voice faded into silence. She took up her mug and sipped at her tea, staring at a place in the middle of the table. "I don't want you to make the same mistakes I did."

Same mistakes? What was his mother talking about? "I'm not getting married and going on a two-month honeymoon around the world. Good night, Mom." He hurried from the kitchen before she started crying. He never could handle that well.

On the way to his bedroom, he passed Maddie's, the light from the hallway shining across her bed where all her stuffed animals sat. He paused in the doorway and flipped on the overhead light. Maddie had never been neat. She rarely kept her room tidy, but lately it had gotten worse. Tonight was no different.

Half of her stuffed animals, all with names, lay scattered on the floor around his daughter's bed, unmade with the coverlet spilling onto the carpet. Clothes littered every surface in her room, flowing out of her open drawers. Shaking his head, he switched off the light and closed the door.

And now, he had to deal with Maddie wanting a tattoo.

⌒

The next morning the smell of a freshly mowed field teased Wyatt's nostrils as he sat on Sergeant Pepper at the fence line to his neighbor's property. Bob must have cut the grass early. He couldn't blame Bob. It was going to be another scorcher with highs in the low hundreds. Which meant he needed to cut his ride short and head to the spot where Lillian's body was discovered. The search for other bodies would take place early before it got too hot to work for long outside.

The sound of hoof beats invaded the quiet morning. He twisted around and saw his daughter galloping toward him on a strange horse. She came to a halt alongside him.

"I forgot today's Friday. I borrowed one of Kelly's horses. I figured you'd be here."

He wasn't sure if he should be pleased she was here or leery. What was behind this unexpected arrival? He didn't want to have the conversation about getting a tattoo right now, even a henna one. If he could, he'd postpone it forever. "How did you do last night?"

"I got first place in barrel racing and second in roping."

"That's great. Did Nana take a video of your performances?" His mother had been gone this morning, and he hadn't had a chance to check with her.

Nodding, Maddie shifted in the saddle, chewing on her bottom lip. "Did Nana talk with you last night?"

So much for postponing it forever. "Yeah, we talked some when I got home."

"And?"

"And what?"

"Dad! She was gonna talk to you about me getting a tattoo."

He opened his mouth to say no way when Maddie launched into an obviously rehearsed speech, "There are a bunch of us girls who are gonna get a small dolphin on our back. It won't be visible most of the time. Please, Dad. Everyone is getting one."

"Are they? If the tattoo isn't going to be visible most of the time, then why have one?"

Her eyes grew large and round. "You don't mind me getting one that everyone can see? I thought you might, so I figured if I did it on my back it would only be seen when I wear my bathing suit. One on my ankle would be even better." She started to lean forward and throw her arms around his neck.

He held up his hand. "I didn't say you could get a big or small one anywhere on your body."

"I can't." She settled back in the saddle, a pout descending. "I thought . . . Why can't I get one? Everyone is."

"That's fine if everyone else does. Just not you."

"Why can't I? What's wrong with it?"

"I'm a Texas Ranger. It's against the law in Texas. What did you think I would say?"

"But I'm getting a henna tattoo. That's okay. It only stays on about three or four weeks. That way I could change where and what I want to have."

A picture of a man's tattoo—a snake entwined around a dagger—filled him with rage. He'd never forget seeing it when the man lifted his gun and shot Rebecca. "You just can't and that's the last we're going to talk about it. I was heading back in. I have to meet someone in an hour." He turned his gelding around to head back to the barn.

"I don't understand. It isn't like a permanent one. So what's the harm?"

"I've given you my answer, and I don't care to have a debate about it." The image of the dagger and snake still burned in his mind as he nudged his horse forward.

Staying still, his daughter pressed her lips together so tightly they were a thin line.

He looked back. "Are you coming? Nana should be back from town and have breakfast ready."

Maddie's face scrunched up in a frown. "I'll pass. I'm riding back to Kelly's." She urged her mare into a gallop and charged across the pasture in the direction of her best friend's house.

If this was any indication of how his day was going to be, he might as well go back to sleep and wake up tomorrow. As he directed Sergeant Pepper toward the barn, he contemplated that thought until a few yards from the corral when his cell blared out his theme song.

"Sheridan here."

"I got the autopsy back," Daniel said, his breathing hard.

"What are you doing?"

"My morning jog before it gets blazing hot."

"What does it say?"

"I'm having it emailed to me. I'll see you in an hour and let you read it for yourself. But she didn't die from an overdose. She drowned."

"Drowned? Not an overdose?"

"Yes. She had drugs in her system, but they weren't what killed her. I don't know more than that until I get the report. See you soon."

After hanging up, Wyatt dismounted and proceeded to take care of his gelding. Automatic movements he'd done dozens of times. But that fact didn't seem to stop him from staring off into space. All this talk about tattoos brought the one memory he never wanted to remember to the foreground.

His wife's murder—one he should have been able to prevent. She wouldn't be dead if he hadn't hesitated that day at the lake.

When would he forgive himself?

Never.

☙

Kate resisted the urge to slam down the phone after another unsuccessful attempt to get funding for the program. She was beginning to suspect her mother had made a few calls and put the word out that this wasn't a project people wanted to sponsor. She might not be able to get anything local so that meant she would have to search nationally for a source of money for Beacon of Hope.

There was a knock at her apartment door. She pushed herself off the couch, hurried toward the entrance and let Wyatt in. "I can't believe it's three already."

"I'm a little early."

"Come in. I just got back from the hospital, made a few calls, and was heading down to my office." She'd decided to talk to possible sponsors in her apartment rather than downstairs where she could be overheard.

"Are you finished with your calls?"

"Sadly, yes." The words slipped out before she realized the implication of them.

"Sadly?"

As much as she wished she could brush off his question, she couldn't. There was something about his kind expression, the way he'd helped her last night that prompted her to say, "My mother pulled the funding for the program."

"Your mother funds this operation?"

"Well, Winslow Foundation does, but she runs it."

"Why did she do that?"

Kate gestured toward the couch while she took a chair across from the coffee table. "Because she heard about Cynthia's suicide attempt. Actually, she'd been looking for an excuse to pull the money. She only gave me the funding in the first place because she thought it would fail and I would finally get the notion of helping these kids out of my mind and get back to being what a Winslow is."

He arched a brow. "What is that?"

"A Winslow contributes to charities, but they never get down in the trenches and work with the people."

"So you've been making calls to try and get funding?"

"Yes, and not very successfully. At best, I need money to tide me over until I can find a more permanent source. But I can't even find that. It requires a lot of money to run Beacon of Hope. I do get some other funding, but not enough to keep the doors open. I still need to house the girls and feed them."

"And I thought I had a tough day."

"The case?"

"Partially, but mostly my daughter."

"Ah, she wasn't too happy you didn't come to the rodeo."

"Actually she didn't say anything about that. She informed me she wants a tattoo. She's only fourteen."

"I gather you disapprove of a tattoo, and she wasn't happy with that." She could imagine asking her mother if she could get a tattoo. She probably would have been disowned. Winslows didn't do that either.

"To put it mildly. And the law thankfully is on my side. She's too young even for a henna tattoo, but that doesn't stop her from wanting one. I've heard of some people having an allergic reaction to the dye. Eighteen is soon enough for her to make that decision—semipermanent or permanent."

"So you're going to turn over the parental role when she turns eighteen?" If only her mother would let her make her own decisions without trying to interfere in everything.

"Not totally. I don't think most parents can. I can't turn my back on her just because she turns eighteen and she's considered an adult."

His statement clearly came out of love, whereas she didn't think her mother was capable of loving that way. Controlling, yes. "What went wrong concerning the case?"

"Nothing per se. The good thing is that the cadaver dog didn't find another body in the field where Lillian was found."

"So Rose could still be alive. That's wonderful news. We have a chance to find her." The hope she'd been desperate to keep hold of grew.

"I wish I was as optimistic as you are. We didn't find her there. But she could have been killed and dumped somewhere else. Tomorrow they'll search the lake to see if they can find anything there. We think that was the original destination for getting rid of Lillian."

She sagged back against the chair. "Then what went wrong today with the case? I figure no news means Rose might still be alive."

"Nothing turned up at the parks. People aren't talking, at least not to me. Also, we got the autopsy back on Lillian. She died by drowning, possibly in a bathtub. There were a lot of drugs in her body, but an overdose isn't the cause of her death. There was no indication she was held under. She wasn't hit over the head and dumped into water either."

"So it wasn't murder?"

"I didn't say that. I think she was given just enough drugs for her to pass out and then placed in water, which is murder in my book. Besides, someone dumped her and tried to bury her so she wouldn't be found."

"What a life these girls get to look forward to. If they only knew what was really in store for them. Next week I'm speaking at a year-round middle school. I try to do that at least several times a month to various groups. I hope one day there's no need for my type of organization."

"If you haven't already, I'd like you to talk to Bluebonnet Creek Middle School where Maddie goes. I'm sure I can get the principal to agree to you talking with the kids."

"That's one I haven't done. Set it up, and I'll be there."

He grinned. "That's the best news I've heard today."

"And the fact Cynthia is doing better. She'll stay a few days, and I've got Jan Barton coming here to work with her. In fact, she has agreed to do more with the other students. I'm excited she's volunteering some of her time. Just as my mother pulls the funding, I'm starting to get more and more top-notch professionals to volunteer their time to help Beacon of Hope."

"Speaking of the other students, I'd like to talk with them, starting with any who are local or from Texas. They might not know anything about Rose, but if I can get a better picture of what's happening from their side, it will help me while working on the task force."

"I have one girl who has graduated and is working at a department store while going to junior college. She was my first success and she is from Dallas. She may know something, and I know she would want to help. Sometimes she goes with me to talk with the kids. Her name is Grace Johnson. I hope once she gets her teaching certificate that she'll come back here to work."

"I'd like to talk to her." Wyatt rose and started for the door.

"Let's get you connected with some of the girls. I have seven from Texas. Two of them from the Dallas area besides Rose."

"Good. Oh, I forgot to mention we do have another lead. A rancher who lives next to where Lillian was found saw a white Chevy parked off the side of the road near where the van went off the highway. He didn't see anyone in the car. He thought someone had car trouble and didn't think anything about it. He remembers seeing the license plate as he passed it. It was a Texas one with the letters H-O-T. He laughed because that's the way he felt already at four in the morning. It wasn't there when we arrived a few hours later, and any tire treads were obscured by arriving police."

"Then it could be connected." Kate opened her apartment door and went into the corridor.

"I'm hoping. There haven't been any white Chevys with that partial license number reported missing." He fell into step next to her. "Who else lives up here? Any of the girls?"

"No. Two staff members and me. Susan, the nurse you met, and Harriet, one of my teachers."

"So, if something happens to Beacon of Hope, you'll need to find a new place to live?"

"That'll be the least of my worries." She pictured herself with her suitcases standing on her parents' front porch begging to come in and stay. That would never happen, but the thought sent a chill down her spine. She and her mother didn't look at life the same. She'd hoped that once she'd grown up she would be able to connect with her mom, but it had never occurred.

"You can set up in one of the classrooms. I'll bring in Beth first. She's been here two years and will graduate at the end of this year. The other one from Dallas is Zarah. She hasn't been here much longer than Rose was." She stopped at the bottom of the stairs. "I just remembered something. When Rose came here, I thought that she and Zarah knew each other. But they kept their distance and other than that first meeting, I never got that impression again."

When Kate left Wyatt in the classroom, she went in search of Beth and found her in the rec room playing a video game with another girl. "Are you sure you're all right with talking to Ranger Sheridan?"

"If it'll help Rose, yeah." Beth chomped down on a big wad of bubble gum.

"There's nothing to be worried about." Kate paused at the door into the classroom.

"I'm not worr—" The seventeen-year-old peered at Kate and laughed. "Okay, maybe a little."

Beth always smacked gum when she was concerned about something. "I know how leery you are of police officers. Ranger Sheridan is different."

"I lived with my mother for almost fourteen years, and she didn't know me as well as you do."

"I figure if you talk to him, the others are more likely to. He wants to help with this whole situation, not just Rose's."

"I'll do my best if it'll stop someone going through what I did."

Kate opened the door. Wyatt rose from his chair and reached out with his hand to shake Beth's. By the time Kate left the classroom, her student sat relaxed across from Wyatt and even took the gum out of her mouth.

⤳

When Zarah, his last girl to interview, came into the classroom, Wyatt smiled and said, "Thanks for agreeing to talk with me."

The fifteen-year-old girl mumbled something and sat across from him.

He stared at the top of her head. "As you know, we're looking into Rose's disappearance. Did she ever say anything to you about seeing someone she knew at Oiler Park?"

Zarah didn't say or do anything for a moment. From what little he saw, her expression was blank. Then she slowly shook her head.

"How did you come to be here?"

The girl finally lifted her head. "The police raided a joint and took me in." The slight upward tilt of her chin and the folded arms across her chest spoke of a person who didn't want to be talking to him. "It was either come here to live or go into the foster care system."

"Where are your parents?"

"I don't know where my mom is. She left my pa years ago."

"Where's your pa then?"

Zarah shrugged. "I ain't seen him either in years. He left me and my sister not long after my ma did."

"Did Rose ever mention a girl named Lily?"

Zarah blinked and slid her gaze away for a few seconds before reestablishing eye contact. "Nope."

Wyatt was sure she was lying. "So Rose did say something about Lily?"

"Hey, didn't I just say no?" She set her mouth in a scowl.

"Had you ever seen Rose before she came here?"

"No, absolutely not." Her teeth snapped together on that last word.

Wyatt stood. "Thank you, Zarah."

She looked up at him. "That's all?"

"Unless you know something else you aren't telling me, yes."

She uncrossed her arms and clamped the sides of the chair to push herself up. "Nope."

When she left, Wyatt sighed and glanced at his watch. Tonight Maddie was going to a sleepover, so she would be gone again. Right now, he didn't want to play games with his mom. She would be looking for her newest project, and he didn't intend to become that project. Maybe he could see if Kate would grab something to eat with him, and they could talk about her work with the girls in the program. Today, he'd seen a handful of young teens with new perspectives on their prospects thanks to Beacon of Hope. Beth was 100 percent sold on what the program was trying to do to help her, while Zarah was just marking her time until something better came along.

"How did it go with Zarah?" Kate poked her head through the entrance into the classroom.

He noted the dark circles under her eyes, the dullness in her gaze, and the slower movements. What was happening was taking its toll on her more than she probably cared to admit. A few hours away from here would be good for Kate. "Not very communicative."

"No. She doesn't want to be here."

"And that's okay with you?"

Kate stepped through the threshold into the room. "No, but I don't have a choice. I've had some who haven't in the past. A few I managed to change their mind. A couple left and went back to their old life. I focus on the ones I can help."

Like he did on his cases. If he didn't, he might have given up long ago. "Are you hungry? Would you like to go grab something to eat? To talk about what the girls said," he added the last hastily.

Smooth, he thought, when he saw her eyes widen. Obviously, he still needed lessons in asking a woman out—not that this was a date. He didn't have much time to date with his job and family commitments.

"I've got a better suggestion. Let me fix something for us to eat in my apartment. I'd rather stay nearby, and besides, it gives me a chance to show off my cooking skills."

His mother once said that to him when she came to stay with him and Maddie, and he'd been sick for two days with a stomach ailment he was sure had to do with the undercooked meat and questionable potato salad. "Are you sure? I don't want you going to any trouble, especially after last night with Cynthia."

"This is just what I need. I love to cook and don't get to nearly enough. I took cooking lessons one summer in Paris."

"French cuisine?"

She laughed. "I know how to do meat and potatoes too."

Good, at least he hoped so. "How can I pass up a home-cooked meal? I'm not a cook."

"Come on. I'll even have you earn your food."

"Maybe I should reconsider then." Grinning, he slowed his pace.

"I thought a Texas Ranger was adventurous and daring."

"What do you have in mind?"

She winked. "You'll see."

⁓❧

"I'd gladly help with the dishes anytime you want to ask me over to eat." Wyatt captured her full attention at the sink and then gave her a wink. "I hope I'm not being too subtle."

"Why, I think I understand perfectly what you want, Ranger Sheridan." Kate passed him a wet plate to dry.

"I will admit this wasn't what I was thinking I'd have to do. Most places have a dishwasher in the kitchen."

"Oh, and what did you think I had in mind?"

"I had visions of having to peel tons of potatoes or dicing onions. It isn't a pretty picture seeing a grown man crying buckets."

"I'll have to remember that in the future." She scrubbed the pot, rinsed off the suds, and then handed it to him.

"You know we haven't yet talked about what we were going to."

The carefree, relaxed atmosphere that started when she and Wyatt had returned to her place came to a grinding halt. "No. I can put on some coffee, and we can talk then. Are you sure you don't have to get home? I don't want to be responsible for keeping you from your family two nights in a row."

"You aren't. Maddie is at a birthday sleepover."

"How about your mom?"

"Probably at this moment she is plotting something with her girlfriends. She goes out every Friday night with three others for dinner, and I'm not sure I want to know what else. She's been doing it for years and nothing has interfered with the four of them getting together, not even a man. That's when I knew her third marriage wouldn't last when her soon-to-be third husband never got to take her out on Friday night."

"I'll trade my mother for yours. Wait. I can't do that. I need your help finding Rose, and if you got to know my mother, you'd keep your distance."

He chuckled. "I've dealt with tough people before in my job. Your mother doesn't scare me."

Kate gave him the last dish to dry. "She should. Little stands in her way, including my father. Whereas your mother sounds like a sweet lady."

"She is that, but I never know what to expect from her. Once I came home from a three-day conference and found the house totally redecorated. How she managed that I don't know. She'd moved everything around. I couldn't find anything of mine for months. It drove me crazy."

"How do she and Maddie get along?" Kate hosed down the sink, ran her dishcloth around it, then hung it up to dry.

"Great. If you discard your sanity, there's little not to love about Mom."

Kate made the coffee. "I'm not looking forward to tomorrow's luncheon. I'll try one last time to convince her not to pull the funding, but I might as well hit my head against a wall for all the good it will do. I'd hoped to approach some people at the luncheon who support different charities, but I've gotten the impression my mother has said something to them. I called some today, and from what they said, I don't think they'll go against her wishes."

"I'm sorry that's happening. After talking with some of the girls, I understand what you're doing and how valuable it is. If you can get even half of these teens off the street permanently, you're doing better than most. Beth has such plans for herself. You've given her a chance to think about that future."

His comment sparked an idea in Kate. She moved to the coffeepot and poured two mugs. It could work. Right now, anything was better than doing nothing. When she gave Wyatt his drink, she asked, "What do you think about having an open house and inviting people to see and hear from the girls what kind of effect this program can have on changing lives? I have several who have left here and are functioning well who I think would talk to others about Beacon of Hope."

"You could get the media involved too."

"If I can broaden my sources of financial support that will be better than depending on one major funding source." Kate sank into the chair at the table in the kitchen, the long day finally catching up with her. "I was wrong to do that. I took the easiest way out when Mother agreed to support the program. She thought she could control me and has found out she can't. In fact, today that was exactly what I was trying to do again. I need to change my game plan."

"Like the old saying goes, don't put all your eggs in one basket."

"Yes. In the past, I've played this low-key for the girls' sakes. I've worked behind the scene with the police, courts, and on the streets. Not anymore. This is a problem that the public needs to know about. The more I let the public know about the problem, maybe the more support I can get financially and with professionals volunteering."

"I could help you. I have a few connections in the media that I think would jump at the chance to cover something like this."

The smile and warmth in his eyes flowed over her in comforting waves. "I'll take any help I can get. I'm finding out I can't do this alone. The more involved the better."

"Then I'll make some calls tomorrow and get back to you."

"There'll be press at the luncheon. Mom always has some attend these functions. I can talk to them and see if they're interested. Now all I have to do is plan a big open house, look for Rose and—"

"What do you mean look for Rose?"

"You said you weren't successful at the parks. Probably because you are a Texas Ranger. They might not talk to you, but they might talk to me. I know a few people who frequent Oiler Park who wouldn't talk to the police but will me."

"Homeless?"

"A couple are."

"I don't like you going out alone and trying to find Rose."

"Then you come with me, but you can't dress as you are now." She let her gaze roam down, then up him—he was dressed in brown boots, tan slacks, white long sleeve shirt, a striped tie in different shades of brown and his silver star. "You'll have to dress down—way down."

"Where are you planning to go?"

"Into the areas my mother couldn't imagine existed in Dallas. Did the interviews with the girls help you any? I've talked with them and Rose's disappearance has shocked them. They don't think she's staying away willingly because she was happy to be here."

"That's the impression I got. But I think Zarah knows something. She lied to me about not knowing anything."

"Zarah isn't sold on the idea of being here, but why do you think she would know something about Rose's disappearance?"

"Her body language when I asked certain direct questions."

"She might have just been intimidated by you."

"I didn't get the impression Zarah gets intimidated that easily. I've been around people like Zarah. She's used to looking out for herself. She's street smart."

"I'll talk to her again after you leave. Maybe I can find out what's going on."

Wyatt finished the last of his coffee. "Let me know what you find out. I'm going to check into Zarah. Talk to the officer who brought her in." He stood and grabbed his mug. "I'd better be heading home. Thanks for dinner. I especially like the steak, baked potato, and salad. My kind of food."

"That's what I figured. Plus, it's easy to throw together fast. I'll have to have you back one evening when I have time to plan a real meal."

"Oh, that was real to me. I don't know what you put on the steak, but it was delicious."

"A secret spice blend I came up with."

Wyatt set his mug in the sink. "Don't forget. I'm coming with you when you go talk to the people you know on the street." Pausing in front of her, he took her hands. "Promise me you won't go and do anything without talking to me first. Rose is caught up with some very dangerous people who won't hesitate to murder."

His touch spurred her heart to beat faster. His concern washed over her and gave her hope that things would be all right. "I won't. I don't fancy myself a detective, but I do know some people who are aware of what's happening on the streets. It's taken me over three years to develop these contacts, and they might know something to help us."

"Us?"

"Okay, you. But I'm involved whether you want to acknowledge it or not."

He brushed her hair back from her face, his fingers lingering on her cheek a few extra heartbeats. "I don't want to have to search for you, too."

She smiled, feeling not so alone. "I don't want that either."

He gently squeezed her hands then released them. "Good night. I can find my own way out."

"I'll walk down with you partway. I'm going to have a talk with Zarah now."

On the second floor landing, Kate watched Wyatt continue on downstairs. At the bottom, he turned around and waved at her. As she made her way to Zarah's room, the sensations his touch had produced in her—a quickening of her pulse, a super awareness of her surroundings, an expectancy in the pit of her stomach—clung to her. If her life wasn't so complicated right now, she could see herself falling for him.

At Zarah's room, she knocked on the door. She waited a minute and repeated the knock. Where were Zarah and her roommate? She placed her hand on the knob when the door opened to reveal Zarah's roommate, her eyes red from crying, wet tracks still on her cheeks.

"What's wrong, Audrey?"

"Zarah packed her things and left a little while ago."

7

When?" Kate asked Audrey as she moved into the room and looked around.

"Half an hour ago."

The closet was wide open and revealed one side empty except for hangers on the rod. Everything else seemed as it was because there had never been any of Zarah's personal touches. Most girls slowly added them as the months passed and they remained. Not for Zarah, even after seven months. "You should have come and gotten me."

"I wasn't sure she left until I came up here. I saw her leave by the side door. She goes outside sometimes at dusk. Told me once she likes to watch the sunsets. I thought that was strange, but then Zarah is. When I looked out the window of the rec room a few minutes later, I saw her getting into a white Chevy."

White Chevy like the one seen at the dumpsite for Lillian Harris? "Did she have a bag with her when she left by the side door?"

"No. She was empty-handed when I saw her going outside, but when she got into the car, she had a bag with her."

"So she must have hid a bag outside earlier?"

Audrey lifted her shoulders, her palms facing upward toward the ceiling. "I haven't been up here since breakfast. I guess she could have packed earlier and snuck the bag out. She didn't have too much. She left some things."

"Did you see who was driving the car?"

"The windows were too dark."

"So you didn't see anyone in the Chevy when she got in?"

"Nope. She went around to the other side."

Kate felt her front pants pocket for her cell. It wasn't there. She'd left it on the counter in her apartment. "Did she look upset? Frightened?"

"Not much was different than usual. Not happy. Not sad. Not much on her face. I started to go outside to catch her before the car drove off, but the second she slipped inside, it sped away."

"Thanks, Audrey. You did all you could." Kate hurried from the room and took the stairs to the third floor two at a time. She needed to call Wyatt and get him back to Beacon of Hope. Even if Zarah went willingly, something didn't feel right.

Inside her apartment, she snatched up her cell and quickly punched in Wyatt's number. When he answered, she said, "Zarah's gone. Please come back. I think the same car that was spotted near where that girl was dumped picked Zarah up about thirty-five minutes ago." The last sentence rushed from her mouth in a single breath. All she could think about was Lily/Lillian being found in the field buried in a shallow grave.

"I'm turning around. I should be there in ten minutes. I'll call the police and report it. I'll go through my contact on the task force, Detective Finch."

Someone knocked on her door. "See you soon."

With her cell still in her hand, she went to the door and let Audrey into her apartment.

"I forgot to mention something." She took several steps inside then whirled to face Kate. "Because the car sped away so fast, I didn't get all the license plate, but I wrote down on my hand most of it." Audrey showed Kate her palm.

The letters H-O-T S-T were written on her skin in blue ink. A definite connection to the vehicle sighted near Lillian's dumpsite. The implication heightened Kate's fear for Zarah. "Thanks. I'll let Ranger Sheridan know."

After Audrey left, Kate called Wyatt again. "It's the same car. I'm sure of it. Audrey wrote most of the license plate down. HOT ST."

"Great. I'll pass this along. We're short one letter or number but having five out of the six will narrow our search even more. I'll have Detective Finch put out a BOLO on the car."

"I'll meet you downstairs," Kate said right before she disconnected.

As she made her way to the ground floor, she felt as though she were being attacked from all sides. First, Rose vanishing, then Cynthia's suicide attempt followed by her mother pulling the funding, and now Zarah leaving. The girls weren't guarded, but how was Zarah able to plan all this? Someone purposely came to pick her up at a certain time. She must have snuck her clothes out earlier, which meant it wasn't a spur of the moment decision. Zarah didn't have a job, so as far as she knew she didn't have a cell. The phone the students used who didn't have their own was in the rec room. Not a lot of privacy. When they needed it, they came to her office and used hers. Zarah hadn't done that in the past few days.

Zarah wasn't the first girl to leave the program. She'd had four others in the three and a half years Beacon of Hope had been opened. They had been older and on their own longer than Zarah. She was barely fifteen with a lot of anger issues that she'd started to reveal lately in bits and pieces during her group therapy session.

Kate had thought with time she could reach the teen. Now her time had run out. It appeared as though Zarah had chosen to return to her old life. *Why, Lord? Why couldn't I help her?*

Those questions weighed on her as she waited for Wyatt to show up. She paced the foyer, aware that several girls paused near the staircase, observing her. News of Zarah's disappearance would spread quickly, and she would have to deal with the fallout. She jumped when the buzzer on the intercom sounded behind her. She quickly answered it, the screen showing Wyatt standing out front. She punched the button to open the door.

The sight of him brought immediate ease to her. He'd know what to do about Zarah. The connection to Rose and Lily made finding Zarah all the more important.

"Thanks for coming back." Kate crossed the foyer to Wyatt. "I know it hasn't been long, but is there any news about the car?"

"Not yet but there's a regional alert on the white Chevy. I'm treating it as an abduction, since we don't really know the circumstances behind Zarah's leaving and the fact that she's fifteen."

"I don't think she was forced, but I don't know that for sure. Why would she leave like that?"

"There could be several possibilities. She knew something and was scared to stay. She was involved in Rose's disappearance somehow. Her old life appealed to her more than a chance at the future you could give her. Or the people running this ring have a hold over her." Wyatt glanced over her shoulder then nodded toward the staircase.

Kate rotated around and faced the twenty-one girls left all standing on the steps, watching them. Worry and fear marked each teen's face. Tears streamed down Audrey's and Beth's.

Kate moved forward. "Let's meet in the rec room." She'd talked to each student individually, but not as a group. It was time to let them know exactly what was going on. She owed them that.

As the girls filed down the stairs and headed for the rec room, Wyatt came up beside Kate. "What are you going to tell them?"

"Everything."

"Do you want me to wait out here?"

"No, they may have questions for you. I want them to realize you're here to help them. Some of them don't have a great opinion of the police."

The girls all sat on either the couches, chairs, or the floor waiting for Kate. Audrey and Beth had stopped crying, but the expressions of fear and worry were still in place when Kate entered the room.

"By now you've heard that Zarah has left Beacon of Hope. Audrey saw her willingly get into a car this evening and drive away. Some of her belongings are gone, so it doesn't look like she is coming back. This is a program with certain security procedures in place, but more so you're safe—rather than keeping you locked up like criminals. You aren't criminals. You're girls who I hope will grab at the second chance you've been given."

"So you're gonna just let Zarah walk away like that?" Jana, one of the oldest students, snapped her fingers.

"No. Every effort to bring Zarah back will be made. Ranger Sheridan has a search out for the car Zarah left in. She's here, as some of you are, because of the courts. I'm her guardian, and I'll do *everything* to see she's safely back here."

"What's going on? First Rose and now Zarah." Beth's voice could barely be heard from the back of the room.

"We're not sure. Rose got a call from someone she knew. I think another girl was in trouble. Rose went to help."

A few of the students murmured how that sounded like Rose.

"That was stupid," Jana said over the voices of the others.

Audrey shot to her feet. "Shut up. We have a problem here. We have to work together."

Jana rose slowly and faced Audrey. "Doing what?"

Audrey stared at the older girl across the room, then swiveled her attention to Kate, a plea in her eyes.

"I need each one of you to think long and hard about the last few weeks. Anything you can remember about Rose or Zarah. A call they took. A person they saw. Something they said. You never know what might be important. If you think of anything, please let me know. It might help us find who is behind this. Has Rose or Zarah ever talked about what happened to them before they came here? I think whoever has them is someone they knew from their past, especially since they're from this area of Texas."

"When we went on a field trip last week, I saw a guy talking to Zarah. She said she needed to go to the bathroom and left the group to do that. But she took a wrong turn and went down a different hallway. I had started to tell her when I saw her talking to him. He stroked her arm. She smiled at him," Georgia, a quiet student who had been at Beacon of Hope for a year, said from the couch. "I ducked out of the hallway before she saw me."

Kate wished Georgia had told her when it had happened, but she wouldn't say anything in front of the group. Georgia rarely spoke up, especially when more than one or two people were around. "Could you describe him?"

"I think so."

Wyatt stepped forward. "I'd like you to work with a sketch artist. Will you give it a try?"

Georgia nodded.

"This kind of information might help us. So if anyone else has something, please let me know." Kate scanned the faces of each girl, some in thought, others' expressions blank. When no one said anything else, she continued. "There is one more thing I think you should know."

Several students tensed. Audrey sank back down to the floor while Jana remained standing, her hands balled at her sides.

Her throat clogged with the words Kate needed to say. These girls had done and seen things most people wouldn't in their lifetimes. She'd owed them respect and faith in them if she wanted it returned to her. "I wish I didn't have to tell you this, but the majority of the funding for this program will be cut off at the end of the month."

"How much?" Jana asked, her hand flexing and closing at her sides.

"Seventy-five percent." That was how much the Winslow Foundation contributed to Beacon of Hope.

A few whistled. Others scowled and grumbled while a couple of their mouths dropped open.

"As I know you've figured out, it would be impossible to run the program on what we have left." Kate felt Wyatt's presence right behind her as though he were lending her his support.

"Haven't you said all things are possible through the Lord?" Jana shouted, with several agreeing with her.

"Yes and that's true. That's why I have come up with a way I think we can get the money."

"Yeah, like rob a bank?"

Kate didn't see who said it, but she answered the group with, "We're going to have an open house and invite people who can donate money to the program. I want them to see what we're doing here. Talk to you all and see what you're doing. That can be the most powerful message we can give them. But I won't be able to do it without your help."

"When will we have the open house?" Beth asked.

"I thought in three weeks. That'll give us time to come up with the plans for it and for me to send out the invitations. I'll be including the media. You all have overcome so much. I hope that one day there's no need for a program like this. In order for that to happen, we need to get the message out. Whoever wants to be part of that is welcome to join me if we have permission from your guardian, but I won't ask anyone to do anything they don't want to. If nothing else, the other staff and I can show people the program and testimonies can be given unanimously too."

Georgia immediately dropped her head and stared at her hands as they twisted together in her lap. Several others averted their gazes, their brows furrowed.

Jana stepped through the maze of girls and came to the front. "I ain't putting myself on display." She continued her way toward the door.

Beth stood. "I'll help. If it weren't for you believing in me, I'd probably be dead by now."

A couple of older girls nodded their heads and agreed to help too.

Kate raised her hands to quiet the discussion among the students. "This doesn't have to be decided tonight. Let me know if you want to be involved. The ones who don't can go on a field trip that day."

"If we don't help, does that mean the doors will close on this place?" the newest girl asked, biting her bottom lip.

"No matter what, I'll do everything I can to keep that from happening. Remember my door is always open."

When there were no more questions, Kate decided to leave the students to talk among themselves.

Out in the hallway Wyatt said, "I'd like to see Zarah's room. Maybe she left something behind that might give us an idea who she went with or where she went."

"This way." Kate climbed the stairs to the second floor. With each step, she felt as though she dragged the weight of the world up with her.

In Zarah's room, Wyatt checked the closet, then her desk, and finally the drawers she used. Some of her belongings were crammed into a couple of the bottom ones.

When he straightened after going through what Zarah left behind, he shook his head. "Nothing."

"Do you think the guy Georgia saw Zarah with is involved in all of this?"

"Let's hope so. We could use a break."

The notes to *The Good, the Bad and the Ugly* blared. Wyatt quickly answered his cell.

As he listened to the caller, a frown deepened on his tan face. "Okay. I'll be there."

"What's happened?" Kate's chest constricted, capturing her next breath in her lungs.

"A police officer saw the white Chevy with the license plate HOT STF on it. He tried to stop him. The car wouldn't pull over. A high-speed chase occurred, ending in a crash. One person got away. While another officer went after the man who fled, the other stayed to check out the car. A young girl who fits Zarah's description, was found shot in the front seat."

"Is she . . . is she dead?"

"No, but it doesn't look good. The ambulance is taking her to Mercy Cross. I'll drive you."

His news hit her like a knockout punch. Everywhere she turned lately, she ran into a barrier as though Satan were toying with her. She wouldn't let him win.

❧

King clenched his fists and glared at the man cowering in front of him. "You fool! You were supposed to get rid of her. Never to be found. She can link us to Rose."

"Before I ran, I shot her in the head. She's dead."

King snorted. "My contact just informed me Zarah was taken to the hospital. If you don't clean up this mess, you'll regret being born. That's a promise you know I'll keep."

"I'll go to the hospital and make sure Zarah doesn't make it."

"You do that."

Tony averted his gaze, his hands stuffed into his pockets. "Boss, there may be one little problem."

"You mean besides Zarah is alive and in the hospital?"

Tony nodded. "She has something hidden she says could cause you problems. She knew about the connection between you and Rose. She wanted some money. Before I could do anything, though, the cops came after us."

"You shot her instead! Before you could find out where the information was?" King made his hands into fists, wanting to pound some sense into the man.

"I didn't know what else to do. I couldn't see her running from the cops in those heels she was wearing. I took her purse after I shot her, then got out of there before the cops caught me."

"Nothing was in the purse?"

"No, there wasn't anything about you or Rose in the purse. Zarah probably was bluffing. She ain't too smart."

Neither are you. "You better hope that's the case. Make sure it is."

Tony straightened. "Yes, sir."

"Now be useful and bring Rose up here."

King prowled the bookcase-lined room. Energy surged through him as if he'd touched a live wire. This whole affair had become a ball of rattlesnakes feeding on each other. He'd known from the first day his wife's niece, Rose, came to live with them, that she would be trouble. Too beautiful for her own good. Too innocent to be true. But he would have done anything for his wife—even take in her niece. Now his wife was dead, and he was left dealing with the girl. She'd earned her keep as a recruiter for his prostitution ring, but everything changed when she brought Lily to him. He'd been ready to teach her a lesson when one of her johns beat her up and left her for dead. In fact, he'd thought she'd died until Zarah had let Tony know about Rose.

Had Tony in his dealings with Zarah let something slip? Was that why Zarah knew about the connection between Rose and him? Most of the people in the trenches didn't know King's real name, so he should be all right. But if Tony didn't clean up this mess soon, he would live to regret it.

He ceased pacing at the large window overlooking the pasture where quarter horses grazed. He knew his prize mares were there even though he couldn't see them in the darkness of night. The knowledge his ranching operation ran smoothly comforted him. Now if only he could get his other enterprise in line, he would be content. If he didn't get a better handle on it, his partner would—

A noise out in the hallway interrupted his thoughts. He quickly pulled the blackout shade down, then slowly turned. King confronted Rose. Her eyes were still adjusting to the bright lights glowing in his office. The sight of her curdled his gut. He'd had a good thing going. Until Rose turned up alive—a connection to him he couldn't afford for the police to discover.

After Tony shut the door, leaving him and Rose alone, he strode toward his niece—nothing like his wife who he missed every day—standing in the middle of the room, her arms hugging her body, her eyes no longer blinking. She tilted up her chin and glared at him.

"Ah, I see the Deprivation Room hasn't done its magic with you yet. Not to worry. It will. But for the time being I feel generous. You'll be allowed to eat dinner with me. None of that gruel you've been eating. All your favorite dishes."

"Your mind games aren't gonna work with me anymore. I know what you're doing. I've read all about it."

"While you were at Beacon of Hope." He spit the last words out as if they were poison on his tongue.

Her lips thinned. Her eyes became mere slits.

"I fed and clothed you for eight years. You owe me."

Her hands dug into the flesh of her upper arms. But she didn't reply.

He let the silence lengthened until he noticed Rose shifting from one foot to the other.

"Why am I here? I didn't say anything to anyone about you," she muttered between gritted teeth.

It would have been only a matter of time before she had. "You still haven't paid me back for all the money I've spent on you."

"I had a job. I could have paid you back with that money."

He laughed. "Yeah, at the rate you were going I'd be an old man by that time. No, I have a much better use for you."

"I won't recruit girls for you anymore."

"I know. There are other ways you can make money."

Rose's eyes rounded. Her arms slipped to her sides. "Not that again."

King took the few feet separating them and put his thumb under her chin, lifting her gaze to lock with his. "You have no choice now. I have you back where you belong. I'm the one who decides when you can leave." He pinched his thumb and forefinger together, watching tears well in Rose's eyes. "Don't forget that. I'm the King." Then smiling, he released his grip and caressed the red mark he put on her chin. "Let's go eat."

❧

Curled on her side, Rose lay on the hard floor, her arms cushioning her head against the stone. The food she'd forced herself to eat solidified in her stomach, its churning and gurgling the only sound in an otherwise void netherworld.

Blackness pressed in from every side as if her eyes were closed. She could no longer smell the dank musky odor that had assailed her when she'd first been put in the room. Her senses were so dulled even the stone beneath her was smooth.

While with King, she'd tried to figure out what time of day it was, but the windows were blacked out. There were no clocks or references to when it was. No clue at all. The thought she was losing track of time sent a wave of panic through her.

Everything changed once her aunt had died, leaving her with King. She would never think of him as her uncle because he wasn't really. For years he'd ruled her life. Even when her aunt had been alive, she'd kept her distance from King. Then right after Aunt Belle's funeral, her world had crashed down on her.

Tears quickly followed. Always there just below the surface—since she'd arrived at the ranch. No one for miles around.

King's place was big. She let the tears flow. It was useless to keep them inside anymore. She was utterly alone.

No, I'm not. She scrambled to her knees and bowed her head.

Lord, I'm sorry. Please forgive me. I was wrong to help King, but how was I to fight him? Please help me. Kate says You'll listen when we're in trouble. I'm in trouble. I need You.

The ever-present silence mocked her attempt at praying. She sank to the floor and clasped her legs to her. Sobs tore at her body like vultures stealing pieces of her flesh.

I'm alone.

❧

"I'm sorry. Zarah didn't make it," the man in the white coat said.

The same doctor, the same waiting room as with Cynthia the night before. Kate sank onto the chair behind her. So much death. *Why, Lord?* This latest one shook her faith. *I don't understand.*

"Thank you, doctor." Wyatt cut into the heavy silence. "I've notified Detective Finch of the Dallas Police. He may want to talk to you."

She heard him speak, but the sound seemed so far away. It was as if he were whispering on the other side of the room. But he stood in front of her, shaking the doctor's hand. She observed the older man leaving the waiting room. When he disappeared from view, Kate took in the rest of the room, noting the couple in the corner waiting for news about their son and the old man sitting with his shoulders hunched over, his hands folded as though he were praying.

Slowly the sound of her name filtered into her brain, and she peered up at Wyatt. As last night, he was here for her with concern on his face and a softness in his eyes that reached out and wrapped her in an embrace of comfort.

She couldn't say anything, not even thanks for being here. Tears crowded her eyes, and the image of him wavered.

He took her hands and tugged her to her feet. "Let's get out of here."

She nodded.

He hooked his arm around her shoulder and cuddled her against his side.

As he started for the door, Kate wiped her hand across her eyes. She needed to hold it together. She would have to tell the girls about Zarah.

When she emerged from the hospital, the summer heat clung to the night, thick and suffocating, pressing down on her chest. She stopped and bent over, inhaling large gulps of the oppressive air. She couldn't get enough. Gasping, tears stinging her eyes, she let Wyatt guide her toward a wooden bench.

But instead of taking a seat, he drew her into his arms and held her against him. "You aren't alone. I'll be here to help."

The soothing calmness of his voice slipped into her mind and eased the panic she experienced. Her head cushioned against his chest, she listened to the rhythmic, steady beat of his heart. Its sound wove through her and fused itself to the frantic tempo of her own. Slowly her heartbeat returned to normal. She became aware of his lime-scented aftershave, his gentle hand stroking the length of her back, the sound of cars in the background, the glow of the security light a few feet from them.

Kate stepped out of his protective embrace and put several feet between them. "I'm fine."

One eyebrow lifted. "You are?"

"I don't know what came over me."

"I do. The past few days are catching up with you. You won't be able to help your girls if you don't take care of yourself."

She wanted to bristle at his advice. She wanted to put more emotional distance between them—until her gaze reconnected with his and she glimpsed the caring in his expression. She hadn't had that in a long time—certainly not as a child. The urge to go back into the circle of his arms overwhelmed her. Clamping down on her teeth, she curled her hands into fists to keep herself from moving toward him.

"I'm taking you home. You need to get some sleep. Tomorrow won't be an easy day for you. Besides the luncheon with your mother, Detective Finch will pay you a visit first thing in the morning. He's going to wait until then. He agrees with me there's more going on here than we know and in the end it may help us break up a big prostitution ring working in this part of the state."

"Please come with me to the luncheon." The request tumbled out before she realized what she was saying. She'd never taken a "date" to one of those affairs, which would put her mother on alert. She didn't need that right now, and yet the prospects of him attending with her felt right.

"Weren't you the one who warned me off of your mother?"

"Yes, but you're a big, tough Texas Ranger. I figure you can deal with one petite woman who thinks she owns Dallas. Probably the whole state of Texas."

He cocked a grin. "Now you've piqued my interest."

"Good. I could get used to having backup when dealing with her."

"Hey, I didn't say anything about actually interacting with her. I thought I could stand in the corner and quietly watch her at work. Maybe I could pick up some techniques to use on suspects."

"If intimidation is your game, then she's a master."

He held out his hand. "Come on. Let's get you back to Beacon of Hope. I need to go home and get my beauty sleep if I'm gonna face your mother tomorrow."

A vision of Wyatt at one end of the main street in an old western town while her mother was at the other took over her thoughts. They faced each other. Their hands hovered over their holstered guns. Their gazes gauged each nuance of their opponent. The town clock struck twelve o'clock—high noon, and they reached for their weapons.

His hand moving to the small of her back to guide her into the passenger side of his truck wrenched her away from her daydreaming. Heat scored her cheeks. What was she doing fantasizing about Wyatt even if it was only a scene with him facing down her mother? Next, she'd be fantasizing about something much more dangerous—like kissing him.

When he climbed behind the steering wheel and started the engine, he threw her a look that instantly put her back in her fantasy. With his cowboy hat, dark stubble from the beginnings of a beard and his tan features set in a neutral expression, he could be a Texas wrangler from 150 years ago. He linked his gaze to hers and time completely fell away.

"When should I pick you up?" She blurted out the first thing that came to mind.

"You're picking me up? I was going to ask you that."

"This isn't a date, and you're doing me a favor by going. I could use the moral support. Besides, I'd love to see your ranch." That last remark took her by surprise. She liked ranches but didn't generally invite herself to a person's house.

He chuckled. "Sure. I live right outside Bluebonnet Creek two miles on Front Road. My place is called the Lone Star Ranch. What time should I expect you?"

"Noon—I mean eleven."

He pulled out and headed toward the street. "Good. It's a da—what do we call what we're doing?"

"Helping out a friend."

His attention slid to her. "I like that."

The grin that accompanied those words melted any conflict she had for asking him to come to the luncheon. He was just what she needed to make it through the ordeal tomorrow.

⁓ℰ⁓

"Is this all the information you can find on Wyatt Sheridan?" King asked one of his men.

"Yes, on such short notice. Give me a few more days, and I'll come up with more." The baldheaded man plopped the folder down on King's mahogany desk.

"I want you to tail him. I want to know where he spends his time."

"Done."

King flipped the folder open and perused the report and pictures that accompanied it. An idea took hold as he studied the attractive woman who was identified as Caroline Sheridan, the ranger's mother. "Also I want someone to follow his mother and daughter. I want to know where they go, when, how long they stay. Use Tony for that. He needs to be useful."

Beads of sweat popped out on the baldheaded man. He took out a handkerchief and mopped it away. "A Texas Ranger's family?"

King slammed his palm down on his desk, ignoring the sting of the hard contact. "I pay you good money to work for me. I don't like people who question my techniques. Do I make myself clear?"

The man's Adam's apple bobbed up and down. "Yes."

"Report to me any changes in the Sheridan family's whereabouts. Now go." King waved his hand toward the door as he returned his attention to the folder. His full attention fastened on the petite woman with short medium brown hair with touches of red and large gray eyes, fringed in long eyelashes. Not bad as a diversion.

～෨～

"Frankly, Kate, I'm surprised you haven't had more trouble considering the type of teens you work with. You deal with girls who don't make it other places. Or ones who need someone who understands what they have gone through. You have programs to deal with their schooling, counseling, and medical necessities as well as developing their vocational skills. Your setup here with a qualified staff to meet their needs is the best situation they could be in. Judge Adams sees that. And so are other courts and police departments beginning to see it. Not just here but in other states." Mrs. Stutsman, the liaison from Judge Adams' office, rose from the couch in Kate's office. "I mainly stopped by to reassure you everything is all right. I've talked with Ranger Sheridan and Detective Finch. Everything that can be done is being done. Our Memorandum of Understanding still stands."

Relieved the MOU between Beacon of Hope and the court system was still in place, Kate accompanied Mrs. Stutsman to the door. "I'm glad you stopped by. On your day off, at that."

"I've seen your success with some of these girls I didn't think had a chance. I also know how you pour your all into this program. I'm reassured by Detective Finch and Ranger Sheridan taking both Rose's disappearance and Zarah's murder very seriously." Mrs. Stutsman offered Kate a reassuring smile. "Call if you need to talk."

"Thanks."

Kate watched the middle-aged woman, whom she had been working with since Beacon of Hope opened, stroll down the long hall toward the main entrance. As was Mrs. Stutsman's custom when she visited, she stopped along the way and talked with any of the girls she encountered. Beth and Audrey spoke to her for a few minutes before she continued her trek to the exit.

Then Kate's gaze fell on the wall clock. Nine thirty. She quickly shut her office door and hurried toward her apartment on the third floor. She didn't have much time before she had to pick up Wyatt, and she still needed to pay Cynthia a visit at the hospital.

Ten minutes later Kate left the building, wearing a designer dress even her mother would approve of, and slipped into her Mustang. It wasn't even ten in the morning and the day had already been long and emotionally exhausting with visits from Detective Finch and Mrs. Stutsman. But she knew after talking with them everything was being done that could be.

When Kate entered Cynthia's hospital room twenty minutes later, the young girl lay in bed, staring out the window. Sunlight streamed in through the blinds, brightening the soft green walls.

The sound of the door swishing closed brought Cynthia's head around. She rested her chin on her chest. "I want to leave here."

Kate walked to the chair next to the bed and sat. "Good. I want you to come back to Beacon of Hope as soon as the doctor will allow it."

"You do?"

"Of course. Why wouldn't I? You belong there. You're one of us. In fact, I've got some messages from the others." Kate rose a few inches and placed a manila envelope in Cynthia's lap. "They miss you and need your help."

"My help?" Cynthia kept her head down, her gaze focused on the packet Kate had brought her.

"We started planning a big open house to be held in three weeks to raise money for the program. Think of it as one great big party."

"I don't know anything about parties."

"But you have a gift for drawing. I've seen your work. We can always use that skill."

Cynthia raised her head and looked at Kate. "I didn't try to kill myself."

"What were you trying to do?" Kate held her breath, praying the girl finally talked to her about her cutting. She'd once thought when Cynthia had come to a safe place like Beacon of Hope she wouldn't do it anymore. She'd been wrong. Now after talking with Cynthia's doctor and Dr. Jan Barton, she understood more about what was going on with the teen.

"I—I . . ." Cynthia broke eye contact, again staring at her lap.

Kate scooted the chair closer to the bed and cupped one of the girl's hands. "There's nothing you can tell me that would surprise me or make me change how I feel about you. When I take a girl into the program, she becomes part of my family. Maybe it would help if you talked about what was going on right before you cut yourself. What were you feeling? Nothing you say will go any further than me." Dr. Barton had said it was important that Cynthia had someone she could trust enough to share her feelings. Rose wasn't around right now so she prayed that Cynthia would let her take Rose's place.

"I was so angry I didn't stop Rose from leaving." She stared at Kate. "She's dead, isn't she?"

"I don't know. I'm praying she isn't. The police are looking for her. We haven't given up. If she's out there, I intend to find her."

"When we talked at night, it was always about me. She never said much about herself. If I had shut up, she might have and I would know something to help find her."

"This isn't your fault. None of it. You need to believe that." If only she could follow her own advice to the teen.

Cynthia didn't say anything.

"The doctor has agreed to discharge you tomorrow. You will continue to see Dr. Barton once a week. She'll be working with you and me to teach you how to help yourself. She also has a group of teens who cut themselves she wants you to be part of. There are ways to deal with anger that don't involve hurting yourself. You can run, hit a pillow, use a punching bag, dance, scream."

"So if I go running from this place, hitting a pillow and screaming, no one will think I'm strange."

Kate broke out laughing. "I might join you with the kind of day I'm having."

"Concerning Rose?"

"No, just a boring luncheon I need to attend." Kate rose. "I'll be back tomorrow to spring you from this place."

As she closed the door on Cynthia's room, Kate glimpsed the girl tearing into the manila envelope and pulling out the stack of messages from the others. She began reading, and a smile lit her face.

❧

"How many acres do you have?" Kate asked as she finished the brief tour of Wyatt's barn.

"A hundred. Over the years, part of it has been sold off, but I'm determined to hang on to this last hundred. When I retire, I want to raise horses for the rodeo."

"Isn't the idea of retiring to rest and relax? Maybe play a little golf, do a crossword puzzle or Sudoku?"

"If retiring means going from doing one thing to not doing much of anything, then I'll go crazy if all I do is play golf and work puzzles."

"Me, too."

The front screen door banged closed, and a pretty teenage girl bounded down the steps and walked toward Wyatt. "Your daughter?"

He grinned. "Yep, and I see she's dressed for the mall."

"Dad, Nana and me are going to the mall. I need to start shopping for school. It'll be here before you know it."

"Who are you meeting at the mall?"

His daughter shrugged. "A couple of friends. Nana is okay with it."

"Is she staying?"

"Yeah. She's not dropping me off and coming back later. I promise she'll be there."

"I want you to check in with her every thirty minutes."

"She's gonna be there." Exasperation edged the teen's tone.

"Yeah, camped out at the coffee shop while you and your friends are gallivanting all over the two-story mall, looking for boys."

"Daaad! I have a boyfriend, and he isn't gonna be there."

"That's supposed to reassure me?"

"Stop being a cop. Nothing's gonna happen to me."

"Check in every thirty minutes or you can't go."

"I'm fourteen now. I'm not a baby." She blew a frustrated breath out, whirled around, and marched toward the house, muttering something under her breath.

"Maddie," he called out in a tightly controlled voice.

His daughter stopped and turned back.

"This is Kate Winslow. Kate, this is my daughter, Maddie."

"Nice to meet you, Maddie."

"Same here." Wyatt's daughter swung back around and continued her march toward the front door.

"Sorry about that. I should have introduced you before we got into our usual argument about spending time at the mall."

"It's not easy raising kids today. Peer pressure is strong. They all want to do what everyone else is doing. They're desperate to fit in."

"Tell me about it. Last summer I couldn't get her near a store or mall. All she thought about was riding. Maddie is a good kid, but more and more I'm seeing her friends influence her choices. She's usually wrapped up in training for the rodeo events she likes to compete in, but this new trend of spending time at the mall isn't one I like. I guess it's the heat that forces kids indoors."

"More like shopping and hanging with your friends. Ready to leave? I don't mind being fashionably late, but my mother minds if I am."

"Let's go. When you first arrived, you met my mom, so it's only fair I meet yours." He grinned as he slid into the passenger seat of Kate's red Mustang. "My mother is sweet. But that doesn't mean she doesn't drive me crazy. She can't stick with anything for long. I think she's gone through every hobby that ever existed and has started to do some over."

"Stamp collecting?" Kate pulled away from Wyatt's house.

"Yep."

"Scrapbooking?"

"Oh, yeah. You should have seen the house when she was doing that. Her supplies were scattered all over the place."

At the end of his drive, Kate stopped and waited for a dark blue sedan to pass before turning onto the highway that led into Bluebonnet Creek. Her palms dampened, and her stomach contracted the closer she got to her parents' estate. This would be the longest few hours.

❧

King climbed into Tony's new dark blue Ford at the mall. "I want you to stay out here. Watch the car and let me know if they leave."

"Sure, boss. But if they're anything like my girlfriend, they'll be inside for hours."

"Which door did they go in?"

"That one." Tony pointed toward the main entrance on the west side of the mall.

"Which car is Caroline Sheridan's?"

"The one next to you."

King glanced out the side window at the yellow Volkswagen. "Idiot. You don't park next to the car you're watching."

"It was the only parking space around."

"Find another one." King shoved the door open and exited the Ford.

He paused at the Volkswagen, scanned the area, then bent down and released the air in the front left tire. If they left before he could connect with the ranger's mother, that would delay them. Now to hunt down Caroline Sheridan.

8

The temperature outside was nearing one hundred, but inside the solarium at the Winslow estate it hovered around sixty-five degrees. That didn't stop Wyatt from wanting to shed his suit coat, roll up his shirtsleeves, and remove his tie. It constricted the flow of air into his lungs. Either that or the fact that Kate's description of her mother was every bit right on. She was a force to be reckoned with. Her mother had her hands in every important thing that went on in Dallas.

Observing an older version of Kate from across the large glassed-in room, Wyatt sipped his ice water and relished the coolness as it slid down his throat. Laura Winslow moved from each group of guests spread out among the beautifully set tables—just how his mom had shown him when she was going through her decorating phase. Mrs. Winslow had yet to make her way to her daughter. In fact, she seemed to be purposefully avoiding Kate.

Kate rejoined him near the bar, which was doing a brisk business. "I'd like you to meet my dad. He just arrived. I'll introduce you to Mother a little later, after she makes her rounds."

"I don't mind if you want to put it off."

She chuckled. "If only I could. She's saving the best for last. That's always her method."

"The best? Thanks, I think."

"I probably should have said the juiciest. She likes people to squirm while they wait. She's good at that."

"Let's meet your dad. I might offer him my condolences."

"He wouldn't understand. He and Mother are still deeply in love after thirty-two years of marriage. It amazes me at times. My father is the only man my mother has eyes for. I wish I knew how she did it."

Wyatt thought of his deceased wife. Rebecca and he'd had that kind of relationship. He figured a man only got one in a lifetime. He just wished the Lord had allowed him to be with Rebecca longer. Five years wasn't long enough.

"Have you had any success with getting funding?"

"There are a few who said they would come to the open house but nothing concrete. I did connect with some media people who are interested in the program." She tugged on his hand. "Come on. The mayor just left Dad."

Wyatt had seen the distinguished looking older man in newspaper photos on several occasions. His smile as his daughter neared him made him instantly like her father. He gave her a bear hug before turning to Wyatt.

"I understand from Kate you're a Texas Ranger."

"Yes, sir."

"Please call me Bennett. Any friend of Kate's is welcome in my home." He turned his attention back to his daughter. "Your mother told me she isn't going to support your program after this month. Frankly I'm surprised she has for this long. I never thought it was a good idea from the beginning. I don't want my daughter exposed to the unsavory side of life. It's too dangerous."

"Beacon of Hope is in a safe part of town."

"Barely. After what has happened, don't you see what could happen to you?"

"Nothing has. I've been perfectly safe."

Bennett frowned. "Aren't you talking to a low-income-area middle school in Dallas next week? I've heard of shootings occurring in broad daylight there. One just a couple of weeks ago."

"So you aren't going to help me convince Mother otherwise?"

"No. Find another way to help the less fortunate. Work for the Winslow Foundation. I've always wanted you to. Then when your mother wants to retire from the foundation, you can take over running it. That's what both your mother and I want."

"I'm not going to stop helping these girls. I'll find another way if I have to."

The tension spiked between Kate and her father. Wyatt took hold of her hand, hoping to convey support for her. But he could understand where Kate's dad was coming from. The most important thing in his life was to keep his daughter safe. The more Maddie was pulling away from him, the more he wanted to hold her tight.

"Kate, finally I get a chance to talk to you." Laura Winslow stepped up to the group and gave her husband a quick kiss. "I'm glad your meeting was over early. I can always use your help in raising money for the hospital."

Bennett smiled, his look only for his wife. "I cut the meeting short. I know how important this is to you. Let me see what I can do. I see Kenneth Foster has arrived with his wife." Kate's dad shifted toward Wyatt and offered his hand. "It was nice meeting you."

He shook the man's hand. "Likewise."

As Bennett headed for a group of men to the left, Laura looked Wyatt up and down. He was catalogued and assessed in a few seconds. And he'd come up short in Kate's mother's mind. The slight twist to her mouth indicated her disapproval although she had managed to cover it quite fast.

"I hope you're enjoying yourself, Mr. Sheridan."

"Yes, you have a beautiful home."

Laura dismissed him and focused on Kate. "I only have a little time. Let's go talk in the library."

⟶

King found Caroline Sheridan sitting at a table in a café at the mall. Her photo didn't do her justice. She was beautiful, almost innocent looking, even though he knew she'd been married three times. She took a sip of her drink without taking her eyes off the page in the big, thick book she was reading.

He moved closer to her, but stopped short when two young girls converged on her. Caroline smiled at the teens and exchanged some words with them. Her granddaughter hugged her then hurried away with her friend.

King resumed his approach to the café, ordered a latte, and sat at a table next to Caroline Sheridan. He opened his newspaper and glanced at the articles while drinking his coffee. He watched his target out of the corner of his eye. She scanned the restaurant. He looked up as though pondering something he'd read.

His gaze intersected with hers, and he smiled. "Indoors is the only place to be with this extreme heat. Even then, sitting under the ceiling fan makes it barely tolerable."

She glanced down his length, then back up. "From what I heard on the radio this morning, there's no end in sight. All next week they said sunny and the highs in the low hundreds."

"I'd love to pick up and leave for the month of August, but I have obligations."

"I know what you mean. Me, too." She closed her book—a volume on the history of the Alamo.

"I see you are a history buff. Or at least Texas history. Have you read the account of Sam Houston's life by Haley?"

"No." She sent him a grin that made her eyes sparkle. "I have to confess this is the first book on Texas history I've read. I'm planning to take my granddaughter to San Antonio this fall. I want to go see the Alamo and regale her with tales of bravery and heroism."

"There are a lot of accounts of the Battle of the Alamo."

"Yeah, I just got through reading about Davy Crockett."

"Have you read about Colonel William Travis yet?"

"No, not yet. I'd actually heard of Davy Crockett, so I read that section first. Who was Travis?"

"May I join you? I love talking about history, especially with such a charming woman."

Blushing, Caroline nodded.

King picked up his latte and moved to her table, sitting across from her. "He was the commander of the Alamo and had his hands full fighting a Mexican army with overwhelming odds against him." He infused enthusiasm into his voice as if he spoke on a subject he cared about. He hated history, but to get close to this woman, he would say anything.

❧

The second Kate entered the library behind her mother she pounced on Kate. "How dare you use my luncheon to recruit money for your lost cause?"

"You've left me no choice, Mother. I'm not giving up on my girls. They're counting on me."

"Let them count on some other bleeding heart." She marched over to the Queen Anne desk and opened the drawer. After withdrawing a pack of cigarettes, she shook one out and lit it. "See what you're doing to me. I haven't had one of these in days."

"I'm not doing anything to you. You're one of the strongest women I know. If you really wanted to quit, you would."

Her mother inhaled the smoke, then blew it out. "It's obvious you don't know what you're talking about." She took another puff on the cigarette then crushed it in a lead crystal ashtray. "I won't let your behavior govern what I do."

Kate nearly laughed out loud but instead bit down hard to keep from saying or doing anything to further rile her mother.

"I thought when you started your little venture that you would grow bored and stop or at the very least let someone else run Beacon of Hope. But no, you became more and more involved to the point that this year you moved in so you could be there 24/7. This cavorting with prostitutes has got to stop now. Your program has been mentioned in the newspaper several times in the past week."

Must have been a slow news week. Wait until she sees the articles and publicity about the open house.

"This subject can't be taken lightly. One of your girls stole your van and has disappeared. Another has tried to kill herself and now you've got one who ran away and ended up getting shot. A Winslow cannot be associated with that kind of behavior." Her hand clutched the desk conveying the intensity of her anger.

"Nothing is being taken lightly, especially the girls' welfare. I'm working with the police—"

"That's just it. You're involved with the police. You even brought a Texas Ranger to this luncheon. Imagine what people are saying."

Kate stared at the cold expression on her mother's face, her rigid stance. "You don't have a say in the program anymore.

Remember you pulled the funding." She spun on her heel and marched toward the door.

"Come back here. You don't walk out on me."

In the entrance, Kate glanced back. "You do a lot of good in this world so long as it involves things like hospitals and medical research. But I've discovered there are parts of life that can't be wrapped up in a neat little package with a pretty bow on it. These girls have no one but me. I won't walk away from a commitment I made to myself to make their lives better."

Kate took a few steps out into the hallway. The trembling in her hands went through her whole body. She couldn't go back to the party, at least not until she'd pulled herself together. She hastened toward the downstairs bathroom designated for the women to use. Inside, after locking the door, she eased down on the pink settee and hugged her arms to still their shaking. She would not let her mother get to her. But the scene in the library kept intruding.

I've never been able to please Mother. That isn't going to change.

At least her older brother wasn't such a disappointment to their mother. Gerald was right on track to take over the family manufacturing company when their dad retired. He did everything a Winslow was supposed to do, even married a nice young woman from an old Texan family with lots of money. If she'd stayed in the library much longer, the topic of why she wasn't married and pregnant would have come up. Her mother didn't have time for her while she'd been growing up, but Kate had to admit she was a good grandmother to her brother's three children.

You can't please everyone. Stop trying. Her grandmother's advice popped into her thoughts. Of course, Grams was right, but all she'd ever wanted was to please her mother some of the time.

Rising, Kate took a towel and wet it, then dabbed her face. She couldn't hide in the bathroom for long. She didn't want to leave Wyatt alone too long. No telling what her mother would say to him.

When Kate exited the restroom, she collided with State Senator Charlene Foster, one of the few women who wasn't intimidated by her mother. "I'm sorry. I should be watching where I'm going."

"No problem. I'm glad we ran into each other."

"Literally," Kate said with a chuckle.

"Yes, well, I'm sure you have a lot on your mind. I've heard about your troubles at Beacon of Hope."

"It has been a busy week."

"I imagine so, with your mother removing her support. I'd like us to have lunch at the first of next week and discuss me helping with your funding needs. Judge Adams and I are good friends, and he believes in Beacon of Hope. Would Tuesday noon at the Oaks Country Club be good for you?"

For a few seconds Kate thought she heard the woman wrong. Afraid her voice wouldn't work, Kate nodded.

"Good. I've been looking for a worthy cause to support. I'm on a committee in Austin that deals with children's issues. Your program could be just what I need. We'll talk Tuesday about the particulars."

"Thank you, Mrs. Foster."

"Please call me Charlene. I think we'll be spending a lot of time together in the future. I see such possibilities with what you're trying to do." The tall woman with silver white hair smiled then proceeded to go into the restroom behind Kate.

Excitement bubbled up in her. She could hardly contain it. She hurried toward the solarium to tell Wyatt. The program had a chance. *Lord, you are awesome!*

She paused in the entrance into the glassed-in room and scoured the crowd to find Wyatt. He was in a group of men that included the mayor, the owner of a Dallas professional sports team, and Charlene Foster's husband. Wyatt caught her looking at him, said something to the others, then threaded his way through the tables toward her.

"Your mother changed her mind?" he asked when he stopped in front of her.

"Does it show on my face?" She probably had on a big, goofy smile, but she didn't care. God came through for her and the girls.

"You look beautiful."

His compliment took her by surprise and robbed her of her next words. The warmth in his eyes as they met hers heightened her awareness of him. All she wanted to do was escape the luncheon and go somewhere to celebrate. "My mother didn't change her mind, but Charlene Foster, one of the senators from Dallas, wants to help. You were talking to her husband a few minutes ago. I know that Charlene and Kenneth Foster can be quite generous. If I can get them to supply enough money to keep me going while I search for more contributors, I can start thinking about some of the expansions I want to do. So many girls that need a place to go. I serve this whole region. One day I would love to open more of these programs in different parts of the country."

Wyatt leaned close and whispered into her ear, "So can we leave?"

Kate scanned the faces of the people around her. Her gaze landed on her mother's. Their looks locked together. Kate pulled her attention away and smiled even more at Wyatt. "I think that's the second best thing I heard today."

"Why is Ashley always so late?" Maddie leaned against the store window in the mall with Kelly next to her.

"It's not her. Her mom always arrives late. It drives Ashley crazy." Kelly popped a piece of gum into her mouth. "She'll be here soon."

Glancing at her watch, Maddie pushed off the window and turned toward Kelly. "Nana can't stay all day, and I want to get my tattoo." She backed away a few steps.

"You have the coolest grandma."

"Shh. Never use that word around her. She goes ballistic if I ever say it. She doesn't even want me using the word *Nana* anymore. It is Carrie. Not even Mrs. Sheridan." Restless, Maddie swung around to pace and smacked right into a guy—a hot one with blond hair and dark brown eyes like rich, mouthwatering chocolate.

His hands clasped her arms briefly before falling away. "I'm sorry."

"Oh, no, it was my fault. I wasn't looking where I was going." Maddie reluctantly stepped back but not before she got a good whiff of the musky scent he wore.

He grinned, his gaze skimming down her length. "Not a bad way to start the day. I'm Tyler Collins," he glanced at his companion, "and this dude is Chad Wilson."

Maddie tore her attention from Tyler, who was several inches taller than her with his cowboy boots and hat, and looked at Chad. "I'm Maddie and," she peered over her shoulder and waved to Kelly by the window, "that's Kelly. We're here shopping for school."

"So are we. Can't believe school is starting so soon." Tyler's dark eyes twinkled, his look trained on her.

"Where do you go to school?"

"Southwest Academy. You?"

Maddie swallowed and said, "Bluebonnet Creek High School. I'll be a freshman." Okay, she was only lying by a year, but Tyler must be a junior, maybe a senior.

"Junior. Only two more years and I'm a free guy."

While Kelly approached them, Maddie relaxed and gave both boys a smile. "I know what you mean. I can't wait until I can be on my own. No one to tell me what to do."

"Hey, we're going into Worthington to get some clothes. I could always use a pretty gal's opinion."

"Me?" Maddie squeaked out, her cheeks getting warm.

"Of course."

"Maddie, we have to wait for Ashley." Kelly eyed Chad and raised one eyebrow.

"Yeah, we have a friend meeting us here." Maddie angled toward the multiple sets of double doors. "And it doesn't look like she has arrived yet."

"That's a shame. Well, maybe we'll see you around later." Tyler tipped his cowboy hat and sauntered toward the store around the corner.

Maddie watched him swagger, his tight jeans fitting just right, his muscular arms indicating he was into body building or working on a ranch lifting bales of hay. "Did ya see those eyes of his? They are to die for." Her heartbeat increased the more she thought about the guy. "There's certainly no one like him at Bluebonnet Creek Middle or High School. And he goes to Southwest Academy. He must be rich."

"His friend wasn't bad either."

"I'm texting Ashley again. Hopefully, she'll answer this time. Doesn't the girl realize the point of having a cell is to leave it on?" A few minutes later, she got a response from Ashley. "They're just leaving her house. Let's go see what Tyler and Chad are doing. Ashley will be another twenty minutes."

"Are you sure we should leave? What if Ashley comes early?"

"I'll text her we're in Worthington and to come find us. I don't know why I didn't think of that earlier." Maddie's fingers flew over the small keyboard. "There. Let's go."

"Remember we have to check in with your gran—Carrie."

"I'll text her, too. She'll be okay with that even though my dad isn't. The only time I need her is when I go to get my tattoo. I wish my dad trusted me more. Yours doesn't fret over every place you go."

"My dad isn't a Texas Ranger."

"Yeah, lucky me."

❧

"Here we've been talking about the Alamo and other things to see in San Antonio and I haven't even told you my name." King held out his hand. "I'm Jack Reagan."

Caroline fit hers in his grasp. "I'm Carrie Sheridan."

"Would you like something else to drink?"

"No." She checked the clock over the door. "My granddaughter should be back soon."

"You've got a granddaughter? I know this might sound like a line, but I can't believe you have a grandchild. How old? Five? Six?"

Her blush returned to color her cheeks a rosy hue. "Fourteen."

"Fourteen! You're kidding."

"True. I was very young when I had my son." She glanced toward the entrance. "Here she comes. I promised her I would let her get a henna tattoo. We're going to a place in here."

Three teenagers surrounded the table. Maddie inspected him before twisting toward her grandmother. "Ready?"

"Yes. Maddie, this is Jack Reagan. And these other two are Kelly and Ashley."

King gave each girl a big smile, doing his own assessment. Perfect candidate for his side business. As Carrie rose, he did, too. "I'll walk with you. I have to go to the department store down that way before I leave."

"You know the Body Art Palace?"

King raised his sleeve to reveal a heart with an arrow shot through it and a name written across it. He gestured toward Belle. "Belle was my deceased wife's name." He remembered when he got the tattoo. Belle was with him, holding his hand because he didn't like needles. She'd always been there for him until she'd died four years ago.

"I like the heart. Maybe I can get that instead of a dolphin." Carrie's granddaughter giggled with Kelly and Ashley.

The sound grated on King's nerves.

"Whatever you get, you have to get a small one in a place your dad can't see."

"Yes, Nana."

The trio of girls quickened their pace lengthening the distance between them and Carrie. "Your son doesn't know what you're doing?"

"No, but he's being ridiculous. There's nothing wrong with getting a henna tattoo. I'm getting one myself today." At the store, she slowed and added, "Maybe a heart. We should be through in half an hour. Come back and see what I decided." Then she sauntered into the shop with the three teens.

King laughed. This was going to be entertaining. If Wyatt Sheridan continued to investigate Rose's disappearance and got too close, he would have a way to strike back at the heart of the man. He would not tolerate anyone threatening his business.

9

Carrie approached King outside the store. "You waited. I wasn't sure you would."

He peered behind her. "Where are the others?"

"Oh, they're looking at earrings. I told them to take their time." The smile that accompanied those words brightened the woman's face, making her look ten years younger than her age of fifty-five.

There would be no woman to replace his wife, but at least she wouldn't be a bad diversion, especially since he could use her to get close to Wyatt and his daughter. He widened his grin, his gaze focused totally on Carrie. "Did you get a heart tattoo?"

"Maybe," she said with a laugh. "Did you get what you wanted at the department store?"

"Maybe."

She glanced around him for a sack. "It must be small."

"No, very big. I had it delivered to my ranch," he lied, not having bought anything.

"You live on a ranch?"

"Yes, but not around here. I'm in town for a few weeks to buy stock and get some things I need. My ranch is outside

Austin." Another lie rolled off his tongue. He wanted to state a connection between them without really letting her know where he lived.

"I live with my son on a ranch, not too far from here. Lone Star Ranch isn't big, but it has been in his father's family for generations."

"What does he raise?"

"He only has a few horses right now. He's too busy with work to do much more."

"What does he do?"

"He's a Texas Ranger."

King whistled. "There aren't many in Texas. What are the odds I would meet someone whose child is a ranger?"

Carrie's cheeks flamed, and she looked down then up at him through her lowered eyelashes. "He's very good at his job. Maybe you could come out to the ranch while you're in town and meet him."

"Spend more time with you?"

She nodded.

"That would be great. I hate going back to my hotel room every night and trying to find something to watch on TV."

"Why don't you come tonight for dinner?"

"A home-cooked meal?"

She hesitated a few seconds. "Sure. What do you like?"

"Anything you cook would be fine by me. I don't get too many home-cooked meals since I live alone. It's not worth cooking for one."

Carrie dug into her purse for a scrap of paper and wrote some directions on it. "This is how to get to the ranch. Seven tonight?"

"Sounds great. Can I bring anything?"

"No, I'll take care of everything. You're my guest."

"Ah, I see the girls are leaving the store." King rose. "I'll walk y'all to your car then I have to leave. I still need to get to the stockyard."

Amidst the chatter and giggles, King escorted Carrie, her granddaughter, and one of her friends to her car. "I look forward to seeing you later." He pulled out a fake business card he carried in case he needed it and scribbled his cell phone number on the back. "If you need to get in touch with me, call here."

Carrie took it and tucked it in her front jeans pocket. She gave him a smile with a hint of coyness—like a woman who had laid claim on a man.

Which made this all the more enjoyable. King watched her stroll toward her car, waiting for her to discover the flat. She didn't. She kept throwing glances back at him.

When Carrie slipped behind the steering wheel, he gritted his teeth, strode to the vehicle, and pointed toward the front tire. "You've got a flat."

Carrie climbed back out and inspected it. "I don't know how to change one." She looked up at him with a helpless expression.

"I can. Do you have a spare?"

"I'm sure I do in the trunk." She leaned down and said to the two girls, "Jack is gonna change the tire."

"How long is it gonna be?" Maddie asked as she exited the car.

"Fifteen minutes." King walked toward the trunk as Carrie popped it.

"Can we go get a drink? Right inside the door there's a place." Maddie pointed toward the area.

"Sure. Bring me an iced tea. It's hot out here." She wiped her hand across her forehead. "Would you like something, Jack?"

King withdrew the spare tire and tools. "No, I've got everything I need to do the job." He was definitely set. Carrie was so easy to manipulate it would make this a breeze.

⋘

Wyatt angled toward Kate in her Mustang. "I enjoyed this afternoon."

"Do you mean once we escaped Mother's?"

"No, I actually enjoyed the whole time. Meeting your parents was—interesting." He rested his hand against the back of her seat.

His fingers were inches from her, and that fact kicked her heartbeat up a notch. "I appreciate you coming with me. I don't know if I would have made it long enough to speak with Senator Foster."

"Now you have a chance with your program."

"Nothing is firm, but she sounded like I would after we talk on Tuesday. She's friends with Judge Adams, which will help my case."

"Let me know how it goes."

"You'll be the first one I call." The sound of a car coming down the gravel road intruded. Kate glanced back. "Company?"

"No. Mom and Maddie are back from the mall."

Wyatt's mother pulled up to the side of the house, and the second she'd parked, his daughter jumped from the car and hurried toward the Mustang.

When Maddie bent down and peered inside, he rolled the window down. "Did you put me into debt?"

"I tried my best but only found one outfit for school. I guess that means I need to go back next week." Maddie looked beyond her dad. "Hi, Miss Winslow."

"Hi." His daughter's expression was far different than it was earlier. Kate tried to remember when she was Maddie's age. Two words describe that period in her life: drama and angst. She didn't envy Wyatt having to deal with a teenage girl.

"Ask Nana about her date," Maddie said in a loud whisper as her grandmother approached the car.

"Maddie, I think you forgot some packages in the trunk."

The teen grinned and whirled around. "Oh, yeah."

Her grandmother tossed her the keys, and she set out across the yard. "Don't forget, Dad."

"Forget what?" The older woman's forehead wrinkled as she glanced toward Wyatt.

"Maddie says you have a date."

A rosy hue brushed Carrie's cheeks. "Sorta."

Wyatt exited the Mustang. "Are you going out with a man tonight?"

"Not technically." The color deepened.

"So what's happening?"

Kate pressed her lips together to keep from laughing or even smiling at the exasperated tone in Wyatt's voice.

"Jack Reagan is coming to dinner here tonight. I'm cooking."

"Who is Jack Reagan?" Wyatt's body language reflected the tension in his voice.

Kate felt as though she had a front row seat to a family drama. But she wasn't going to leave, at least not yet.

"A man I know."

"You just quit dating Chuck a few days ago. How long have you known this man?"

"A while. Chuck and I weren't exclusive. I can talk to other men." She huffed. "Really, Wyatt, I am your parent. Not the other way around." She stomped toward the house.

Wyatt buried his face in his hands then rubbed his finger-tips into his brow.

Kate slipped from her car and rounded the hood. "Okay?"

"Great. I thought she might mourn Chuck's departure for at least a week. But as usual my mother can't be without a man for longer than a day or so. What makes a person so needy?"

"Beats me. I've only had a couple of serious relationships, and the last one was enough to put me off having one."

"Exactly." He plowed his fingers through his hair then kneaded the cords of his neck. "My deceased wife was my one true love. If you're lucky, you get one in a lifetime."

"Who said that?"

He looked puzzled. "Well . . . I just figured a person shouldn't be too greedy."

"Love often has to do with how open you are to it. Right now my girls require so much of mine, but maybe one day . . ." She hadn't realized she harbored the notion she might fall in love at some time in her life. Paul had pretty much killed the desire to search for a man who would love her unconditionally and without strings.

Wyatt got his cowboy hat out of her car and plopped it on his head, setting it low to mask part of his expression. "I don't think this new man will last."

"Why do you say that?"

"She said she's cooking dinner. I guarantee that will chase him off. If it doesn't, something is wrong."

She put her hand on her waist. "Have you thought he might like your mom? She is nice. Remember my mother."

Carrie came out onto the porch. "Wyatt, I need you to go to the store for me. We need some groceries."

He groaned. "No matter what she buys, it isn't going to help."

Kate circled around Wyatt and crossed the yard to the porch. "I love to cook. I've even studied cooking in Paris. Can I help you, Carrie?"

"Bless you, child. You're an answer to my prayers."

⁂

His hands clasped behind his back, King stood at his office window and stared out at the pasture where some of his horses were grazing. Raising quarter horses was a front. He had enough men to work his ranch to keep up any pretense he was a rancher, but their real jobs were to guard his main form of income: the girls. He would do anything to maintain his current level of income. Actually, there wasn't much he hadn't done so far—including once his wife died, forcing Rose to join his business.

A knock sounded at the door. He turned and said, "Come in."

His sister's oldest boy, a young man who looked sixteen but was really twenty-one, entered his office, a pleased expression on his face—a face that had lured many girls into his operation. "She took the bait."

"Ah, good. What name did you use this time?"

"Tyler Collins. All the girls I recruited under that name are still in our control. The cover with the Southwest Academy is a good one if anyone checks. So far they haven't." His nephew, Gregory, slumped onto the couch, lounging back.

King strode to his liquor cabinet and poured two glasses with several ounces of whiskey, the expensive kind that slid down a man's throat smoothly. He gave his nephew one and then sat across from him in a wingback chair. "How did Brad work out? Do you still think he's right for this job?"

"He's good. He's hungry for the money, so he'll do just about anything to earn the bucks he's getting. He used the name Chad Wilson for this job."

King crossed his legs and savored his drink. "I'm going out tonight to see Carrie Sheridan. Give it a couple of days then call Maddie and set up a time to meet her."

"Do you want me to take her then?"

"Not yet, unless something changes. I'll let you know. Right now Carrie and Maddie are my insurance policy that Ranger Wyatt Sheridan stays out of my business. If we have to focus his attention in a different direction, then we'll take Maddie and get her out of state before her daddy even realizes she's gone."

Gregory chuckled and took a gulp of whiskey. "My pleasure, Uncle."

❧

"Dessert anyone? I made a Pineapple Upside-Down Angel Food Cake. It's light after that heavy meal." Carrie stood, took Jack's plate, and stacked it on top of hers.

"I didn't know you knew how to make that cake." Wyatt's eyes twinkled.

Kate kicked him under the dining room table. "I gave her the recipe." All through dinner he had subtly teased his mother about "cooking" the dinner. Technically, Carrie had, but with step-by-step help from Kate.

"I'd love some, but I'm watching my weight."

Wyatt studied his daughter. "Since when?"

"Since I gained a pound."

"Body weight fluctuates a couple of pounds during the day." Wyatt shook his head. "I don't understand why you and your friends are always on a diet."

Maddie shot to her feet and tossed down her napkin. "Since when do you know about dieting? I doubt you've ever been on one. Have you?"

"No, but I still know your weight can go up a pound or two during the day. You're fine, sweet pea."

Maddie slanted a look at Jack, then back at her father. "Don't call me that. I'm not a baby anymore. Excuse me." She dropped her head and stormed toward the hallway.

"Okay, Kate, Jack, or Wyatt, any cake?" Carrie piled some more plates on top of the two she had.

"I'll take a piece and," Jack rose, "I'll help you clear the table."

"But you're our guest."

"Who would like to help."

"Wyatt? Kate?" Carrie asked, all the while her gaze was transfixed on Jack.

"I'm stuffed and besides, I need to leave."

"Mom, I'll have some later."

"We can clean up the dishes, then have a piece." After Jack took the stack of dishes from Carrie, he started for the kitchen.

Carrie grinned from ear to ear and mouthed the words, "And he does dishes." She waved her hand in front of her face, leaned down near Kate's ear, and whispered, "Such a gentleman. Where has he been all my life?"

Kate chuckled as Carrie left the dining room. When she shifted toward Wyatt, she caught his frown.

"Who is that man?" he asked, staring a hole through the closed door to the kitchen.

"Someone your mother is interested in."

Wyatt groaned. "Here we go again. You wait. She has a knack for attracting needy men."

"He seems pretty confidant to me."

"Since he isn't from here, maybe it will die quickly. But then if it isn't Jack, it's someone else."

"Do you resent your mom having a boyfriend?"

A frown darkened his features. "Is that what it sounds like?"

"You tell me."

"It's more frustration than anything. I've always wanted my mom to have a marriage like I did with Rebecca. She didn't even have that with my father. She may pretend she did because after every marriage she goes back to using the Sheridan name, but they weren't good marriages. No one pleases her for long. This man will follow the others."

Sad. Although she and her mother didn't get along, Kate had seen firsthand the depth of love her parents had for each other—sometimes to the exclusion of her. She would love to experience that, but her luck with men hadn't gotten her close to that. And now, her focus had to be Beacon of Hope, especially with all that had happened lately. She could pour her love into the girls. They certainly had little of it in their lives.

Kate stood. "I really need to get back to Beacon of Hope. Monday we're holding a memorial service for Zarah at the church down the street. The girls need it."

"What time?"

"One."

In the living room, Kate grabbed her purse and strolled toward the foyer. Wyatt was a step behind her. He reached around and opened the front door, then proceeded onto the porch with her.

Although dark for an hour, heat still infused the air with its suffocating grip. Taking a breath was an effort. She descended the steps, her car parked only a couple of yards away. Quiet reigned. Stars littered the night sky with only a slither of the moon hanging above the trees to the left.

There was a part of her that didn't want to end the evening yet. She enjoyed Wyatt's company, his support. Today she hadn't felt so alone. If they had met at a different time, maybe there could—she shook that thought from her head. He had made it clear he wasn't interested in getting involved seriously, and she didn't do casual.

An owl hooted, disturbing the silence. She stopped at the driver's side of her car and turned toward Wyatt. He was closer than she'd realized. Only inches separated them. His male scent vied with the earthy aromas lacing the air. In the light from the porch, she could barely make out the slight uplift to his lips, the intensity in his eyes. Or was that imagined? She just knew that she couldn't move. Didn't want to.

He brushed her hair behind her ear, then cradled her face between his large hands. The touch seared his palms into her cheeks as if he'd branded her. "Thanks for helping Mom cook this evening. That was a sweet thing to do." His mouth tilted up another notch. "I'm not much of a cook either. I enjoyed the pot roast."

"I seem to remember you telling me you're a meat and potatoes kind of guy." She wasn't even sure how she could string a coherent sentence together. Her heart hammered an increasingly fast tempo against her ribcage. Her skin felt on fire from the slow caress of his thumbs on her face.

"Yeah, I liked it very much." He bent his head nearer.

"I'm—glad."

Their breaths tangled. Everything else fell away, leaving only him and her. Her mind ceased trying to put her thoughts together. All she could concentrate on was the feel of his fingers on her, the warmth of his breath flowing over her lips—tingling in anticipation. She slid her eyelids close and hoped he ended her torture soon.

When his mouth settled over hers, she melted against him. His arms clasped her to him. His chest rose and fell in a deep breath as though he was finally content to be where he was. All Kate knew was she didn't want the kiss to end.

But all too soon it did. He pulled back, his embrace loosening about her. Then he stepped away, ending their connection.

"I'm sorry. I shouldn't have done that."

His words hurt. "Why did you?"

"Because I've been wanting to all day." He opened her car door. "I'll be in touch. Drive safely."

She climbed into her Mustang. His declaration still rumbled around in her mind, leaving her frustrated and confused.

Wyatt backed away from her vehicle but stood at the bottom of his stairs waiting for her to leave. She fumbled inside her purse until she found her car key then tried to put it in her ignition. It didn't go in. She lifted it and in the light from the porch saw it was the key to her apartment.

"Okay, Kate. It was just a kiss. Pull yourself together."

This time she used the right one and started her Mustang. She had a long way to go and she needed her mind focused on driving—not the kiss that rocked her clear down to her toes.

A minute later she turned onto the road in front of Wyatt's ranch and headed toward home. She had wanted the kiss to continue; he had ended it abruptly with regrets. No matter how much she tried not to think about what happened, she couldn't banish it from her thoughts.

Until two miles away from Wyatt's ranch. A car came flying up behind her with its bright lights on. The glare blinded her. She slowed to allow the vehicle to pass her. It decreased its speed, too.

Then it surged forward. Its bumper connected with her back one, jolting Kate. Panic flooded her.

10

Kate floored the gas pedal, gripped the wheel with one hand and reached for her purse on the seat next to her. Her fingers clamped around her phone, and she pulled it out.

Another bump against her car raced her heartbeat as fast as the Mustang was going. The brightness of the headlights behind her allowed her to see the keypad enough to punch in 9-1-1.

When the 9-1-1 operator came on, Kate rattled off, "Someone is trying to run me off Front Road about four miles outside of Bluebonnet Creek."

The vehicle thumped her again, jarring the cell from her grasp. On the straightaway, she swerved her Mustang from side to side, trying to shake the car off her bumper.

When her gaze skimmed over a sign along the road, for a few precious seconds the implication of its warning didn't register, then the fact that a dangerous curve was up ahead slammed into her. Little droplets of sweat coated her forehead and hands gripping the steering wheel. She had no choice. She slowed her speed, hoping it was enough to make the S curve. She took the first part of it, her car veering off into the other lane but still on the highway.

Please don't let anyone be coming.

Perspiration rolled into her eyes and stung them. She blinked and kept her gaze glued on the pavement in front of her. As she went into the second part of the curve, the vehicle smashed into her with more force than before, clipping the back part of her right side. The impact sent her flying across the road toward the other side and a drop-off. Her damp palms slipped on the wheel. She managed to grip the plastic tighter as she went over the edge. Her Mustang bounced down the small incline and across a flat piece of land.

The thudding of her heart, as though it banged against her skull, drowned out all other noise. Looming before her was a fence. Before she could do anything, she plowed right through it. The sound of her Mustang pulverizing the wooden structure competed with the thundering beat in her head.

The glow from her headlights illuminated the field before her. With a pond only yards away. She wrenched the wheel to the right.

Too late.

Her Mustang came to a stop with its front end submerged in water and tilted at a left angle. Everything went pitch dark.

Leaning over, she fumbled for her bag and cell. She clasped the leather strap and pulled her purse toward her then continued the search for her phone. She couldn't find it. When she felt the first cool rush of water over her feet, she gave up looking for it and hoped she didn't need it, that help was on its way.

As the liquid quickly covered her shoes and moved up her legs, she pushed at her door. She couldn't open it. Panic clawed its way up her chest into her throat—quickly, like the water rising. She couldn't let it take over.

Lord, help.

She tried the driver side door again. Nothing. It didn't even budge an inch. The water was up to right below her knees. She unbuckled her seatbelt and crawled upward toward the passenger's seat. She pushed hard on the handle. It gave way, swinging outward as more water tumbled into the interior.

After looping her handbag on her shoulder, she pushed past the rushing water filling the Mustang and away from the quickly sinking vehicle. She swam a few feet until she felt the muddy bottom. Dragging herself from the pond, she collapsed against the soft cushion of the grass and wanted to surrender to the exhaustion that was replacing the surge of adrenaline.

But a hundred yards away lights announced she wasn't alone. She rolled over and saw a large man silhouetted in the glow of a car's headlights. The one who ran her off the road? Or help?

∽❧∾

His mother and Jack's voices coming from the kitchen drifted to Wyatt. He stuffed his hands into his jeans' pockets and stared out the front window at the dark landscape. His mom's laugh sounded, light, full of joy. And sad. Most of his life she had been looking for love and had never found it for long. At least he'd had it for a short time before his wife was snatched from him. He knew what it was like to be totally in love.

A picture of Kate invaded his thinking. Her full lips taunting him to kiss her. Her scent drove all other thoughts away. Holding her deluged him with sensations he wanted to deny. How could any woman replace Rebecca in his life?

He pulled the blinds, shutting the black night out. He shouldn't have kissed Kate. That a mistake. He had thought by kissing her, his curiosity would be sated, and he could totally focus on the case when he was with her. Now he couldn't get the kiss out of his mind.

As he turned away from the window, his phone rang. He hastened across the room to answer it. "Sheridan here."

"This is Deputy Olson. We got a call from a woman between you and town who said someone was trying to run her off Front Road."

Wyatt stiffened. *Kate?*

"I'm fifteen minutes away, on the other side of Bluebonnet Creek. Is it possible—"

"I'm on my way." Wyatt slammed down the receiver and headed for the door.

As he jogged toward his truck, his mom and Jack came out onto the porch.

"Where are you going?" his mom shouted.

"Someone's in trouble on the highway." He jumped into the cab and switched on his truck.

Please, Lord, let me get to her in time.

⤷⤶

The large man on the road started down the incline.

Friend or foe?

Not sure what to do, Kate scrambled to her knees, the effort sapping what strength she had left after the terror of the chase. She could stay where she was and hope he came to help or— she scanned the area. Where could she hide? Did he see her?

In the distance, the blare of a siren sliced through the night.

Halfway down the slope, the man above her spun around and hurried back up to the road. He disappeared from view— a few seconds later the sound of his vehicle cranking up and the crunch of tires as they spun on the shoulder of the high-way blended with the siren.

Foe.

Kate closed her eyes, her wet clothes weighing her down, and sank back to the edge of the pond. She couldn't stay here. She needed to get to the road so the police would see her.

She struggled to her feet, the darkness spinning around her for a moment. She planted one foot in front of her, then the other. Slowly she made her way through the pasture and through the busted fence, stumbling over a slat of wood in her path. When she went down on her hands and knees, a piece of the fence pierced her palm. Pain radiated up her arm.

After clambering to her feet again, she cradled her injured hand against her and continued scaling the incline. A few hundred yards away bright lights glowed, coming toward her from the right. Had the man returned in spite of the police coming? Which way had he gone? Right or left?

Right. She was sure of it.

She searched the side of the road for a place to hide.

❦

A dark car sped past Wyatt. He couldn't tell the make or see a license number. The urge to swing around and give chase overwhelmed him until he shoved it down. First and foremost, he had to find Kate or whoever was being pursued. As much as his cop instinct was screaming the person in that vehicle was involved, he couldn't follow through.

Wyatt fumbled for his cell, called 9-1-1, and reported the little information he had on the vehicle speeding away then returned his full attention to finding the person in trouble. Driving along the highway, he searched both sides of the road.

He tried Kate's cell number a couple of times. Nothing. His gut solidified into a rock.

He headed into the S curve, slowing as he rounded the first part of it, half expecting to come upon her crashed car. When he hit the second part of the dangerous curve, his lights illuminated tire tracks heading off the side of the highway into the darkness. He stomped on the brake, his tires screeching, and pulled off the road. He got out of his truck with his high-powered flashlight and walked to the top of the incline. Shining his light down into the pasture, he saw the downed fence and the pond forty feet from it. A couple of yards out in the water, the back end of a car stuck up. The rock in his gut plummeted.

He started to charge down the slope when he heard a voice to the side of him say, "Wyatt."

He whirled around and spied Kate coming toward him, wet, muddy, and alive. In three strides, he gathered her to him. "You okay?"

"No, someone ran me off the road," she murmured against his chest then shuddered, "intentionally."

He comforted her for a moment, then pulled back to check if she was physically all right. That was when he saw the wound on her palm and clasped her hand. "What happened? Anything else wrong? I need to get you to a hospital to be checked out."

Over the din of the siren nearing the scene, she said, "It's nothing. I had a run-in with a piece of that fence. Otherwise, I'm fine. Wet, angry, scared, but fine."

"That's Deputy Olson. He called me to help. After I talk with him, I still think you should be checked out."

"No."

"Then I'll take you back to my house—"

"No, I need to get to Beacon of Hope."

He opened his mouth to protest.

She laid two fingers over his lips. "If anything is wrong, the nurse there can help me. The girls are my responsibility, and I've got to make sure they're all right. As I said, someone deliberately ran me off the road. Why?"

❧

"Are you sure she's going to be okay?" Wyatt paced in Kate's living room while Susan tended to her.

"Yes. I got the piece of wood out of her palm. I promise I'll make her see a doctor if something shows up later." Susan finished winding white gauze around Kate's hand and taped it.

"You two, I am sitting right here, and I can assure you I'm fine. A few bumps and bruises. That's all."

Wyatt stopped and pivoted. "That's all? You could have been killed."

Images of the wreck paraded across her mind. She shut the door on them. It was wasted energy to relive it. "But I wasn't. I'm fine, and that's all that is important. That, and who was the person who tried to run me off the road? And why?"

"Yes, we need to talk about that." He looked pointedly at Susan.

"That's my cue to leave."

"Susan, are the girls all right?"

"You saw for yourself. Nothing new has happened. We're locked up tight."

"Thanks." Kate gave her friend a smile then collapsed against the back cushion of the couch as Susan let herself out of the apartment.

"I'm staying tonight." Wyatt towered over Kate, determination on his face.

"We're fine. I have our private security patrol we use coming by more frequently to check on us and there's a night attendant on duty."

"But—"

"Wyatt, it's important you find out where Rose is. You can't do that guarding me. I won't take unnecessary risks. But I can't go into hiding either." Kate sighed. "I have underestimated the people involved in child prostitution. I can't have them coming to get their girls back. The first thing I'm going to do when I get new funding is to get an even better security system with cameras on the parking lot in back and on the entrances. "

Wyatt folded his long length into the chair across from her. "Which makes me wonder why did someone go to such lengths to take Rose back? What did Rose know that had someone concerned?"

"I don't know. She never said anything to me. I kept hoping she would. I thought she'd blocked a lot of what happened and couldn't remember."

"Maybe but what about that girl she was talking to at the park? Cal thought Rose knew her and then the call from Lily. It's clear she remembered parts of her past at least. So you don't know anything about where she lived before she got caught up in the prostitution ring?"

"Noth—" Something nibbled at the edges of her mind. A conversation she and Rose had a month ago.

"Do you remember something?"

She closed her eyes and tried to visualize them talking in the rec room. About one of the field trips? No matter how hard she tried she couldn't grasp the thread dangling in front of her—just out of reach. Frustration knotted her stomach. She rubbed her fingertips over her face.

Still nothing.

She shook her head. "Maybe it'll come to me when I'm not trying so hard."

"It's not like you haven't been through an ordeal. Everything leads back to Rose. I need to find out about her. I'll put a man on it. Maybe we'll get lucky and discover something."

"The courts and police couldn't locate any information when Rose was found. That's why she ended up here." Exhaustion battered her. She rested her head back against the cushion and stared at the ceiling. "Too many people depend on Beacon of Hope. I've got to find out what's going on."

"No, you don't."

"Yes, I do." She leaned forward. Their gazes clashed over the expanse of a few feet.

"I'll look into it. Not you. Look what almost happened to you tonight. You could have been killed."

"I think you pointed that out to me already. I get it. Even if I don't do another thing, I don't know if my girls or I are safe until we figure out what's really going on and catch the guy responsible for all of this."

"It's *my* job." His tightly controlled voice didn't mask his anger.

"It's my job," she thumped her chest, "to protect these girls."

His glare burned into her.

She rose and strode toward the front door. "Let's agree to disagree. Now before I fall asleep sitting on that couch, I'd better go to bed. Thanks for helping me tonight."

His eyes still locked on her, he covered the few yards to her and stopped. "I think you should get some sleep. I'm sure when you're rested you will think more reasonably."

Her mouth fell open. "I'm not unreasonable."

He raised an eyebrow.

"If you don't want me to go off on my own, then you'd better keep me in the loop. I know this world you're investigating. I can help."

His mouth twisted into a scowl, and he mumbled something under his breath about stubborn women.

She opened her door. "Good night. We'll talk tomorrow."

After he left, she sank back against the wood and nearly slid to the floor in her weariness. So much of what he'd said was right, and yet she couldn't walk away from the situation and not try to do something to find Rose, to keep the rest of the girls safe.

As she trudged toward her bedroom, she decided to turn the problem over to the Lord. He would direct her with what He wanted her to do.

⸙

Standing in the middle of a pasture with sunlight showcasing the beauty surrounding her, Kate drew in the aroma of wildflowers, grass—horses. Lots of them. All racing toward her.

Only a hundred feet from her.

She spun around to run away. A tree branch suddenly appeared, and she tripped over it. The hard impact with the earth knocked the breath from her lungs. The sound of hooves striking the ground echoed in the air.

She rolled over and sat up. The horses were a couple of yards away. She scooted back and tried to scramble to her feet.

The first animal was right above her, its hooves ready to come smashing down on her . . .

Kate bolted straight up, her raspy breathing breaking the quiet of the night.

She scoured the blanket of dark in front of her until she made out the faint outline of the end of her sleigh bed.

Only a dream.

Why horses and a pasture? Because she'd been at Wyatt's?

Why not the wreck?

She brought her knees up to her chest and clasped them, then rested her cheek on them. Staring at the faint light leaking through a couple of slits in the blinds, she tried to remember the beginning of the dream. Rose materialized in her thoughts.

"That's it!"

She glanced at the digital clock on her bedside table. She'd only been asleep for an hour. Wyatt wouldn't have been home long. Maybe he was still up.

Flipping on the lamp, she reached for the phone and called his cell.

He answered on the second ring. "Sheridan here."

"Wyatt, I know what Rose told me about her past. She used to live on a ranch with horses, probably somewhere near Dallas."

11

"What did Rose say? Did she tell you where?" As he spoke with Kate on his cell, Wyatt strolled into his house after the long trip back from Beacon of Hope and a brief revisit to the scene of the wreck. He glanced toward the living room and discovered his mother and Jack sitting on the couch. He nodded toward them and kept walking toward the kitchen at the back.

"We were talking about possible field trips. Things to do when the weather got cooler. Rose mentioned how much she loved to ride horses. That she used to do it a lot when she was a little girl."

"Then why do you think she lived on a ranch?" He switched the phone to his other ear, moved to the stove, and poured himself some still-warm coffee.

"I quizzed her a little farther before she clammed up. She mentioned having to take care of her horse. I supposed she could have lived in town and boarded her horse, but I got the feeling that wasn't it. I tried a couple of days later to talk with her, but she wouldn't say anything else. I know it's not much, but it's a place to start."

"Why somewhere around Dallas?" He was still upset with Kate and her insistence on being involved in finding Rose. He didn't doubt she would try on her own if he didn't keep her involved in some way. The key was letting her think she was helping but keeping her out of harm's way.

"Because from the beginning she always gave the impression she was from this area. She knew a lot about Dallas. Again, I guess she could have learned that from working the area, but I don't think so. Her accent is Texan."

"There are hundreds of ranches in this part of Texas." He sipped the lukewarm coffee and winced. Would he ever learn about his mother's coffee-making skills?

"I know. I just thought it might help."

The weariness in Kate's voice dissolved his anger. She had been through a lot in the past week and was still fighting strong for the teens at Beacon of Hope. He had to admire that about Kate even if it scared him. He didn't want anything to happen to someone he cared—

The realization he cared about her more than he should sucker-punched him. He sat down wearily in a chair at the table.

"Wyatt?"

"Yeah?"

"Just wanted to make sure you were still there. You were so quiet. Still mad at me?"

"No. It's hard to stay mad at you for long."

"Then you'll let me help you?"

"I'm beginning to think I don't have a choice."

The sound of Kate's laugh floating through the phone wiped away any remnant of anger that lingered.

"I didn't get to tell you that I'm bringing Cynthia home tomorrow. We had a good talk today. I'm going to put her with

Audrey since both girls need a roommate. I don't want them alone. They might be able to help each other."

The door to the kitchen opened and his mother entered, a dreamy look on her face. Wyatt glanced behind her for Jack, but he wasn't there. "I'd better let you go. I'll talk to you tomorrow afternoon. Bye."

"Good night, Wyatt," Kate said as though she was trying to stifle a yawn at the same time as talking.

He clicked off and peered at his mother who stood a few feet inside the room, lost in thought. "Are you all right?"

"I'm more than all right. Isn't Jack wonderful?"

Wonderful? That wouldn't be his word for the man. "Mom, he isn't going be here long. Don't get too wrapped up in him." *You're just going to be hurt again.*

"Austin isn't that far."

"Mom, promise me you'll take it slow this time. Get to really know the guy." *Before deciding you're in love.* How was it he had a mother who could fall in love almost instantly, and he couldn't see himself doing it but once? Yes, he cared for Kate. But caring and loving were two different emotions.

"Sure, hon, if you'll promise me you'll not give up on loving someone again."

"I can't do that." He tried to declare it with his usual force, but the words trickled out in a weak stream.

His mom crossed the room and kissed his cheek. "I love you. I want you to be happy. Rebecca would want that. It's been nine years."

He wanted to shout, "You don't know what Rebecca would have wanted. You were halfway around the world with husband number three." He gritted his teeth and kept the words inside, but they boiled in his gut.

"I'm going to bed. Jack is coming to church with me tomorrow. I wish you would come, too."

"I've got things to do around here."

She headed for the door. "Don't give up on God."

"I haven't." *He's given up on me.*

༜

Rose's eyelids flew open. The ever-present blackness entombed her. The verses of the Twenty-Third Psalm kept playing through her thoughts. *Even when I go through the darkest valley, I fear no danger, for You are with me.*

No matter how much she tried, she couldn't get the Psalm from her mind. "What are You trying to tell me? That I'm not alone? I am."

Tears leaked out of the corners of her eyes and rolled into her hair. The hard stone beneath her—so like her life—constantly reminded her of what lay ahead for her.

Unless you do something about it.

"What? I tried to escape."

First, get out of here, then the rest will come.

She had to be going crazy. How was she supposed to get out of the Deprivation Room?

The door crashed open. Rose sat up and blinked as light flooded her prison, silhouetting King in the entrance.

He settled his fists on his waist. "Have you had enough of this? Or do you want to stay in here longer? I'm losing my patience."

This is your chance. As she stared at King, trying to adjust to the sudden brightness, the words ran over and over through her mind and wouldn't stop.

"You've won," she murmured, the admission bitter on her tongue.

He cackled. "It's about time. You're family. I should be able to count on you."

Her skin crawled as though thousands of spiders covered her. Acid roiled in her stomach. She would never think of King as her aunt's husband and certainly not as an uncle. He was not family.

"I don't have all day. Let's go."

She struggled to her feet. Her legs nearly collapsed under her. She'd been lying on the floor for so long she wasn't even sure she had the strength to move forward.

Yes, you do.

She placed one foot in front of her, then the other. At the door King sidled away to allow her to go through the entrance.

When she passed him, he grabbed her arm and yanked her toward him. "I'm not fooled by your meek behavior. I'll be watching you. If you ever cross me again, there are places far worse than here that I can put you."

The words weren't what pushed the nausea up from her stomach into her throat. It was the scent of peppermint. She bent over and threw up on his boots the little she'd been permitted to eat.

❧

"We've got an open house planned for the last Thursday of the month. We're opening the place from two to five." Kate turned onto the street that ran in front of Beacon of Hope. She glanced over at Cynthia. "I'd love for you to help but only if you want to and we have your parents' permission. This open house is voluntary."

"I'll help. I owe you. My parents don't care so long as I'm not their immediate problem. You were here for me. Not them. I guess I should be content they called each day while I was in the hospital," the teen whispered in a husky voice.

"I've kept in touch with your parents about your situation. I'll continue to do so." When she'd talked with them that morning, she'd heard frustration in their voices and resignation that it might take a long time before Cynthia was healed. Kate drove into the lot behind Beacon of Hope and parked near the door, then angled around to look at Cynthia. "You don't owe me anything. Help if you want but don't feel like you have to."

"I want to." Cynthia sat forward, her head down, her fingers entwined together.

Kate placed her hand over hers, half expecting the girl to flinch or draw away. She didn't. "You are what is important to me. Don't forget that, Cynthia."

A tear splashed onto Kate's skin. Her throat closed. She and her mother might not get along, but her childhood had been nothing like Cynthia's and a lot of the girls'. So many of them had been throwaway kids. No one to love or care for them. At least she could do something about the girls in the program.

"I should never have run away from home. I thought that was the answer to all my problems. It was only the beginning." Cynthia's last word caught on a sob. "My parents weren't great, but they were better than my pimp." The teen straightened. "I want to help Beacon of Hope."

"Audrey asked me if you could be her roommate. Do you want to?" Kate squeezed Cynthia's clasped hands then sat back to let the teen gather her composure.

"She does? Why?"

"You need to ask her that, but you need a roommate." She prayed Cynthia chose to agree, because she couldn't stay by herself.

Through shimmering eyes, Cynthia peered at her. "Are you afraid I'll cut myself again?"

"All I can do is pray you won't, be here for you, and provide you with the help you need to work through your problems.

When you feel the urge to hurt yourself, come to me. Talk to me about what's bothering you. I'll be here for you any time you need me."

"Why do you care?"

Kate could remember Rose challenging her with that question the second month she'd been at Beacon of Hope. She would tell Cynthia the same thing. "Because once I had a chance to help someone and was too frightened to do anything but stand and watch. I won't do that again. I lost a friend that day. She was sold by her family to a man who ran a prostitution ring in Costa Sierra."

"She was?" Those two words came out with a long breath. Sadness reflected in her eyes, Cynthia averted her gaze. "That's what my pimp did to get money for drugs."

"I'm sorry, Cynthia. You're safe now." She hoped. She had to find Rose and show the girls no one was going to force them to sell their bodies again, that their life was in their own hands now.

"But what about Zarah and Rose?"

"That's a fair question. Rose left to help someone. I believe Rose would have brought Lily back here if something hadn't happened to her. I'm not giving up looking for her. She's too important to me, as you are. And as far as Zarah is concerned, she left on her own. She didn't want to be here any longer. I would never have sent her away." If Senator Foster didn't support the program and she couldn't find others to fund it, then she would go back to her mother and do whatever she had to in order to get the money she needed.

"I've been thinking lately. I had a lot of time in the hospital to do that. When I told Rose about getting mad at my parents and running away, she got this funny look on her face. Then she smiled at me and told me how much she'd loved her parents. I asked her what happened. All she said was her life became a nightmare when hers were killed in a fire."

"Did she tell you where this fire was? How long ago?" Excitement bubbled up in Kate. Maybe Wyatt could use this tidbit to narrow his search down even more.

"No, but I got the impression it was years ago."

"If you remember anything else, let me know. Every little bit helps." She would call Wyatt and let him know after she got Cynthia settled. "Let's go in. Dinner will be in an hour. Pizza."

Cynthia grinned. "I love pizza."

"I know."

The teen's eyes grew round for a few seconds. Then she pushed open her door.

When they entered the building, colorful streamers were hanging from the ceiling and a banner welcoming Cynthia home stretched across the hall leading into the foyer from the back door. The girl stopped. Her mouth fell open.

Finally, she glanced over her shoulder at Kate, her eyes glistening with tears. "You did this for me?"

She shook her head. "It was Audrey and Beth's idea and the other girls wanted to help them."

Cynthia shuffled forward, her attention glued to the banner. When she stepped out into the large front foyer, all the students and staff were there standing in a semicircle around a table laden with chips, dip, cookies, a cake with Cynthia's name on it, and platters of pizzas. The girls began cheering and clapping.

Cynthia froze, her gaze sweeping from one person to the next.

Kate put her hand on Cynthia's shoulder. "They wanted you to know they cared." She moved to her side.

Tears ran down her face. The students swarmed Cynthia and tugged her toward the table, half the girls talking all at once.

Through the crowd Kate's gaze paused on Jana off to the side, her arms folded over her chest. *Lord, I need to reach her somehow. I don't want to lose her like Zarah.*

Kate felt someone come up behind her. Even before she turned, she knew it was Wyatt. His presence made her whole body tingle. His scent enveloped her. She smiled. "I'm glad you're here. I was going to call you."

"Oh?" he said with one brow raised.

"Cynthia told me something she remembered about Rose."

He took her elbow and drew her off to the side away from the others. "What?"

For a moment, all she could focus on was his hand touching her. She wanted more. She wanted him to kiss her again. "Uh . . . Rose's parents died in a fire, probably years ago. She was happy until then. After that, she said the nightmare began. Cynthia didn't know exactly how long ago it happened."

"It should help. We can do a search of the past twelve years where a man and woman died in a fire and left a little girl. If it was in Texas, we have a good chance of finding something. If it was somewhere else, it will take a lot longer."

"So why did you come?"

"To see how you were after the crash last night."

"You could have called. Saved you the time coming all the way down here."

"Maybe I didn't want to save time."

"If you don't have any dinner plans, you can have pizza with us. As you can see we are celebrating." Kate waved her arm toward the people in the foyer.

"Don't mind if I do. Maddie and Mom went to some sappy movie this evening. Didn't even ask me if I wanted to go."

"Did you?"

"Nope. Mom likes to take my daughter out once a month. She calls it their girls' night out."

"Sounds like you want to be included."

Mock horror seized his face. "No way. The movie is called *Love Lessons*. I don't think so."

"Are you more a western fan?"

He shook his head. "I like thrillers."

"That would have been my second guess. If we want any pizza, we'd better grab some now. It'll be gone in no time." Kate grasped his hand and hauled him through the crowd of girls.

After getting a plate full of food, Kate directed him to the stairs. "Let sit down. It's been a long week. And this one coming up doesn't look any less busy." As she eased onto the step, her body protested the movement, her aches a constant reminder of how close she'd come to dying last night.

"I noticed your car was towed out of the pond when I went by today."

"And carted off to the junkyard. One of the things I have to do is get a car. I've got a rental for the time being. What I hate is the Mustang was paid for. Now I'll have monthly payments again. Any leads on who tried to run me off the road?"

"No, but I'm pretty sure it had to do with Rose's case. Which leads me to telling you again, you've got to be careful. Avoid going anywhere after dark and especially any place where there aren't many people."

"I'm carrying pepper spray and starting to upgrade the security system here even more than it is. I think if you had your way you'd put me under house arrest." She bit into her Canadian bacon and extra cheese slice.

He grinned. "If only that were possible. I wanted to let you know that tomorrow several other rangers and I will be around this area paying the local law enforcement agencies a visit about Rose. See if anyone knows her. I'll also ask about fires where a couple died, too. It'll take us a couple of days, but we'll cover the surrounding towns. I got some good news. There were fingerprints found in the car Zarah was in that wrecked. A match was found for one set. Tony Langford. His driver's license photo matched what Georgia gave the sketch artist. He's the same person who approached Zarah on the field trip."

Kate washed some pizza down with a soda. "Have you located the man?"

"No. He hasn't been at the address we have for him in two years. I'm also going to go talk to the neighbors and see if anyone might know where he is now."

"Things are starting to look up. I have my meeting with Senator Foster on Tuesday and you've got some leads to run down. A toast to our success this week." She held up her can and tapped it against his soda, suppressing a groan from moving her sore arm up.

After tossing her empty paper plate away, Cynthia and Audrey neared the stairs. Cynthia's dull eyes met Kate's. "I'm going to go to my room." She threw Audrey a look. "I mean our room and lie down. I didn't realize how tired I am."

Kate released a long breath. "So you two are going to share a room?"

"Yes, it made sense. We both don't want to be alone." Audrey took the first step. "I'm helping Cynthia move her things into my room."

"Good. Do you need me to help?"

Cynthia's attention shifted from Kate to Wyatt then back to her. The dullness in her expression brightened. "No, you look busy. We can manage. I don't have a lot."

MARGARET DALEY

As the two girls passed Kate on the stairs, she heard their giggles and whispers. Heat flushed her cheeks. Kate returned her attention to the other students and noticed most of them were watching her and Wyatt. Suddenly, it felt as if fiery flames licked her face. She noticed the quiet and the speculation in each girl's gaze.

Wyatt leaned closer and whispered into her ear, "I think it's time for me to leave."

"Chicken," Kate muttered back.

"Yep. Remember I live with a fourteen-year-old, and she often has her friends over. I know those looks we're getting."

❧

Kate sat by a bank of floor-to-ceiling windows that over-looked the golf course at Oaks Country Club, staring at the vibrant greens that were dotted with large oaks, elms, and maples. She wrapped her hands around the ice-cold tea and waited for Senator Charlene Foster to return from taking a call. Other than greeting each other and ordering, they hadn't discussed the program yet. She was wound so tightly she was afraid she'd snap any second. So much hinged on whether the senator meant what she said on Saturday.

She watched the senator and her husband making their way toward the table.

"Kate, you know my husband, Kenneth. He finished playing a round of golf and thought he would join us. I hope you don't mind. He's quite interested in your program too." Charlene slid into the chair across from Kate while Kenneth sat next to his wife.

"I don't mind. I'm glad you're interested in Beacon of Hope." Directing her look at Kenneth, Kate attempted to smile, but the corners of her mouth quivered and her stomach churned. She couldn't pretend this was a casual lunch.

"Charlene is excited about this new project. That's all she has been talking about the past few days." When the waiter approached the table, Kenneth ordered a chicken salad sandwich.

The senator spread her napkin on her lap. "I'm so glad you sent a messenger over with your budget yesterday. Last night I looked over your numbers. I had Kenneth look at it, too. I'm willing," she slanted a glance at Kenneth, "I mean, we're willing to donate 65 percent of your monthly budget. I realize the Winslow Foundation was contributing 75 percent from what you had written on the paperwork you gave me. I wish I could go higher, but I can't."

"I've been working on broadening my base. I've approached various organizations and foundations and have filled out their applications. I'm applying for some grants, which I hope will come through in the next several months. But all of this takes time. This will help keep the program going. If the grants come through, then I can do some of the expansion I want to do." She might have to make cutbacks, but it gave her time to strengthen her contributions for the future. In hindsight, she should never have depended on one source—even if it was family. She'd learned a lesson and would work extra hard to become schooled in the financial end of running a charity.

"I have one stipulation, however," Charlene said.

"What?" Kate gripped her hands together in her lap, her breath held tightly in her lungs.

"I want to be involved with the program. It would help me to understand these girls' plight better if I work with them. I could do something a couple of times a month. Maybe teach them about government."

Kate let out her breath slowly. "What a great idea! Who better to teach about our government and how it works than someone who has been a part of it for twenty years. A young girl being exploited isn't new. In fact, the number in the United States is growing and is alarming, not to mention what is happening in other parts of the world."

Charlene grinned. "Great. With all that settled, we can enjoy our lunch before I have to get back to work. I leave for Austin this afternoon. I'll talk with my attorney and get the details worked out and to you."

The waiter appeared with their salads and placed the plates in front of them. The knots in Kate's stomach unraveled one by one as she ate. This was going to work out. For the first time in over a week, hope blossomed inside her. *Thank You, Lord.*

Charlene sipped her coffee. "I understand you've had a bit of trouble at Beacon of Hope."

Tension twisted inside Kate, and the bite of salad she'd swallowed burned in her throat. "One of my girls is missing and another ran away recently."

"Does that happen often?" Kenneth asked.

"No, thankfully. I've only had a few over the past three and a half years. Most want to be in the program. I work hard to make them feel like they're not in a prison."

"Have you found either girl?" Charlene forked a piece of lettuce.

"The police are looking for Rose who is missing. Zarah was in a car wreck and died shortly after she arrived at the hospital."

Kenneth's gaze shifted from his wife to Kate. "So you still have one missing? Why did you say she is missing and not a runaway?"

"For one, she didn't take her possessions with her. Rose was happy where she was and was making plans for the future. That wasn't the case with Zarah."

Charlene leaned forward. "See. That's what I need to find out. What makes one girl want to leave and another stay? Why was Zarah drawn back to her old life? That kind of information will help me in my work at the state level and should also help you." She took a piece of hot bread and buttered it. "Tell me about the girls."

~~⚘~~

Tuesday afternoon Wyatt pulled up to the police department in Lake Royal, the fourth one he had visited that day. The sun beat down upon him relentlessly as he climbed from his truck and made his way toward the entrance into the building.

Part of being in law enforcement was tracking down leads. Most didn't pan out. But Wyatt only needed one person to recognize Rose.

He approached the officer behind the counter when he entered the small station. "How's things going?"

"Slow but I'm not complaining, Ranger Sheridan."

"Is Chief Taylor here?"

"Yup. In his office. Go on back. He always has time for you."

Taylor's office door was open, and Wyatt poked his head inside. "Got a minute?"

The police chief glanced up from his computer. "Yeah, I need a break after working on this computer for an hour. I thought it was supposed to make my job easier. I spent the first twenty minutes trying to find the file I needed. I forgot what I named it."

Wyatt sat in a hard-backed chair in front of Taylor's desk that took up most of the small office. "I know what you mean. I have to go to my fourteen-year-old daughter for help. I don't know what I would do otherwise."

"So I need to hire some teenager to help me with my job?"

"Don't you have a grandson?"

Taylor's expression brightened. "Yeah and he's twelve. Maybe he could help his grandpa."

"Worth a try." Wyatt slipped the photo of Rose from the manila envelope and slid it across the desk toward the police chief. "Does this girl look familiar?"

He studied the picture and slowly shook his head.

Wyatt removed the second photo and handed it to Taylor. "This is a computer-generated photo of what the girl might have looked like at nine or ten. Does she look familiar?"

Again, the police chief scrutinized the image. Longer this time. "Nope. What's this all about?"

"She's missing."

"You don't usually come around showing me a photo of a missing child, especially one this old." Taylor flicked the paper.

"We're looking into a ring involving child prostitution."

"Is she part of it?"

"She figures into it. Not exactly sure where."

"Sorry I can't help you." He pushed the photos back toward Wyatt.

"You keep them. Show them around to your officers. Maybe one of them has seen her. If so, get in touch with me."

"I sure will. I don't cotton to people using children for their pleasure." Taylor rose, taking the pictures out to the bulletin board in the work area of the station and tacking it up. "I'll make sure every one of my officers checks these out."

"Thanks. I knew I could count on you." Wyatt shook the chief's hand.

"Anytime."

Another dead end. If Rose had ever lived around Lake Royal, Chief Taylor would probably have seen her. The man had an uncanny ability with faces. He never forgot one.

On the way out of the station, his cell blared. "Sheridan here." It was his mother.

"Wyatt, I'm stuck in traffic. There's a bad wreck on the expressway. Are you near to pick up Maddie at Ashley's house? I'm not supposed to be there for another hour, but Jack and me are way across town near Fort Worth. I know I can't make it even in an hour. Maddie has tumbling lessons. If you can drop her off, I'll pick her up."

Jack and his mom were out again. Maybe this was more serious than usual. "Sure." He started mentally rearranging his schedule. "I'm not far from Bluebonnet Creek."

"Thanks, hon. See you later. Jack and me are bringing home dinner. I confessed that I'm not a very good cook. We laughed about Saturday night."

"That's nice, Mom. Bye." He heard more than his mother's words. Behind the words, he glimpsed his mother's attraction to Jack, stronger than to anyone recently. Maybe he'd better do some checking into Jack Reagan—to make sure his mother wouldn't get hurt. He'd put it on his to-do list. Most likely, by the time he discovered anything, Jack would be old news.

He hopped into his truck and made a U-turn in front of the police station then headed toward Bluebonnet Creek. This wouldn't be much out of his way since he had to go near the town to get to Silverwood, his next stop on his list. Fifteen minutes later, he pulled up into Ashley's driveway. Laughter and shouting echoed through the hot afternoon air. Ashley had a pool and no doubt the girls would be outside swimming, just as any sane person would be, given the opportunity on a day like this.

He made his way to the side yard and through the iron gate. He followed the sounds of merriment.

"I can do a bigger cannonball than that," Kelly was saying when Wyatt rounded the corner of the house.

Kelly jumped high into the air, rolled herself into a tight ball and landed with a big splash into the pool.

His daughter put her hand on her waist. "Nope. Ashley's was bigger. But I can beat—"

He didn't hear the rest of what Maddie said because his gaze zeroed in on a dolphin tattoo peeking out of the low-riding waistband of her bikini. He wasn't sure what upset him more—the skimpy bathing suit or the tattoo.

12

"Maddie," Wyatt said in a surprisingly calm voice while inside he raged. His daughter had gone behind his back when he'd expressively told her no bikinis or tattoos.

Maddie spun around, her eyes huge.

He stalked over to her bathing suit wrap lying on a chaise lounge and snatched it up, then tossed it to her. "Put this on. You're leaving. Now."

"I have to get my stuff inside."

"Get it. Meet me out front." He strode back the way he'd come.

He sat behind the steering wheel, gripping it so tightly pain shot up his arms. The heat in his cab without the air-conditioning vied with the heat suffusing him when he remembered seeing both the bikini and tattoo. Even worse, he hadn't realized how much his little girl was turning into a young woman. Where was the child he used to read bedtime stories to and hold when she hurt herself falling off her horse?

The passenger door opened. Maddie climbed up into the truck and faced forward, her hands clasping the strap of her gym bag.

Anger tied his thoughts into a knot. His teeth ground together.

"Dad, I can explain."

"I doubt it."

"Nana knows about the bikini and tattoo. She said it was okay."

"I see. So then it's all right to go against what I asked you not to do?"

"Well, I . . . You're being unreasonable. Everyone has one. No one wears a one-piece suit anymore. And as I told you, the tattoo is a henna one. It will fade with time."

"So that's what makes it all right for you to disobey me?"

"I didn't say that. You don't understand what it's like to be a girl. You don't . . ." Her voice faded into a tearful sound.

He wondered when she would try that. He hated to hear someone cry, but that wasn't going to change anything. "I'm taking you home to change out of that," his gaze slanted toward her still in her bathing suit and cover up, "swimsuit. Then I'm taking you to tumbling class. Your grandmother will pick you up from there. We'll talk about this later."

Maddie sighed.

"Don't think you're off the hook for disobeying me. If I grounded you right now, your friends wouldn't see you until your tattoo wore off."

"That's weeks—Oh." Maddie snapped her mouth closed.

⁂

"In conclusion, be cautious when approached by strangers whether female or male, young or old, especially at places like a mall or where teens hang out. Before doing something with a person check them out with friends like an employer checks out a prospective employee's references. You can never be too careful." Not until Kate finished the last word of her presentation did she stop shaking. Giving a speech had never been one of her favorite things to do, but she felt so passionate about this subject she had no choice but to do this. "Are there any questions?" She scanned the audience of middle-schoolers. A skinny boy in the back of the auditorium waved his hand. "Yes?"

He stood up, all six feet of him. "Why are guys having to listen to this?"

A few snickers erupted around the student, and he grinned. The principal moved down below the stage to position himself in front.

Kate pasted a smile on her face, half expecting this question. The boy wasn't the first one to ask her that. "Because predators don't confine themselves to girls only. Boys have been caught up in the kind of situations I've discussed. And I think it's important to raise everyone's awareness about what's happening to some of the kids in this country. Thousands and thousands."

The teenager slinked back into his seat, his face flushed red.

"Any more questions?"

A girl at the end of a row in the middle rose. "What can we do to protect ourselves?"

"As I said, check people out. What school do they go to? Who are their friends? Listen to your gut. So many times something bothers you, but you dismiss the feeling. Don't. If you're having a problem at home, talk to a school counselor, your pastor, someone who can help you. Running away is not the answer. So many runaway teens end up on the street in horrible situations they can't get out of."

Ten minutes later Kate shook the principal's hand then headed for the back of the auditorium and the exit. After the luncheon and this presentation, all she wanted to do was sleep, but she needed to go back to Beacon of Hope and work with the students on the plans for the open house.

Leaving the building, she crossed the west parking lot toward her rental car. Waves of suffocating heat came off the asphalt making it difficult to take a decent breath.

"Ms. Winslow?"

Kate halted at her car door and turned toward a girl, probably sixteen or seventeen. "Yes?"

"I need to talk to you about what you said to the kids."

"Do you go to this school?"

"No. I go to Roosevelt High School. It's not one of the year-round schools. But I heard you were going to be talking today. I don't live far from here."

"What do you need to talk about?"

"My sister, Zarah, called me last week. I just found out that she's dead. A car wreck. She told me to come to you if anything happened to her."

⟿

Wyatt pushed through the door into the Silverwood Police Station. The last stop on his list of police departments. He hoped one of the other rangers was more successful than he had been. He'd come up with nothing. Maybe Daniel's database search for Rose's parents would go better.

Silverwood wasn't one of the police departments he worked with on a regular basis, but he knew the police chief had been serving the town for almost ten years. He'd found that in small towns with a police force that didn't change much there weren't many people in the area the officers didn't know. He was counting on that to help him find where Rose came from.

If he knew how Rose ended up a part of a prostitution ring, he might be able to track the people behind it.

He saw Police Chief Bo Jeffers a few steps inside the front door. Wyatt held out his hand and said, "We met last year on the Lindaman case. I'm Ranger Wyatt Sheridan."

The six-foot three-inch man with graying hair at the temples and a barrel chest shook Wyatt's hand. "Yes, I remember. Glad I could help with the case. What brings you around these parts?"

"I'm looking for a missing child." Wyatt withdrew the two photos. "Have you ever seen this girl around here?"

The police chief examined both pictures then gave them back to Wyatt. "I wish I could say yes, but I can't. How long has she been missing?"

"Over a week."

"She may be long gone by now. So many teens who've gone missing are runaways. How old is she? Sixteen?"

"Yes."

"Why do you suspect foul play?"

"The van she took was found abandoned in a field with a dead girl nearby."

"Maybe she killed the girl and fled. After you've been in this business long enough, you see all kinds of things. Kids killing kids is one that has been hard to accept."

"Yeah, I know what you mean. But I don't think that's the case here. I'd like you to show your officers these photos and have them be on the lookout for this girl." He slid the pictures into the folder and held it out for Chief Jeffers.

"Sure. If we find out anything, I'll give you a call."

Wyatt withdrew his business card and passed it to the police chief. "I appreciate—" The sound of "The Good, the Bad and the Ugly" interrupted him. "Excuse me." He pulled out his cell and walked a few steps away to answer the call from Kate.

"I'm sitting in a coffee shop with Zarah's older sister. They almost look like twins. She called Beacon of Hope today to check on Zarah. That's when she found out that her sister had died. The girl answering the phone told her I was speaking at the middle school. She came to find me. I think you should hear what she has to say."

"Where are y'all?"

"At a Starbucks but I'm taking Amanda to Beacon of Hope to give her Zarah's things."

"I'll meet you there then." He turned toward the police chief. "I appreciate any help you can give me." He touched the brim of his cowboy hat then left the station.

It would take him a while to get there with the rush hour starting. Dallas traffic wasn't his favorite thing to negotiate.

Fifty minutes later, he pulled into a parking space in the back lot and headed into the building. Wyatt found Kate in her office with a beautiful young girl, dressed in jeans and a University of Texas T-shirt with the same long curly brown hair and dark eyes that slanted at the corners slightly like Zarah's.

Kate rose when he entered. "Amanda, this is the Texas Ranger I was telling you about. Wyatt Sheridan."

The corners of her mouth wobbled with a smile. "I can't stay too much longer. I work at a restaurant and have to be there tonight by five thirty." She touched her finger to her upper lip.

Wyatt took the chair at the round table across from the teenager. "Kate said you've been in contact with Zarah."

"We used to talk some before she ran away from her last foster home. Then I didn't hear from her for several years until last week."

"Why do you think she ran away from her foster home?" He lounged back in his seat, watching Amanda as she talked.

The teen stared right at him. "She was being sexually abused by the husband but was scared to tell anyone."

"Why didn't you say something?"

Tears welling in her eyes, Amanda looked away, rubbing under her lower eyelid. "She begged me not to. Said she was going to take care of it. A few weeks later I heard she'd run away."

Kate reached over and patted the girl. "Predators prey on fear."

Amanda's gaze slid to Kate's hand on hers. The girl shifted in her chair and stared at the table. "I was so lucky. I was adopted and had a good home. But I couldn't do anything to help her. I can now."

Something was wrong. Amanda said the right words, almost as though they were rehearsed, while her body language indicated there was no truth behind what she was telling them. Or, at the most, only partial truth. "Why did she call you after all these years?"

"She thought something bad might happen to her. At first, I thought she was talking about the man who sexually abused her. That he found her."

"But you don't think that was the case?"

Amanda lifted her gaze. "No. I did some checking. The foster parents she lived with last have moved away from here."

At least that much was true. He had looked into Zarah's background before she'd run away and ended up on the street turning tricks. "Even though she took part of her possessions, you don't think she willingly left here? Got into that car?"

"Why would she? She said she was safe here. She said she loved being here." Amanda scratched the side of her neck and shifted again, uncrossing her legs and recrossing them.

Kate flinched and leaned back, her eyes narrowing on the girl. "So why do you think she wanted you to come see me?"

"To tell you she was scared? She just said to come see you. She wasn't real clear why. Maybe she wanted me to have her things. I don't know why. She said she didn't have much." The tears returned and a few coursed down her face, flushed with a rosy hue.

"Most of the girls come to us with little. Zarah had only been here seven months."

"I appreciate being able to take her things. I don't have anything of Zarah's. We were separated when she was five and I was seven."

Too many red flags were waving in the air. Wyatt stood and peered down at the young woman, wanting the height advantage. "Cut the lying. Who are you really? Why are you here? Is it Zarah's possessions you want? Why?"

The teen blinked rapidly, hugging her arms to her body, her gaze wide but never looking at him. "I don't know what you mean."

He placed his hands on the table and leaned close to the teen. "We know that Zarah has a sister and her name is Amanda, but you aren't her. Yes, you two have similar coloring. I give you that, but I can tell you're lying. I've been around enough to know when someone is. And frankly, you aren't very good at it."

"I came here because Zarah asked me to. But I don't have to stay." The impostor bolted to her feet and whirled around, racing for the door.

Wyatt leaped forward and cut off her escape by blocking the door. "On the contrary. You do have to stay until we have this figured out."

He escorted her back to the table, and she sat down hard in the chair, both arms folded over her chest. "I am Zarah's sister."

Zarah did have an older sister but from the records Daniel accessed the family had moved to Louisiana years ago. Had they moved back, and Daniel hadn't discovered that yet? "I want you to call your parents. They will need to come here and pick you up. And while we wait for them, I'm going to be doing some checking on what you told us." Hovering over her, he drilled his gaze into her, hoping to intimidate her.

A glint sparked in her eyes, and she tilted her head back to look straight at him. She clamped her lips into a tight line. Her expression issued him a challenge.

"Better yet, I think this would be better handled at the police station. You have just become a person of interest in a kidnapping case."

"Kidnapping? Zarah is dead."

"And she was involved in a kidnapping."

The color siphoned from the young woman's face. Her grip on her arms went slack. "I don't know anything about kidnapping. This was just supposed to be a simple job. Act like I was this girl's sister and get her things." The impostor tossed her head toward Kate. "That's all. No harm. The girl's dead. You said yourself she didn't have a lot."

"Who are you really?"

"Emma Banks."

"How much are they paying you to do this?"

"Five hundred dollars."

Wyatt skirted the table and delved into the box with Zarah's possessions inside. What was so important about them? He dumped its contents on the table and was even more puzzled by what he saw. He unzipped the black backpack and pulled out articles of clothing—three T-shirts, a pair of jeans, a bag of makeup, and several lacy pieces of underwear. He checked all the side pockets. Nothing.

Wyatt gave Kate a questioning look. "Not much."

"That isn't all of it. That was all the police gave me that was with her when she was found."

"No purse?"

"No, and she did have one that's missing." Kate slanted a look toward the teen then back at Wyatt.

"Where are her other possessions?"

"In the storeroom. I hadn't gone and gotten that box yet. This one was delivered yesterday and was still sitting on the table when we came in here."

Wyatt came around to Emma and lounged back against the table, his hands clasping its edge. "Once you got Zarah's stuff, what were you supposed to do with it?"

"Call a number and let the person who answered know."

"How old are you?"

"Nineteen. I look young for my age."

"Do you live with your parents?"

"No, I'm taking theater classes at a community college."

"How were you picked to do this?"

Emma dropped her head. "I can't say."

"Why?"

"I don't want to get her in trouble."

"I'm sure if you cooperate you won't be charged with anything, but if not, like I said, you might be considered an accomplice after the fact to a kidnapping."

Emma's hand trembled as she brushed her long brown hair behind her ears. "I met her a couple of times in the Student Union and we got to talking. She knows I need money and that I act in school productions. I guess that's why she approached me."

Thankfully, the girl had not mastered the art of lying convincingly, which took practice. "Who is she? Which college? Is she a student there?"

Emma bit into her lip. A minute passed before she answered, "East Dallas Community College. Her name is Liz Taylor. We even joked about her name being the same as a famous actress.

I assume she's a student there. She had some books and was studying the first time I saw her."

"Which class was she studying for?"

"Freshman English." Emma shifted toward Kate. "I've never been in trouble with the law before, but I needed the money. I even dyed my hair brown like she told me. I wouldn't get paid until I brought her Zarah's belongings so I followed everything she said to do."

Walking across the room, Wyatt took out his cell and placed a call to the Dallas police detective he was working with on the task force. After he talked with him, he made another call to the community college and set up a time to meet the Admission Director.

When he rejoined Emma and Kate, he sat across from the teen again. "Detective Finch is coming to take you down to the police station until we check out your story. Kate, can you get the rest of Zarah's possessions?"

"Yes."

After Kate left the room, Emma began crying. "I didn't do anything wrong."

"You attempted to steal Zarah's possessions. You were caught before you could succeed. You may know who is behind the kidnapping of a young girl. Those tears won't accomplish anything. I have a daughter who tries them."

Emma sniffled and swiped them away, then collapsed back in her chair and glared at him.

The mention of his daughter brought Wyatt's thoughts back to the earlier problem he'd have to deal with when he got home. Not just with Maddie but his mom. He loved his mother, but it was becoming obvious she wasn't the best person to raise his daughter, especially when she blatantly ignored his wishes and let Maddie do what she wanted.

After Detective Finch took Emma with him, Kate emptied the second box of Zarah's possessions on the table in her office. Sad that a kid's life could be contained in two small cartons.

Wyatt fingered a ratty stuffed monkey. "This is Zarah's?"

"Yeah. It was one of the few things she had with her when she came here."

"It doesn't fit the image of her. She came across tough as though she didn't need anyone."

"I once found her asleep on the couch in the rec hall after hours with this stuffed animal clutched to her chest. When I woke her up, she was angry and hid it behind her back. That was the only time I saw it except that first day she came here."

"Maddie had one. A bear called Teddy. She named him when she was two and a half. I finally had to throw it away. It was falling apart and smelled. She cried all day about what I did. I even tried to find a new one exactly like Teddy. I finally did, and she wouldn't have anything to do with it."

"What could be in these things?" Kate waved her hand over the articles of clothing, a pair of sandals, and the monkey.

He shook his head. "You got me." After examining each piece of clothes, he tossed them back into the box. "These are all dead ends. Maybe whatever someone wants was in the purse that's missing." He finally picked up the stuffed animal and began checking each limb and body. The insides made a crunchy sound when he squeezed the head.

Kate stared at the stuff animal. "That's different."

Wyatt inspected it closer. "The seam at the back has been re-sewn." He took out his pocketknife and slit it, then dug around in the stuffing. When he withdrew a key wadded up in a piece of paper, he peered up at Kate. "Interesting hiding place." Unfolding the paper, he read. "Locker 5RB."

"Where? What does 5RB stand for?"

"Don't know. The key doesn't have any writing on it. But it definitely might be something someone didn't want us to find."

"Depending on what is in the locker."

Excitement gripped him as it did when he felt he was on the right track or had gotten a big clue in a case. "Now all we have to find out is where. Maybe this Liz Taylor can help us. I'm heading to the college and see what I can find out."

"What do you want me to do with her belongings?"

"I'll take them with me. Maybe there's something else we're overlooking or a hint somewhere that tells us where the locker is or what in the world 5RB means."

"The only places that come to mind are gym lockers and the ones at the bus station. I could see Zarah using a bus station. Not likely a gym."

"We can start a search around here."

"What if she did it before coming here?"

"Where she was picked up for solicitation?"

"Possibly. While you're tracking down Liz Taylor, I'll do some checking with the officer who arrested Zarah originally. Also, I'll talk with her case manager. I've worked with the woman one other time concerning a girl picked up for prostitution like Zarah."

"Great. I'll call you later tonight after visiting with the college Admission Director and having a long talk with Maddie and Mom."

"That doesn't sound like something you're looking forward to. What's happened?"

Wyatt sighed. "My mother isn't thinking like a parent but like a friend. I love her, but I'd forgotten how easy it was for me to talk her into doing something I wanted to when I was growing up. Maddie has discovered she can do that too. Remember when I was talking about Maddie wanting to get a tattoo? Well, she has one now thanks to my mom. Granted, only a henna one, but she went against my wishes. What do I do?"

Kate began putting Zarah's possessions back into the carton. "I found when I'm angry with my mother or one of the girls I have to give myself a cooling-off period before I talk with them. When I can calmly discuss the issue in question with them, then I'll approach them." She flashed him a mocking grin. "Of course, it works better with these teens than with my mother. I want to show these girls how to deal with their anger in a constructive way, so I'm especially careful with them. Calm and cool are two words I keep repeating to myself as we talk about the problem."

"Good thing I didn't have time to deal with the tattoo earlier." He touched her shoulder, relishing the connection with someone who understood. "Thanks. Sometimes with my mom, I feel like I'm raising two children. She doesn't think before she acts. I know how much she loves me and Maddie, but she always hated making those tough decisions a parent sometimes has to."

A smile shimmered in her eyes. "You'll do fine."

On the drive to the college, Wyatt thought about his conversation with Kate. He hadn't had that kind of relationship with a woman since Rebecca. He didn't realize how much he had been missing. His daughter needed more than what he could give her. She was becoming a young lady and needed a role model. Kate would be a good one.

At East Dallas Community College, the receptionist showed him to the office of the Admission Director. The woman greeted him with a handshake.

"How can I help you, Ranger Sheridan?"

"I need to talk with one of your students involving a case I'm working on. Liz Taylor."

"Let me check our student roster." She shifted toward her computer and brought it up on the screen. As she scanned the list, the furrows in her forehead deepened. "I don't see anyone by that name or by Elizabeth Taylor, even with a middle name of Elizabeth or Liz."

13

When Wyatt pulled up to his house an hour later, he stayed in the truck, his hands still clamped about the wheel. Dread weighed him down, keeping him glued to the seat. Today wasn't a good day—one of the few leads in the case only ended up complicating the whole mess. Then there were Maddie and Mom. Anger began to fester in the pit of his stomach. His fingers tightened even more around the plastic.

What do I do? He rested his forehead against the steering wheel.

Calm and cool.

Kate's words seeped into his mind like the heat from outside did into the cab. For a moment he felt as though Kate was sitting next to him, laying her hand on his arm to let her know she supported him.

With a gulp of the now stifling air, he pushed himself out of the truck and strode toward the porch. His mother met him at the door, her expression full of concern.

"I can explain everything, son."

She rarely referred to him as her son unless she wanted to play the parent card. He moved past her into the kitchen. "Where's Maddie?"

"In her room."

He walked to the coffeepot and tossed away the remains in it, then set about to make a fresh brew. It was going to be a long night. "So what is your explanation?" he asked.

Her teeth digging into her bottom lip, his mother picked up a wet dishcloth and began wiping the kitchen surfaces.

His patience slipped down a notch. He gripped the counter's edge. "Mom?"

She huffed then threw the cloth in the sink. "Okay, I messed up." Fully facing him, she ran her fingers through her hair then played with some strands. "All the other girls in her group were getting one, and I hated to see Maddie left out."

"All?"

"Well, Ashley, and I think Kelly will be able to talk her mother into it."

"But she doesn't have one?"

"Not yet."

"You know that isn't really the issue. You helped my daughter disobey me, and we aren't even talking about the bikini. What kind of message does that send to her?"

His mother hung her head. "I don't want her to hate me. You two are all I have."

He drew in a steadying breath. "Giving into her isn't the answer. I know how much you love us, but loving a person means doing what is best for them whether they know it or not. If Maddie still wants to get a tattoo when she is eighteen that is her business, but I wanted her to make that decision when she was a little more mature and not swayed by her peers as much."

"I got a tattoo with my third husband. There's nothing wrong with them. And hers will wear off in three or four weeks. It isn't permanent."

"I know that. Again, that's not the issue."

"You need to give her some room to make her own deci-sions—and for that matter, her own mistakes. She's growing up and will be an adult before you know it."

"I'm still the parent here." The image of his wife's killer's tattoo tried to intrude into his mind and shove him back into the past. He shook it away and said, "Mom, I have to know you support me 100 percent with Maddie. I can't worry that you're countermanding what I tell my daughter."

She lifted tear-filled eyes to him. "Do you want me to leave?"

"No."

"I was wrong. I shouldn't have gone behind your back. It won't happen again. Promise."

He covered the short space between them and hugged her. "We're family. We stick together no matter what, but I am Maddie's parent and what I say goes."

She kissed his cheek. "When she asked me, all I could think about was when I was her age and trying to fit in with my friends." She took a step back. "I've learned my lesson."

Wyatt bit the inside of his cheek to keep from saying, "How long?"

"I'd better go get ready for my date."

"With Jack?"

"Who else? He's such a gentleman. I haven't met a man like him." While the aroma of coffee infused the air, she sailed out of the kitchen in her usual "on to the next project" manner.

He poured himself a mug then sat down at the table. He couldn't bring himself to talk to Maddie yet. His conversation with his mom had zapped some of his patience, and he needed to replenish his store of it before seeing Maddie. Plus, he really didn't know how successful he was with his mother. She said all the right things, but would she remember them when she needed to?

He pulled out his cell and called Kate. "The college was a dead end. There wasn't a student named Liz Taylor enrolled."

"So does that mean Emma was lying about that, too?"

"Maybe. I'm having her give a description of the girl to a sketch artist. If we can't get the person when Emma calls the number she was given tomorrow, then I'll show the picture around the college and see if anyone recognizes the girl that recruited Emma. So far what we've discovered about Emma supports her story."

"How about finding Zarah's sister? I know we tried for the memorial service but didn't get anywhere."

"We know the family who adopted Zarah's sister, Amanda, moved years ago to Louisiana. I'll put some of my resources into that. I'm not sure she can give us anything, but we need to check everything out." He sipped his coffee, hoping the caffeine gave him a jolt of energy to tackle this next problem.

"Have you talked with Maddie and your mom yet?"

"Mom was waiting for me when I walked through the door. We talked. I think she heard what I said. Only time will tell on that one. She's getting ready for another date with Jack."

"If you want to talk afterwards, call. I'm doing some paperwork for Senator Foster."

"Bye." He pictured Kate sitting at her desk, her long hair falling forward as she wrote. Her lips puckered in concentration. Lips he wanted to kiss again.

He had to put a stop to that thought. He had to keep focused on the issue with Maddie. After finishing off his last swallow of coffee, he rose and made his way to his daughter's bedroom. He rapped his knuckles against the door.

When Maddie opened it, she stepped to the side to let him into the room. Her eyes were puffy and red, which should have made him feel better that she was upset about what she'd done.

It didn't. It should never have come to this. How was a parent supposed to stay on top of everything in his child's life?

He crossed to the bed and sat while Maddie took the chair at her desk, curling her legs up to her chest and locking her arms around them. *Calm and cool.* "Why did you do it?"

She rested her chin on her knees. "I wanted one. It's my body. I'm the one who has to live with it. Not you. Besides, it wasn't a permanent one so what harm was done?"

"You're saying I should let you do anything you want even if I think you should wait or it's not good for you?"

"There's nothing wrong with a tattoo—even a permanent one."

"And when you're eighteen, you can get one if you still want one. But as long as I'm responsible for you and you live here, you have to follow the rules. Even the ones you don't like."

She stood, her arms stiff at her sides. "What's so wrong with a tattoo? A dolphin is a beautiful animal."

"I don't like tattoos." The memory nudged its way forward in his mind. *No, I'm not going there.*

"That's all." She clenched her hands. "Just because you don't like one, I have to suffer and not have one until I leave home. That's not fair."

"Life isn't always fair." Was it fair an escaped felon murdered his wife?

"That doesn't make what you said right."

The arm lifting up and the gun pointing toward Rebecca's heart filled his vision for a few seconds. All he saw was the dagger tattoo, menacing and evil looking. He closed his eyes.

"Why do you hate them?"

The noise of the Magnum .45, his gun, thundered in his mind. The sight of Rebecca crumbling to the floor would stay with him forever.

"Dad, why?"

The same rage he'd experienced when the man shot his wife washed through him, leaving him quaking. *Calm and cool.* He gritted his teeth and realized he'd lost that when he'd walked into the bedroom. He shoved to his feet. "School starts next Wednesday. You're grounded until it does."

"Grounded! For getting a tattoo!"

He strode toward the hallway but paused at the threshold and said, "No, for disobeying me."

He continued his trek down the corridor. The sound of the door slamming behind him reverberated through the air with his daughter's anger. He should have told her the reason behind his feelings concerning a tattoo. The words had lodged in his throat as though his wife's murderer had his hands around his neck and was choking the life out of him.

At the end of the hall, his head swimming with painful images of Rebecca with her murderer, he reached out his hand to steady himself. *His* gun had killed her. *He* was the one who had insisted they take a long weekend at the lake. Rebecca had wanted to stay home. *He'd* needed to get away, especially after an especially difficult murder case. She was dead because of him.

The ringing of the doorbell forced him to straighten, to pull himself together. His mother sashayed toward the foyer. The stone lump in his gut grew. He quickly disappeared into the kitchen as his mother, wearing a black cocktail dress and three-inch high heels, greeted Jack.

❦

Later that night, Kate turned over in her bed and punched her pillow. Sleep evaded her. All that had happened earlier tumbled through her mind, churning her frustration.

When she'd listened to Amanda—no Emma—talk about Zarah, she'd been happy that at least Zarah had been able to go to her sister. That she hadn't died so alone. Then she'd found out that Emma had been lying.

Father, why can't things be simple? Be what they appear to be?

No answers came to her. And she hadn't expected any because life wasn't simple. It was full of complications. She'd learned that repeatedly while trying to get her program going. Thankfully, Charlene Foster had given her hope she could keep Beacon of Hope and possibly even expand it in the future.

The sound of her doorbell echoed through the apartment. Jerking up in bed, she threw back the covers and stood. She'd put the bell in so she could hear if someone was at her door even in the middle of the night. She'd meant it when she'd told the girls she was there for them 24/7. Sometimes when a new teen began the program, she would test that. She hoped that was all it was tonight. She didn't need another problem after the past ten days.

When she opened the door, she found Cynthia standing in the hallway, biting down on her lower lip to the point Kate worried she'd draw blood. Kate took the girl's hand and tugged her into the apartment. "Come in."

Cynthia's large gaze skimmed down Kate's length. "I shouldn't have bothered you. You were asleep."

"I may have been in bed, but I wasn't sleeping. Sit. Tell me what's going on." Kate made her way to the couch and patted the seat next to her.

Cynthia hung back for a long moment, still chewing her lower lip.

"I was thinking of getting up and doing some reading. When I can't sleep, I hate just lying there." She smiled at Cynthia, hoping that would reassure the girl. "Can I get you something to drink? I know it's probably still ninety degrees outside, but

I was thinking about getting a hot cup of chamomile tea. Do you want that?"

The teen shook her head and plodded to the couch. "I'm scared." The words slipped out on a whisper, Cynthia's head down, one hand kneading the lower part of her arm.

"And you want to cut yourself?"

She nodded.

Kate slid her arm around Cynthia. "I won't let anything happen to you."

"But look what happened to Zarah and Rose."

"Remember, Zarah chose to leave. Rose, I think left to help a friend and got caught up in something. I won't stop looking for her until she's found." *Hopefully not dead.* "Both girls were from this area, but you aren't. You're from Kansas. That's a long way off for your pimp to come looking for you. The security is good here, but I'm going to beef it up even more."

"How? Isn't Beacon of Hope in trouble?"

"Not anymore. I have the money to keep it open, and we're going to get more starting with our open house."

Cynthia lifted her head and stared at Kate. "You've got someone to help us?"

"You bet! Senator Charlene Foster is going to support the program. She's been working in Austin to strengthen the laws against people who harm children. We couldn't ask for a better person to help us."

"Can I tell the girls? They've been worried."

"I was going to tomorrow when Senator Foster comes to Beacon of Hope, but go ahead and spread the word. I don't want you all to worry—or be scared. You've got a safe haven."

The tense set of the teen's shoulders relaxed. "I've never had that."

Emotions clogged Kate's throat. She swallowed several times before saying, "You do now. For as long as you need it."

Cynthia stopped rubbing her hand up and down her lower arm. "You're really not mad I came so late?"

"Nope. How are you and Audrey getting along?"

"Okay. We don't talk much."

"She's a quiet person."

"So am I. Rose always did all the talking." The mention of her friend's name brought a frown to Cynthia. "Do you really think you'll find her?"

"I'm not giving up. Just like I won't give up on you."

"My parents did."

"I'm not them."

Cynthia yawned. "I guess I should get to bed."

Kate rose. "Come on. I'll walk you back to your room."

By the time they reached Cynthia's room on the second floor, the redness her kneading had produced on her arm had vanished. At her door, the teen gave Kate a small smile that evolved into a yawn.

"Thanks, Kate."

Before Cynthia went inside, Kate said, "Remember, I'm available. Anytime you even think you want to hurt yourself, come see me."

As the girl disappeared into her room, Kate prayed the teen would come see her before hurting herself.

܀

Kate positioned herself at the classroom door as Charlene and her husband talked with Harriet, then moved around speaking to different girls independently working on their level in English with the teacher's assistance when needed. From the interested expression on the senator's face, Kate inhaled a relieved breath. This initial visit had gone well. Charlene and Kenneth had enjoyed eating lunch with the girls and answering questions from them. In turn, she, and even her husband, had asked them some. Most of the girls shared how they had ended up as prostitutes and what they felt now that they weren't. Jana and another remained stony quiet.

Charlene thanked the class and Harriet, then threaded her way through the maze of tables and chairs to Kate, while Kenneth remained talking with the teacher. "I hate to leave. This has been so enlightening. I'd like to volunteer when my schedule permits."

"We'd love to have you."

"Kenneth thought he would stay a little longer, if that's okay."

"Sure."

"I need to grab my purse and get moving before I miss my afternoon meeting." Charlene started down the corridor toward Kate's office.

The older woman entered first and came to a halt a few feet inside. Kate peered around Charlene to find her mother sitting at the round table, glaring at her benefactor.

"So the rumors are true. You are funding Beacon of Hope." Kate's mother rose as though she had not a care in the world, but the tightening about her mouth and the hardness in her eyes belied that impression.

"Yes. It's a worthy cause—one I believe in. I'm not fair-weathered like some I know." Charlene marched to the couch and picked up her purse, then moved back to the door, turning her back on Laura Winslow and facing Kate. "You'll receive the first check next week. I'll encourage my friends to attend your open house. This is something they should get behind."

"Thank you for seeing that. I feel the same way."

When the sound of the senator's footsteps faded down the hallway, Kate closed the door and turned toward her mother. "Why are you here?" The calmness in her voice conflicted with the tension mounting inside her.

"I needed to hear from you that you went behind my back and solicited funding from someone you know I don't like or get along with."

How could you? was left unsaid but definitely implied. "Mother, you left me no choice. You won't support the program, and I won't give up on it. Weren't you the one who taught me if I started something I needed to finish it? Well, I'm doing just that."

"To spite me." Her mother clutched the leather straps of her purse, her chin tilted up.

"No, to help these children who most people have ignored, or worse, exploited."

Not one hair out of place, her makeup perfectly done, her mother strode toward her. "You've made your choice about who is more important to you. Good-bye, Katherine."

The finality in her voice froze Kate. She shuddered and watched her mother head toward the foyer, her shoulders thrust back, her head held high. Tears smarted in Kate's eyes, quickly blurring her vision. She shifted away and closed her office door. She didn't want any of her students to see her falling apart.

But the last sentence her mother had uttered made it clear she wouldn't welcome Kate at the house. Or in her life. Hurt swamped her. The constriction in her heart sent waves of pain outward.

Somehow, she found her way to her desk and collapsed in the chair. Fighting the tears, she scrubbed away what few had slipped down her cheeks. "I'm not going to let you get to me. Dad will make you change your mind." Her father might not like the idea of Beacon of Hope, but he would never cut her off because of it.

Scooting her chair up to her desk, she switched on the computer to work on sending out invitations to the media for the open house. As she composed the press release, the phone rang. "Hello," she said, noting the call was from Wyatt. A smile chased away her earlier gloom. She cradled the receiver against her ear and lounged back in her chair. "Any news?"

"No, but we're leaving to stake out the café where Emma is meeting her contact, this Liz Taylor or whatever her name is. Maybe I'll have something later."

"Great. I hope so."

"How did the meeting go with Charlene Foster?"

"Good until my mother showed up. I'm surprised you didn't see the fireworks go off where you are."

"Nah. It's still daylight. You need to have those kinds of confrontations at night," he said with a chuckle. "Seriously, are you okay?"

"Other than my mother washed her hands of me, yes, I'm fine. Call me and let me know what happens with Emma."

"I've got a better idea. Why don't I pick you up and you come to the ranch? I can tell you all about the stakeout."

"You can do that over the phone. What's the real reason you want me to come to the ranch?"

"Am I that transparent?"

"Afraid so."

"To be a buffer between Maddie and me."

"That's all?"

"I want to see you."

The implication of what he was saying melted any resistance she might have. "Only if you let me cook. I rarely cook for just myself, and I enjoyed helping your mom last weekend."

"You won't get an argument out of me on that. We can stop by the grocery store and get whatever you need."

"See you later then." When she hung up, she realized he'd lifted her spirits as nothing else could have.

She was falling for Wyatt Sheridan.

❧

Wearing cowboy boots and hat, blue jeans and white T-shirt, Wyatt entered the busy café right across the street from the East Dallas Community College and took the table off to the left of the door with a direct line of vision to Emma. A Dallas female police officer greeted him as though they were a couple. After giving his order to his waitress, he relaxed back, smiling and nodding his head toward his "date" while scanning the restaurant and noting his surroundings.

At a back table, Emma sipped a soda and watched the entrance. She'd already shredded one paper napkin and was working on the second one. The waitress approached Emma with the check and laid it down on the table along with an envelope. After the woman left, Emma finished her drink, put some money on the table, then got up and ambled toward the exit.

The gym bag full of Zarah's belongings remained on the floor where Emma had placed it when she came in. Daniel covered the right side of the café while he did the left. Waiting for Liz Taylor to appear. Two guys, college age, took chairs at the table but didn't seem to notice the bag by the seat between them.

Keeping an eye on the pair, Wyatt nursed a cup of coffee and picked at his piece of pecan pie, his favorite, for ten minutes. When two girls joined them, the heavyset male saw the gym bag, picked it up, and stood. Wyatt tensed, readying himself to follow the guy. But he detoured toward the counter and gave the bag to the waitress that served him.

Great. Emma received her money, but no one came for the bag. What was going on?

"Something's wrong," came through his earpiece. "The envelope was stuffed with paper, not money."

14

Kelly, he called. He wants to meet me, and I'm grounded."
Maddie plopped down on her bed and sat back against her
pillows. She moved the cell to her other ear so she could grab
her Dr. Pepper.

"What are you gonna do?"

After taking a long sip of her drink, she placed it on the
nightstand. "I don't know. Dad didn't say anything about not
being able to ride Star Champion. In fact, I'll have to because I
have a rodeo in a couple of weeks."

"Then you're gonna meet him?"

"Yeah, and remember his friend with him at the mall? He
told me Chad thinks you're cute. You and I could meet them at
the stream near the fence that separates our ranch. It's near the
road. Easy for them to spot and get to. How about it?"

"Do you think we should?"

"I'm not leaving the ranch. What's the harm? We'll be
together."

"They are sooo cute," Kelly said with a giggle. "Oh, I'm getting the shivers just thinking about seeing Chad again."

"Me, too. Tyler is such a hunk. I'll give you a call back and
let you know when we'll meet."

After Maddie hung up with her friend, she pictured the high school junior she'd met at Ashland Mall. A sigh slipped from between her lips. Her dad would never approve. He would say Tyler was too old for her because he was in high school. Three years had separated Dad and Mom. But her father treated her as if she were a child. She wasn't. And, she wasn't going to do anything stupid. Meeting Tyler and Chad at the ranch was perfect, especially with Kelly there. It wasn't like she was meeting Tyler alone somewhere.

Satisfied with her plan, she punched in Tyler's number to set a date and time to meet him.

❧

The waitress' eyes grew round as Wyatt and Daniel approached her in the back near the kitchen.

While Daniel headed to the counter to get the gym bag, Wyatt stopped in front of the young woman and held up his badge. "I need to talk to you in private."

"Why?" Her blue gaze fixed on his ID.

"I have some questions about who gave you the envelope you passed on to the girl sitting at that table." Wyatt pointed toward the one Emma had been at.

"I—I . . ." The waitress swallowed hard.

Wyatt guided the woman toward a deserted alcove near the restrooms. He remained silent. He'd found that often worked better with witnesses.

She shifted from one foot to the other and back. "Some— woman asked me to give it to the lady who sat there. She gave me a twenty to do it. More money than I've made so far in tips."

"Was the lady at the table when the woman asked you to do that?"

"Yeah. I'd just taken her order. One lousy drink. Wasn't gonna make much on that. I didn't see any harm in taking the twenty and giving the lady the envelope. I didn't do anything wrong."

"Does this place have a security camera?"

She shrugged. "I guess. There's a camera over the door, but I haven't been a waitress here long. I don't know if it even works."

"Is the owner here?"

"Yep. In his office in the back."

"I need you to come with me to see him."

"Why? I was just trying to earn a buck." Fear tensed her face into a frown, puckering her red lips.

"If the camera works, I need you to ID the woman who gave you the envelope."

Wyatt followed a step behind the waitress to a door with "Office" stenciled in black letters on it. He reached around the woman and knocked.

A deep husky voice shouted, "Come in."

Wyatt pushed open the door and waited until the waitress entered before he came in. Withdrawing his badge and ID, he presented it to the owner who rose.

"What's going on? Something happen?" The baldheaded man looked from Wyatt to his employee.

"Does your security camera over the door work?"

"No."

Couldn't something go their way in this investigation? Wyatt expelled a deep breath in agitation.

"But the one on the wall behind the counter does. I need to get the other fixed." The bald-headed man came around his desk.

"I would like to see the tape for the past hour. There was a customer this waitress interacted with that is involved in an ongoing case. We need to have her ID the woman."

The owner scowled at his employee. "Did Bonnie do anything wrong?"

The waitress tensed next to Wyatt. "No, in fact, she'll be a big help to us."

The rigid set to the man's shoulders relaxed. "Sure. It's over here. I can pull up the footage for you."

It took the owner a few minutes to set up the tape, then he moved back and let Wyatt control the speed of viewing.

"Bonnie, let me know when you see the woman."

The waitress leaned in close. Halfway through the footage, she said, "Stop. That's her." She tapped her red fingernail against the TV screen.

Liz Taylor as Emma had described her to the sketch artist. She existed. For a moment when everything had fallen apart, he'd wondered if Emma had lied the whole time to him. Now her story was confirmed. Although they weren't any closer to finding Liz. "May I take this tape?"

"Sure anything to help the Texas Rangers."

Wyatt removed the tape, an antiquated system for security but one that worked in this case. He handed the waitress a card. "If you remember anything else about the woman, please contact me."

⟿⟾

Maddie galloped toward the stream and grove of trees close to Front Road and Kelly's ranch. A perfect place to meet with Tyler, Chad, and her best friend. *Technically I've done what Dad wanted—staying at the ranch.* The thought brought a grin to her mouth, and it grew the closer she approached the rendezvous. Dad wouldn't be home for hours. So long as she was back before dark, he wouldn't realize she'd even left her room, and if he did, she would just tell him she needed to exercise Star Champion. She wasn't even lying. She did need to ride her horse to keep him in shape for the competition.

Tyler moved from the stand of trees and waved at her. Maddie increased her speed into a flat-out run. A minute later, the drop-dead gorgeous hunk helped her dismount by placing his hands on her waist and easing her to the ground. And she let him as though she didn't know how to get off a horse she'd been riding for years.

"Where is Kelly and Chad?" she asked when he stepped away from her, much to her disappointment.

He flipped his wrist toward the stream. "Over there. They've got their feet in the water."

Maddie brushed her fingers across her forehead, their tips drenched in perspiration. "It's hot. I wish we could have met somewhere cooler."

"Why not? We could go for a ride in my car and find some air conditioned café to sit and talk."

The temptation to leave and go get a soda enticed her to say yes. What harm could that be? The sun beating down on her shoulders only reinforced that. A tall, ice cold—

Tyler tugged her hand. "C'mon. Let's see if Chad and Kelly want to go. I can have you back any time you need to get back."

The smile he sent her, as if she were the only girl in the world, urged her to say yes. She checked her watch and calculated how much time she would have.

❧

"I love Italian food. Lasagna sounds great." Wyatt made a right turn into his driveway.

"With garlic bread and a salad, it's one of my favorite meals." Kate took in the expanse of green pastures on either side of the gravel road. Being out of the city was a nice change of scenery. She'd never realized how much she liked the country. The quiet. The stretch of land all around. The fresh air with a hint of grass, pine, and earth.

"I think it will be nice not to think about the case for an evening," he slid her a look, a corner of his mouth quirking, "or at least until after dinner. I don't want to say anything in front of Maddie."

"I wish you'd caught Liz today."

"We've got a pretty good picture of her on the video. We're going to distribute it and see what turns up. Emma confirmed the woman the waitress picked out. I'm going back to the college tomorrow and show the photo around. Also, places near the college. Maybe something will happen."

"Your job isn't like on TV, is it?"

"You mean, where I solve the case in an hour or two? No, not usually unless you catch the assailant standing over the victim with the gun in his hand and you have several witnesses to confirm he pulled the trigger. But then you have all the paperwork to still fill out." Wyatt parked next to a Lincoln Town Car. "I see Jack is here again."

"We have enough for him."

Wyatt frowned.

"You don't like him?"

"He's okay. Mom's doing her usual thing—falling headlong into a relationship without any reservations. She's fifty-five, and I doubt she's going to change anytime soon. I just wish she would take her time getting to know a person. It seems so desperate to me."

"Maybe it is."

He angled toward her. "What do you mean?"

"There are some women—men, too—that need that connection all the time. They don't like being by themselves. Another person is what defines them."

"That's Mom. I've tried to show her I love her. That she's important to me and Maddie."

"It's not the same thing. To some women a man completes them."

"That explains the three husbands and countless relationships over the years." He shoved open his door and hopped out, then grabbed both bags of groceries sitting on the front seat.

"Like I said before, we could always swap mothers." When he looked at her as if she'd gone crazy, she laughed. "Or maybe not. I don't blame you. My mother would be difficult at best."

He headed for the porch. "I know you told me about your mom disowning you, but surely she'll change her mind when she calms down."

"I don't think so. She feels I've betrayed her by having her archenemy Charlene Foster fund the program."

"What were you supposed to do?" He waited until Kate entered the house, then followed her inside and led the way toward the kitchen.

The sound of country music, not blaring but turned up slightly, drifted from the direction of the bedrooms, momentarily drawing Kate's attention. Her mother would never allow her to listen to that, only classical. Just another aspect of her life her mother had wanted to control.

"Kate, you okay?"

She focused on the man beside her. She started to say yes, then realized that was yet something else her mother had insisted upon—slang wasn't permitted in the Winslow household. "Yeah, I'm fine. What I was supposed to do was what my mother wanted in the first place, not have the program. I thought over time she would get used to the idea and see the good being done. But she could never see beyond the fact these girls had been prostitutes at one time. She blamed the girls, not the people who preyed on them. She never took into consideration they were still children."

Wyatt shouldered his way into the kitchen. "That's where the media can come in and inform people."

Kate's gaze strayed to Jack and Carrie at the table, sitting next to each other, drinking what looked like iced tea. "I'm hoping so." She smiled toward the pair. "It's nice to see you again."

"I didn't know you were coming tonight, Kate. I haven't even thought about dinner." Carrie's gaze latched onto the bags Wyatt carried. "Do those mean you're going to cook?"

"Yes, unless you want to." When Wyatt's mother's eyes widened, Kate continued. "But I was looking forward to cooking for more than one for a change."

Giving Kate a wink, Carrie waved her hand in the air toward the stove. "Oh, in that case please do. It's nice not to have to cook for an evening." She patted Jack on the arm. "He knows that cooking is not my strong suit."

Wyatt crossed the room and set the bags on the counter, then began emptying them. "How did it go with Maddie today? I half expected to get a phone call from either you or her."

"She's been quiet. Staying in her room. She came out at lunch, but as you can hear, she's been listening to music most of the day. Good thing I like what she likes. I'm giving her space."

"Probably wise." Wyatt finished putting away the food that wasn't needed right away.

Jack took Carrie's hand. "I'd better be going. I have business to see to."

"Are you sure you can't stay for dinner? Kate's a great cook."

Jack rose. "I wish. But something has come up, as you know. Can't stay. I can't ignore the call from my partner." He tugged Carrie to her feet. "Walk me out."

When they left, Wyatt scowled by the sink with his arms folded over his chest.

Kate strolled to him and placed her palm on the bunched muscles of his biceps. "Now it's my turn to ask. Are you okay?"

"It's one thing knowing how Mom is and another seeing her in action."

"I think it's cute," Kate said, remembering the adoring look in Carrie's eyes when Jack took her hand.

"She's fawning all over him."

"Some men like that. He didn't seem to mind."

Wyatt snorted and turned toward the sink. "I can help with a salad."

Kate stared at the taut lines of his broad shoulders and felt the frustration pouring off him. She began to lay her palm against his back, wanting to help him, but his stance conveyed: Do not touch.

❧

Carrie kissed King good-bye, then stepped back from his Lincoln Town Car. He drove away watching her waving to him in the dim light of dusk through the rearview mirror. For fifty-five she was in good shape, beautiful and a free spirit, much like his deceased wife. Too bad not much would come of this relationship. This was business, pure and simple. But in spite of that thought, the touch of her lips against his stayed in his mind until his phone rang.

"Yes." King dismissed from his mind the picture of Carrie as he left the ranch, the wind blowing her long flowing skirt about her shapely legs, her feet bare, her hair dancing about her face. He forced his concentration on the call from his nephew.

"Everything is on schedule. I met with Maddie but had to do it at her ranch. I almost got her to leave to go get something to drink, but at the last minute she decided she'd better not, in case someone saw her and said something to her dad."

"Probably a good thing you didn't go out together around Bluebonnet Creek."

"Her friend came along, so I brought Brad aka Chad. I think we can recruit both girls."

"No, not Maddie. Not yet."

"How about Kelly?"

"Wait. I may need them for leverage against Maddie's father. From what I hear he's making progress. Set up another time to see Maddie. She's grounded. You may have to wait until after Tuesday. I don't want you going to the ranch again. Try to do it alone with her this time."

"It won't take much to get her to do what I want. She's angry with her father and desperate for a guy's attention. I think her dad keeps a tight rein on her."

When King hung up with his nephew, he finally returned his partner's earlier call. "I was with Carrie Sheridan and couldn't talk freely."

"Do you know what you're doing?"

The question, spoken with censure, iced his blood. "Yes. I'm keeping track of the investigation."

"You should have killed Rose six months ago."

"She's my niece."

"By marriage. She should never have gotten away from you."

"If anything happened to her, she could be tracked back to me. I took care of that john who beat her and left her for dead."

"Yes. Before you found out where he left her."

From what he had gotten out of the man, he thought the john had killed Rose—until Zarah contacted Tony. "I finally got her back, and I'm keeping her alive to show the other girls what can happen if they defy me. They can run, but I'll always find them."

"My contact in San Antonio needs four young girls—fresh, preferably."

"By when?"

"End of the month."

"Okay." He instantly thought of Maddie and her friend. He might have to call his nephew back.

"No more mess-ups. I want you to take care of Tony. They're getting close to him. They know he was driving the car that crashed with Zarah. They found his fingerprints in it."

"Do you believe Zarah had anything on the operation written down somewhere?" A pair of headlights came toward him in the other lane. He noticed darkness was quickly descending. Night, his favorite time of day.

"She told Tony she had and demanded that money. I'm working on finding out if she was bluffing."

"How?"

"I have my connections. But even if she did, Tony was her handler, and once he's gone any tie to us is broken. Remember to take care of him." The line went dead. As dead as Tony would be by this time tomorrow. Although the air conditioner blasted him with a steady stream of cold, King shuddered. Suddenly the darkness he loved didn't comfort him. His partner didn't tolerate too many mistakes in anyone, even him.

⟡

Now that he was calmer, Wyatt intended to talk with Maddie about why he hated tattoos. He knocked on Maddie's door, loud so she could hear him over the music. Nothing. He tried the handle, but she'd locked the door. "Open up, Maddie." He waited another half minute. "Now!"

She might be upset with him, but she didn't ignore him like this. She knew better. He went to his room and dug around in his top dresser drawer for the skeleton key he had. Then he walked back and opened the door, only to find the window cracked a few inches and his daughter gone.

15

$\mathcal{F}$ear bolted Wyatt to the floor for a few seconds. He spun on his heel and quickly searched the rest of the house, calling out Maddie's name. When he came back to the foyer both Kate and his mother stood there. Their expression reflected their confusion and worry.

"What's wrong?" his mom asked.

"Where's Maddie? She isn't in her room. Or the house." In two strides, he cut the space between them. "Did you let her go somewhere?"

His mother paled and shook her head. "I don't know where she is."

"What have you been doing all day? Spending time with Jack rather than knowing where your granddaughter is?"

His mom gasped. "I realize you're upset and don't know what you're saying, but Jack had only been here a half an hour before you came home."

He swung around and passed Kate who looked at him with a mixture of worry and disbelief. Going straight to the kitchen, where he kept a list of Maddie's friends' numbers on the cork board, all he could see was Lillian buried in a shallow grave.

That could be Maddie if she did something stupid. He called Kelly first. The girl's mother answered.

"Wyatt, Kelly should be home about now. She went riding. She said something about meeting Maddie."

"Thanks. When she comes in, please have her call me on my cell." After Wyatt gave the woman the number, he slammed the phone down. What she said should have eased his worry, but he couldn't shake Lillian's image from his mind.

He stormed out of the back door and across the yard toward the barn. *Please, Lord, let her be in there.*

When he entered it, its emptiness mocked him. Walking through it, he noted Maddie's saddle was gone. He opened the back doors and stepped out into the rosy orange glow of the sunset. He checked the back pasture where Star Champion was kept. The gelding wasn't there.

For a moment, he debated whether to go out looking for her or wait in the barn or house for Maddie to return. He closed his eyes and tried to draw in a decent breath. He couldn't. *What if something happened to her? She knows never to ride after dark, and while it wasn't night yet, it was close enough that her horse could stumble or—*

"Wyatt?"

The lilting sound of Kate's voice sliced through his haze of anger and fear.

"Is her horse gone?"

He slowly turned to Kate who could make him forget the pain of his past, the mistakes he'd made. "Yes. Kelly went out riding to meet Maddie. They usually ride together in the morning."

"Maybe Maddie needed to get out of the house after staying in her room all day."

"She's grounded."

"To the house?"

"Well, I didn't exactly say that."

"Then she probably thought she had to stay on the ranch. I found with kids you have to be specific, or they'll find the loopholes."

"She met Kelly. Grounded means no friends over. That much she knows."

Kate came up to him, her smile easing the tight knot in his gut. "Why don't we wait for her at the house? The lasagna is baking and should be ready in half an hour. We can wait out on the porch." Kate held out her hand for him.

He took it and relished the warmth in her touch. He saw so much evil in this world that sometimes he forgot that there was good too. This case was wreaking havoc with him. His daughter was just a year younger than Lillian. If he lost his daughter, he didn't know what he would do.

❧

Maddie hurried through taking care of her gelding and letting him out into the pasture. Darkness surrounded her as she headed toward the house. She was late. Being with Tyler had been wonderful. He understood the problems she was having with her dad. She could talk to him. He'd had the same kind of trouble with his father.

Then she remembered him giving her a leg up although she didn't need the help. She'd been mounting Star Champion by herself for years. But Tyler's touch on her thigh as she settled into the saddle sent a tingling through her. The only thing she regretted was he hadn't kissed her. Maybe next time she saw him. She'd never been kissed unless she counted the one Johnny snuck back in fifth grade.

Nearing the back of the house, she headed for her window and the crate she'd put there to use. She groped around in the dark, but she couldn't find it.

"Missing this?"

Heartbeat racing, she whirled toward her father, his face hard to see in the light from the house and the shadows of night, but she noticed the tic in his cheek twitching.

"I saw you leave the barn."

Surprisingly, his voice sounded calm, which concerned Maddie more than if he had yelled at her. "I needed to exercise Star Champion."

"You were out alone after dark." He spoke with an even tone, but the rigid set to his shoulders was at odds with his composed voice.

"Yes. I had some thinking to do, and before I knew it, I realized it was dark."

"So you didn't meet Kelly tonight?" He moved closer, his eyes hard, piercing, his jaw clamped down so hard the cords of his neck tensed.

Oh, no. He knows. He probably called Kelly's house when he found I wasn't home. She stared down at the small space separating them and tried to come up with a reason she lied. "I needed to talk with Kelly. She's my best friend."

"So you ignored that you were grounded. I see."

She lifted her gaze. "Do you? I have no one to talk to around here. Kelly understands me. You don't."

"Do you understand? I was worried about you when you weren't where you were supposed to be. Not until I called Kelly's and her mom told me she went out riding to meet you, did I have any idea where you were. You could have been kidnapped or hurt somewhere. I didn't know." His voice rose with each sentence, his hands opening and closing.

"I didn't leave the ranch."

He took a deep breath and released it slowly. "True. But you met with Kelly and you were grounded, which means no friends over either. You don't go anywhere or see anyone when you're grounded. I didn't think I had to explain the conditions of being grounded. I was wrong. Do you understand what it means to be grounded now?"

She started to reply, "I'm not a baby. I understand," but swallowed those defiant words. She remembered what Nana said about a smile getting her more than a frown. She wiped all anger from her expression and tilted her head down. "I'm sorry. I understand. No friends over and I can't leave here without your permission."

"Good. I'm tacking on another week to your grounding. Nana and I can't be worried about what you're gonna do all the time. That's something you can think about while you're here. If you want to leave the house, you must tell us, even to go tend to your horse."

"But the first big party of the school year is that weekend."

"Actions have consequences. You should have thought about that when you were meeting Kelly to talk. A phone might have been a better way to talk to your friend." He turned to leave.

She remained rooted to the spot, fighting down the anger that would only get her into more trouble. But words begged to be said. *It isn't fair. All this because of a tattoo. There's nothing wrong with one. I can do what I want with my own body.*

He peered over his shoulder and in his calm voice asked, "Are you coming inside? Nana saved you some dinner."

Frustration churned her stomach. *He can do what he wants, but I can't. It isn't fair.* "I'm not hungry." She charged around him and stomped into the house.

She stopped when she saw Kate sitting at the kitchen table, drinking a glass of iced tea. At the place next to her set a plate full of delicious smelling food. *Lasagna, my favorite.* Her stomach rumbled its hunger.

"I nuked it while your dad was talking to you. I figured you would be hungry after a ride." Kate smiled and gestured toward the dinner.

"I didn't know you were here."

"Your dad invited me. I told him I would come only if I could make dinner. I hope you'll try it. A lot of the girls at Beacon of Hope like this recipe. Occasionally I relieve our cook to make dinner."

Maddie opened her mouth to tell her she wasn't hungry, but before she could say it, Kate stood and moved to the oven to withdraw some French bread. "Your dad told me you love lasagna. I don't get to cook for others as much as I would like."

The pangs of hunger cramped her stomach. "I'm not very . . ." Kate's openness appealed to Maddie. "Okay." After washing her hands, she slumped into the chair, the aroma from the dish assaulting her senses, stirring her appetite. She was starving, but being mad at her dad wasn't a good reason not to eat. Why should she suffer any more?

Maddie picked up her fork and dug into the lasagna. As she ate, her father came into the kitchen through the back door. She tensed, but ignored him, all the while savoring the wonderful taste of the meal, trying not to appear too enthralled with its delicious flavor.

"I have some calls I need to make before I take you back to town," her dad said to Kate, then strode from the room.

Maddie's tenseness relaxed the second he left, and her shoulders sagged forward.

"Are you all right?" Kate asked.

She wasn't going to say anything, but she looked into Kate's face and saw understanding there. She took another bite and said, "I don't see what the big deal is about having a tattoo. Dad is making such a BIG deal out of this. He won't even see it."

"My mother wouldn't let me pierce my ears in more than one place. I wanted to wear studs in the top of my earlobes. I didn't even mention I also wanted one in my bellybutton."

"Did you get your ears pierced?"

"Yes, behind her back, and she was furious at me. I had a friend pierce them. One of my ears got infected, and I felt like I had done something terribly wrong even though she never said anything to me about it. I could never wear my studs when she was around until I left home. But you know something, the whole incident took the pleasure out of wearing them."

"I love my tattoo. I wish I could get a permanent one. I don't understand why there's a law against that. I'm old enough to make that kind of decision." Maddie lifted her chin and sat up straighter. No one was gonna make her feel bad about doing something she should have been able to do in the first place.

Kate curled her hair behind her ears. "I love wearing all my earrings now. But at the time, I think what bothered me was that I purposely went against my mother. In the end that didn't set well with me. It hurt my relationship with her. She didn't trust me for a long time after that, and trust is important to me. Working with teens now, I understand the importance of trust."

Maddie finished the last bit of her lasagna. "Did you get your bellybutton pierced?"

"Nope. It took me three months for my ear to heal."

"Well, I went to a professional place so that shouldn't be a problem."

"Have you talked with your dad about why he doesn't like them? Why you want one?"

"All my friends are getting one."

"That's not enough. Why do you want one? Some of the girls at Beacon of Hope aren't always happy with my decisions, but they know at any time they can come talk to me about it."

"Do they?" Tearing off some French bread, Maddie popped it into her mouth.

"All the time."

"You don't get angry at them for challenging your authority?"

"I don't see it that way. I see it as an opportunity to have a dialog with them and share what I'm thinking and for me to understand what they're thinking."

"Do you change your mind?"

"Sometimes."

Maddie plopped back against her chair. "Dad doesn't."

"Never?"

Maddie thought back to last year when he did and let her go on a mission trip to New Mexico. "Not often."

"Have you ever been responsible for something like a pet?"

"My horse and the dog we had until recently."

"Did you ever have to do things for them that they didn't like but were good for them?"

Maddie thought of the shots that Chester, her dog, used to hate or the fact that if Star Champion was allow to, he would eat until he got sick. "One time Star got into some feed, and I had to call the vet. He ate so much he got sick. So now I am extra careful and aware of his ability to open a gate if I don't put the chain up to keep him inside. Simply latching it doesn't work."

"Ah, I bet he wasn't happy about that."

"You should have seen him at first. He pawed the ground, snorted, and tried to get out anyway. No, he wasn't too happy with me."

"But you did it because you thought it was best for him?"

Maddie gathered up her dishes and rose. She didn't like where this conversation was going. "It was obvious it was best for Star. He got sick. I'm fine. Nothing is wrong with me because I got a tattoo."

"That's good. Some people have allergic reactions to henna. I knew someone whose tattoo got infected. It can happen just like it did with my earlobe. A caretaker, whether a pet owner or a parent, makes decisions on what they think is best. Most of the time they are right, but sometimes they aren't. Talk to your dad when you both aren't so upset."

"If my dad wasn't a police officer, he probably wouldn't be so uptight about everything. He always thinks the worse. Real life isn't like that." Maddie crossed the kitchen toward the hallway. At the doorway, she paused and said, "You can fix lasagna anytime for me. It was great. Much better than Nana's."

"I'm glad you liked it."

Maddie made her way to her bedroom without seeing her dad. She heard him on his phone in the den but was glad he didn't see her. He would never understand about Tyler. She wasn't going to say anything to him, but she hoped Tyler called her soon like he said he would.

⁓≈⁓

"Ready to go home?" Wyatt asked a few minutes after Maddie left the kitchen.

Kate rinsed off Maddie's dish and placed it in the dishwasher. "Yes, it's been a long day. I seem to be saying that a lot lately." Drying her hands on a towel, she shifted toward Wyatt.

"A lot is going on." He took the dishtowel from her and tossed it on the counter, then caged her against the cabinet, leaning in. "I appreciate the lasagna, and the companionship while I waited for Maddie to return, but most of all you caring enough to try and talk to her. I have a feeling she had a few choice words to say about me. I grounded her for another week. She wasn't happy with me."

"No, she wasn't. I suggested she talk to you when you both aren't so upset."

"I'm not changing my mind."

"You don't have to, but if you let her feel her opinion means something to you even if you don't change your mind, she is more likely to come to you when she has a problem. My dad always listened to me, but rarely went against Mother. But she never would listen to me. She told me something and that was it. No discussion. No listening to me. Communication is key to a good relationship. There is none in my relationship with my mother. It's her way or the highway, even now that I'm an adult."

Wyatt smiled. "Duly noted. I'm always ready to look for the worst in a situation. It might not always be the best way." Inching closer, he wound his arms around her and tugged her against him. "How did ya get so smart?"

She leaned back and looked up at him. "I'm not so sure about being smart. Look at my relationship with my mother. But when dealing with twenty plus students who have seen more of life than a lot of people, I've had a crash course. And I've made my share of mistakes. I should have anticipated Cynthia's reaction to Rose's disappearance. She should never have cut herself so badly if I had been there more for her."

"How's she doing?"

"I think Audrey and her rooming together is a good match. Which reminds me. I want to check in with them before they go to bed. I've been doing that, and I think it helps."

He kissed the tip of her nose. "I get the hint. Time to go."

But before he loosened his embrace, he settled his mouth over hers, and for a moment she forgot everything but him.

She wanted to weld herself to him and give in to the security she experienced in his arms, but she had her girls who needed her, especially now with all that had been happening. Pulling back a few inches, she cupped his face and stared into his beautiful eyes, feeling herself being pulled further in.

She glanced away. "It's getting late. We'd better go."

"I'll let Mom know I'm leaving. Be back in a sec."

Kate sighed and leaned against the counter. As she panned the kitchen, taking in its warmth and homey feeling, she couldn't shake the sense of belonging. She had enjoyed cooking dinner tonight for them. Even with what happened between Wyatt and his daughter, she felt the love she had never felt in her own childhood home. Her dad loved her, but he wasn't around much. To her mother, all she had been while growing up was an inconvenience. Her older brother could do no wrong in their mother's eyes, but it was rare that she did what her mother thought she should do.

⌀

At dinner, Rose sat at the long table in King's dining room with him at one end and his nephew, Gregory, across from her. She picked at her food, the few bites she'd taken stuck in her throat.

"I'm disappointed in you." King lifted his water glass and took a sip. "I thought you were a survivor. A survivor would eat and build up her strength."

"I guess I found a new way of dieting."

King laughed, the sound slithering down her spine like the snake he was. "You're too thin. You need meat on your bones. I hope, Gregory, the girl you're bringing me isn't as thin as Rose."

King's nephew smiled, and if Rose hadn't known what kind of person he was, she would be drawn in by the grin on his handsome face. "Maddie will be perfect for our purposes."

Her stomach clenched tightly, masking her hunger pangs.

"Once we fill this latest order, I'm moving our operations. I've got plans in the works."

"In Texas?" Gregory caught Rose's attention and winked.

Her skin crawled as if rats skittered over her.

"My partner prefers it and provides certain benefits to staying here. Besides, we're near the Mexican border and a port for shipments outside the country."

Partner? She'd always thought King was working alone.

Gregory chuckled. "I can see why you feel that way. Protection is important in this business."

King raised his glass. "To another year as profitable as this last one."

When Gregory lifted his drink, anger as she'd never felt deluged her, shaking her whole body. She sprang to her feet, her chair crashing to the floor. "Why are you doing this? Why are you keeping me here? You two aren't even human."

King slowly rose and tapped his chest. "This human is hurt deeply by you. After all I have done for you. I took you in when you lost your parents. I fed and clothed you."

"You'll never get thanks from me. I would have been better off on the streets by myself."

"Tsk. Tsk. You know what happens to pretty, young girls who are on the streets. I promised your aunt I would look after you when she was dying. I don't go back on my word."

She swept her arm across her body. "You call this taking care of me? I'm a slave."

"You are alive—fed and clothed." King edged toward her. "And because of your Aunt Belle, you will remain alive—for the time being. Don't make me go back on my word to my wife. I never have, and I don't want to start now. I love her and want to honor her wishes."

Staring at the menacing look on his face, Rose clutched the table to steady herself. She'd loved her aunt, who had been good to her. If Aunt Belle only knew what her husband was really doing, the kind of man he was. When King ran a finger down her cheek, hatred stiffened her posture. Revulsion soured her stomach.

"May I go to my room?" she asked in as strong a voice as she could manage.

"Of course, my dear. You are free to leave the table." King returned to his seat and continued to eat.

Rose rushed from the room, only to find her guard outside waiting for her in the hall. As she trudged up to the third-floor bedroom that had been hers since her aunt died, she scrubbed her hand against her cheek trying to wipe away *his* touch.

Inside her old room, she listened as the lock was turned in the door. She stared at the window. If there had been a fourth or fifth floor, King would have put her up there. He relished the fact she hated heights and had taken such pleasure in moving her from the ground floor to this one when her aunt died. Ever since she had been trapped on the second floor in a burning house, she had been scared.

Fear is in your mind. You can overcome it when you want to. When the Lord is with you every step, you can do what you have to do. Kate's words came to her mind as she made her way toward the one window in the room. She'd told her that after finding her for the fourth time sleeping on the couch in the downstairs rec room. Kate took her hand and walked her up the stairs to the second floor. Finally, she'd been able to go up to her bedroom without Kate, but she never looked out the window. King knew that. He knew all her weaknesses and used them against her.

She inched up to the drapes that she kept closed and fumbled for the cord. After opening them, she peeked out of the corner of the top glass pane. Orange and yellow streaks painted the dark blue sky with the rays of the setting sun. Gorgeous. Mesmerizing. She eased forward a little more to see its full beauty. Threads of rose weaved through the other bright colors.

She inhaled a fortifying breath, held it in, and peered down at the ground. Her heartbeat thumped against her ribs, picking up speed the longer she looked. Perspiring, she backed away and tried to draw air into her lungs, one gasp after another. Finally, the rapid heartbeat in her chest abated. She wiped her wet hands together and approached the window again.

There was only one way out of this room. With the door locked, this was it. *I either overcome my fear or be a prisoner until King has me killed. I don't want him to win.*

She stared at the ground three stories down with large boulders sprinkled among the rocks in the garden beneath her window taunting her to try. King hadn't even locked it, but then she could understand why he was sure of himself. She'd lived in this room for almost two years and had never attempted to escape out the window.

Sliding the bottom pane up, she glanced around before sticking her head out and assessing her situation. Not good. Impossible. A sheer drop to the ground without anything to use to climb down. No trees nearby. The only possibility was on the other side of the house where the roof slanted down to the second floor and there was a drainpipe.

What good was that for her? She was stuck in this room. She turned away from the window and slumped to the floor. Even if heights didn't frighten her, how was she supposed to get down?

Pulling her legs up, she rested her chin on her knees and stared at her prison—a cold, impersonal room with a double bed, a table and chair, and a dresser. Nothing on the walls, no knickknacks, no rugs on the floors. She closed her eyes and pictured what she'd seen out the window. A thought nibbled at her mind.

No, she couldn't get on the roof. It was too difficult. One slip . . .

What do you have to lose?

My life.

Do you want to live like this? Anything is possible. Just have faith.

Before she talked herself out of it, Rose leaped to her feet and clutched the windowsill. There was still enough light left for her to try. She would need some, at least at first. Once she was on the roof, she knew where she needed to go.

She crawled out onto the small ledge, in a crouch, still clasping the bottom of the raised window. *Don't look down. Look at where you need to go—the second floor roof ten feet to the left. If I can jump over there, I might make it.*

Her heartbeat thundering in her ears, Rose dried her hands on her jeans, closed her eyes for a few seconds, and pulled in a shallow breath. Then another.

If You exist, God, I need You.

She pushed off and took a real leap of faith. Sailing through the air, she kept her gaze glued to the roof where she needed to land. When she crashed into the tiles at the edge, the air whooshed from her lungs. She gripped the gutter, her legs dangling over the side while dragging breaths into her. Aware of the noise she'd made, she hoisted herself up and onto the roof. She scoured the growing darkness for any sign of one of King's men.

But this part of the house was on the west side away from where King usually was at this time of night. Her eyes now adjusted to the dimness, she saw no one. Turning her head away from the ground, she scrambled up the roof and over it. When she started her descent, her foot slipped out from under her, and she went down, tumbling forward. She clutched the air, her fingers connected with a vent pipe, stopping her slide. She tightened her hands around it while her body shook, and she squeezed her eyes closed.

Dizzy from the pounding of her pulse, she stayed like that while night settled completely over the landscape. Once she tried to let go and couldn't pry her fingers loose. She counted to ten then twenty and willed herself to release her grip. Her hands remained locked about the pipe.

C'mon. I'm almost there. I have to do this or . . .

She refused to think of the consequences. Nothing was worse than staying King's prisoner. One. Two. Three huge breaths and she flattened herself on the roof and inched toward the downspout.

When she reached it, she thanked the Lord for getting her that far and for the blackness that surrounded her. She couldn't see the ground, which helped her lower her legs over the side of the roof. Using the drainpipe, she shimmied down it. Her feet hit the dirt, and she collapsed to the earth, all energy siphoned from her.

Scooting behind some large holly bushes, she rested, leaning her back against the brick of the house. She would wait until most everyone went to sleep then make her move. She couldn't go on foot because King had a dog that was used for tracking. She needed a car.

Closing her eyes, she let the chirps of the crickets and the night song of a bird somewhere nearby lull her almost to sleep . . .

Rose's eyes popped open, and at the same time she sat forward, her heart racing with fear she'd let her exhaustion lure her into a deep sleep. But it was still pitch dark. Still time for her to get away.

Crawling out from behind the bushes, she slipped around the side of the house to the circular front drive where King often kept his two-seater sports car at the ready, as though he might need it to make a fast getaway. She smiled when she saw it. Now it would be her getaway car. And she knew where he kept a spare set of keys, because he had once locked himself out.

She found and retrieved the keys from the magnetic key box in front of the left rear wheel, She moved quickly, wanting to put as much distance from her and the ranch as possible before dawn. On the small incline, Rose turned the key without starting the motor, disengaged the clutch and pushed the car as far as she could before jumping behind the steering wheel and starting the engine. She pressed the accelerator and drove the vehicle without the lights on toward the highway, thankful King had let her drive this car a few times as a reward for doing her job well.

Almost there. The black iron gate loomed ahead. She found the remote control clipped on the visor and punched the button. The last barrier standing in her way of freedom opened slowly. She zoomed out onto the highway that led to Silverwood or Dallas. She swerved the car toward Dallas, and Kate. Pressing her foot on the accelerator, she relished the sense of accomplishment.

Until she drove up an incline in the road and topped it. Below her sat two patrol cars across the highway as though they had been waiting for her. She'd seen the police chief at King's before and couldn't take a chance. She braked and made a U-turn, only to discover three vehicles converging on her. Trapped.

She realized a ditch along both sides of the road made escape impossible. Bright headlights from both directions came at her as she stopped. Wrenching open the door, she fled on foot. Down into the ditch and up the other side. Between two slats of a fence. Across a pasture until someone tackled her from behind, sending her flying forward. The man smelled of peppermint. King.

Flattened on the ground, she felt all hope shatter. He leaned close to her ear and whispered, "You are mine. Have you not learned that yet?"

⋙⋘

The next morning as Wyatt headed for the kitchen, he passed his daughter's closed door, paused, and started to knock. He stopped and dropped his arm back to his side. He wasn't ready to have the conversation they needed to have, and he doubted she was either. But, soon, he needed to have a father/daughter talk. What was happening now could not continue.

Kate's advice about making sure he listened to Maddie's opinion settled in his thoughts and wouldn't let go as he drove toward Dallas. The police had found Tony Langford's residence earlier, and he and Byrd Finch, the Dallas detective on the task force, were paying the man a visit. This might be the break they needed. Nothing had come up yet concerning Rose's whereabouts before she became part of the prostitution ring, but he would give each law enforcement officer he had contacted a reminder call later.

He pulled into the driveway of a small house that desperately needed a fresh coat of paint and the yard of weeds mowed. Wyatt climbed from his vehicle and met Detective Finch at the steps to the small porch. Two uniforms skirted around to the back to stop any exit that way.

"Is he home?" Wyatt asked, getting a feeling the place was deserted.

Finch shrugged. "No activity this morning. No car in the drive. I've got the warrant. Even if he isn't here, we can search the house."

"Let's do it."

Finch pounded on the door. "Police. Open up."

Wyatt went to the front window. Through a slit in the curtains, he glimpsed an empty room. "I think he's vacated this place too."

Finch tried the knob. The door opened. "I guess we won't have to break in."

When Wyatt stepped inside, he realized his assessment had been correct. Tony Langford didn't live here anymore. "Another dead end."

"But at least this one is more recent. He paid the rent on it for August so he was here lately."

"Let's do a walk-through—maybe he left something behind."

Wyatt checked the two bedrooms, one with a bed, a small table, and a chest of drawers. The other had no furniture, and both of them had empty closets. The bathroom was cleaned out too. He lifted up the bare mattress and found nothing. Heading back into the living room, he met Finch coming out of the kitchen.

"I found a jar of pickles and a six-pack of beer in the fridge. Otherwise, nothing."

"Me, too. Nothing. I'm beginning to hate that word."

In the living room Wyatt ran his gaze over a lounger, a small table next to it, and a brown couch. "Was the furniture his or the landlord's?"

"Landlord's."

Wyatt crossed to the couch and lifted the cushions. Beneath them a quarter and some peanuts lay hidden. "I don't see us finding him with a jar of pickles and peanuts."

Finch upended the lounger and bent down. "But this might help us." He held up matches. "Maybe someone there can help us."

Wyatt read the name, Cattleman's Bar and Grill, and went cold. "That's in Bluebonnet Creek. That's their new logo."

"How new?"

"About three months ago."

"So that puts our Mr. Langford at the Cattleman's Bar and Grill in the past three months."

Wyatt took a whiff of the room. "Or someone visiting him. This place doesn't smell like a smoker lived here."

"Maybe he smoked outside."

"Yeah, why would he in this kind of heat?"

"In the lease agreement?" Finch flipped open his cell and made a call while Wyatt strolled into the kitchen and bedrooms again.

A few minutes later Finch found Wyatt in the bedroom with the furniture. "Not in the lease. The owner didn't even think about something like that."

Wyatt smelled the curtains hanging in the room. "He didn't smoke in here."

"So maybe he didn't smoke, but that doesn't mean he didn't pick up the matches."

"I'll take his picture by and ask."

"I'll check with impound about the wrecked car. See if any cigarette butts are in the ashtray. Then continue canvassing any of his known associates. The problem with that has been there are so few of them we've heard about in the past couple of years."

"That we know about. It sounds like he reinvented himself a while back. Why? Because of who he is working for now."

⋘⋙

Wyatt showed Langford's photo to a Cattleman's Bar and Grill waitress he knew had worked there for years. "I haven't seen anyone like that in here. I don't forget a face. He looks like a weasel. I'd remember him," she said, confirming what the other employees and the owner Wyatt had interviewed told him.

He tipped his hat. "Thanks, ma'am. Have you seen anyone new recently."

"We don't get too many strangers in here. We're off the beaten track. The last one I saw was about a week ago. Nice looking, tall, wearing expensive clothing—black boots, designer jeans, and a black Stetson. He was with a younger man. Now that one was downright handsome—movie-star type, with gorgeous brown eyes and blond hair."

"Do you know who they were?"

"Nope. Paid cash and I haven't seen them since. I was hoping they were new to the area and would become regular customers. These tired eyes got a thrill watching them, especially that young one."

Wyatt withdrew his business card and gave it to the thirty something waitress. "If you see this guy around here, please give me a call."

"Gotcha. Better get back to work before my customers riot," she said.

Wyatt left the restaurant. The early afternoon sun blinded him until he put his shades on. The heat shimmered on the black asphalt parking lot as he made his way to his truck. In the cab, he inserted his key into the ignition. The blare of *The Good, the Bad and the Ugly* filled the interior.

"Wyatt here," he said, noticing the call was from Detective Finch.

"Tony Langford has been found dead."

16

"So that will be our menu for the open house. Any other suggestions?" Kate stood at the end of a long table with the girls who had wanted to help make the food.

"Oh, I forgot all about the no-bake cookies I used to have as a little girl. I'd like to have some of those. I'd like to make them," Beth said.

Kate wrote that on the white dry eraser board. "Anything else?" Turning, she looked at each of the eight girls who had volunteered for this job. "Then we are set on what we will serve. This is your open house. I want to showcase you all even if you decide not to participate that day."

The students filed out of the classroom while Kate jotted down what they had suggested. When she sensed someone near her, she glanced up and smiled. "I'm glad you have decided to help cook, Cynthia. I understand you are quite good."

The teen shifted her gaze away from Kate and murmured, "I love to cook."

"So do I. On one of the cook's days off, we'll have to make something for the girls."

Cynthia looked straight at her. "I'd like that."

"So would I." Kate gathered up her pad and pencil and started for the door.

Cynthia hung back.

Kate turned toward her. "Is there something else you want to talk to me about?"

"I don't know if this means anything, but I remember Rose talking to me about when she was growing up, she had trouble getting to sleep because of the planes that flew so low over her house some of the time."

"It might. I'll pass the info on to Ranger Sheridan."

Cynthia shuffled past Kate. "I'm scared it's too late even if it could help."

"I'm not giving up hope we'll find Rose. As long as we haven't heard anything otherwise, there is room for hope." Out in the hallway, Kate shut the door to the classroom. "The Lord gave us the ability to hope. It's a precious gift. Without it people would give up. Once you give up, it's over."

"Then I'll pray Rose has hope wherever she is."

"Me, too."

⁓

"Tyler, I'm glad you called. I've missed you." Maddie looked at her wall calendar with five Xs drawn through the days since she last saw him. "School is starting soon and I figure you'll be so busy . . ." She was making a mess of this. She sounded too needy. Biting her bottom lip, she shifted her cell to the other ear.

"Kelly told me what happened with your dad. I was afraid to call and get you in more trouble. I miss talking to you."

She dropped back on her bed and stared up at the white ceiling. "I'm glad you called. Dad hasn't restricted my calls. I just can't go anywhere for another week and a half."

"That long?"

The disappointment in Tyler's voice brought all of Maddie's anger at her dad to the foreground again. She was so bored she could scream and she might when she got off the phone. "Yeah, he was pretty ticked off at me."

"I want to see you. Is there any way?"

"I wish. I—"

"Oh, Maddie, I've got to go. Chad's here. There's an orientation at school. I have to be there. Talk to you later."

"Bye," she said to the dial tone.

She clicked off and tossed the phone onto her covers. He was going to be at school with all his classmates while she was stuck here in her room doing nothing. Her cell phone was an old kind without access to the Internet and no games on it. She could only make calls using it. Boring. Then to add insult to everything, her father had taken her computer out of her room. He said she would get it back when she started classes in a few days. Until then, she was going crazy. The only time she could leave the house was to take care of Star in the morning while her dad was at the ranch. And, what was worse, for once her grandmother was following her son's dictates. She seemed to barely think about Maddie. She was so wrapped up in her new guy, Jack.

Maddie turned over and pounded her fists into her pillow. It was a good thing her dad was working a lot lately. She might say something to him that would get her in more trouble.

❧

"Why did ya say that to her?" Brad grabbed his latte from the clerk and made his way to a table in the front of the coffee shop that had a view of people walking by in the mall. "We don't have any junior orientation. We don't have anything to do but hang out here."

"I know that. It's a ploy to keep Maddie guessing about my intentions." Gregory chuckled and sat. "I can't appear too eager to see her all the time, especially if I'm gonna persuade her to run away, to meet with me against her father's wishes. I'll give her another day of silence, and she'll be calling me, begging to see me."

"Are Kelly and Maddie going to be part of the San Antonio cargo? If not, we still need two more to fill that order."

"King hasn't made up his mind yet about Kelly. Yes, to Maddie, but I need to get her away from the ranch. Things are heating up and King wants to take the ranger's mind off the case."

"Okay, then we need to scout out another girl."

"Yeah, the younger the better."

Brad nodded toward two teenage girls. "How about one of them? I think the blond would work. Let me do this one. I could use more money."

"Sure."

Brad scraped back his chair and threaded his way through the tables to the exit. Gregory leaned back and watched his protégée make his move on the girl, probably no more than fourteen. Brad's thirty thousand dollar gambling debt would keep him working for a long time—at least until he could no longer lure young girls.

He observed Brad stroll out of a store at just the right moment so that the blond teen collided with him. Gregory's cell went off. "Littleton here."

"Have you found another girl yet?" His uncle asked.

"Working on it. Why not Kelly?"

"I've found it's easier to take one at a time. Keeping a girl separated from anyone she knows is better too."

"So Maddie is still slated for San Antonio."

"Yeah, those girls won't be staying in the United States long. Perfect revenge for Ranger Sheridan for sticking his nose into my business. Son, when someone strikes you, you have to strike back. Hurt him where it counts."

"Of course," Gregory hung up and slipped his cell back into his pocket. When his father went to prison eleven years ago, his uncle took him in and raised him. There was no one else in his family who would. He would do anything for King. He was the father he never had.

⬥

"The firefighters pulled Tony out of the warehouse before he was burned so we were able to ID him." Detective Finch walked toward the stretcher where a body bag lay and unzipped it.

The stench wafted to Wyatt. Not something he hadn't smelled before, but he was glad it wasn't a charred corpse. At least now they knew what happened to Tony. "Any idea what the cause of death is?"

"No knife wounds, gunshots, or obvious blunt force. I suppose it could have been smoke inhalation, but I don't think he would lie there and not try to get out. The firefighters said he was lying on the cement floor of the warehouse in the corner behind a stack of crates. That doesn't sound like someone trying to get out of a burning building."

"Let me know as soon as the medical examiner determines cause. Do you think the crime was committed here?" Wyatt waved toward the partially burned building, one of several deserted warehouses in this part of town.

"Probably not. If so, we may never know. The place is a mess. If an anonymous person hadn't called the fire in, this warehouse would have been destroyed. When the fire department got here, it was going fast."

"Do we know who called 9-1-1?"

Finch lifted his shoulders in a shrug. "He didn't stick around, but this area has its share of bums. I'll have some officers canvas the ones they can find and see if anyone will admit to calling 9-1-1 or seeing anything connected to the dead body. We'll check the company who owns these warehouses, but I suspect it will be a dead end."

"Yeah, from the looks of the other two, not much security around here." Wyatt noted the broken windows and one door ajar on the building next to the destroyed warehouse.

"I'll continue to dig into Tony's background. Find out who he has been working for. Check with his neighbors." Finch zipped up the body bag.

"Whoever killed Tony, cleared out his house. That will make it more difficult, especially following the money trail."

"Someone probably has seen something we can use. Some unusual activity at his place. He lived there for almost two years. The bad thing is that he paid his rent in cash."

"Do you think he did everything in cash?"

"Possibly. There might not be much of a money trail to follow."

The tension in his neck gripped it in a viselike hold. Wyatt kneaded the taut cords. "The news is just getting better and better. The matches didn't lead anywhere. No one had seen Tony at the bar. While you concentrate on him, I'm going to continue trying to track down where Rose lived before she got caught up in the prostitution ring."

"Daniel is looking into the Liz Taylor connection at the college. Let's hope one of these pans out for us."

"Yes. I'm heading to Beacon of Hope. I need to find a locker that goes with a key. At least that's what I think it is. We checked the bus stations nearby. Nothing."

"You think it's near Beacon of Hope somewhere."

"I'm starting there then checking out the area where Zarah was last picked up. Otherwise, it could be anywhere in Dallas."

"That's a big haystack."

"And a tiny needle." Wyatt withdrew the key—too small for a door. "If you come up with any ideas, I'm open to them." He strode toward his truck, his ring tone blaring. Seeing the call was from Kate, he quickly answered. "Hi, I was telling Detective Finch I was on my way to see you."

"You are?"

"Yep. I was going to start at Beacon of Hope and work outward, trying to come up with a place that has lockers."

"For Zarah's key? With all that has been happening, I'd forgotten about that. I'm going to ask some of the girls. One of them might know where she could have gotten a locker."

"They seem to open up to you better than me. Anything to narrow down where to look would be great."

"The reason I called is that Cynthia thought of something else that might help you in finding Rose's parents. She once told Cynthia that she used to have a hard time getting to sleep because of the planes that flew overhead."

"So Rose lived near an airport. That might help when trying to exclude people who died in a fire. Tell her thanks from me."

"I'll let you tell her. I think it will be great coming from you. See you soon."

When he slid into the cab of his truck, he caught a glimpse of himself in the rearview mirror and the grin that spread across his face like some teenage boy in love. He couldn't be in love. There was no time or place in his life for love. At a stoplight, drumming his fingers against the steering wheel, he tried to visualize Rebecca in his mind. The image wavered and vanished.

As he neared Beacon of Hope, his thoughts filled with Kate. Her smile that encompassed her whole face. Her eyes that twinkled when she was happy. The sound of her voice when she talked about the girls she was trying to help—full of dedication and love for her job and the people she worked with.

Maybe his mother was right. Nine years of mourning his dead wife was enough. Was it time to move on? But then, that advice came from a woman who had been married multiple times and still hadn't found a man who made her forget all others.

The sight of the place up ahead made him smile in spite of himself. Knowing Kate, she would be near the foyer waiting for him. After he parked, that thought spurred his steps faster. He needed a bright spot in a tough day.

As he thought, Kate stood talking to Audrey in the foyer. The animation on Kate's face told him she had more good news for him. Did Audrey know where Zarah would have found a locker?

"Good afternoon," Kate said with a big grin. "Audrey may be able to help you. She remembers Zarah talking about the recreational center. She was thinking of going over there and swimming. Audrey doesn't know if Zarah ever did, but she's pretty sure they have lockers in the dressing rooms."

"She never *actually* said she went swimming?" Wyatt asked Audrey.

The girl shook her head. "On our free afternoons she would sign out, but I know for a fact she didn't go where she said she was. Once I went to the same place as she had signed out for and she never came. I don't know where she went." Audrey swung her attention to Kate. "I'm sorry. I know I should have said something, but I had to share a room with her. She was difficult at best. I didn't want to have to deal with her if she found out I ratted her out."

"How often do the girls have a free afternoon?"

"They earn them up to one a week, and there were stipulations of how they could use them. Zarah only earned a few of them in the months she was here."

Wyatt turned to Audrey. "Is that the rec center in connection with Oiler Park?"

"Yes. I did see her once in the park. I don't know where she had signed out to go."

"Thanks, Audrey. This might really help us. It's a place to start looking."

Beaming, Audrey ascended the stairs to the second floor.

"Let's go see if the key fits a locker." Kate started for the door.

"You're going?"

She paused near the entrance. "You bet. I was with you when we found the key. I want to know as much as you what she could have hidden in a locker."

He held up the key. "*If* this fits a locker. We don't know for sure."

"Have faith. We've got to have a break soon."

"We. You keep saying that." He covered the space between them and opened the door.

"That's because I have a stake in this investigation. I owe it to Rose to find her."

"You don't owe her anything except to keep yourself and these girls safe."

"As long as that prostitution ring is working out there, we aren't safe, especially young girls in the area."

"The sad thing is if we shut down this one organization there will be another to fill the gap."

"Every time you put these criminals away, you send a message to the bad guys."

He climbed into his truck. "I know. I can't stop, but sometimes it's discouraging."

"One step at a time, Ranger Sheridan."

Ten minutes later, the woman who ran the rec center showed Wyatt and Kate into the women's locker room. "We have several people who come regularly and leave their clothing here for a workout. Most are used for just a few hours while they are here."

"So you don't know if a locker is being used on a regular basis or only one time?" Wyatt scanned the three rows of lockers with one on top and the other on bottom—about ninety lockers in total.

"We haven't had any complaints. So long as things run smoothly, I don't see any reason to monitor them. That takes manpower we don't have with budget cuts. We've always had the option of cutting the lock off if need be."

Wyatt opened his hand to show the woman the key. "Would this fit one of your lockers?"

The young woman swept her arm to indicate the three rows. "Most have a combination, but I think there are a few that need a key. Feel free to check them all out."

"Any with 5RB on it?"

"No. Nothing like that."

Wyatt walked down the first row while Kate took the last one. He found one locker that required a key to unlock. When he fit his into its slot, it didn't go all the way in. He moved on until he heard Kate call him.

On the bottom of the last row Kate stooped in front of one. He passed the key to her, and she tried it. It went in but wouldn't turn.

"She's right. Most of these are combination locks." Kate rose.

"I know. This shouldn't take too long." Wyatt rounded the corner and examined the lockers on one side of the middle row while Kate took the other.

Five minutes later, Wyatt pocketed the key, disappointed. "I thought this might be the place."

"So did I. I thought Audrey was on to something."

Wyatt thanked the woman who ran the center and left with Kate. Out in the parking lot next to the building, he stood at his truck and made a slow circle. "Where do we go next? You know this area better than I do."

"If Zarah hid it recently, then it should be near Beacon of Hope. She wouldn't have a lot of time or money to go very far. Let's drive around. Move outward from our building."

Two blocks from Beacon of Hope, Kate leaned forward and pointed toward a large structure on the left. "The Striker's Bowling Lanes. About a month ago, we came over here one afternoon and bowled. The girls had fun. I think they have lockers in their restrooms—at least the women's. She might have used one of them."

"Did Zarah come?"

"Yes." Kate tilted her head and thought a moment. "I remember Zarah being unusually quiet. When she came back, she said she got sick in the restroom but was fine now."

Wyatt made a sharp left turn into the lot next to the bowling alley. When they entered the building, he pressed the key into Kate's hand. "You go in and check the women's restroom for lockers. I'm going to talk with the people who work here. See if they remember Zarah coming here recently."

As Kate made her way toward the restroom, Wyatt strolled up to the large round counter in the middle of the bowling alley. The workers had a good view of both sides of the building's sixty lanes. Some teenage boys were playing video games in the room off the main hallway. The aroma of French fries and hamburgers saturated the place and stirred his hunger.

At the desk, Wyatt removed a picture of Zarah and slid it toward an older man whose shirt had manager under his name, Donald. "Have you seen this girl around here?"

The manager studied it for ten seconds and said, "Nope. We get a lot of kids in here." He nodded his head to the group of boys, talking loud and cheering their companions in their quests on the video games they were playing. "If I remembered all the kids who come through here, I'd have no room in here," he tapped his temple, "for anything important."

"I'd like to ask some of your employees."

"Sure."

Wyatt approached several workers, and by the time he had talked with the third one, Kate came out of the restroom, a huge grin on her face.

"I saw her about two weeks ago here," a young woman with carrot-colored hair said. "I remember her because she slammed the pay phone down real hard and then stomped into the ladies' room. I got kinda worried and started to go in there to see if she was okay. But she left before I had taken two steps."

"Did she leave the bowling alley?"

"Yeah. Kept her head down and plowed her way through some teens and out the front door."

"Thanks." Wyatt turned away from the employee and bridged the short distance to Kate. "You found it?"

"Yes. It was on the right side of the room on the bottom row fifth locker from the door. That's what 5RB stands for." She held up a small pad, similar to what he used to write down information about cases.

"Let's eat lunch here and go through this. That was the only thing in the locker?"

She nodded.

"I think she left it two weeks ago. At least it sounds like she did after talking to that lady over there." Wyatt gestured toward the woman cleaning the area behind lanes one through ten.

After they took a seat side by side in a booth and placed their orders, Kate flipped the pad open to the first page. "If u r reading this, I'm dead. Take this to the police." Kate glanced at Wyatt. "She never said a word to me. Everywhere I look, I find I've let down my girls. I should have known Zarah was scared about something, but she always acted like nothing bothered or scared her."

"False bravado."

"It seems so," Kate murmured in a low voice, a frown scrunching her forehead. "Maybe I have no business running Beacon of Hope."

Wyatt slipped his hand over hers. "Remember your successes. You have saved some girls from a life on the streets. You have given some of them hope. A hope they hadn't had in a long time, if ever."

Kate sniffed and turned the page. "I'm trying, but so much is at stake here."

Wyatt's gaze lit upon Zarah's next words. "I never knew Rose's real last name—not sure Rose is even her real first name. When she came to Beacon of Hope, I knew who she was. I'd seen her a couple of times. She's the boss's niece—a recruiter for him. She denied it, but I know she's involved with King. This might be my way out of here. I don't belong here."

She leaned forward. "King? Have you heard of anyone connected to this case by the name of King?"

"No."

"I wonder if that is the man's real name."

"If someone like Zarah knew that name, I doubt it. But I'll ask the rangers in this area and Detective Finch to check with the Dallas Police, especially vice."

On the next page Kate picked up the narrative written by Zarah, "I called Tony. I told him I'd tell him where Rose is if he got me out of this place and give me a thousand bucks. I figure that's OK on account of Rose being family to King. I don't know who the big guy really is, but she does. My silence should be worth something. I could start over someplace else."

"Now I see why Zarah was shot." Wyatt tapped the word thousand. "She was blackmailing Tony and King. Not smart— even with this as insurance."

Kate continued reading, "Tony is coming 4 me soon. I'm putting down everything I know about King. Rose is gone. Her uncle must have gotten her. I'll use this to get what I want from Tony when he comes. He better have my $$ with him. What I heard from some of the girls is King is good looking, owns some ranch here in Texas and is rich. A couple of the girls were kept at the ranch. Not me." She closed the pad. "That fits with what we know about Rose and her riding horses when she was younger."

"Okay. We think Rose lived in this area of Texas, maybe on a ranch near an airport. It burned down and her parents were killed in the fire. We don't know when, but it had to be some-time between two to eleven or twelve years ago. If she was too young, she wouldn't have been riding horses. Then it sounds like she went to her uncle's ranch. A man who is handsome and rich. If we can find the first, we should be able to find the second ranch. This will be my priority, especially now that we know the connection between Rose and this King."

"Wait. What if Rose was talking about riding horses and the airport and she was referring to this King person's ranch? Maybe at first she wasn't used in the prostitution ring because she was too young."

"You think he drew a line at when he would use his niece?"

"Maybe."

Wyatt snorted. "You're giving this man more credit than I can. Remember what your girls have gone through. These kinds of people have no morals. You know that some parents have sold their children into this type of life."

"You're right. But I'll always have hope that a person can change. I have to." Kate sighed and relaxed back against the brown vinyl cushion. "At least this is a solid lead."

❧

"I'd love another cup of your coffee." King gave his mug to Carrie.

"It's nice to have a man appreciate my coffee. I'm going to check on those sweet rolls. It's Kate's recipe. You'll have to tell me how they are." She headed toward the kitchen. "I'll be back with breakfast."

King waited until she disappeared through the doorway, then hopped up and moved toward the window that looked out over the porch. Sheridan had gone outside a few minutes ago when he had received a call from another ranger. He positioned himself at the corner of the window, hidden by the drapes, and leaned as close as he could.

Although most of the conversation was hard to make out, King heard a couple of phrases. "Expand our search . . . all of Texas. Got to be . . ."

What search? He needed more information. His gut told him something was going on that was connected to him.

He heard Carrie returning. King scrambled away from the window and stood in front of a painting—amateurish—odd colors with geometric shapes. He noted "Caroline" was written in the corner.

Turning when she came back into the living room, he closed the space between them and took the tray she carried. "Did you paint that picture?"

Carrie blushed. "What do you think?"

"You've got talent. I like your use of colors."

"My son didn't want me to put it up in here. I insisted. It took me two days to do it a few years back."

"Have you got any more paintings?"

"No, Wyatt isn't into that kind of stuff. I gave them away. That was my favorite one. I kept it, and in spite of his protests, it's hanging in here."

"I offered to hang it up for you in your bedroom." Wyatt said from the foyer. He picked up his cowboy hat and set it on his head. "I'm leaving. I'll probably be late again tonight."

"Hon, you need to slow down. You've been putting in a lot of late nights. I worry about you."

"It's this case. Hopefully it'll be over soon." Wyatt kissed his mother's cheek, nodded to King, then left.

Carrie released a long breath, shaking her head. "He will never change."

"Why do you say that?"

"He's like a pit bull. He won't let go no matter what. That's him when he's working a case that means something to him."

"All cases don't?"

"No." Carrie walked to the couch and sat in front of the tray, then patted the cushion next to her. "Come, eat. I need someone to appreciate my attempts to learn to cook decently."

King took the place next to Carrie and selected a sweet roll from the plate. After tasting it, he closed his eyes and licked the sugar from his lips. "Hmm. This is good. Too bad your son is missing this."

"He's missing a lot. His daughter is unhappy, and his way of dealing with it is to be gone. I'll be glad when school starts tomorrow. At least she can leave the house to go there. This grounding is my punishment too. I get to witness her moping around all day. I don't feel I can go anywhere so I'm basically confined here too." She leaned back and slid her arm through his. "I'm so glad you're all right about coming here to see me."

"When I'm not having to work, I'd much rather spend my time here. You're prettier to look at than the walls of my hotel room."

She playfully punched him in the arm, the color of her cheeks deepening to a bright red. "I bet you say that to all the women you date."

He schooled his expression into a look of seriousness. "I haven't dated since my wife died. You're the first to tempt me to give up my bachelor ways."

She laughed. "You're just saying that to get another sweet roll from me."

"Nope. The honest truth." King held up his right hand as though he was swearing in court, then he winked at her. "But there is another one on that plate that is begging me to eat it."

"Go right ahead. You better than me. You don't have to watch your calories like I do."

"Ha. Are you wanting another compliment? I could do it all day. It's easy to give you compliments."

She put her hand to her cheek. "Oh, my. You know how to sweet talk a gal."

"With you, it's a pleasure." He reached for another roll and leaned back with his arm around Carrie.

"You said your granddaughter is home. It's awfully quiet for a teenager."

"That's because she's sleeping. I don't think she's gotten up before noon since she's been grounded."

"Doesn't she ride her horse in the morning?"

"Not lately. It's like she doesn't care about riding anymore. I told Wyatt, but he seems to think she's just pouting and everything will be all right when she's no longer grounded. I don't know about that."

"What's this big case that takes him away from the house so much?"

"I don't know much. Just bits and pieces I've heard him say on the phone or to Kate."

"Kate, the lady I've seen here? She works for the police?"

"Oh, no." Carrie angled more toward him and snuggled closer. "She runs Beacon of Hope in Dallas for troubled girls."

"Troubled? How so?"

"Girls found on the streets selling themselves."

"What's your son got to do with that? Isn't that Dallas Police's problem?"

"He's on a task force involving human trafficking— especially children that prostitution rings move all over the place. It's alarming what's going on."

King brought his other arm up to encircle Carrie, hopefully giving her a sense of security. "Is this a big problem around here?"

"It's a big problem all over the United States. I think Wyatt is getting close to finding a major supplier in this area."

"He is? That's great."

"Yes. I can't wait until this is over with. I hate thinking there are people out there preying on young girls. I heard him talking to Kate about something one of her girls wrote about the ring she was in."

Zarah. So it wasn't a bluff. If only Tony hadn't gotten into a wreck, they would have the information she had threatened them with. It wouldn't have taken long to get it from Zarah. She had no idea who she was up against. Tony paid for his mistakes, but King had to deal with the consequences.

King slipped his arms away from Carrie, then reached for his coffee and forced himself to take a sip. "I wish I could stay longer, but work calls me too. Hopefully not for too long."

"When are you leaving Dallas?"

"Soon, but that doesn't mean we can't keep in touch. Unless you don't want to." King put his mug on the tray, the bitter coffee assaulting his taste buds.

"No. Austin isn't that far away."

King rose. "That was what I was thinking."

Carrie walked him to the front door. He dipped his head toward hers and kissed her. When he left and descended the steps outside, he dug into his pocket and withdrew a peppermint. Popping it into his mouth, he savored its sweet flavor that drove the taste of Carrie's nasty coffee from his mind. The things he did for his business. He shook his head. It would be over soon. In fact, sooner than he had planned.

After he climbed into his sedan, he called his nephew. "We're moving everything up. Call Maddie and arrange to meet her tomorrow."

17

"I'm miserable and so bored." Maddie lay on her bed, her cell to her ear.

"I saw Kevin and Andrew today in town. They were telling me about freshman orientation. I can't wait till next year," Kelly said, excitement in her voice.

"Yeah, middle school sounds so dorky."

"Well, we don't have to wear uniforms like Chad and Tyler."

"Did you talk to Chad lately?"

"Yeah, he called me last night and again a little while ago. Haven't you heard from Tyler?"

"No, I feel so isolated. There is nothing to do. Every web site I want to go to Dad has blocked, and now I can't even use the computer until I'm off being grounded. Tyler told me he had a way to get around those blocked sites. I'm dying to learn how." *If only he would call.*

"Chad told me they start school day after tomorrow. They're lucky they have an extra day of freedom."

"Yeah, but they have uniforms. I'd hate that. You should see the outfit I have for tomorrow. I'm gonna have to wait until Dad leaves to put it on. Lately, he's been leaving early so he should tomorrow too. He wouldn't like what I'm gonna wear, but Nana won't care. She helped me pick it out before *he* grounded me."

"What happens if he does see you in it?"

"He'd ground me another week probably. I've hidden it in my closet so I'll just wait until he leaves."

Kelly giggled. "The things we have to do. My mom is pretty good about things like clothes, but my dad isn't."

"At least you have a mom. My dad would have me wear armor if he could."

"That would set off the metal detectors."

The picture of her going through them and all kinds of bells clanging and going off brought a smile to Maddie's lips until she thought of the long night ahead with nothing to do. "I'd better go. Nana said dinner would be soon. See you on the bus tomorrow."

Maddie put her phone on her coverlet, her smile dying as thoughts of being in this house for another week, except when she was at school flooded her mind. *Dad is being so unreasonable!* Anger welled up in her. Her hands curled into fists, and she pounded them against her bed. *He still thinks I'm a little girl.*

I'm not.

Nana rapped on the door, then eased it open and peeked in. "Dinner is ready."

"Is Dad home yet?"

"No, but he should be here any minute."

"I'm not hungry."

Nana came into the room. "Sure you are. You're just mad at your dad and don't want to eat with him."

"Bingo. I thought he was going to be late again."

"He called and said he got through early." Her grandmother sat on the bed and patted Maddie's arm. "I think he misses seeing you. You've done a great job of avoiding him. Staying mad at him won't make the situation better. You need to talk to him."

"Yeah, so he can dictate something else for me to do."

"He loves you. He has your best interest at heart. Honey, do it for me. Please."

"Sure. But it's not me. It's him."

"I was wrong to go behind his back about the henna tattoo and bikini."

"But, Nana, you understand. I should have control over my own body. What harm is a tattoo, especially one that isn't permanent? No one even sees it unless I have a bathing suit on."

"That's not the issue. I went against your father. He is your parent."

Maddie scooted up and sat back against the headboard clasping her legs against her chest. "But you're my grandmother. You're a woman. He isn't and doesn't understand."

"Then help him to understand. Dismissing him and his concerns won't make this better." She rose. "He should be here in five or ten minutes."

Maddie pressed her lips together, refusing to say another word. Her dad had gotten to Nana. She couldn't even depend on Nana's support anymore. When her grandmother left, the door remained ajar. All she wanted to do was go to it and slam it closed. But then her stomach tightened with a hunger pang.

The cell on the bed beside her rang. She picked it up and saw Tyler's number. As she answered it, she jumped up, hurried toward the door, and closed it quietly.

"Hi, Tyler. I can't talk long. Dinner is about ready."

He chuckled. "Hello to you, too. I won't keep you long. I miss you so much. Can we see each other soon?"

"Why haven't you called?"

"I tried to stay away. I hate talking to you and not getting to see you. All I do is think about you."

"Me, too. I've been so bored. I want to see you."

"Is there any way you can get away? Tonight?"

"Tonight? I don't know about that." She pressed her ear to her door and heard voices—her grandmother talking to her dad.

"Tomorrow, when your dad goes to work? We could spend the day together. We could meet at Ashland Mall. I have some shopping to do. We could have lunch there. I need to see you."

The urgency in his voice made her legs go weak. Maddie leaned back against her door, her heartbeat accelerating at the thought of seeing Tyler, defying her father. "School starts tomorrow, but actually that might be the best day to skip. They don't keep good attendance the first few days. They don't call parents about students not being there until next week. And Nana goes to her ladies' church group in the morning."

"Great. What time do you think you can get to the mall?"

She wished she hadn't told him she drove. Thinking about how she could pull it off and not get caught, Maddie slid down the wall, drew in a deep breath, and finally said, "Ten o'clock."

"I'll see you there at the northeast entrance. I can't wait."

"I can't either."

"We're gonna have so much fun."

A knock alerted her right before her dad opened the door. She shot to her feet and quickly said, "I have to go. Dinner is ready. See ya." She shut down her cell and slipped it in her pocket of her shorts.

"Who was that?" Her dad remained in the entrance.

"Kelly. About school tomorrow. I'll finally get to leave this prison."

One corner of her father's mouth tilted up. "At least it's not solitary confinement. It could be worse."

She saw no humor in his comment. "Not much."

"Hon, things don't have to be like this. All I ask is that you respect my wishes and follow my rules."

"Is that all?"

He frowned. "Yes. I was a teenager once. I know things aren't always black and white, but you can't just break a rule of mine without consequences. What did you expect me to do?"

"Understand."

"I do understand what it's like to be a teenager."

"A girl? You don't know the first thing I'm going through."

"Then help me understand."

"I've tried. You don't listen. You think I'm a little girl. I'm not."

"You aren't an adult yet either. I'm still responsible for you."

"How am I gonna ever learn responsibility if you are always smothering me?" Her voice rose several levels.

Her dad's expression evolved into a scowl, his brows slashing downward. "Watch your tone, young lady."

"Yeah, fine. I'm hungry." She skirted around him and stormed down the hall. All she wanted to do was eat, go back to her room, and plan her meeting with Tyler tomorrow.

❦

"Did I just hear Dad leave?" Maddie came into the kitchen, headed for the refrigerator, and took out the orange juice.

"I'm not sure you should wear that outfit," Nana said, buttering a piece of toast.

"Remember when we went to the mall to get my tattoo, I showed you this and you liked it."

"It was on the hanger when I saw it. I didn't realize how short the skirt was and that the T-shirt doesn't completely cover your midriff. Does that meet the dress code?"

Maddie tugged the shirt down. "I'll be fine, Nana. All the girls wear stuff like this."

"I don't know—"

"Young lady, you go back to your room and change. That is not appropriate for school, and you know it."

Maddie pivoted toward the doorway into the dining room. Her dad stood just inside the kitchen, the hard line of his jaw conveying his feelings. One hand clutched the countertop nearby while his gaze cut through her.

"But, Dad—"

"Now."

Fury sped through her veins. She stomped toward the hallway. "I'm gonna be late for the bus."

"I'll drive you to the bus stop. If you miss it, I'll take you to school."

With those words, she increased her pace. She couldn't have her father take her to school. She flew into her room, threw on a pair of jeans and a long plain T-shirt, and returned to the kitchen to retrieve her book bag and a piece of toast with peanut butter on it. Her dad watched her as she started for the back door.

"Aren't you going to have something to drink?" Nana asked before Maddie put her hand on the knob.

"I've got to go."

"Get some orange juice. I'll drive you to the bus stop."

She opened the door. "No, I'm fine. I'm not thirsty." Then to prove her point, she took a big bite of the toast and chewed it as she went out on the stoop.

She half expected her father to follow her and demand she ride with him. She didn't want to be around him. He had an uncanny way of knowing something was up. The less she was around him the better she was. At the edge of the yard before ducking between the slats of the fence, she spied her dad leaving in his truck. As he drove away, she followed his progress toward the road, not releasing her breath until the back end of the truck disappeared from her sight.

Maddie glanced over her shoulder to see if Nana was watching. The coast was clear. Maddie darted back toward the house and hid behind the toolshed, waiting for her grandmother to leave, too. Thirty minutes later she finally took her car and headed for the highway. Relief trembled through Maddie. She gave Nana an extra five minutes because sometimes she came right back because she forgot something.

She snuck back into the house, hurried to her room, and changed into the outfit she had worn earlier, then went in search of the keys for the old pickup used around the ranch. She'd learned to drive it this past year, only using the gravel and dirt roads on their property. Now it was time to take her real debut road trip.

The keys were where they always were in the drawer in the desk in the kitchen. She took them and made her way to the barn where the old truck was kept on the west side of the building. The pickup had to be at least fifteen years old with over a hundred and fifty thousand miles on it. It needed a paint job to cover the rust showing through the black paint. But it would get her where she wanted to be and back home.

She settled behind the steering wheel and started the truck. It came to life, then sputtered to a stop. She waited a moment, remembering what her dad had said about flooding the engine. When she turned it over this time, it hummed like it always did. Maddie smiled and patted the dashboard.

Glancing at her watch, she noted she had an hour to get to the mall. Plenty of time. With a sigh, she backed out of the parking space next to the barn and directed the pickup toward the highway. If she remembered all her driving lessons and kept under the speed limit, she would be fine.

Halfway to the mall, she gripped the steering wheel so tight her hands ached. Sweat beaded her forehead. She'd forgotten there wasn't any air-conditioning in the pickup, and the hot wind blowing through the cab with both windows down wasn't enough to cool her off. On top of that the thick traffic caused her heart to hammer in her chest at a maddening pace. At a stoplight she tried to calm down.

Last night while she plotted her great escape, it had seemed simple. Now she wasn't so sure. When someone honked behind her, she released the brake slowly. She crept forward while a car sped around her, then another one did, too. The driver glared at her.

Five miles below the speed limit was better for her than going over it. The thought of a police officer—someone her dad worked with—pulling her over chilled her, even in the hot pickup. She knew kids at school who had skipped before and nothing had ever happened to them. But rivulets of sweat ran into her eyes, stinging them. What was she doing? Why was she taking the chance? Panic nibbled at her resolve to do this.

Then she saw Ashland Mall up ahead, only a block away. She tried to relax her grasp on the steering wheel, but she couldn't. She turned into the parking lot on the east side of the mall not far from the northeast entrance. All she had to do was find a parking space and—

The pickup sputtered to a stop in the middle of a parking lot row, blocking some parked vehicles from leaving. She wasn't far from where she should be, but suddenly it seemed miles away. She thought of leaving the truck and going inside to find Tyler, but as she sat in the cab, she couldn't bring herself to open the door. Her limbs felt weighed down, keeping her glued to the seat.

She pulled her purse to her side and dug inside it until she found her cell, intending to call Tyler and tell him where she was. But again, she couldn't do it. Her fingers poised over her phone, but instead of punching his number in she found Kate's stored in her cell from when she'd called a few days ago to see how she was doing. She'd been surprised, but now she was glad Kate had checked on her.

"Maddie, I thought school started today for you," Kate said when she answered.

"Please come pick me up at Ashland Mall near Bluebonnet Creek. The pickup died in the middle of the parking lot. It's blocking other cars from leaving."

"Did you call your dad?"

"No, and promise me you won't. I'll explain everything when you get here. I'm two rows north of the northeast entrance."

"Maddie, you need to call your dad and tell him what's going on."

Tears jammed a lump into her throat. She swallowed several times and said, "I will. I promise when I get home. I did something foolish." Her voice broke. "Help me make it right first."

"I'll be there. Probably thirty minutes. Don't leave the truck. What color?"

"Black. It's old and beat up. We only use it around the ranch."

"Lock the doors and stay put." Kate clicked off.

Maddie checked her watch. 9:40.

⁓❧

In his office, Wyatt stared at the list of his search results. Only three couples' deaths in a fire in the past eleven years in Texas fit the parameters of what he was looking for. Terry and Laura Alexander, Robert and Vickie Maxwell, and Randy and Debra Rhea. One couple lived within fifty miles of Dallas—

the Rhea family. The other two were hundreds of miles away. He would start with the nearest one and pray the couple was Rose's parents.

Before he left, he started calling his sheriffs and police chiefs about the photos he'd left with them of Rose. He wanted to emphasize the importance of the case by following up with them.

The first three assured him that no one had recognized Rose from the two photos. With the fourth call, the police chief promised he would talk to his men again.

The rest of his calls went about that way. Not one lead. By the time he reached his last one, discouragement frustrated him to the point he was glad he was getting out of the office after this call.

"This is Ranger Sheridan. Is Police Chief Jeffers in?"

"No, sir, he's gone today. This is Officer Bowen. Can I help you?"

"I was checking back on the two photos I gave him to show around. Have any of you recognized the girl in the picture?"

"When was this?"

"Last week."

"We haven't seen a photo of a girl. What age?"

"One is of a sixteen-year-old. The other is a computer-generated photo of that same girl maybe at the age of ten or eleven."

"I haven't seen it. Just a sec. I'll ask a couple of the other officers."

Wyatt drummed his fingers on his desk while he waited. This same situation had happened at another two offices.

"No, sir, we haven't."

"I'm faxing you another set of pictures in a few minutes. Please pass them around and call me if anyone knows anything."

"Will do."

Wyatt hung up and stood. He strode to the fax machine and sent the photos to the three offices that hadn't followed through on the pictures. He realized how good intentions could be forgotten when some other situation came up and took a law enforcement officer's whole attention. That was why he always called to check on any progress made.

⌣⌣⌣

Five minutes after ten, Kate's rental car pulled up behind the pickup, and Maddie watched her get out. Another woman sat in the passenger seat. As Kate strolled toward her, Maddie opened the door and climbed down.

"Who's with you?" Maddie wiped her hand across her wet forehead.

"Susan. She works at Beacon of Hope. If I can't get this truck started, I'm going to wait here for my car service to come get it while she takes you to school."

Remembering the confrontation this morning with her dad and even Nana about her outfit, Maddie gestured at her clothes. "I can't go to school like this. They would send me home."

"Why are you dressed like that? Why are you skipping school?"

The sun beat down on her as if she was being grilled under a hot spotlight. Sweat dampened her midriff T-shirt. She peered toward the entrance of the mall where the air-conditioning worked.

"We're not going anywhere until you tell me what's going on. I didn't call your dad, but I can now."

Tears flooded Maddie's eyes. "Don't. Not yet. Dad is gonna be so disappointed in me. I messed up. Big time."

"Why are you here?"

"To meet a boy."

"His school didn't start today?"

"No, he goes to Southwest Academy. He doesn't start until tomorrow."

"He's in high school. A freshman?"

Maddie shook her head.

"How old is he?"

"He's a junior."

"Where did you meet him?"

"Here at the mall a few weeks ago."

Kate didn't say anything for a long moment. "Is he a friend of a friend?"

"No."

"Tell me about him. Have you seen him a lot?"

"How could I? I got grounded. I've talked to him on the phone, and he came to the ranch once."

"Oh, so your dad has met him, and he is okay with him being a junior in high school."

Maddie straightened. "What's wrong with that?"

"Does he know about—what's his name?"

"Tyler Collins, and no, he doesn't."

"Has your grandmother met him?"

"No. I met him at the stream between our ranch and Kelly's. She was there."

"Did he ask you to skip school today?"

Maddie dropped her head. Anger and embarrassment warred within her. "We haven't gotten to see each other in a while. Nothing happens at school the first day or so."

"What's he look like?"

"He is gorgeous with the prettiest chocolate brown eyes. When you look at him, that's what you see first. He's almost six feet, a great tan. I can't believe he's interested in me. He probably could have any girl at Southwest."

"How did you meet at the mall?"

"I bumped into him, and we started talking. He had a friend with him, and Chad likes Kelly."

"Did Kelly skip school, too?"

"No, but then she hasn't been grounded like me. I just wanted to have a little fun. If the truck hadn't died, Dad would never have known about it."

"Why didn't you get Tyler to help you?"

The question hung in the hot air between her and Kate. What made her call Kate, not Tyler? She'd been ready to call him and ask for his help. "I don't know."

"It didn't feel right?"

Maddie shrugged. "I guess so. I started thinking about Dad. I . . ." She didn't know what to say because she couldn't really explain her actions.

"Come on. Let's get you to school. Later this afternoon you and I need to have a long talk with your dad."

"He is gonna be so mad at me."

"Yes, he will be, but in the end you stopped and thought about what you were doing. If you hadn't, you wouldn't have called me." Kate started toward her rental car. "What time do you get home from school?"

"Four."

"Then I'll be there. Don't worry about the truck. I have a car service that can tow it to a mechanic I know. He won't work on it until your dad knows."

As they approached the rental, Susan exited the passenger side and rounded the front of the car.

"Susan, this is Maddie, Wyatt's daughter. She needs to go to school after she goes home and changes. I'll let you know if you need to come back here or to Bud's Garage to pick me up. It depends on how fast the tow truck will get here. I'll call you."

Susan nodded then turned to Maddie. "Are you ready?"

Maddie peered back at the mall. She made a big mess of everything. "Yes." She'd never see Tyler again. Her dad would probably never let her out of his sight. Why did she call Kate?

As she settled into the front seat of the car, Maddie relished the cooler interior, but a blanket of perspiration still covered her. Her head throbbed. Her mouth was so dry.

Susan started the engine. "Are you okay?"

Maddie rubbed her temples. "I've got a headache."

"Probably from the heat. We'll stop and get some water on the way."

"Why are you and Kate being so nice to me? I screwed up bad this time." She'd never done something like skipping school. Her dad would ground her for months.

"Because you're still a child and you're learning what's right and wrong. We've all messed up in life. Kate and I work with girls who have, and they're trying to make something better for themselves. At least most of them."

"Not all of them?"

"There are some that want to keep their old way of life. They get caught up in the sex and drugs. I wish we could reach them all."

"How in the world do they let that happen to them?"

"Some are runaways and are on the street, trying to find a way to live. Others are recruited."

"Girls are approached to be a prostitute and agree?"

"I suppose some are, but a lot are kidnapped and forced into it. They're drugged or beaten into submission."

And my dad is trying to do something about it. The idea made her think about him differently. He didn't talk about his work much at home. He'd always steered the conversation to something else—like her friends, training for the rodeo competition. "Is Kate helping my dad?"

Before Susan could answer, Maddie's cell rang. She noticed it was Tyler's number and thought about not answering it. What should she tell him?

"Aren't you going to get it?"

It stopped ringing. "I don't know what to say to him. It's the boy I was meeting."

"You tell him the truth. You changed your mind." Susan flashed her a grin. "We have the right to change our minds."

When it rang two minutes later, Maddie answered her cell.

"Where are you?" A thread of strain ran through Tyler's words.

Maddie tightened her hold on her phone. "I had truck problems."

"Why didn't you call me?"

"I didn't—I didn't know what to do."

"Baby, I can come and pick you up and help you." His voice lowered to a slow drawl that melted her insides.

She should have called him. Then she wouldn't be in such trouble with her dad. "It died in the middle of a row in the parking lot and the pickup is blocking several cars. It's got to be moved as soon as possible or some shoppers will be mad. I panicked and called a friend to come help me."

"A friend? Who?"

"Kate Winslow. She has an auto service that's coming to get the truck and tow it away. She's with the truck until they do. Her friend is taking me to school. I didn't want to call my father, and yet it had to be moved. Dad's gonna find out and . . ." The words spewing out came to a halt when she thought of the consequences of her actions.

"You could have called me. I would have helped you."

The hurt in his voice nipped at her composure. She was continuing to make more and more bad decisions. "I'm sorry."

Tears swelled into her throat, closing it off. "Bye." She clicked off. After this he would think she was a little girl.

When her cell rang again, she checked the number and didn't answer.

"Is that the boy?"

"Yeah. But I wouldn't say he's mine anymore." Her tears flowed down her cheeks. Maddie let them fall onto her lap.

⁂

Gregory clenched his cell, resisting the impulse to throw it. "She isn't picking up."

"What are we gonna do now?" Brad asked as Gregory charged toward the northeast exit in the mall.

"Call King. See what he wants me to do. We need two more girls to fill the order." Gregory punched in his uncle's number.

"How did it go? Got her already?" King asked.

Gregory hurried out of the mall and found a secluded area so he could talk to his uncle privately. Brad stood guard. "No. She had car trouble and had Kate Winslow come pick her up. She's going to school while Kate stays with the pickup until an auto service comes to tow it. I think we've lost our chance. Once her dad finds out what she was going to do, he won't let her out of his sight."

"Kate Winslow. That's great. She'll do in Maddie's place. I've seen Sheridan with Kate. I think they're involved. Besides, I can use Kate to bring Rose under control. Go see if she needs any help. Then take her and bring her to the ranch."

Gregory glanced up and down the rows near the mall entrance and found Maddie's pickup stalled in the middle of the back of a row, two over. "Are you sure? She won't help us fill the order for San Antonio."

"Yes, I'm sure. She's the reason I'm having such a hard time with Rose. I don't think I can do anything with Rose. Besides, if I get rid of Kate, that's the end of Beacon of Hope."

"Fine. I'll bring Kate to the ranch."

⁓⊙⊱

"Thanks, ma'am." Wyatt tipped his hat at the older woman who had lived next door to the Rhea family whose house burned down six years ago. He descended the steps and walked back to his truck.

Another dead end. Rose didn't look anything like the daughter of the deceased couple. Now he would have to wait for the two rangers interviewing the neighbors of the other victims who fit the criteria of what he was looking for.

He received a call as he drove toward the highway that led back to Dallas. "Sheridan here."

"This is Officer Bowen in Silverwood. Our secretary knows the girl in the photo you sent me."

"What did she say? Is she there for me to talk to?"

"She went to lunch but will be back in forty-five minutes. The girl used to come to town with her aunt. She hasn't seen her around in years."

"I'll be there to talk with her. Probably be at least an hour."

"I'll tell her."

Wyatt merged with the traffic on the highway connecting Fort Worth and Dallas. The hairs on his neck tingled. When a case began to come together, he always got this feeling. He tried to tamp down his excitement. It could just mean that Rose visited one of her aunts occasionally. He didn't know if she had lived in the Silverwood area.

⁓⊙⊱

Kate leaned back against the front of the pickup, the sun beating down on her. Even waving her hand in front of her face did nothing to relieve the heat. The tow truck should be here in the next half an hour. Maybe she should go into the mall for a while to cool off. But what if he came sooner than he thought he could get there?

She pushed off the hood and looked longingly at the mall where air-conditioning existed for days like today.

A blond teen, wearing sunglasses, headed toward her. Was one of these blocked cars his?

The guy frowned and stopped a few feet from her. "That's my Firebird. Can you move the pickup?"

"Sorry. It's stalled. I've got a tow truck coming soon."

"How soon?" He checked his watch. "I've got a job interview. I can't be late."

Kate's gaze flicked down his tall length. Well, then he should have dressed a little better if he was looking for a job. "If you want to try and push it out of the way, I'll steer."

He grumbled under his breath and started toward the back of the pickup. "I guess I have no choice."

Kate moved toward the driver's door. A blue car turned into the row and drove toward them. She flattened herself against the pickup to let the person go on by, but he braked. Before Kate could react, the blond teen had the blue car's rear door open and the boy driving jumped out and pushed her toward the back seat.

Kate swung her fist toward the blond as the other climbed back in the front. She connected with the teen's jaw, knocking his sunglasses off. She stared into brown eyes that reminded her of pieces of rich milk chocolate. It was only seconds but long enough that he brought a rag up and covered her nose and mouth. A sickly sweet smell of chloroform assailed her, shoving her toward a void.

18

$\mathcal{W}$yatt arrived at the Silverwood's police station and approached the officer behind the counter. "Where's Bowen?"

"He's gone on a call. Probably be gone for a while."

"Did he said anything about me coming by?"

"No, but then I wasn't here when he left."

"Where is your secretary?"

"Which one? We have two."

Wyatt noticed one at the copier and pointed toward her. "I need to speak with her." If she wasn't the one Officer Bowen was talking about then he would find the other secretary.

"Betty, a ranger is here to talk to you."

The young woman looked across the main room at Wyatt. When she saw him, she smiled and said, "Come on back." She brushed her long black hair behind her ears. When Wyatt was a few feet from her, she put her papers down and squared her shoulders. "What can I do for you?"

He removed a picture of Rose from the envelope he carried with him and showed it to the woman. "Do you recognize her?"

She studied the photo of a younger version of Rose. "No."

Wyatt passed her the other one of Rose after she arrived at Beacon of Hope.

She shook her head. "No. Sorry."

Wyatt peered over his shoulder at the officer at the counter watching them. Wyatt stepped closer to the young woman and lowered his voice, "Where's the other secretary?"

"Gladys is in the back. I'll go get her for you."

The officer strolled over to Wyatt when Betty left. "Is there a problem? Maybe I can help you."

Wyatt showed him both photos. "Have you seen this girl around here? It would have been several years ago."

"I can't rightly say. I've only been here for a year."

Wyatt spied an older lady coming from a back room. Her gaze latched onto his, and for a brief few seconds he thought he glimpsed fear in her eyes. But a smile spread slowly over her features, and she held out her hand for him to shake.

"Officer Bowen told me you might want to see me," the woman said, her gaze darting to the other officer next to Wyatt.

"Yes. I thought he would be here."

"The police chief needed some backup. He went to help."

"Can you tell me about seeing this girl here? Bowen said you recognized her."

"I saw her a couple of times in town with her aunt, but I don't know her name. That was years ago."

"How many?"

"I can't rightly remember—maybe five or six."

"Who is her aunt?"

"Lydia Johnson."

"Where does she live?"

"She doesn't. She died several years ago."

"She's dead?" Was this going to be another dead end?

The sounds of his ring tone blasted the air. Gladys chuckled. "I'm a Western fan. Good movie."

Wyatt walked away a few paces and turned his back, then answered his cell.

"Mr. Sheridan, this is Ashland Mall's security. A black pickup registered to you is parked in the middle of a row blocking several cars from leaving."

Black pickup? The old one is at the ranch? "Is it pretty beat up with rust spots in the hood and back left side?"

"Yes."

"I'll be right there."

"Thank you, Gladys." He handed her his card. "If you can think of anything else regarding this girl, please let me know." Wyatt strode toward the exit, paused halfway, and swung back toward the older secretary. "Was Lydia Johnson married?'

Gladys glanced from the officer at the counter to Wyatt. "No."

Wyatt tipped his hat, saying, "Thanks, ma'am," and continued his trek to the front door.

The officer behind the counter asked, "Did you get what you needed?"

"Yes." Wyatt didn't break stride. Outside, he quickened his pace even more toward his truck, deciding he would be back to talk with the police chief and Gladys without that officer looking on. The glance she'd sent the man at the counter bothered him. Something didn't feel right, but, at the moment, he had to see about why his ranch pickup was stalled at the mall.

As he drove away from the police station, he phoned his mom. "Where are you?"

"At church."

"I just got a call from an Ashland Mall security officer. Our pickup is stalled in their parking lot. I need you to go home and see if it's gone, then let me know." Although from what the man said, it was. "You're closer than I am. If it's gone, check for the spare keys in the kitchen and for anything else missing."

All kinds of alarms were going off in his head. None of them good. Next, he called Maddie's school because he couldn't see someone coming to the ranch and stealing that beat-up truck even if he had left the keys in the ignition—which he hadn't. He prayed she was there, and this was all a mistake.

But when the secretary at the school notified him that Maddie wasn't there, his heart began slamming against his chest. *What has Maddie done?*

❧

Maddie stared at her house as it came into view. When Susan stopped the car, Maddie sighed and pushed the passenger side door open. "I won't be long."

"Good." Susan climbed from the car and followed Maddie to the porch. "I'm calling Kate while you change. I thought I would hear something by now."

"Maybe she forgot." Maddie headed for her bedroom.

"Not Kate. More likely, the tow truck hasn't come yet."

Maddie hurried to her room and grabbed what she had on earlier when her dad made her change. Dorky, but at least it would be acceptable at school. *Why are there so many rules I have to follow? Like I don't have a mind of my own?*

She pulled on her jeans. Her cell rang, and she saw her dad's number. He never called during school hours since all cells had to be turned off. Did Kate call him after all before she had a chance to tell her dad? Anger seeded itself in her heart and grew.

"Yes?"

"Where are you?"

The tightly controlled voice of her father made her shiver, then her body stiffened. "I'm at home."

"Why?"

"I skipped school today."

"Did you drive the pickup to the mall and leave it?"

Her legs going weak, Maddie sank onto her bed. "Yes, but Kate was going to take care of it. Have a tow truck take it to a garage. I was going to tell you about it this afternoon." When her dad didn't say anything to her explanation so far, she plunged forward. "Her friend, Susan, from Beacon of Hope, brought me home to change and she is taking me to school."

Again, a silence that knotted her stomach fell between her and her dad. Her grip tightened about the cell. "Dad? Are you there?"

"I had to pull over so I can continue this conversation. Let me see if I get this straight. You skipped school and drove without a license to the mall in the pickup. What was so important that you would do something like that?"

Maddie could imagine the fury on her father's face. Every word he said dripped with it. "I was meeting a boy." She closed her eyes and waited for the explosion.

"Nana is coming home. You wait there and do not go to school. Ask Susan to wait until your grandmother comes before she leaves."

"I can stay by myself," she said before she really thought about it.

"You can? Only someone I can trust can do that. Follow my directions to the letter. I'll take care of the pickup then be home. Understand? Don't go anywhere."

"Yes." When she disconnected, the cell slipped from her fingers and fell into her lap. Any anger in her vanished as she heard the disappointment in her father's voice. Would he ever forgive her?

❧

Wyatt pulled back into traffic. He was now fifteen minutes away from the mall. At the first stoplight, he called Kate's cell. It rang and rang until he was asked if he wanted to leave a message.

"Kate, this is Wyatt. I'm heading to the mall. I got a call about the pickup from security. Call me if you get this before I arrive."

Later when he drove into the north end of the mall, he headed for the northeast entrance. He saw the security officer next to his car behind the black pickup. An angry customer gestured wildly at the stalled vehicle. When Wyatt parked behind the mall vehicle, he climbed from his cab and strode toward the security officer and a petite lady with her white hair in a bun. Her words blistered the air.

The security cop saw Wyatt and gave him a weak smile. "Ma'am, we're trying to move it. A tow truck is on its way."

"Officer, why don't we push it out of the way so she can back out? I'm Ranger Sheridan."

Relief washed over the man's face. "I'm so glad you're here."

"I'll push. You steer."

Five minutes later the petite lady backed her Lexus out of the parking space, gunned her accelerator, and sped away.

The security cop shook his head. "I had been listening to her for ten minutes about how she was going to be late for her doctor's appointment, and if he charged her for not making her appointment, she was going to send the bill to the mall to pay."

"My daughter said that a friend of mine was staying with the pickup. Where did she go?" He needed some answers to what was going on.

"There was no one here when I arrived thirty minutes ago. In fact, the driver side door was slightly open."

"Who called the tow truck?" Wyatt nodded at one coming down the row toward them.

"That's not the one I called. The mall uses Mulligan and Sons."

When the truck stopped next to them, Wyatt walked over to the driver, a man in his fifties. "Who called you?"

"Miss Winslow. I would have been here sooner, but there was a wreck I got caught behind. Where is Miss Winslow? Is that the pickup she wanted me to tow to my garage?"

"Yes. Did she say she was going to be here waiting for you?"

"Yeah. I can't imagine her leaving without calling me. I have to have her permission to transport the pickup."

"How long ago did she call you?"

"Fifty minutes ago."

So, there was twenty minutes between her calling for the tow truck and the security officer's appearance. What happened in that time? Acid roiled his stomach. In the heat of an early afternoon, a chill blanketed him as though it was suddenly winter. Something was wrong. But what?

"I'll sign for the truck to be towed. It's my pickup. I'm Wyatt Sheridan."

The man shook Wyatt's hand. "I'm Bud Masters. Do you want me to see what's wrong with it and give you an estimate to fix it?"

"Yes." Wyatt withdrew a card and passed it to the tow truck driver. "Call my cell when you know it, or if you hear from Kate Winslow."

As Masters hooked the pickup to his tow truck, Wyatt swung toward the security officer and gave him a card, too. "If you hear from Kate Winslow, please let me know and have her call me. If you hear anything about where she might be, please let me know. Also, I need you to send me any security coverage from this area of the parking lot for the past hour and ten minutes until you arrived on the scene. The email address is on the back."

Then Wyatt climbed into his vehicle and immediately placed a call to Beacon of Hope. Maybe she had to get back there and didn't have her cell with her. But even as he thought that, he knew what Harriet, who answered, would say.

"No, the last thing we knew was Kate and Susan were going to pick up your daughter. We haven't heard from either Kate or Susan. Do you want me to try calling both of them?"

"I'll take care of it. Susan is at my ranch. I'm on my way there now." *To get answers from my daughter.*

❧

Her mind a blur, her head pounding, Kate slowly opened her eyes to pitch blackness. A stone floor lay beneath her back. The fear of being trapped in a small space shot a rush of adrenaline through her. She lifted her arms and swept them in a wide arc. Hitting flesh—a leg.

"Who's there?" Her roughened voice, as though she hadn't used it in a long time, barely sounded above a whisper.

"Kate, you're awake finally. I was so worried about you."

"Rose?" Kate groped until she grasped arms, praying it was Rose. That she had found her alive.

"Yes." The teen fell into Kate's embrace. "I thought you were really hurt. I didn't know what to do. I've been praying you'd wake up."

Although her head still throbbed, she ignored it and struggled to sit up straighter. The haze lifted a little. The damp coolness of the stones seeped through her clothes and shot ice through her veins. "Where am I?"

"You're in the Deprivation Room at the ranch. King's favorite place to put people who don't follow his rules." Rose clasped Kate's upper arms and drew nearer.

"How did I get here? I was at the mall, then suddenly two guys threw me into a car and put a cloth over my face."

"That was probably my uncle's nephew and his friend."

"Your uncle? You have an uncle? Why didn't you tell me?"

"At first I didn't remember a lot of what happened to me, but as I healed from the beating, I began to remember how evil King is and that he's the reason I was left to die at the side of the rode. He's the person behind the prostitution ring. I was afraid. He told me if I ever crossed him, he would make me pay and anyone I cared about. That he knows people who can protect him. He's been doing this a long time. I believe him." Rose's voice quavered in the dark. Her hand on Kate's arm tightened.

"Why did he kidnap me?"

"I suspect because you were getting too close to the truth."

Kate found both of Rose's hands and held them, wishing she could see the teen, make sure she was physically all right. "What is the truth? Where are we? You said a ranch. Where?"

"A ranch outside of Silverwood. It's big. King owns a lot of land. He is powerful, and he's done everything he told me he would do. I should have realized he wouldn't let me go."

"Listen to me. We'll get out of this somehow. We're not going to let him win."

"How? I've tried to escape two times, and he has stopped me each time. I think he likes to see me try and fail."

Like she's his entertainment. And now she would be too. Kate gritted her teeth, fighting the fear eroding her composure. She couldn't fall apart. *Rose needs me.*

Rose's tears sounded in the unearthly quiet—like a tomb.

"We aren't alone, Rose. God is with us." Kate squeezed the teen's damp hands. "Lord, anything is possible through You. Help us get away from King and bring this man to justice. Show us the way. Amen."

"I'm not worth His time. Look at all I've done wrong. Lily is dead because of me. I recruited her for King. I'll never be able to forgive myself for that. I'm paying now for it, but you shouldn't have to. I deserve this. Not you."

"No one deserves this. You might not be able to forgive yourself, but the Lord forgives you. We have something King doesn't have. We have the God of hope and love on our side."

Rose threw herself into Kate's arms again and sobbed, "Will that be enough?"

❦

Wyatt strode into his house and spied Maddie, his mother, and Susan sitting in the living room. Silence ruled. Somber faces turned toward him as he entered.

"I can't get hold of Kate. I've tried calling several times, and it always goes to voice mail. She never leaves it off like that in case something happens at Beacon of Hope." Susan pushed to her feet, clasping her purse to her.

"I've tried, too. I think something has happened. Susan, go back to Beacon of Hope and if you hear from her call me immediately. There may be a perfectly good reason she's out of pocket." But he didn't believe it. "To be on the safe side, Detective Finch and a couple of patrol officers are headed to Beacon of Hope to make sure nothing happens to the girls."

The color blanched from Susan's face. "I'd better get back there now. The girls will need me when they see the police."

"Keep me informed of anything that happens." Wyatt walked the nurse to the front door and watched her until she climbed into her car and drove away.

He came back into the living room, taking a chair across from Maddie. With her head down, she twisted her hands together in her lap.

"I need to know everything Maddie. Who were you meeting at the mall? Why would you skip school? This is very serious. Kate is in trouble." He felt that deep down as though Kate's life was ticking away quickly.

"I'm so sorry. I'm . . ." Maddie cried, burying her face in her hands.

His mother started to move closer to Maddie. Wyatt waved her away. "Mom, I could use a cup of coffee and something to eat. I haven't had lunch."

His mother's eyes widened. "Okay."

He waited until she had left the room before saying, "Maddie, I don't have time for hysterics. I need your help in figuring out what might have happened to Kate. I have the police checking the morgue and hospitals, but I don't think she'll be there."

Maddie paled. "The morgue? Hospitals?"

"She's disappeared. She wasn't at the pickup at the mall."

"It was hot in the mall parking lot." His daughter raked a trembling hand through her hair. "She's probably perfectly fine somewhere having a late lunch."

"It's been several hours. People have tried calling her. No answer. She isn't where she is supposed to be and said she would be. That's not Kate." He fortified himself with a deep breath. "Let's start with the name of the boy you were meeting."

"Tyler Collins."

"Why the mall? Why today?"

"That's where I met Tyler a few weeks back." Her eyes shone with unshed tears. "We hadn't seen each other because I've been grounded." She sniffed. "I was angry at you."

Wyatt wrapped his hands around the arms of the chair in such a tight grip his knuckles whitened. "You've only known this Tyler a few weeks? You didn't know him from school?"

Maddie shook her head.

"How old is he?"

"He's a junior at Southwest Academy. They don't start school until tomorrow."

"He's three years older than you. A high school student." Somehow he managed to keep his voice level, but for a few seconds he felt his control slip. He scrambled to shore up his composure or he would never get to the truth of the matter.

"That's not that much older than me. You were three years older than Mom."

"That isn't what we need to talk about right now. I need information. Did Kate know about Tyler?"

"I told her this morning about him, and she made me promise to tell you today. I was going to when you came home."

"How did you meet this boy?"

"I bumped into him at the mall—literally. We started talking. He asked me to help him shop for school. I couldn't believe such a hot guy was interested in me."

"Did you see him other than that time at the mall?"

Maddie averted her gaze, rubbing her hands over her jeans.

"Maddie?"

"Yes, that night I came in late when I was grounded."

"So you snuck out to see Tyler. Where did you meet him?"

"By the stream near Kelly's ranch. I never left here. That's the truth."

"Did anything happen I should know about?"

"Dad!" Maddie's face reddened. "Kelly and Chad were there too. Nothing happened."

"Who is Chad?"

"A friend of Tyler's."

"Did Kelly skip school today too?"

"No."

"What do you know about this Tyler besides what you've told me?"

His daughter opened her mouth to say something but snapped it closed.

"Maddie, this is important. Where does he live? Bluebonnet Creek? Dallas?"

"I don't know," she said each word slowly as though until she'd spoken it out loud she hadn't realized how little she knew about the boy she skipped school for.

"You were willing to break the law by driving without a license and skipping school for a boy you don't really know?"

"I know his cell number."

"Call him right now."

"Why?"

"I'd like him to come over."

"Dad!"

"This isn't debatable."

Maddie dug into her pocket and made the call. Her forehead crunched, and her eyes narrowed. When she hung up, she looked at him. "The number no longer works. I just called it a couple of hours ago. I don't understand."

"I know a guy who is a sketch artist for the sheriff here. I want you to work with him and come up with a good likeness of this Tyler Collins."

"I don't understand. Why? He didn't do anything wrong. We didn't even see each other this morning."

"I want the number that no longer works. Does he drive?"

"Yes."

"Then anything you know about his car."

"Why?"

"Because Tyler may not be who he says he is. Because I'm worried about Kate."

"You think they are connected? Dad, that doesn't make . . ." Maddie covered her mouth with her hand, her eyes huge.

"What's wrong?"

"I told Tyler I called Kate to help me with the stalled pickup. He was angry that I didn't come get him. I told him I was going to school, and Kate was staying to have the truck towed. He wasn't happy with me. Do you think that's why his phone doesn't work?"

"No, I think there's much more going on here."

❧

"Maddie has finally calmed down," Wyatt's mother said when she came into the dining room where Wyatt was meeting with several members of the Child Rescue Task Force.

He wouldn't leave the ranch until he knew that his daughter and mother were protected, because if what he feared was true, the people behind the prostitution ring he had been hunting down took Kate. When his wife had been killed years ago, he'd almost fallen apart. Only the fact he was a single parent and responsible for his daughter had kept him together. He wasn't going to let a criminal take away someone important to him again.

"Does anyone else need more coffee?" his mother asked the group around the table.

Several immediately replied no, but Daniel held up his mug. "I could use some."

Wyatt stared at the FBI agent. "Are you drinking the same thing I am?"

"Yes, I happen to like mine extra strong."

Wyatt shook his head and returned to the sheet in front of him. "The cell this Tyler Collins used was untraceable—which sends up a huge red flag to me. We've checked with Southwest Academy and discovered there isn't a Tyler Collins going there. Someone of that description registered a few months back as an incoming junior, but when we dug a little deeper, all the information given was false. Everywhere we've turned has been a dead end as far as this guy is concerned. Which leads me to think he was sent to recruit Maddie. When she didn't go along with his plan this morning, he very likely took Kate instead."

"Why? She doesn't fit the description of the usual females they go after," a fellow Texas Ranger said.

Wyatt stared at the photo of Kate that Susan had provided him. "I don't know. To get back at me. I've been pushing hard on Rose's case. We do know Kate hasn't been seen by any of her colleagues, friends, or family in the past nine hours. That isn't like her. With the footage from the parking lot at the mall, we don't actually see her being kidnapped, but there are five cars that went down that row in the twenty minutes from when she called the tow truck to when the security officer showed up. We're running those cars down now and hopefully will hear something soon."

"What have Kate's parents said? Has she ever done anything like this?" Daniel took the mug from Wyatt's mom. "Thank you."

"I have talked at length with her father who assures me she has never done something like this. She is very responsible, and this isn't like his daughter." Wyatt wouldn't tell the team around the table what her mother had said. *I knew something like* this was going to happen. *When my daughter works with people like the girls in that program, it was bound to get her into trouble sooner or later.* "Her father has talked with the governor to make sure we do everything possible to get his daughter back."

"What if she just got tired of it all and went off by herself for a while? A lot has happened in the past few days to make anyone stressed."

Wyatt glared at the young FBI agent who assisted Daniel. "We have to assume the worst. If we don't, by the time it is confirmed she could be dead or shipped out of the country."

The man shifted in his chair and avoided eye contact with Wyatt.

"I'm going to follow a lead I got this morning." Wyatt went on to tell the group about what happened at the Silverwood police station. "I'm going to pay the police chief a visit at his house this evening. Something isn't right there. Call it a hunch. I do know Rose visited there five years ago. That is the best lead we have right now. In the meantime, I want to know everything there is about a Lydia Johnson who used to live in Silverwood."

"I'm coming with you." Daniel said as he stood up when Wyatt did. "You're going to need backup if this lead pans out."

"Keep working on tracking the cars. I know one only had a partial plate number because of mud. I would concentrate on that one. We've all seen that trick before. I think Tyler Collins is obviously an alias, but check that name out in the Dallas area. Y'all have a drawing of what Tyler looks like from my daughter and Kelly. Continue to press for information about the other two house fires on ranches in Texas. We need to find out who Rose's parents were. If I can't find out anything in Silverwood, that may be the only way we find Rose's real name and her uncle."

"Didn't you say that Gladys at the police station said Rose visited her aunt? Maybe that is the uncle involved?" Daniel passed a photo of the sketch of Tyler to each team member.

"Gladys said the aunt Rose visited in Silverwood wasn't married." Had the older woman lied? He couldn't shake the feeling she had been scared this morning. "Call if you get anything important."

⤻

"Mrs. Jeffers, is your husband at home?" Wyatt asked, standing on the police chief's porch outside of Silverwood.

"No. He probably won't be back until late tonight."

Daniel moved into the light. "Is there a way to get in touch with him?"

"He's fishing and camping with a friend. He does it every year. They are out of cell phone range."

"Please have him contact me as soon as possible." Wyatt pulled out a business card and gave it to Mrs. Jeffers.

The large woman with short white hair pocketed it, then stepped back into her foyer and shut the door.

Daniel glanced at Wyatt. "I didn't get any warm fuzzes from her."

"More like biting Arctic winds. And someone is lying in this town. This morning Officer Bowen was supposed to be helping the police chief with a case. But his wife claims he's fishing and camping. They need to get their stories straight." Wyatt descended the steps. "I looked up Gladys's address. I'd like to pay her a visit away from the office. I got some weird vibes today. I don't think she was telling me everything. Like where Officer Bowen and the police chief were."

On the drive to Gladys's house, Wyatt received a call from the Texas Ranger at his house. "There hasn't been a Lydia Johnson in Silverwood in the last fifteen years."

"Thanks." Wyatt hung up and told Daniel.

"So the woman lied. Why?"

"We're about to find out."

Wyatt drew up to the curb in front of Gladys's small A-frame house. There was one light on in the front room. *Lord, I need Your help. Something is going on here. I know I've let the anger over Rebecca's murder push me away from You. But I don't know where to turn. I feel the danger Kate is in. I don't want to lose her too.*

As Wyatt strode toward the place, an image of Kate in a tomb tortured his thoughts. *She can't be dead. Please, God, I need her.* His heartbeat slowed to a painful throb.

At the front door, he rang the bell. The sound of the chimes drifted to Wyatt on the porch. A few minutes later, he pushed the button again.

Daniel wandered over to the window, the drapes pulled. "I can't see much of the living room, but no one is in there that I can tell."

Suddenly the click of the lock being turned riveted Wyatt's full attention to the door opening. Gladys stood in the entrance, her brow wrinkled, her gaze darting about until it latched onto Daniel.

The woman's stress hit Wyatt in the face. "May we come in, Gladys?"

"No."

"Why not?"

"Please leave. I have nothing else to say to you." She clutched the door, her fingernails digging into the wood.

"Please. This is a matter of life and death. Do you want a woman's death on your hands?"

Gladys began trembling. Her grip clasped the edge of the door even tighter. "I can't. I . . ."

Wyatt took a step closer. She tried to straighten but collapsed against the wood she held.

"I'm going to come in and you're going to tell me what's going on." Wyatt sensed Daniel right behind him as he moved forward.

"I don't really know. They will . . ." She compressed her lips into a thin line, but she backed away from the threshold.

Inside, Wyatt shut the door after Daniel entered, then faced Gladys. She folded her arms over her chest, but she still quivered. "Who are you afraid of?"

"If you ask too many questions, you might disappear. It's happened before."

"Who was Rose's aunt she visited? We know it can't be Lydia Johnson."

"Belle Littleton."

"You said she's dead. Is she?"

"Yes, that was true. Like I said several years ago." Gladys waved her hands toward the front door. "Now go before . . ." The older woman swallowed hard.

"Was Belle married?"

Her teeth gnawed her lower lip. Moisture on her forehead glistened in the light of the foyer. "Yes. To Duke Littleton. He has a big spread a few miles outside of town. He owns half of Silverwood. You don't mess with him. He has a mean streak."

"Does he own the police chief?" Daniel leaned back against the front door with his legs and arms crossed.

Gladys flitted a glance toward Daniel then returned her attention to Wyatt. "I need protection. If Chief Jeffers knew you were here tonight, I would be in a lot of trouble. He and Officer Gilmore were not pleased with me today."

"The police officer who was at the station when you and I talked?"

The older woman nodded.

"Why wasn't Gilmore pleased?"

"I was told to mind my own business or else."

"Or else what?"

"He didn't have to say. Like I said, a couple of people have disappeared when they crossed the police chief. Of course, it was said they decided to move, but I don't know if that's the real truth, not with what has been happening lately."

"Why hasn't anyone come forward to complain? We deal with law enforcement corruption in Texas."

"Eight months ago someone tried. His house was burned down with him in it. It was ruled an accident, an electrical short. But some of us have wondered."

"Then why are you working for the police chief?" Wyatt pushed from the door.

"To find some kind of evidence I could take to the authorities that the police chief can't refute."

"What is Chief Jeffers doing illegally?" Daniel asked.

Gladys lifted her shoulder. "Don't know for sure. But he is tight with Duke Littleton. What Duke wants, he gets. No one dares cross him."

Wyatt thought about what little he knew about Bo Jeffers. There had been suspicion of using excessive force once a few years back.

"What's Duke's ranch called?" Wyatt moved to a window next to the front door.

"The HRH Ranch."

"What's that stand for?"

"Someone said once His Royal Highness, but I don't know if that's true."

"I take it that Duke isn't well liked around here." Parting the blinds, Wyatt scanned the street.

"More like he is feared. His ranch is guarded by a small army."

Wyatt peered at Daniel. "We need to get Gladys somewhere safe and see if we can get a warrant to search his place."

"Not with the evidence we have."

19

*F*rustration twisted Wyatt's gut. He knew they didn't have enough evidence, but instinct told him something was going on at that ranch. "Then we'll need more evidence to prove our case. Gladys, pack a bag."

"I'll see what I can find out about Duke Littleton." Daniel removed his cell from his pocket and made a call.

When Gladys came back into the room with a small duffle bag, Wyatt took it from her. "I want you to tell me how to get to HRH Ranch. I thought before we leave the area I'd drive by and get a look-see."

"You aren't going to stop, are you?" Her voice quavered.

"No, I don't want them to know I'm interested."

"Then I can show you an old back road that leads to a hill that overlooks the ranch. It's not in great shape, but it might be a good place to check its layout."

"The road isn't on Littleton's property?"

"It runs along his western border. You won't see much at night, but it would be a nice spot to observe from tomorrow."

Wyatt chuckled. "I like the way you think, Gladys."

"I've been working for the police chief's office for nearly thirty years. I've picked up a few pointers along the way. And

I'll tell you right now, young man, I haven't liked the changes that have taken place in Silverwood and in the police chief the last eight years or so. About the time Duke Littleton came to town with all his money."

"It's people like you who can make a difference and make my job easier."

After Daniel hung up and joined them, Gladys crossed to the front door. "I'm sorry I didn't say anything at the station earlier today, but Officer Gilmore was looking on. I should have done it before this. That man uses fear to control people."

"Most predators do." Wyatt stepped out onto the porch after Gladys and Daniel then made sure everything was locked up before going to his truck.

Before Wyatt climbed behind the steering wheel, he scanned the area. Nothing seemed out of place, but the stakes were high. He had to be extra cautious. If the person behind this ring took Kate, then he would do anything to stop Wyatt and the task force discovering the truth. A lot of money was involved. Human and sexual trafficking was big business.

Wyatt followed Gladys's directions over the rough dirt road to the overlook and parked his truck so no one from the ranch could see it. "You stay in here. Daniel and I will check it out."

She nodded, then hunkered down in the backseat.

Wyatt retrieved a pair of night vision binoculars from his equipment box. He and Daniel crawled up to the rise that gave them a view of the ranch below. As he swept the area below him, Wyatt noted the main house, barn, stable, and a couple of outbuildings—one with armed guards around it. The police chief's vehicle sat in front of Littleton's mansion, along with the same car Maddie had described as Tyler's and another small sports car. "Other than men with weapons patrolling near a building in the back, everything seems normal for a ranch."

"So what's in that building that Littleton's guarding?"

"Good question. We'll ask him when we see him." He passed the binoculars to Daniel. "I see the police chief has returned to Silverwood earlier than his wife expected."

"Wonder what Jeffers and Littleton are talking about?"

❧

King needed to know what was going on. He picked up his phone and called Carrie, slipping into his Jack Reagan persona. On the fifth ring, she answered, breathless.

"Is something wrong, darlin'?" King asked, cradling the receiver between his face and shoulder.

"No, I was in the other room and had to hurry to get the phone. I thought . . ."

"Thought what?"

"Oh, nothing. I didn't expect to hear from you again this evening."

"I'm sitting in my hotel room getting lonely. I was hoping I could pick you up and go for some coffee. Maybe the Cattleman's Bar and Grill. I love their apple pie. Just thinking about it makes my mouth water. What do you say?" He lowered his voice to a husky drawl. "I need to see you, darlin'."

A long pause then Carrie said, "Well—tonight isn't a good time. Things are happening here and I shouldn't leave."

"What's wrong? Is everything okay?" He made sure just the right amount of concern sounded in his voice.

"Wyatt told Maddie and I to stay put. My granddaughter did something foolish today."

"But why should you have to stay put? I didn't want to tell you this, but I have to go back to Austin tomorrow. I have to deal with some business right away, and I don't know when I can come back to Dallas. I don't want to leave without seeing you."

"Just a minute," Carrie said to him, and then she must have turned away from the phone because her voice was muffled and sounded far away. All he heard was Carrie say "a friend" and murmurs of male voices in the background. A minute later, she came back on. "Sorry. Wyatt has some colleagues over here. This isn't a good time. I need to be here for Maddie."

"You're worrying me. You sound frazzled."

"Let's just say this hasn't been a good day. My granddaughter did something stupid and my son is beside himself. He's rallying the troops to take care of a situation that's quickly developing. I wish I could tell you more, but I've mainly been in the back with Maddie. Please call me tomorrow. Maybe things will be better by then."

"Very well. Good night." He waited until she hung up before he slammed down his receiver. The urge to throw the phone across the room inundated him.

"We've got trouble." King peered at the police chief sitting in a chair in front of King's desk. "Send Officer Gilmore to pick up Gladys. We can't afford to rely on fear anymore. We need to tie up loose ends and move this operation. Now."

❧

Sheridan's daughter was lucky today. She could have become a statistic if she had met that guy at the mall.

After Maddie overheard the Texas Ranger in her dining room, she shut her door and crumpled against it, surrendering to the trembling, to the tears. Tyler was going to kidnap her? Why?

No, he cares for me. He might be mad because I didn't show up, but he'd get over that and call me.

But as much as she wanted to believe that, the conversation of the Ranger and the other police officers only underscored her naiveté. Hadn't her dad warned her enough? Not to be so trusting. So gullible. So impulsive.

A knock on her door startled her. Maddie gasped and scrambled to her feet as her grandmother opened the door and came in.

"Hon, I'm sorry you had to hear that."

"Is it the truth, what he said?" Maddie backed up until her legs hit the bed and she sank onto it.

"Yes. They have analyzed some more security footage they just received from the mall and isolated the picture of the man who pushed Kate into the car. He looks just like the sketch drawn from your description of Tyler."

"I'm the reason Kate has been kidnapped." Tears flooded her eyes. An unbearable pain constricted her chest. "She was there to help me."

Nana hurried to her and sat beside her. "You didn't know that was going to happen."

Wet tracks coursing down her cheeks, Maddie looked at her grandmother. "If I hadn't been so stubborn, selfish, she would be okay. How in the world did I think someone like me could have attracted someone like Tyler?" She hit the side of her head. "Dumb. Dumb."

Her grandmother grabbed her hands and held them. "You're a beautiful young lady who can attract anyone she wants. It isn't you, honey. It's this Tyler. He's a predator who knows what he has to do to lure girls like you to him."

"I fell for everything he told me. I can't believe it."

Nana wound her arm around Maddie. "Let me tell you. I've done my fair share of falling for the wrong man. I've never been able to find someone to replace your granddaddy. I've spent so much time running around after every man who will look at me twice that I've neglected you and Wyatt. I've made a few mistakes in all of this." She cradled Maddie to her. "I can't change what's happened, but I can learn from it. When I see your father, I have some apologizing to do."

"Me, too." Maddie swiped at the tears, but they kept falling. "Do you think he'll find Kate?"

"All we can do right now is pray he can in time."

"Will that be enough?"

"It's in the Lord's hands now. Our prayers will help."

❧

"We need to get out of here," Kate said, pacing the perimeter of the Deprivation Room, using her hand to feel the wall as she walked.

"I've tried two times. There's no way out."

The defeat in Rose's voice broke Kate's heart. The girl had been through so much. She should be going to sleepovers with her friends and only worrying if she was going to pass the next algebra test. Not how to get out of a dungeon-like room. "How did you try?"

Rose explained both ways to Kate. As she listened to the teen talk, an idea came to Kate's mind. "I have a hair clip. Can you use it to pick the lock?"

"He has cameras at all his doors that lead into this house. I don't think it's possible to get out of here."

Kate moved toward the sound of Rose's voice. She stretched out her arm until she encountered the girl. "It might not be, but we have to try. We'll never know otherwise. If you get us out of this locked door, then I'll find a way out. How about a window?"

"Bars on the ones downstairs."

"Locked?"

"From the inside," Rose gripped Kate's arms. "We might be able to get out that way." Excitement built in her voice. "The key has to be nearby because of the fire hazard. Aunt Belle insisted on that after what happened to my parents. If not, I can try picking the lock."

"Then we'll get out that way. See you know more than you realize from your years living here." Kate reached up and removed her hair clips from each side. "Here, see if you can use these."

For ten minutes, Rose worked on the lock. Kate stood behind her, praying over and over. *Lord, anything is possible through You. Help us escape. Please.*

Rose hit the door with her fist. "I can't do it. I can't—"

"Try one more time. We're not alone in this." Kate settled her hand on Rose's shoulder, the teen's body quivering, her skin clammy.

"But what if they come down to check before I can open it."

"You're such a capable young lady. Concentrate on what you need to do. Nothing else."

Rose went to work again. Five minutes later the lock clicked, and she eased the door open. "It's clear. At least down here."

Again, Kate heard a defeated tone in Rose's voice. Her uncle had really done a number on her. He had so much to pay for. "That's a good start. We'll make it."

Kate followed Rose out into the dimly lit basement and up the stairs, only silence from above them. What time of day was it? Where was everyone? Why so quiet? Worry attacked Kate from every angle.

Trust in the Lord.

At the top of the steps, Kate paused and closed her eyes for a few seconds, imaging giving her worries to the Lord. The frantic beat of her heart eased. *We're not alone.*

Inch by slow inch she pushed the door open, then she and Rose crept out into the hallway. Light washed over Kate. She blinked, adjusting her eyes to the brightness, and flattened herself against the wall. Her heart sped so fast the hall before her spun.

After checking the empty hallway, Rose gave her the okay sign, then started forward. Kate passed a shut door and pointed to it. Rose shook her head and gestured toward another closed one up ahead. Taking several more steps, the door behind Kate opened. With no place to hide, Kate along with Rose whirled around to face the threat.

Kate braced herself to fight. Rose grabbed her arm, tugged her back before the person stepped out into the corridor. The teen dropped Kate's arm and continued her flight down the hall. But when Rose rounded the corner at the end, she plowed right into Jack Reagan. He clasped her, anger deepening the grooves on his face.

A few paces behind her, Kate froze for a few seconds when she glimpsed the man who had been dating Wyatt's mother. What was he doing here? Was he rescuing them?

"Haven't you learned your lesson, Rose?" Thunder descended over him, a storm brewing in his ice-cold eyes.

The smooth Casanova replaced by a cold-hearted killer? The need to protect Rose gave Kate clarity. She grasped a vase on a hall table, charged Jack Reagan, and smashed the porcelain into his head. "Run."

Kate grabbed Rose and raced toward the front door. Behind Kate, Jack or whoever he was groaned then yelled for help. She didn't dare look back. Her escape loomed before her.

Five feet.

Two.

⁓⧫⁓

Wyatt spied the front door to the house fling open. Two people flew out of the place—two females. Focusing his binoculars on the pair, he went rigid. Kate? It was too far away for him to see much detail on her face, but it was Kate. He was sure it was. Behind her was another woman—no, a girl—running toward the field near the main house.

Bolting to his feet, he started down the hill, saying to Daniel, "Get help. Kate's in trouble." Two men came out of the house, one holding a gun. "One of the guys is carrying a gun—all the more reason to move in now. I can't wait for backup."

Hurrying down the hill, Wyatt slowed enough to lock his binoculars on the men barreling down on the women. From the porch light, he could make out Chief Jeffers a few steps behind . . .

Jack Reagan?

❧

With no thought other than to try and escape, Kate followed Rose who headed toward the darkness surrounding the large house and yard. In the blackness, they might be able to find a place to hide then get away.

Kate heard deep, angry voices shouting behind her. She kept running, not even glancing back because that would slow her down.

In the next instant, the sound of a gun firing filled the air.

❧

The sight of the man his mother had been dating, who had sat at his dinner table, fueled Wyatt's fury. He couldn't give in to it or he wouldn't be effective. He continued his plunge down the hill toward the women.

The sound of the gunshot froze Wyatt for a microsecond. When Kate went down, his heart plummeted, but he increased the speed of his descent.

No, God. Not again.

He released the binoculars and they dropped on the strap to his chest. Reaching for his weapon, he concentrated on each step. He couldn't afford to falter. Each second counted. The pounding of his heart vied with the pounding of his footsteps.

❧

Fire seared through Kate's shoulder, but fear propelled her up and forward. Rose stopped, spun back, and grabbed hold of her to help her.

"I'm okay. Keep going." Kate pulled away from Rose, the fence and field beyond only twenty feet away. "Hide, then get away. Get help."

Finally, Kate glanced back and noticed one captor was close. The man called Jack. Another in a police uniform jogged three or four yards back from Jack. Her legs weighed her down, energy draining quickly. The metallic scent of her blood saturated the air she breathed, highlighting her weakened state. One step, then one more.

I can't let Rose down.

When she looked one more time over her shoulder as her pace slowed even more, the man in the police uniform lifted his gun and squeezed off another shot. It struck the ground a foot from her.

Only a little way to the fence.

Rose scrambled over the fence and jumped to the ground on the other side. Kate faced the obstacle in her path to freedom and didn't know if she could get over it. The pain intensifying with each jarring step she took.

Kate reached the barrier and gripped hold of a wooden slat with one hand. The other throbbed from shoulder to fingertips. Placing her foot on the bottom board, she tried to hoist herself up. If she could get to the top . . . Her mind swirled. Blood ran down her arm. Her grasp slipped.

༺ཀ༻

Wyatt reached Rose and grabbed her. "Get down."

Rose yanked back.

"I'm a Texas Ranger. I'm here to help."

Her arm still taut, Rose ceased pulling away. "Kate's been shot. King and the cop are after her."

Jack is King/Duke Littleton. "I know. Stay down. I'll get her." Wyatt kept low running toward the fence.

Police Chief Jeffers lifted his weapon again and aimed toward Kate. Wyatt stood, braced his feet, and pointed his Wilson Combat pistol at the man. "State Police. Drop the gun."

Armed men running from the bunkhouse and the back of the house invaded the yard. All carrying guns.

༺ཀ༻

The sound of Wyatt's voice gave Kate a boost. With all the energy she had left, she pulled herself up with one arm. In the moonlight, against the darkness of the pasture, she made out Wyatt's outline, and she trained her gaze on him. If she could get to him, she would be all right.

But behind her, she heard more shouts and doors slamming close. She glanced back. Men poured out of the buildings. The sight of them shot a surge of adrenaline through her. The top of the fence pressed into her stomach. With effort, she pushed forward and tumbled down to the ground, her good shoulder taking most of the impact. But still, pain flashed to every part of her, her mind wavering then going blank.

⁓e2⁓

"It's too late. Duke Littleton and Chief Jeffers, we know what's going on here." Wyatt hoped to bluff enough to spook the men.

Another man, younger, rushed out of the house. The light from the porch illuminated him but not enough for Wyatt to tell who he was.

"Wyatt, I'm coming up behind you," Daniel said and appeared at his side.

"You called it in?"

"More help is on the way. The first group from the sheriff is probably five minutes out."

"Can we trust the sheriff?"

"We have to, but the state police and FBI are right behind them. The sheriff and his deputies are coming in the front. I figured you might need some help down here. We're outnumbered."

"Yeah, about ten to one."

The man he knew as Jack Reagan laughed, holding up his arm as though to stop the chief from shooting. "If you're wise, you'll drop your guns. It's not looking good for y'all."

The sound of sirens in the distance echoed through the night.

King swiveled his attention toward the road that led to the main gate. He took a step back, then another. "Take them out," he shouted to his men.

Wyatt dropped to the ground and belly crawled toward Kate while some of King's men opened fire. Daniel got off a few rounds.

Jack ran toward the nearest car, about ten yards behind. Jeffers spun around and followed suit. The sirens grew louder. The sound of a helicopter in the distance scattered the men.

Wyatt reached Kate and turned her over to face up. In the dark, he couldn't see much. *Please, Lord, let her be alive.* He felt for a pulse, his breath caught in his lungs.

20

Kate's pulse beat beneath Wyatt's fingertips.

He saw bright lights slicing through the darkness. Three sheriff cars sped down the road and screeched to a halt while a helicopter with a spotlight came in from another direction.

Rose and Daniel came up to Wyatt.

"Is Kate alive?" Rose asked, kneeling next to her.

"Yes."

"We need to stop Littleton and Jeffers. They are fleeing in the sports car. There must be another way out of here." Daniel pointed in the direction Littleton's vehicle was heading—toward the back part of the ranch.

"King has an airstrip back there and a plane he uses sometimes."

"Where?" Wyatt asked Rose.

"The northwest corner. I can stay with Kate and make sure she gets help."

Torn between staying with Kate and going after Littleton, Wyatt hesitated, his hand still holding hers. The scent of her blood demanded justice for these men. He turned to Daniel. "Let's have the chopper land. That's the only way we'll get back there in time."

Daniel made a call, and a minute later the helicopter swung around and began to land. While the sheriff and his men went after the fleeing hired guns, Wyatt and Daniel headed for the open space where the chopper was setting down. Wyatt held his cowboy hat down so the wind from the blades wouldn't whip it off.

He climbed in after Daniel who sat in front and took a seat catty-corner behind the pilot. He put on earphones and said, "An airstrip is in the northwest corner of this ranch. That is probably where the fugitives are heading."

The pilot lifted off and swung his helicopter toward that direction. Wyatt scanned the landscape below with his night vision binoculars. He spied the sports car with its lights off, coming to a stop.

Wyatt gestured toward the area. "That way."

The pilot swung down low flying over the treetops. Through the binoculars Wyatt spied two men hop out of the car and race toward a plane sitting on a grassy runaway.

Maybe four or five football fields away from them. Wyatt didn't want an air chase.

Time ticked away. Time they needed to stop Littleton.

The propellers on the twin-engine plane started. The aircraft was already in position to go down the runway as if it had been readied ahead of time for just such an escape. As it started down the strip's flat grassy ground, the chopper pilot set his helicopter down halfway. Thirty yards the plane, still picking up speed, came right at the helicopter.

Wyatt gripped his seat.

With the plane only ten yards away, the pilot lifted the helicopter off the airstrip, veering to the right. The plane kept going toward the end of the runway while the chopper pilot swung back around to pursue the fleeing craft. It took off, gaining elevation but not fast enough. Its bottom skimmed the top of some tall pines at the end of the airfield. Then plunged down toward the ground.

At the stand of trees, the chopper pilot put his helicopter on the ground. Wyatt and Daniel leaped from it and rushed toward the crashed aircraft, flashlights and guns out. Wyatt slowed his pace the closer he got to the plane.

Until he saw a large limb piercing through the windshield. Littleton's head was smashed into the side window, blood on the glass, the scent of fuel in the hot air.

✌

In the hospital waiting room, Wyatt stared down at his cold cup of coffee. Exhaustion had replaced the adrenaline he'd needed hours ago to take down Littleton's operation. Now all he wanted to do was sleep. Days if possible.

But he wouldn't until he knew Kate would be all right— until he had seen her and assured himself with his own eyes. She'd gone into surgery and the doctor was now talking to her parents. It had been clear they didn't want him involved.

"Daddy!"

Wyatt lifted his head and saw Maddie in the entrance to the waiting room. She chewed her bottom lip and hesitated. She hadn't called him that in years. If it weren't for Kate, his daughter could have been taken and on her way to some place. . . . He swallowed the tightness in his throat.

Putting his cup on the table next to him, he rose, opening his embrace for her. She rushed into it, pressing her face against him.

"Daddy, I'm so sorry for everything. I couldn't wait until you came home to tell you. I begged Nana to bring me down here. I hope it's all right." Maddie leaned back and looked up at him through eyes brimming with tears.

"Where is Nana?"

"Out in the hall. How's Kate?" Her last sentence came out on a sob, and she again squeezed herself against him. "Please tell me she'll be okay."

"Hon, she just came out of surgery, but the doc indicated she would be fine in time." That was all he got before her parents whisked the man out into the corridor.

"I've messed up so bad. I . . ."

Listening to his daughter's tears struck down the fragile composure he had been maintaining for the past half a day. All barriers to the emotions he'd been holding inside him since his wife was killed crumbled.

He moved Maddie to the couch behind him and sat. "Honey, I should have told you something to help you understand me. When I lost your mother to a murderer, I was determined I would never lose a loved one again. I've seen some ugly things in this world, and I never wanted it to touch you. One of my jobs is and will be to protect you. The decisions I make are often based on that. Sometimes you may think I'm being over-protective, but if I lost you, I don't know what I would do." His last words, whispered in a raw voice, brought his daughter's head up. "I love you."

"I know. I love you, Daddy." She threw her arms around his neck.

"This doesn't change that you and I need to deal with you skipping school and defying me."

"I know."

"What do you think I should do about it?"

Maddie jerked back and looked at him as if he'd gone crazy. "You're asking me?"

"Yep. If you were me, what would you do?"

"I'd make me face the consequences at school for skipping, and I would ground me for another two weeks."

"Done. That sounds fair. But this time no phone, computer, or TV especially since part of your day will be spent at school."

"Dad!" Anger flared into her eyes. She stared at him a moment then sagged her shoulders. "You're right. That's fair."

"We're going to use some of that time to talk. We've gotten out of the habit. I never want you to feel you can't come to me with something, particularly a boy you're interested in. You know I was a teenage boy once. I know what's going on in their heads."

Maddie giggled and buried her face into his shoulder. He hugged her and savored this moment because he knew there would be other battles in the future. But for the time being they were communicating.

"There's something else I needed to tell you, Maddie. With all that's been happening lately, I haven't told you everything about your mom's death."

"That's okay, Dad. I know that's got to be hard to talk about."

"This concerns my feeling about tattoos."

Maddie pulled back, her forehead puckered. "What's tattoos got to do with Mom's death?"

"The man who murdered her had a tattoo on his arm—a snake wrapped around a dagger. There were many nights after her death that I woke up from a nightmare where all I could remember was that tattoo. I just wanted you to know why I have such an aversion to them. I can't stop you when you become eighteen and it's legal for you to get one, but you have a right to know why I don't want my daughter to have one. I should have told you from the beginning, but it really became an issue of you doing something against my wishes."

"My tattoo wouldn't be anything like a dagger and snake. I don't even like either one of those things."

"I know, but—"

"That's okay, Dad. I understand."

"You do?"

"It hasn't been easy for you since Mom died. That's why I'm glad you're seeing Kate. She's a special lady."

"Yes." He remembered seeing her collapsing to the ground after she'd been shot, and a part of him died in that second, thinking he was losing someone he loved all over again.

"Nana, are you okay?"

Maddie's question wrenched him back to the present. He spotted his mother approaching them in the waiting room. Her face drained of all color, she sank in the chair next to him.

"Jack was the head of a prostitution ring? The same man who had been in our home?" his mother asked in a monotone.

"Yes, Mom. He was being brought here when he died. I'm sorry . . . " He didn't know what else to say to his mother about the man she'd been dating, falling in love with.

"He was a scumbag. The lowliest of the low. I can't believe how two-faced he was. That's it. I'm not dating again." His mother dusted off her hands. "Done."

Maddie leaned around Wyatt to look at her grandmother. "Nana, really?"

"Well, at least for the time being. I'm thinking instead of going back to school. I dropped out of college when I was a sophomore and met your grandfather. It's about time I finished what I started all those years ago."

Wyatt bit the inside of his cheek. How long would that last? Knowing his mother, maybe a semester. He didn't care. His family was safe. Kate was safe. That was all that mattered to him.

Kate took a sip of water from the glass her mother held up to her. "I'm going to be all right. You heard the doctor this morning." *Where's Wyatt?* She knew he had been at the hospital, but she hadn't been able to talk to him. Her parents had stayed with her most of the day.

"When you leave here tomorrow, I want you coming home with us." Her mother stepped back from the bed and stood next to her father who had said little all day.

"No, I'm going back to Beacon of Hope, to my apartment."

"No, you can't! You need to be taken care of. You were shot. Do you not realize that?"

"Mother, if anyone realizes that, it's me. I feel it every time I move."

"Do we need to increase your pain meds?" She moved toward the call button.

"Don't, Mother. I'm okay. I can take care of it."

Her mother settled into the crook of her father's arm. "We've been talking. We think this is a great time for you to come on board with the Winslow Foundation. You can even use some of the money from the foundation to help these—these girls you insist on helping."

"No, I'm staying with Beacon of Hope. I have plans in the future to expand. I know now I will get the funding somehow. God will provide. This is what He wants me to do. The whole time I was held captive, He was with me."

"Fine. Expand the program. Just don't be involved in the day-to-day running of it. Live in a nicer part of town. Have others do the everyday things that are needed," her father finally said, his voice inflexible, his expression set in a frown.

"No. I won't compromise on this. These girls need me. I'm not giving up on them as so many others have. If you all want to be in my life, it has to be on my terms. It's my life. Not yours."

Her mother opened her mouth, made a strangled sound, and shut her mouth, her lips forming a thin, hard line.

Wyatt stuck his head through the door opening in the hospital room. He spied her parents and started to back out.

"Don't go, Wyatt," Kate called out to him, desperation in each word.

He paused, looked at her then her parents, and moved further into the room. "I had to go in and file my report. It took longer than I thought it would."

"Oh, good, you can stay." Kate shifted her attention toward her parents. "Thank you all for being here. I need to talk to Wyatt privately."

Her mother swung around to leave. "This is not over, Katherine."

"Yes, it is." Kate didn't take a decent breath until her parents left. "The past few hours have been intense, but at least they came."

"What happened to you shook them up. Your mother had to leave the waiting room once because I believe she was losing her control and was going to cry."

"Mother? I don't think I've ever seen her cry."

"I didn't witness it, but her eyes were red when she came back into the room with your father."

"That's not going to change my mind. I'm not going to live the way they want. I'm not going to stop doing what I'm doing."

Wyatt averted his gaze for a few seconds. "You could have been killed last night."

"You could have."

"It's my job."

"Beacon of Hope is my job. The doctor assures me I'll be well enough to still have the open house next week. There's so much to do."

"And you have plenty of people to help you, including me, if it'll help you to rest."

She smiled. "I'll take you up on that offer. I saw Rose this morning. Susan came and picked her up to take her back to Beacon of Hope once the hospital released her. She was dehydrated, but much better by the time she left."

"Yes. Right now she's giving the police her statement. Susan is there with her."

"Where is Jack Reagan?"

"Also known as King and Duke Littleton. He died on the way to the hospital. Chief Jeffers was in the plane with him when it crashed, but other than a broken arm and leg he will make a full recovery to stand trial. We found Officer Bowen being held at the ranch in the back building with some girls Littleton used. Bowen is going to help with the cleanup of Silverton's Police Department."

"So the prostitution ring has been rounded up."

"We're working on it. There was a lot of information in Littleton's house, and we're wading through it. We'll be busy for a while. We rounded up most of the men working for him. Quite a few are talking for lesser sentences. I feel we'll get everyone before it's over. Your Rose has been a big help. One remarkable girl."

"Yeah, she is. She held it together when most would have fallen apart. I'm so proud of her. How's Maddie? Tell me nothing happened to her."

Wyatt pulled a chair to the bed and settled into it. Taking her hand in his, he sighed. "She's at school, facing her principal because she skipped yesterday. She came earlier to make sure you were all right. I had to take her to the police station to make her statement before taking her to school. She had to ID Tyler, whose real name is Gregory Littleton. The sheriff caught him trying to escape the ranch."

"My parents didn't tell me much, but that things were settled. I'm glad you came. I know they thought they were protecting me, but I had so many questions I wanted answered and they were not in the mood to answer."

"In all fairness they probably didn't know the answers."

Kate laughed, "I can't believe you're defending them."

He bent forward, a smoldering look in his eyes. "We have a lot—"

The door swung open and Susan, Rose, Cynthia, and a couple of more girls flooded the room, carrying flowers and balloons. "We are here to cheer you up."

✑

"Jack's nephew hasn't said anything yet to the police?" Kate said coming into her living room and making a full circle. "How do I look?"

Wyatt grinned. "Are you fishing for a compliment?"

"Yes. Do you think I can wow the media in this?"

"If you're talking about the sling, it should get some sympathy coverage. Your story has been in the news quite a bit lately."

"I didn't know I had to get kidnapped to get donations. I prefer not having to repeat that in the future. Not a fundraiser I would recommend." She adjusted her black sling lying over her white lacy blouse. "I'm ready to conquer—" She turned toward Wyatt and stopped in mid-sentence.

The strong set of his jaw attested to his equally strong emotions. "We've both been so busy this past week with all that has happened. We've never talked about what happened."

"Yes, we did. King is dead. Rose is safe. You are rounding up all the people involved."

He bridged the distance between them but paused a couple of feet from her as though not sure if he should come any closer. "When you were kidnapped, all I could think about was I would lose another person I was in love with. I didn't think I could—"

"Hold it." She cut the space between them. "Did you just tell me you love me?"

"Yes, but that's not—"

Sheer joy infused every inch of her. She wrapped her arms around his neck and tugged him toward her. "You can stop right there. I don't need to hear anything else." Their lips met in a deep kiss.

Finally, he pulled back, setting her at arm's length. "But I need to tell you something." He sucked in a deep breath. "I'm not very good at this. You saw the mess I made with Maddie. Nine years ago, my wife was killed right in front of me by an escaped convict, and I couldn't stop it. I shut down my emotions—if I didn't feel, then it wouldn't hurt so much. But you came along and I couldn't continue to do what I was doing and not feel. The Lord had something else in mind for me. He sent you to wake me up. Then you almost died and again, I couldn't stop it. I saw you go down and I thought I was hit. I wish it had been me, instead of you."

Kate's heart swelled. She moved to him and laid her fingers over his mouth. "Shh. Don't you want to know I love you. I didn't think I had time for my program and love, but somehow I want it to work out. I can't see living without you in my life."

A softness touched his eyes as he hauled her against him and kissed her again. "I want you in my life too."

"I want that too, but Wyatt, I'm going to run Beacon of Hope. Will you be all right with that?"

He smiled. "That's who you are. I expected that. Lately I've been thinking. What about moving Beacon of Hope to my ranch?"

"Your ranch?"

"I think the girls would benefit from living somewhere like that. Away from the city. It's nothing that has to be decided right away, but a thought we can consider."

We. She loved that word. A team. Yes, it felt so right. She gave him another kiss, wishing there weren't people downstairs waiting for her.

A knock at the door parted Kate and Wyatt. "The masses are demanding our appearance. I wonder who it is, Rose or Cynthia?"

Wyatt took her hand and headed across the living room. When he opened the door, he laughed. "Neither one."

Kate smiled. "Maddie, I'm so glad you could come. Where's your grandmother?"

"Downstairs helping put the food out. The first guests are here. Are you ready?"

"Yes." Kate calmed herself as she made her way down to the first floor.

❧

Gregory sat next to his lawyer in the interview room at the police station. He just wanted to get this over with after a week sitting in jail. On the advice of his attorney, this was his best chance to still have a life after he served his time—if he gave them what they wanted.

"The DA has agreed to the terms if the information you provide leads to Littleton's partner," Detective Finch said across the table from him.

"You won't regret it. My uncle said his partner was the brains behind the setup in the first place years ago."

"Who is this partner?"

⟅⟆

Two hours later the recreation room was crowded with media, some of the teenage girls who wanted to be personally involved with the fundraiser, helpers, and people interested in Beacon of Hope. Kate watched her mother move through the throng as if this was an event she'd planned. For the past week, Kate had been the darling of the press in the area, and her mother was slowly coming around to the fact that her daughter wasn't going to change. She had even agreed to match the money raised today. It was a start.

The only damper on the event was the open animosity between her mother and Charlene Foster. Even across the room, Kate felt the tension between the women, although both smiled and, when forced, conversed. But the look in their eyes—hard, assessing, calculating—told a different story.

"Time for my little spiel." Kate slanted a look at Wyatt. "I speak in front of groups all the time, but I wasn't counting on Mother being here."

He took her hand. "You'll do beautifully. Everyone in this room wants Beacon of Hope to succeed, including your parents."

Kate started for the front of the room. Turning to face the media and potential donors, she smiled and signaled for quiet. As the conversation tapered off, Detective Finch and another officer entered and worked their way toward Wyatt. When the detective spoke to Wyatt, he scowled and glanced toward her, then headed for her with Detective Finch behind him.

Her heartbeat slowed. Something was wrong. She stiffened, preparing herself for bad news. But Wyatt and the detective stopped short of Kate in front of Charlene Foster and her husband.

"You're under arrest for child prostitution, trafficking, and conspiracy," Wyatt said to Mr. Foster while Detective Finch locked handcuffs around the businessman's wrist.

Charlene's mouth dropped open. All color siphoned from her face. "This is a mistake. Tell them, Kenneth."

"Of course, this is a mistake," the man said while flashes went off as the reporters moved in.

Kate remained back while people swarmed forward, eager for the scoop. Wyatt pushed his way through the crowd toward her as Detective Finch and the officer took hold of their suspect and headed toward the exit. The noise level in the room rose to a din.

Kate sank against the podium, the muscles in her neck bunched and knotted.

Wyatt put his hand on her shoulder and kneaded it. "Littleton's nephew just gave up Kenneth Foster as his uncle's partner in the prostitution ring. His trucking company is involved in the transportation of their victims to different parts of this country as well as into Mexico."

"I can't believe it."

Wyatt nodded toward Charlene Foster. "It looks like his senator wife can't either."

"Do you think she knew what her husband was doing?"

"Littleton's nephew was very specific and told the police where his uncle kept records on his dealings with Kenneth Foster. But I suspect her career in government is over with."

"What about Beacon of Hope?"

"Have you stopped and added up the amount the people have been pledging to the program?"

"No, but the contributions I've received have been substantial and I was notified yesterday about that grant."

"See, you're going to be all right." Wyatt peered across the room at Kate's parents, watching as Kenneth Foster was hauled away. "I have a feeling your mother and father aren't going to let you down either. That wouldn't look good in the press."

Kate went into Wyatt's arms. "Anything is possible through the Lord."

Discussion Questions

1. Kate Winslow had trouble dealing with her mother. She never felt like she could please her. What kind of relationship do you have with your parents? How have you dealt with problems with your parents? How can you improve your relationship with your parents?

2. Rose was determined to save Lily, even to the point of putting herself in danger. She felt guilty about Lily's situation. What are some things you've done to make yourself feel better when you felt guilty?

3. Who is your favorite character? Why?

4. Wyatt Sheridan is having problems with his daughter. She wants more independence, but he isn't ready to give it to her. If you had been in Wyatt's situation, how would you have dealt with Maddie's disobedience? How do you let a teenager become independent but still safe?

5. Kate tries to help girls that many people have written off. She tries to give these girls a second chance. If you were asked to help girls like Rose, what would you do?

6. When Rose was held captive, she kept remembering Kate's advice. What Kate said gave Rose hope and courage. Do you have something or someone who gives that to you? Have you done that for another? If so, what have you said to them?

7. What is your favorite scene? Why?

8. Did you know who was King's partner? If so, what gave the partner away?

9. Maddie defied her father and went to meet Tyler. Something told her not to call Tyler when the truck stopped in the middle of the parking lot. If she had, she

would have been kidnapped. Have you ever felt something wasn't right, but you couldn't say why? What was the situation? How did it turn out?

10. Our children are our future. How can we protect our children from predators in our society? How do we teach them to be careful, to be wary of predators?

11. In this story, the importance of forgiving is explored, especially with Wyatt and what happened to his wife. Why is it important to forgive others and ourselves? What happens when we live in the past rather than look forward to the future? Which do you focus on— past, present, or future? Why?

12. This is a book about hope in the time of tragedy. How can we give hope to another in his or her time of need?

13. Cynthia cut herself. She didn't have a constructive way to express her frustration and anger. What could she have done besides cutting herself to relieve her frustration and anger? How do you deal with your frustration? With your anger?

14. Kate had a strong faith, but there were times during the story when her faith wavered. What has caused your faith to waver? How do you get it back on track? What strengthens your faith?

Shattered Silence

Book 2 of Men of the Texas Rangers Series

❧

1

*D*ay One

No one sees me. They walk right by me and don't even know I am here. I'm invisible.

But that's all going to change today. The woman who has agreed to marry me will be here soon. The world will finally know someone cares about me. It was worth all my savings to bring her across the border. I'm tired of being alone. Being nobody.

I'm getting married. I won't be invisible anymore—at least she'll see me.

❧

Maria Martinez lay flat on the dust-covered wooden planks, her right eye pressed against the hole in the floor of the abandoned house. *Pedro won't find me here. I'll win this time.*

A sneeze welled up in Maria, and she fought to stop it. She couldn't. Quickly she looked through the small opening to make sure Pedro hadn't come and heard her. Her older brother always thought he could do everything better than her. Not this time. He'd never think to look here. He'd think she was too afraid to hide here. A rattling behind her sent a shot of fear through her. She went still. Her lungs held her breath and wouldn't let go.

There's no such thing as ghosts. He just told me that to scare me. I'm not a baby. I'm eight.

Her words fueled her courage, and she popped up to look over her shoulder. Nothing. Just the wind blowing through the broken window. Maria sank to the floor in relief and took up her post again. Watching through the hole. If Pedro came into the house, she'd be ready to hide. He was *not* going to find her. For once, she would have the last laugh. He was just two years older, but the way he acted, you'd think he was Papa.

Another sound caught her attention. Down below. Footsteps. She started to hop up and scramble to her hiding place nearby, but a gruff, deep male voice stopped her. *Not Pedro. Who?*

With her eye glued to the hole again, she waited to see who it was. Another voice—a woman's—answered the man then she laughed. A funny laugh—like Pedro when he made fun of her.

"Dumb. Evil eye," the woman taunted in Spanish.

The man raised his voice, speaking in the same language so fast Maria had a hard time keeping up. Mama insisted on only speaking English at home. Now she wished she was better at Spanish. But she heard some words—the ones he slowed and emphasized, repeating several times in a louder voice a few cuss words that got Papa in trouble if he said them at home. The deep gruff voice ended with, "You will pay."

The woman laughed again, but the sound died suddenly. "What are you doing?" she said in Spanish.

Maria strained to see the two people. The lady moved into her line of sight as she stepped back, shaking her head, her long brown hair swirling in the air. Maria glimpsed the top of a tan cowboy hat that hid the man's face from her.

The beautiful lady held up her hands. "No!"

The fear in that one word chilled Maria.

Before she could think of what to do, a gunshot, like she'd heard on TV, blasted the quiet. The lady jerked back. She glanced down at her chest, then up, remaining upright for a few heartbeats before crumbling to the floor.

Maria froze. Her mind blanked.

The man came closer to the still lady on the floor, her unseeing dark eyes staring right at Maria, pinning her against the wooden planks. She saw the gun as he lifted his arm and aimed it at the woman. He shot her in the stomach then the forehead.

Maria gasped.

The man must have whirled away. Suddenly he wasn't in her line of vision. She bolted to her feet as the sound of heavy footsteps coming up the stairs echoed down the hallway.

Terror locked a vise about Maria and held her in place.

Then her gaze latched onto her hiding place—one she'd found when she'd first come to the house. She'd laughed out loud that her brother would never find her there. Now she wasn't so sure it was perfect.

But the approaching footfalls prodded her into action. She had no other choice. She clambered toward the couch as quietly as she could. She ripped the seat cushion off and squeezed herself into the small place someone must have used before. The pounding of her heartbeat in her ears drowned out the sound of his footsteps.

The man threw open a door at the end of the hall. The slam of it against the wall startled Maria as she set the cushion over her like a shield a knight used in a movie she'd seen. When he stormed a castle hundreds of arrows rained down on him. He had survived. Could she?

The scent of mold and dust threatened to set off her sneezing. She held her hand over her mouth and nose praying that would stop her from making any sound.

As the man's footsteps came nearer, her heartbeat reverberated against her skull, again overriding all other sounds. Surely he could hear it. Find her.

Please, Lord, help me. Mama said you protect children.

But not her prayers or her fear calmed her thundering heartbeats. The racket grew louder inside her chest and clamored in her ears. Her head spun. She uncovered her mouth to try and breathe deeply. She couldn't get enough air.

The door opened, slamming against the wall.

She flinched, hoping the seat cushion hadn't moved.

Please. Please, Lord. I'll be good.

The footsteps approached the center of the room.

Lightheaded, Maria closed her eyes as if that would hide her from the bad man. Something scurried over her leg. Something big. A rat? The urge to flee her hiding place robbed her of any thoughts. She curled herself into the tightest ball she could and prayed, her chest rising and falling so rapidly the darkness continued to swirl behind her closed eyelids.

An eternity passed. A brush of whiskers reinforced her fright. She tensed, expecting any second the cushion being wrenched off her hiding place or sharp teeth sinking into her flesh. A warm gush between her legs and the odor of pee heightened her terror. He would smell it and . . .

I'm going to die. Mama . . .

❧

Liliana Rodriguez sat across from her older sister at the Bluebonnet Cafe in Durango, Texas, waiting for the waitress to bring their sandwiches. She leaned across the table and lowered her voice to a fierce whisper. "I don't want to hear those bruises are from an accident, Elena. We both know who did that to you. Samuel, your low-down excuse for a husband."

Her sister's dark eyes clouded, her brow knitted. "Oh, no, I really did get up in the middle of the night and run into the wall."

"Yeah, after he tripped you." Liliana lifted her iced tea, hoping the cold drink would cool the fire in her belly.

"No. No, don't say that. He's a good husband and father. Like Papa."

Liliana choked on the swallow of liquid sliding down her throat. Coughing, she nearly dropped her glass as her eyes watered.

"Are you okay?" Elena started to stand.

Liliana waved her down. "Fine," she managed to get out while sucking in deep breaths of air that didn't fill her lungs. When she could talk, she caught her sister's attention and added, "But you aren't. Your husband is an abuser just like—"

"Don't. Papa disciplined us when we needed it."

When it rained, Liliana's left arm still ached from her father's form of discipline that ended in a broken bone.

Want to learn more about author
Margaret Daley and check out other great
fiction from Abingdon Press?

Sign up for our fiction newsletter at
www.AbingdonPress.com
to read interviews with your favorite authors, find tips
for starting a reading group, and stay posted on what
new titles are on the horizon. It's a place to connect
with other fiction readers or post a
comment about this book.

Be sure to visit Margaret Daley online!

www.margaretdaley.com